*The first monster a director can use
to scare his audience is himself.*

"I'm not that kind of monster." Max frowned. "I'm not. Right?"

Either way, he found himself threading a fresh roll of film into the camera. He watched his hands mount the camera again on the sticks.

"It's not me doing this," he said.

The voice didn't answer.

Obeying the dark impulse, Max aimed the lens at the door.

By Craig DiLouie

How to Make a Horror Movie and Survive

Episode Thirteen

The Children of Red Peak

Our War

One of Us

Suffer the Children

Tooth and Nail

Strike

The Alchemists

The Great Planet Robbery

The Infection Series

Crash Dive Series

Armor Series

The Aviator Series

HOW TO MAKE A
HORROR
MOVIE
AND SURVIVE

CRAIG DiLOUIE

REDHOOK

Redhook Books/Orbit
Hachette Book Group
1290 Avenue of the Americas
New York, NY 10104
hachettebookgroup.com

First Edition: June 2024

Redhook is an imprint of Orbit, a division of Hachette Book Group.
The Redhook name and logo are registered trademarks of Hachette Book Group, Inc.

The publisher is not responsible for websites (or their content) that are not owned by the publisher.

The Hachette Speakers Bureau provides a wide range of authors for speaking events. To find out more, go to hachettespeakersbureau.com or email HachetteSpeakers@hbgusa.com.

Redhook books may be purchased in bulk for business, educational, or promotional use. For information, please contact your local bookseller or the Hachette Book Group Special Markets Department at special.markets@hbgusa.com.

Print book interior design by Bart Dawson

Library of Congress Cataloging-in-Publication Data
Names: DiLouie, Craig, 1967– author.
Title: How to make a horror movie and survive / Craig DiLouie.
Description: First edition. | New York, NY : Redhook, 2024.
Identifiers: LCCN 2023039620 | ISBN 9780316569316 (trade paperback) | ISBN 9780316569330 (ebook)
Subjects: LCGFT: Horror fiction. | Novels.
Classification: LCC PS3604.I463 H69 2024 | DDC 813/.6—dc23/eng/20230830
LC record available at https://lccn.loc.gov/2023039620

ISBNs: 9780316569316 (trade paperback), 9780316569330 (ebook)

Printed in the United States of America

LSC-C

Printing 1, 2024

To all lovers of horror

DESIRE

Nothing's ever real until it's real.

George A. Romero
Director, *Night of the Living Dead*

ONE

If you aren't horrified, you aren't paying attention. If you aren't terrified, you aren't really living. That's what Max Maurey believed.

In fact, Max loved horror so much that he'd devoted his life to making it. Which explained why he donned a tuxedo and rode a rented limousine to the Cinerama in Hollywood on a sultry August evening.

To celebrate the making. A new movie, to be exact.

Powerful searchlight beams swayed in the twilight, the iconic signal of a premiere. In this case, one of the most highly anticipated horror releases of 1988.

Moments later, his limo pulled up to the curb.

And outside—

The red carpet stretched under an illuminated marquee.

The theater's geodesic concrete dome loomed over the scene.

Covered in *Jack the Knife III* splatter logos, the step-and-repeat publicity wall stood ready to serve as backdrop for celebrity photographs.

Max put on a grin and stepped onto the pristine carpet like he owned it, which tonight he pretty much did.

Entertainment journalists craned their necks to see who'd arrived. The fans buzzed. Some of the guys sported leather jackets and shades like the titular Jack. Some of the ladies wore cardigans, skirts, and bobby socks to cosplay the bygone era in which Jack returned from the dead.

This party was just getting started.

Wearing his own tux, Jordan Lyman greeted Max with a puff of cigar smoke. With his curly mop of hair and mirrored sunglasses, the burly producer exuded the overblown masculinity of a porn star who didn't know the seventies were over.

On set, Max might be a creator god, but even he answered to a higher power—the moneyman. As he loathed Jordan for this alone, he couldn't resist a barb.

"Even when you dress up, you only look seedier."

"And you look like something that's afraid of daylight."

"Ouch." Max's hand jerked to pat his silver-streaked hair, which waved in random directions like a mad scientist's. "At least I look the part."

"Crazy eyes, baby," the producer confirmed.

"Crazy eyes?"

"Back when I met you, you were a man possessed by a vision. It's why I gave the first *Jack the Knife* the green light back in '79. And here we are."

"Here we are," said Max.

On top of the world. He'd traveled a long, hard road to reach it.

Working his way up the ladder in the New Hollywood of the seventies, Max had worn many hats. He'd messengered dailies, cut film as an editor, and wrangled sets as an assistant director. His dream of directing his own movies remained elusive, however, in an industry where the bigwigs didn't like to say no but enjoyed making you wait. A way of doing business that prompted Pauline Kael to label Hollywood the one place you could die of encouragement.

Then Max at last won his big break when Jordan wrote a check for $350,000 to develop *Jack the Knife* into a feature-length horror movie.

The pitch: Steven Spielberg's *Duel* meets the supernatural. Back in the fifties, a young man named Jack drove in a drag race on the Fourth of July. As a result of sabotage, he died in a fiery wreck. Decades later, he returns from the dead on Independence Day as an angry spirit of vengeance aimed at the town's teens.

Working twelve hours a day, six days a week, Max had shot the film over three weeks, hustling through a backbreaking twenty to thirty camera setups each day. He squeezed every angle out of the tiny sets. He rigged an Oldsmobile to pass as Jack's on-screen 1957 black Chevy Corvette. When the final movie printed, two-thirds of the end credits were pseudonyms to make the skeleton crew look bigger.

Despite all the sweat and love Max gave his film, he hadn't expected much. But this was 1980, two years after *Halloween* made lightning in a bottle. John Carpenter proved you didn't need massive budgets and Hollywood stars to make a successful horror movie. You only needed to deliver horror.

In *Halloween*'s wake, the major studios poured cash into low-budget productions. The slasher era had arrived. In the end, Jordan sold the domestic and foreign distribution rights to New Line Cinema in a profitable deal.

Jack the Knife went on to gross $12 million worldwide, an actual hit. Eight years later, Jack now held fourth place in the slasher pantheon behind Jason Voorhees, Freddy Krueger, and Michael Myers. And Max, always a misunderstood outcast, had become an important director.

"Do I still have them?" he asked in a quiet voice.

"Have what?" Jordan said.

"Crazy eyes. I'd like to know if you still see them."

"Every time I visit the set or offer a suggestion you don't like." The producer regarded him with a thoughtful expression. "You're actually nervous."

"It's just production hangover," Max said.

The emptiness and loss he suffered when the intense process of making a movie ended. But no, that wasn't it, not this time.

As he approached forty, he'd begun wondering if he'd accomplished enough. He could feel the slasher era coming to an end. This was the last *Jack the Knife*. Soon, he'd have to lead or follow on the next big thing. For the first time in nearly a decade, the future offered a blank page, ripe for a fresh story.

He didn't share this with the producer, who wouldn't understand. Jordan toked on his cigar. "It's your night. Enjoy it while it lasts."

Max nodded, despite this sounding a bit ominous.

Limousines now packed the front of the Cinerama Dome. The fans screamed as they spotted celebrities.

Douglas Avery had arrived, the veteran B-movie actor and discount David Carradine. He played the role of Harbinger, warning the kids not to meddle with dead things, which they of course ignore. Also attending was the beloved, gravelly-voiced Wolfman Jack, who'd reprised his *Jack the Knife II* cameo as an earnest local radio DJ who fears the worst for his town.

Under the deepening dusk kept at bay by bright lights, the cast promenaded on the red carpet, stretching out their minutes of fame. Some paused to chat with fans and sign autographs while the rest headed to the step-and-repeat wall for press photos. Flashbulbs popped. Pumped on happiness overload, everyone wore a strained, bewildered grin they couldn't turn off.

Then the crowd *really* went wild.

Stepping out of their limo, Ashlee Gibson and Nicholas Moody smiled and waved. The Final Girl and Jack had finally joined the party. Seeing them holding hands, the fans howled even louder.

Max pictured the starry-eyed, hungry mob surging over the velvet ropes to caress and kiss and bite their idols. Rip them apart and devour them in grisly mouthfuls while the actors kept on grinning until nothing remained.

Imagining the worst shattering the normal had always been an occupational delight for the director. Looking at his leads, he felt little pleasure now. The crowd should have been cheering *him* for wrangling their difficult personalities into usable footage.

But no matter. Max didn't need the fans' love.

He needed their terror.

As long as they feared him, he was happy.

The cast and critics filed into the theater. The crew and extras had already claimed their seats. They'd entered through the stage door to form a boisterous gang nipping at flasks in the back rows. Most of the actors parked in the back as well, ceding the limelight to the story that would soon appear on the screen. Entertainment press and bigwigs filled the rest of the seats.

As for Max, he sat in the front row alongside Jordan and the producer's taciturn Saudi financiers. He let the hubbub wash over him and liked what he heard. The positive energy in the air had grown palpable. He checked his watch.

Time to get this show started.

Standing to face the crowd, he smiled as their applause washed over him.

"Welcome to the premiere of *Jack the Knife III*," Max said. "Horror's favorite highwayman returns. The *Jack* attack is back and better than ever."

The audience erupted in cheering. Next, he focused on the grumpy critics, who liked to tie movies to a resonant theme or trend.

"But really, this is a film about America reclaiming its lost innocence through violence in the Reagan era, only to discover it was never innocent to begin with. As aways, the franchise asks who the real monsters are."

Laying it on thick, though it wouldn't affect the outcome. Reviewers and critics tended to prejudge horror films based on whether they enjoyed the genre.

After catering to them, he next addressed the cast and crew.

"On a final note, it's well understood in our business that no man makes a motion picture. From the talent to the gaffer, a team makes the picture. That means there's a bit of every single one of you in this film. Thank you all for your hard work. Being your director has been an honor. Give yourselves a hand."

As the energetic applause faded, Max finished, "Now, get ready for America's favorite horror story to continue. As the wise men say, the third time's the charm. And so, ladies and gentlemen, I give you: *Jack the Knife III*."

With that, he cupped his hand and called out to the projectionist: "Roll film!"

The moviegoers whooped one last time. As the lights dimmed, the crowd settled down. The standard fifties doo-wop theme started up, tinny and distant as if haunting the present from a lost era.

A LYMAN ENTERTAINMENTS PRODUCTION

The words flared as if on fire before disappearing.

The black screen came to life with a vehicle point-of-view shot revealing yellow roadway lines zipping in headlight glare. A V-8 engine snarled, filling the theater's Dolby Stereo system with a wall of sound. In an instant, the viewer became transported to a lonely road on a humid summer night.

JACK THE KNIFE III

As the opening credits neared their end, Max smiled.

DIRECTED BY MAX MAUREY

He hoped the critics *did* hate it. He hoped they told America that *Jack the Knife III* made them puke up their popcorn and Jujubes. He hoped parents forbade their teens to see it and nuns ended up picketing it.

The more "normal" society shunned and feared him, the more power they gave him. Taboo and censorship packed theaters. Public disdain tribalized horror fans into rabid devotees. Because at the end of the day, society wasn't normal at all, and horror wasn't lowbrow.

Horror was populist.

When the industry considered your genre one step above pornography in terms of respectability, it became a license to do almost anything you wanted. And horror flourished in rebellion and pushing boundaries.

It was the Midnight Movie, the drive-in double feature, the titillating exploitation film, the vision to do something crazy and powerful with little money, its grit and amateur rough edges only making it scarier. It was an evil grin and a middle finger delivered to society's comforting fictions, a fractured mirror held up to the human condition. It was leering monsters, moldering corpses, strange bumps in the night, forbidden knowledge, steamy sex in the backseat under a frosty murderous gaze, an eerie children's choir setting the mood to venture into a derelict mansion on a dare.

In short, horror screamed punk rock, and it served as Max's sharp playground.

The open credits finished, the story began. With a real budget of $1.75 million, *Jack the Knife III* boasted a higher body count than its predecessors and three times the car wrecks. The additional shooting days and locations showed in the final product. The film flowed clean and smooth on the screen without any problems.

Back in 1980, production for the original *Jack the Knife* had ended with a raucous wrap party but no glittered and starred premiere. Instead, Max had bought a ticket at a seedy downtown theater to catch it in the wild.

He remembered the projectionist forgot to flip the Dolby switch. The bottom of the frame was cut off. Bits of dust blemished the imaging. Mortified, Max had sunk in his seat, his popcorn and soft drink ignored.

Then he'd heard the first anxious chuckle in the dark. He stopped watching the picture and just listened to the audience. A little more nervous laughter. Then sharp gasps. Long stretches of tense, pin-drop silence.

At the first horrifying kill, a woman had cried out, *Oh my God!*

Max smiled again at the memory. That night had made all the hard work worthwhile, a far bigger payoff than the money that started coming his way.

Tonight, the crowd reacted differently to *Jack the Knife III*.

They cheered.

They laughed.

When a hissing cat sprang off a shelf for the picture's early fake scare—a genre convention Jordan insisted on including—they let out a playful scream.

Everyone was having a great time.

Max produced an irritated growl.

He knew they were amping up their reactions for the benefit of the critics. He both encouraged and expected that.

That wasn't the problem.

The problem was that *they were cheering and laughing at all.*

When Jack doo-wopped around the walls and ceiling of Tina's bedroom—a technical feat involving shooting a revolving room—the audience went wild. An organ-rich, New Wavey interpretation of "Mack the Knife" with modified lyrics crooned from the Dolby system while the villain sang:

This monster has such sharp teeth, kid
And they grin oh so bright and white.
Just a switchblade has our Jack, kid
And it gets hungrier every night...

The blood drained from Max's face. "What have I done?"

The crowd wasn't scared. They were *entertained.*

They *rooted* for Jack to dispense his Greek-myth style of justice to a bunch of teenagers guilty of being jerks and having clueless parents. They wanted to see the monster deliver what these stupid kids deserved.

Happy with what he heard, Jordan smirked.

"They're *laughing*," Max complained.

Laughter didn't bother him. Horror and comedy had always been kissing cousins. A little nervous laughter defused the tension. Whistling through the graveyard. But this wasn't that kind of laughing. They were yukking it up.

And this wasn't horror. It was campy self-satire.

Jordan tilted his head to murmur, "You're talking over your own movie."

"I shouldn't have listened to you. All these changes you forced me into."

Giving Jack so much screen time that he stopped being scary, a rakish mix of James Dean and Jack the Ripper. Having him deliver one-liners after his kills that had the audience cracking up in the rows. The new Beauty and the Beast romantic attraction with the Final Girl. Phones ringing but ominous silence on the other end. A severed head discovered in the refrigerator.

Elements ripped off so many times they'd become standard tropes, capped by blatant Pepsi and Kentucky Fried Chicken product placements. Max had been so immersed in the project that he hadn't realized what he'd done.

"They made the movie better," the producer said. "Evolve or die. Listen to the people, Max. They love it."

"They hate it. They just don't know they hate it."

"I think we might actually squeeze another sequel out of this."

"We've taken the real fun out of it, and replaced it with— with—"

"Money's fun," said Jordan.

"It's just like every other slasher flick. Gimmicks. Cinematic junk food."

The man nodded sagely. "That's beautiful, how you put that."

"You think it's—?"

"Formula sells, baby. It's comfortable. And it's for everybody. Not just misanthropic freaks like you."

Max couldn't believe anyone paid for a ticket to a horror film to experience comfort any more than they hopped on a roller coaster to feel safe. They wanted to push outside their comfort zones.

The crowd kept cheering regardless of what he thought.

As *Jack the Knife III* neared its end, the dog everyone thought had died off-screen defending its master reappeared, ready to bravely chip in again during the final showdown. A bit of emotional manipulation that Max didn't mind, as he'd made a rule to never kill off animals in his movies. He could practically hear the audience grinning and tearing up behind him, though he couldn't bring himself to enjoy even this.

When in the final moments one last shock popped out of nowhere to suggest the story might continue—another Jordan "innovation" ripped off from other horror films—they all cried out. Then gave the closing credits a rousing ovation.

Even some of the grumpy critics were smiling.

"Christ," Max groaned. "I'm a hack."

"Cheer up," the producer said. "It's a birth, not a funeral. Mazel tov. Now stand up like a professional and take a bow."

Glowering, he obeyed, feeling about as punk as a cup of decaf coffee.

TWO

Max was born on a stormy night in 1950 while *Sunset Boulevard* and *The Breaking Point* showed in theaters. He grew up in Binghamton, New York, where his father worked as a shipping manager and told a joke every night at dinner.

One night, Dad said, "We had to fire one of our employees today. On his way out the door, he told me all along he'd been moonlighting as an actor on the side."

Mom filled six-year-old Max's plate. "Oh, is he any good?"

"I think he's fantastic. I mean, all these years he's been at the warehouse, he convinced me he was actually working."

While Max laughed, Dad face-planted in his pork chops and mashed potatoes.

"Dad?"

A sudden and massive heart attack had killed him.

For Max, it left a permanent psychic imprint. A dark truth learned too young.

The world isn't fair, he thought.

At the funeral, the pastor told him his father had ascended to a better place.

Max stared at him. "Better than my house?"

"He's in heaven," the pastor said. "Heaven is perfect. He's happy there."

"Because of God. God can do anything."

"That's right. It's why we pray."

For the first time in his life, Max wondered why God allowed bad things to happen to good people. On the spot, his child's mind reasoned that one of two axioms must be true. God couldn't stop evil, which made him weaker than evil. Or God could stop it but didn't want to, which made him kind of monstrous himself.

Max's first taste of cosmic horror.

Mom squeezed his hand. "Dad isn't really gone. He's smiling down at us right now."

Max sensed a con everyone agreed upon to make everything bad about life actually feel nice. Like the actor at Dad's warehouse pretending to work.

"Tell me a joke," he said.

On the drive home, he looked out the window at the pink houses flashing past. Everyone else's lives seemed perfect. More of the big con? They had to be hiding something behind all those curtains.

If they weren't, then he must be a freak.

Mom went back to work to support them. At school, Max curled into a ball under his desk during a duck-and-cover drill to practice surviving an atomic war. He lay there expecting the bombs to drop this time, but they never did.

At home, he watched television hoping someone might articulate the thoughts and ideas that felt way too large for him. The world seemed oblivious and happy. As he got older, his belief this was a lie grew.

Then he discovered *Shock Theater* on channel 7.

At a nocturnal hour, Cool Ghoul John Zacherle introduced old Universal horror movies with macabre humor. Tiptoeing downstairs after Mom turned in for the night, Max sat two feet from his TV set to gape at *Frankenstein*, *Dracula*, *The Mummy*, and *The Invisible Man*.

Watching gave him a delicious thrill. Not only was he breaking the rules, but the films struck him as forbidden and arcane knowledge. A glimpse of real taboo. A window into his own troubled soul. These fictional monsters mirrored the dark truths and questions he wrestled with in his life.

Afterward, he went to bed quaking over what might be under his bed. The greatest of fears, he learned, wasn't what you saw but what you didn't.

The nightmares came soon after.

When Mom caught him staying up and then discovered his stash of EC Comics and *Weird Tales*, she flew into a rage. She worried whether his obsession with horror affected his development and whether the nightmares damaged his brain.

"It's not healthy for you," she yelled.

Max disagreed. These stories didn't hurt him.

They were *saving* him.

Either way, he grew into a tall, gangly, and pasty kid who didn't fit in. A boy who preferred the serenity and quiet desperation of the night to the earnest, social day. After the sun went down, the shadows recast the familiar as the unfamiliar, a breeding ground for terrors both imaginary and real.

As for the nightmares, they'd transferred to his waking hours, during which he reimagined the mundane world as scenes in horror movies.

At school, Max felt like a freak. Even the outsiders shunned him. Then he discovered *Famous Monsters of Filmland*.

The first issue he read had the great Vincent Price on the cover along with a bold invitation to catch pics from *The Pit and the Pendulum*. Max bought and hid it under his mattress, where other boys stashed *Playboy*.

The magazine told him he wasn't weird at all. Okay, he was still weird, but he wasn't alone—there were many other weirdos like him.

In fact, there was a *community*.

While America sank into Vietnam, Max avidly consumed movies and TV shows like *Thriller*, *Way Out*, and *The Twilight Zone*. He read every issue of *Eerie* and *Creepy*. When he caught *Psycho* as a rerun at a late-night theater, he began to admire the artistry behind the stories he loved.

The forty-five-second shower scene in Hitchcock's masterpiece had taken a week to shoot, he learned, and involved seventy-eight camera setups. The next time Max cracked open *Famous Monsters*, he didn't just see a community. He heard a clarion call to contribute and lead.

He wanted to direct movies.

As the sixties reached their messy end, Max arrived at the School of Theater, Film and Television at the University of California, Los Angeles. His education in filmmaking welcomed him like a blank page, full of potential but also intimidating. He loved it all, right down to the iconic palm trees and four-hour-long classes at Melnitz Hall, where he learned things like Freudian interpretations of *Citizen Kane*.

Even here, however, he found himself an outcast. The weird and twisty kid who wanted to direct horror movies. Another milestone in what would be a lifetime of horror shaming.

The censorial Production Code had died a few years earlier, resulting in an explosion of gore before the New Horror of the seventies refined the genre for the emerging yuppies. Eager to push boundaries, Max shot his first student film in his dorm room in grainy 16mm using bell lights fitted with wax paper as homemade diffusers. Titled *Martyr*, it told the story of a man tortured by his malicious doppelgänger. He turns the tables and kills it, one bloody piece chopped off at a time, only to discover he literally fought and killed himself by suicide.

Max's snooty classmates loathed it, wondering who allowed this uncultured, blue-collar weirdo into the same film school as the next crop of Kubricks and Fellinis. Behind his back, they called him the "enfant terrible," a man out to break not society but film itself. When they reached the real world, many of them would one day try their hand at horror as an easier path into directing, but for Max, it had always been his sole destination. His professor also hated the short, declaring that Max's ambition far exceeded his years and that he confused art with bad taste.

Nonetheless, Max had found his home in every meaning of the word.

By the end of his film school years, the blank page with which he'd started had filled to bursting. The school of hard knocks awaited him. Long was the way and hard, but he never gave up on his dream. With *Jack the Knife*, he finally grabbed it by the tail and rode it to the top of the Hollywood horror scene.

For Max, the real horrors were nuclear war and Vietnam. Watergate and Charles Manson. The Summer of Sam and the energy crisis. The hostage taking in Iran and AIDS. Blackouts and riots and Three Mile Island. Growing old, not being able to afford rent, bringing children into this world.

Dad dropping dead after telling a killer joke at dinner.

Finding out he had the same heart defect as his father.

Horror helped Max process all of it with monsters he could safely fear. Fears he could face with a sense of wonder. Terrors he wanted to create for others so they could share in its bitter but cathartic medicine.

No more curtains hiding dirty secrets in pink houses. No American exceptionalism to the universal savagery of the human condition. No sweet icing plastered over life's existential turds. No more false justice.

His audiences would see and feel it all in gory detail.

To Max, it was as healthy as eating carrots.

THREE

Grinning with jack-o'-lantern intensity, the Bel Air mansion welcomed all comers to the *Jack the Knife III* premiere after-party. Floodlights articulated the hulking architecture. The silhouettes of partyers flickered like black candlelight in its bright windows. Every time Max visited Jordan's palatial estate, he received a visual reminder of how badly he was being ripped off.

Lookie-loos flocked to Hollywood each year hoping to sight celebrities in their natural habitat. They came for the glitter and went home with the grime. What most people pictured as Hollywood was actually a small group of communities such as Beverly Hills. There, the industry's aristocracy lived in palaces secured in gated glamor and guarded by their own cops. Everything looked clean and beautiful, stretch limos drove date-palm-lined avenues, and the post office offered valet parking. They even painted the fire hydrants silver.

Bel Air wasn't Beverly Hills, but it was very close.

Max entered a spacious vestibule facing a grand staircase. Like a resume of influence and power, awards and photos adorned the entry walls. While celebrities and famous directors provided the face of Hollywood, people like Jordan Lyman ruled it behind the scenes by handling the cash that powered the illusion factory.

Producers could be studio moguls green-lighting projects, execs submitting to corporate boards, or indie companies packaging distribution deals for the big studios. Jordan had worked as all three, making a name at MCA/Universal and Columbia before jumping again to do his own thing as an indie producer. Max considered his relationship with the man something of a Faustian bargain.

Leaving the vestibule, he entered a vast living room overlooking a glowing swimming pool. Here, cast, crew, and friends of *Jack the Knife III* mingled and laughed among sprawling furniture, expensive art, and soft lighting. Caterers circulated bearing trays of hors d'oeuvres. An INXS song piped through the house speaker system. The partyers shined with needy, manic cheer.

Gazing at this scene, Max pictured himself as a director in a horror film who wants to escape before an ancient evil manifests to consume them all. Too late: Blood drips from the ceiling. It plops into drinks, runs like scarlet mascara down leering faces, disappears on shrimp kebabs into chomping mouths. Looking into their red eyes, he realizes the merriment is all phony.

He is already in a trap, and *they* are the evil.

A peal of laughter swept through part of the crowd, and Max flinched.

A familiar gruff voice: "Welcome to the Hotel California."

He sighed. "I think I need a stiff drink."

"You earned it, Maximillian."

Raphael Rodriguez had worked with Max on the entire *Jack* trilogy as special makeup effects master. The man who put the splatter in Max's splatter flicks.

When Tom discovered Pam screaming on a meat hook in the third act and pulled her off, it was Raphael's gore that geysered from her back. When the released counterweight dropped an anvil onto Tom's head and Tom's skull exploded like a watermelon, that was Raph's work too.

Specifically, blood he made from corn syrup mixed with food coloring and other ingredients. Brains from cauliflower, bread, and gelatin.

If Max loomed behind his movies as a master of illusions, Raphael performed as an expert stage magician. He was no celebrity genius like Tom Savini, whose macabre artistry with *Dawn of the Dead* and other horror pictures established him as the Sultan of Splatter. He had skill, though, and he was reliable. Best of all, he could handle Max's shit. In fact, aside from Susan, Max's fluffy Pomeranian waiting for him at home, Raphael remained the only real friend he had in this town.

He couldn't say how their long friendship started. Like him, Raphael had reached middle age, came from a blue-collar background, and was a filmmaking veteran. Besides that, the man had fought in Vietnam and similarly understood horror and death from a personal perspective. In the jungle, he'd learned what a savaged body really looked like, which he now re-created for horror movie directors with latex and in the process purged his own suppressed demons.

"What I earned is a punch in the face," Max said.

"What happened?"

"I let my producer have his way too many times."

Raphael laughed. "You should thank him."

"*Et tu*, Raph?"

"Your movie turned out awesome," he said. "You're actually getting paid to do something you love. Only you would find a way to get all neurotic about it."

"Okay, okay," Max grumbled.

Looking at it one way, he stood at the pinnacle of success. He understood that. He appreciated it. Looking at it another way, he was trapped in the creative echo of the one good thing he did eight years ago, an echo that degraded with each iteration. He pictured his tombstone bearing the epitaph HE GAVE US JACK.

Max didn't care about money or fame or power. He didn't even really care about his fans. He was an artist. He lived for his movies. If they were nothing but cheap, safe, recycled thrills one chuckled through and promptly forgot afterward, what was the point? To him, a movie wasn't two hours of entertainment but an experience. A statement that endured the test of time.

Was success still success if you'd succeeded at the wrong goal?

Soon, he'd be the same age Dad had been when he'd died. Max went to bed every night and awoke each morning with a sense of living on borrowed time.

Before Raphael could lecture him more about his good fortune, he flagged down a good-looking bow-tied kid carrying a silver platter loaded with bacon-wrapped jalapeños. He handed over a crisp twenty-dollar bill, and the young man with the wavy blond hair and prominent cheekbones took it.

"I want you to head over to the little bar Jordan has set up over there and bring back two glasses of the finest scotch he's got," Max said. "I'll take mine neat."

This allowed him to avoid the crowd. He'd nearly burst a blood vessel dealing with these needy adult-size children for months. He had no patience for hanging out with them now.

Nicholas Moody's agent doubled the actor's price per sequel. Ashlee Gibson suffered nosebleeds during shoots from inhaling too much coke in her trailer and once tried to scratch a makeup artist's eyes out. As for the pair's off-screen romance reported in the gossip rags, it was all a publicity stunt.

"A little ice in mine," Raphael said. "If you don't mind."

"Right away, Mr. Maurey." The kid handed back the money. "No need to tip. My name is Johnny Frampton. I'm an actor. I hope you'll remember me one day if I end up in front of you in a casting call."

Max stared at him. The kid pressed on.

"I could really use a break. My granny isn't doing that great, and my one big dream is for her to see me—"

"Sure," said Max. "Fine."

"Awesome!"

Raphael smiled after the kid left. "See that? You're a big man."

Max scowled. "How do you do it?"

"Charm and intellect. Sorry, what are we talking about?"

"Every picture, you wake up and go to work. I say to you, 'All right, Raph, Jack needs half his face to look horribly burned from his fiery car wreck.' You scissor up some bald-cap vinyl, burn it to a crisp, and layer on some K-Y Jelly—"

Raphael bristled with feigned creative offense. "You forgot I also made a small prosthetic—"

"The point is you make it and hand it over," Max said. "You have no say in how it ends up in the final product. And you're okay with that."

"It's the job, man. It pays the bills. And I like doing it."

Max didn't know what to make of that statement. *A job.* It wasn't a job to him, it was a *calling.* More, it was his identity.

He loved being a motion picture director. He also lived it.

"I'll tell you what, though," Raphael went on. "For once, I'd like to do something really big. Maybe an arrow sticking out of a dude's eye. Something that would make ol' Tom Savini go, 'How the hell did he do that?'"

"You've done exceptional things," Max protested. "You're the one who taught me to show a real murder weapon cutting stuff before we substitute the fake one stabbing people. So the audience connects the two and feels like it's real."

The man turned sheepish. "Also Savini."

"Anyway, you know what I'm talking about. A yearning to do something powerful."

"Sure." Raphael shrugged. "But I don't let it keep me up at night."

The actor returned with a tray bearing a pair of snifters filled with scotch.

"Thank you, Johnny Frampton. I'll remember you." Though he doubted it; while handsome, the kid was generic enough to be a script placeholder. Max shot a look at Raphael. "Come with me. I'd like to show you something cool."

Rows of plush red seats faced a silver screen. Controlled by a dimmer switch, downlights softly illuminated Jordan's spacious home movie theater.

"Oh, groovy," said Raphael. "So this is what boo-coo money looks like."

"Let's see what he has in his private collection," Max said.

"I thought you'd been here before."

"We watched a few pictures together. Sometimes, we come here during production to check out dailies."

They pushed aside a dark, heavy curtain and entered the projection room.

Max added, "But he's never let me inside the holy of holies."

A pair of stout projectors stood side by side, ready to trade off the job of keeping the movie rolling. In a corner, another machine awaited its task of rewinding reels.

He didn't care about them. He gawked at the shelves loaded with feature films spooled in shiny sheet-metal canisters. Plucking one at random, he read the embossed lettering on a strip of tape: ON THE BEACH (1959), REEL #1.

"This is freaking awesome," said Raphael.

"I've never envied Jordan for anything until right now," Max said.

He spoke in a quiet, reverent voice. For him, being in this film library demanded a level of awe akin to how a pilgrim felt visiting a holy site.

So many landmark movies were in attendance. The industry's first significant baby steps. The pioneers and groundbreakers of the fifties and sixties. The auteurs and artists of the seventies, the last powerhouse movie era before the studio giants ruined it all with formula blockbusters.

He shivered a little, though it was mostly the blasting air-conditioning.

Raphael wore a surprised smile. "He actually has excellent taste. I see *Taxi Driver, Dog Day Afternoon, Network*—"

"Hold the phone."

"What did you find?"

Max cradled a clunky, heavy can.

"*Mary's Birthday*," he whispered.

Despite *Halloween*'s impact, fans still debated who started the slasher era. With its surprising shower murder, Alfred Hitchcock's *Psycho* kicked it off. No, Herschell Gordon Lewis's schlocky *Blood Feast* did. Wes Craven's brutal *The Last House on the Left*. Tobe Hooper's nightmarish *The Texas Chainsaw Massacre*. The creepy Giallo movement in Italy helmed by the likes of Mario Bava and Dario Argento.

And of course Arthur Golden's *Mary's Birthday*. The tragic, never-released 1972 horror film so apocryphal it was practically an urban legend.

Max opened the platter and inspected the reel. Then his gaze shifted to the projectors.

"No way, pal," Raphael said.

"Yes way."

"First off, I didn't come to a Bel Air party to take in an old movie. Second, Ashlee Gibson is out there doing God knows what without my admiration. And finally, oh yeah, if Mr. Lyman catches us in his library, he'll probably let you off with a slap, but he'll burn my career to the ground. All of which adds up to me splitting."

Max looked at him with wide eyes. "This isn't the actual picture."

"Okay, then—"

"It's the footage of the *accident*."

Before *Faces of Death*, the Mondo series that claimed to depict real death, there was the *Mary's Birthday* tragedy in 1972.

Raphael slowly nodded. "Yes."

"Yes?"

"Right on."

Max set down his drink. From under the projection table, he pulled a pair of cotton gloves and a can of compressed air. Fitting on the gloves, he sprayed the rollers and sockets to blow off any errant dust. Raphael's eyes widened in silent dread, as if he already regretted the horrors that would soon confront him.

Max mounted the reel and threaded the leader into the projector. He flipped the toggle switch. The xenon light bulb flared to life. The machine clattered as the motor sucked the film under constant tension to the bladed shutter and across the hot light beam.

The cast of *Mary's Birthday*, Arthur Golden's schlock classic, suddenly smiled at him from Jordan's theater screen. The grainy footage showed only visuals, as no one had been recording sound. The lack of brightness and color correction only made it more raw and compelling.

The movie's story: When Mary was thirteen, she attended her best friend Jane's birthday party. In a fit of jealousy, she inadvertently caused the girl's death. Now Mary is a recluse about to turn eighteen and host a party at which she hopes to leave her childhood and horrible guilt behind.

No such luck, as reaching adulthood makes her fair game for Jane's angry spirit and her signature weapon—the knife used to carve her birthday cake.

Violence ensues at Mary's party, claiming everyone she loves until she finds a way to make amends with her dead and vengeful bestie. The usual justice theme played to the usual horrific Greek-myth level of disproportion, though Max always wondered if something else was going on with these villains. Perhaps a simple, brutal desire to destroy the cool, popular kids and the pedestal they stood on.

While shot on 35mm with the newest camera on the market, by all accounts, the picture had been assembled so poorly as to look homemade. An overbaked passion project by a wealthy amateur director whom rumor had it dabbled in the occult and might have been insane.

Despite all that, *Mary's Birthday* made history in that it served as a gory prototype for what would become the eighties slasher flick.

It was also never released. Instead, it entered a genre all its own.

According to legend, the tragedy started like this:

On the last night of production, in a grassy field outside Wilkes-Barre, Pennsylvania, Golden and his crew prepared for the martini shot. The final shot that would wrap the film's principal photography—

A mile away, Harry Stinson, an old friend of Golden's, warmed up his helicopter to grab some bird's-eye B-roll footage of the town—

Helga Frost, the nineteen-year-old West German beauty who played Mary, took some extra time in her trailer preparing for the scene. This afforded the director the chance to pull the rest of the cast together to thank them for all their hard work—

And so Arthur Golden set his camera rolling to capture what for him would certainly be an emotional moment as his dark vision neared its realization.

In Jordan's private theater, the projector whirred. The reels turned. The warming air around the machine carried a whiff of ozone. Dust particles danced in front of its flaring beam.

Max absorbed the silent moving images with a fixed, unblinking stare.

Sporting a mix of early-seventies styles from long hair to bell-bottoms, the actors listen attentively in the afternoon sunlight.

Responding to whatever Golden is saying, they break into smiles. Many wipe tears from cheeks. They laugh as some shoot knowing glances at each other.

Jared Bearden, a veteran B-movie actor, accepts their applause with a sheepish grin. He raises his hand for a quick wave as a few of the actors turn to gaze at something off-screen, mouths working.

Someone points. Part of the crowd flinches.

The helicopter appears as a glimpse at the top of the frame. Angled down and out of control due to mechanical failure, spraying gasoline everywhere.

Rotating seven times per second, the blades sweep the actors and mow them to pieces like a giant lawnmower. Blunt blades that crush, mangle, and eventually sever everything in their whirl.

The resulting carnage at Wilkes-Barre is something Hollywood with all its costly modern special effects could never truly replicate.

Blood fountains among smashed bodies and spinning limbs in a rolling wave that slaughters most of the cast of twenty-one in mere seconds. The survivors squirm or sit dazed in the gore. Armless, Bearden thrashes in a pile of body parts, mouth open in a pitiful soundless scream.

The crew rushes forward to help.

Then the frame jumps as the helicopter crashes in a flaring off-screen fireball. It lights a searing barbecue clear across the remaining cast and crew that turns them all into a living, dancing bonfire, though none of them live very long.

The camera stays on the blaze for several seconds.

The screen went dark. The film crackled in the projector.

Max's heart pounded. He struggled to breathe.

"That's it," he gasped. "He turned off the camera."

Nonetheless, the footage continued to roll in his mind. The cast's faces, tired and happy and emotional about wrapping and going their separate ways. The sudden slaughter as the blades mowed them like bloody grass. The horrified crew racing to help only to burn to death in a massive blaze.

Helicopter accidents were sadly somewhat common in Hollywood. During shooting of *The Twilight Zone: The Movie* in 1982, a low-flying helicopter crash killed actor Victor Morrow and two children. *World War III, High Road to China, Braddock: Missing in*

Action III, and other productions all saw tragic helicopter-related deaths in the eighties.

None, however, occurred on the same macabre scale as *Mary's Birthday* back in '72. Max didn't believe in hexes and curses, but if any film had a curse, it had to be that film. Not even *The Exorcist*—which premiered in Italy across the street from an old church that got struck by lightning, causing its cross to tumble smoking to the ground—came close. Or *The Conqueror*, shot downwind of an atom bomb testing site, nearly half of whose crew wound up getting cancer.

Even after receiving so much, Max wanted more.

Raphael blanched. "Jesus Christ, that was horrible. It was *real*, man. Why did I watch that?"

"It's affecting," Max agreed.

"*Affecting?* I fought in 'Nam. Which sucked. The absolute worst sucking ever. And I never saw anything there like what I just watched in that film."

But it *was* affecting. Max couldn't think of a different word.

Actually, he could. *Heartbreaking, tragic,* and *sickening* all came to mind.

Also strangely compelling. Fascinating. Haunting. Beautiful, even.

The car crash you can't turn away from, on a much grander scale.

But *affecting* covered all of it, summed it up.

And more than that: inspiring. Like some kind of gold standard.

Raphael eyed him. "You know, man, you scare me sometimes."

Max blinked, surprised and a little pleased. "I do?"

"Honestly, I wonder at times what you would have ended up doing if you hadn't become a director."

Who knew, really? But Max *was* a director.

His strongest reaction to watching the *Mary's Birthday* accident reel was he wished he'd made it.

FOUR

Sally Priest was a Bad Girl.

Capital *B*, capital *G*, as in the horror movie trope.

And right now, the Bad Girl skinny-dipped at Jordan Lyman's party, swimming laps across the pool and wondering how she'd gotten here.

It all started with the punch bowl—

No, before that.

Nicholas Moody calling her up on the phone babbling about—

Wait. Rewind.

Once upon a time, Sally Priest had been Emily Corn of Orange County, a fresh-faced girl who dreamed of being a professional actor.

After acting school at UCLA, she'd auditioned for her first roles. Long days in windowless rooms in houses, churches, and theaters packed with actors doing crosswords and breathing exercises. When Sally's turn came, she often typed out immediately as tall or not tall, skinny or not skinny, busty or not busty enough, or otherwise lacking that certain something that made her right for the part.

It turned out she was ideal for horror, which she didn't mind at all, as she loved everything about this dangerous and subversive genre. In an era of big-ticket blockbusters, one could still make a profitable horror movie on a small budget, which opened the door to newcomers like her. Now, at all of twenty-three years old, Sally had been decapitated by a shovel in *Razor Lips* and drowned in quicksand in *Mutant Dawn*. Secondary, one-note characters, sure, but solid speaking roles. She'd also worked as an extra in *Zombie U.* and *War of the Wasteland*.

Sally had met Nicholas Moody at the wrap party for *Jack the Knife II*, in which he'd reprised his role as the titular monster. With his perpetually indignant face and chipmunk cheeks that made him look like an overgrown boy who didn't find his favorite toy under the Christmas tree, he'd struck her as strangely compelling. They had a fling that went nowhere—she could never quite trust him—but stayed friends. When he called to ask if she wanted to be his plus-one for the premiere of *Jack the Knife III*, she'd replied, yeah, duh, obviously.

During the show, Nicholas kept leaving for smoke breaks but really because he hated seeing his pudgy face on-screen. Ashlee Gibson hustled out twice to powder her nose. As for Sally, she sat on the edge of her seat ignoring her bladder and hissing to everyone's annoyance, "*Stay in the light!*" and "*Why is she opening that door?*" and "*Don't get in that car!*"

Anyway, that's how she ended up going to this party.

One mystery solved.

But it didn't explain how she turned into a fish.

Something about the punch bowl. Definitely about the Bad Girl.

The Bad Girl had emerged as an important member of the eighties horror pantheon alongside the Scholar, Hunter, Cop, Jock, Harbinger, Token Minority, and of course the Final Girl, who survives by vanquishing the evil killer. Arguably, the Bad Girl stood second in importance to the story as she provided a dramatic foil to the morally upstanding and responsible Final Girl. In fact, the Final Girl could not be truly pure without her moral counterpart.

Besides that, the Bad Girl had more fun. She laughed and

smoked the devil's lettuce and fucked with an utter lack of shame. And she never, ever took the threat of a machete-wielding maniac in the woods seriously because, come on, as if.

The Final Girl may have symbolized female empowerment, but the Bad Girl embodied it, however briefly. Unlike Emily Corn, the Bad Girl feared nothing. Yes, she was a surefire goner, according to the formula. But she left a beautiful corpse, while the Final Girl survived only to anticipate a lifetime of therapy, survivor's guilt, and looking over her shoulder.

Sally studied for her role. One could say she inhabited it.

As a student at UCLA, she'd latched on to the Stanislavski Method, as so many did. This system helped actors inhabit their characters so as to bring realism to their performance through a naturalistic approach. Lee Strasberg's take was to build a well of experience an actor could draw on emotionally to connect with a character while performing. Stella Adler favored imagination. Sanford Meisner taught actors to focus less on the character's internal landscape and more on reacting to the other actors. All of it worthy, though Sally had a masochistic thing for Strasberg.

The only problem was Emily Corn had been raised a nice, pampered girl by a reasonably wealthy family. Even in college, she'd been a straitlaced nerd. As an actor, she wanted to be the best and was terrified she might not be good enough.

Hence Sally Priest was born. And my, was Sally naughty.

The party had swirled around her in excited glimpses and fragments of people faking it in the belief they were making it. They glanced past each other's shoulders to see who else had attended and whom they were talking to. All of them networking, though the people they were doing it with had little to give except encouragement. Which didn't matter, you did it anyway, because everyone knew someone who might help you, and the struggling actor you met who waited tables between the odd Colgate commercial might become the next Brooke Shields.

As Sally had arrived with Nicholas's inner circle, she ended up in something of a receiving line of people who'd reached a higher rung on the endless ladder to stardom. Faces appeared to ask her what she was doing these days.

You know me, I'm always busy! Razor Lips *wrapped principal photography a few weeks ago, and now I'm taking Dan Womack's acting class. I recently did a photo shoot for fresh headshots and updated my sizzle reel. Oh yes! The director wanted me to dye my hair red for* Razor Lips, *I'm glad you like it!*

Sometimes, I drive out into the desert to work on my scream on the Joshua trees. It's really coming along.

They all said they'd love to hear it sometime. What was next for her?

Playboy kept asking her for a shoot, which she'd been putting off. She was looking at some scripts her agent had sent over. She attended the odd boozy lunch with such and such director. She left out that they all sought her for the Bad Girl role, as she didn't want to have to listen to any mock concern over typecasting. Everyone in Hollywood ended up typecast to some extent, and in Sally's mind, it wasn't such a negative to be a go-to gal for certain parts. Nonetheless, she dreamed of being the Final Girl—joining the scream queen sorority and standing alongside Jamie Lee Curtis, Heather Langenkamp, and Ashlee Gibson.

So that's me. What about you? What's in your pipeline? Who's your agent?

Sometimes, the faces changed before she finished talking. Then Ashlee pointed out the punch bowl with a wicked grin.

She called out: "Who among us is brave enough to try the blue sunshine?"

Only a lunatic would drink the mystery punch. The blue liquid had certainly been spiked. No doubt about that. What no one knew was how many people had spiked it and with what.

What would the Bad Girl do?

Pound a glass of it, of course, while Nicholas laughed his ass off.

"This is why we love you, Sal," he said.

She reined back a belch. "I'm trying to understand suffering."

To be a scream queen, one had to. Whatever didn't kill her made her a stronger actor, and she still wasn't strong enough. She could always be better.

"How is that going for you?"

"I honestly don't feel a thing." She didn't, not yet, anyway.

After an hour, she said, "I wish someone would murder me so I'd know what it's like. But not actually die. Because then what would be the point? You know?"

Nibbling on a canapé, Ashlee sniffed loudly, as she'd recently blasted her nostrils again.

"Not at all," she said.

Sally slapped the rest out of her hand.

"Don't eat that! The camera adds ten pounds."

"Goddamnit," said Ashlee. "Nicky, take care of your friend. She's high as a kite."

That's when Sally realized she had no idea what she'd been saying for the last twenty minutes or six hours, depending on whether her watch or intuitive connection to time and space were accurate.

All her old fears had dissipated. She was seeing the world a whole new way. Nicholas began to coil and bob like an improbable species of alien life. Sally went with the flow.

"You all right there?" he asked. "Your pupils look like black dimes."

"And you're an impressionist painting with van Gogh curves and Andy Warhol colors." It was true; Nicholas's face in particular was all kinds of messed up. She licked his pudgy cheek and frowned. "I thought it would taste like apple."

He wiped at his blushing face. "Jesus. Cut it out, Sal."

"You should get that checked out. By a, uh, a—"

"No joke, you're—"

"Gynecologist?" she finished.

"You're sweating, darling," Ashlee pointed out.

Sally looked at her. "And you . . . you're . . . you're such a—"

This uninhibited thought went unfinished, which was probably for the best; Ashlee tolerated her friends but burned her enemies to the ground. Distracted by her own reflection in one of the picture windows, Sally inspected the maniac leering back at her, mascara running like black tears.

"Who is that sexy creature?" she murmured to herself.

"I think somebody loaded that punch with mescaline," said Nicholas. "And God knows what else. I hope this night doesn't end at the hospital."

She noticed the pool beyond her reflection. "Never have I ever been a fish."

"Now, this is getting interesting," Ashlee said.

"She should lie down," Nicholas said.

"Shut up, Nicky. It's a party. Let her swim with the fishes."

"The Jack attack is back." Sally slowly extended her finger and poked his nose, only she missed by a solid nine inches. "Boop."

Then she yelled, "Okay, fuckers, who wants to go skinny-dipping?"

The crowd cheered. Finally, someone had kicked this shindig into high gear. Sally found the door and walked outside into the balmy night, shedding garments like a molting serpent. By the light of tiki torches, she stood pale and radiant in panties at the edge of the diving board, flickering like liquid porcelain.

Then she raised her arms and executed a beautiful dive that broke the surface with scarcely a blip.

Swirling in neon whirlpools, the warm water enclosed her like a velvet womb. Too late, she realized about an hour's worth of poofy hairstyling had been destroyed in an instant. It didn't matter. She felt free of it all at last. Everything, which included the pressure of having perfect hair.

While she breaststroked her first lap, the water exploded as partyers whipped off their own clothes and plunged in flying cannonballs.

Remembering all this, she now thought, *So that's how I became a fish.*

Yes, it was all starting to fall into place.

Who she was, and what she was doing here with these weird people.

No regrets. The water felt lovely. Honestly, she could live here.

But her limbs started to burn. She trembled with exhaustion. On the plus side, the exercise had helped push her past the drug peak. Her brain processed the world in a slightly more coherent way. She could at least think straight.

For example, she thought, *It's time to stop being a . . . a—*

A parasite swimming in the sweat glistening on the scales of a vast slumbering Leviathan curled into a black ball in space—

Okay, maybe she wasn't thinking *that* straight. But she *knew* she wasn't thinking straight, she had that going for her.

Cut to Sally hauling herself over the lip of the pool, where she lay gasping on the warm stone. She studied her hand, now wrinkled with moisture.

"Time's cruel passing," she said with dramatic flair. "I've grown old."

Perched on the pool's edge, a beautiful mermaid smiled at her. No, not a mermaid but a woman. An actor like her, glistening in bra and panties and swishing the heated water with her long legs.

"That was impressive," the blonde said. "You should go for the Olympics."

Sally squinted. "You were in *Cryptopia*. The morgue scenes."

"I played Dead Girl Number Two."

"You look better alive. Can I touch your skin?"

The woman laughed.

"Of course," she said.

Nicholas crouched next to Sally. "Glad you're still with us, Sal."

He handed her a glass of water. She gulped it down and came up gasping.

"Your face is looking a lot more human," she said. "But you're still wearing clothes."

The party had largely moved outside. Many revelers either frolicked in the pool or walked around half-nude, dripping, and gorgeous in the torchlight. The rest danced in the living room to Siouxsie and the Banshees' "Peek-a-Boo."

He winked at the mermaid. "I'm, uh, still working on that. Hello."

"Hi," said the blonde.

Sally heard tense voices. Living in an industry where everyone was enthusiastically cheerful most of the time, she zeroed in on the sound.

"Who's being a bummer?"

Nicholas helped her to her feet and lit a cigarette. A short distance away, Jordan Lyman lounged pink and steaming in a raised hot tub, looking like a giant ham someone dressed in a frizzy wig and mirrored shades and set to boil. His Saudi backers sat ramrod straight in the water like bearded mannequins he hauled around as glowering props.

And nearby, Max Maurey, the director of the *Jack* franchise, paced the deck scowling. Gaunt and wild-haired, Dr. Frankenstein in a tux.

Max growled. "You always said do it Hollywood's way, play the game—"

"That sounds like me," Jordan agreed. "I'm with you so far."

"You also said if I did that, I'd get to make the motion pictures *I* want to do."

"Oh. Well. I may have been fudging a bit about that part."

"I want to make something that is actually horror. Anything else is a fraud."

Sally turned to Nicholas. "My circuits are fried. The director and the producer seem to be arguing about whether the movie they made is good."

"Creative differences. Mr. Lyman said he's mainstreaming horror by making it palatable to the masses. Max is saying the masses deserve genuine terror, something like that."

"What do you think?"

"I don't," he enthused. "I just want to keep making movies."

"Well, I know how to fix this."

Nicholas snorted a cloud of smoke. "I am certain you do not, Sal."

"You don't understand. I really love this genre."

A mischievous expression crossed the actor's face. A smile of pure devilish charm that once won her over for a single night.

"In that case, I'm sure they'd benefit from your scholarship. Give 'em hell."

Sally was already striding forward. "What we're doing isn't horror!"

The men gawked at her with surprise—producer, director, financiers. Nicholas, meanwhile, vanished into the shadows.

"It's something else," she added. "Horror is only horror when it's real."

She wasn't certain whether it had been her or the drugs talking, but sure, she could agree with what her mouth had said. It sounded quite poignant, in fact.

The men only stared.

Then she looked down and realized she was practically naked.

"Oh, crumb," she said. "I forgot."

Well, so what. America had already seen her chest blown up to mythic proportions on massive screens in multiplexes. In her business, she could consider this little scene an impromptu audition.

Lucky for her, she had her resume on her at all times.

A hundred ten pounds, 36-24-36.

Max and Jordan exchanged a slow glance.

"Sally Priest, right?" said the director.

"That's me." She resisted the urge to do a little curtsy.

"Of course you are. I quite enjoyed you in *Mutant Dawn*." He gazed at her as a candidate for kindred spirit. "Anyway, I think you are absolutely correct. Horror is only horror if it's real. I'd love to talk to you about that sometime."

"Later," the producer said. "Come join us in the tub."

Sally understood she had a clear choice about whom to please, what each man wanted, what she might gain, and what it would cost her.

"I have to find my clothes," she blurted.

Stumbling away, Sally managed to locate her suspendered skirt hanging on an azalea bush. The rest had disappeared. Oh well. Fitting the skirt, she positioned the suspenders so they covered her nipples.

"That works." She didn't feel so good.

Jordan and Max had gone back to their arguing while the Saudis said nothing, their eyes following Sally like a creepy painting in an old haunted house movie. Again, Max Maurey struck her as a modern Dr. Frankenstein, though truth be told, each man no doubt considered himself the creator and the other the monster he couldn't quite control.

"Not the picture," the director was saying. "I saw the accident reel."

"Now you're going to go insane," said Jordan. "That film is cursed."

Max stopped pacing. "What do you mean? Are you serious?"

"No, I'm not serious. It's just footage of a tragic mishap. It's sad."

"I think—"

"And you weren't supposed to be in my film library. That's a big no-no, Max. It results in a very real kind of curse you won't like. The 'curse of the director banned from his producer's house'—"

"I think you're wrong. It wasn't only sad, it was the most powerful six minutes of cinema I've ever experienced. What Arthur Golden captured is nothing short of what Sally was talking about. Real horror."

Hearing her name as a cue to get back on scene, Sally padded toward them on her bare feet. "And another thing—"

Then she remembered this wasn't her argument and realized that she had nothing further to contribute.

One of the Saudis smiled and said something in Arabic.

Max ignored her. "I'd love to talk to him. Ask him what he felt."

"You can't," Sally said. "He's dead."

The director's mouth dropped open. "No, he isn't."

"Arthur Golden died, like, two weeks ago. Um . . ."

She mimed shooting herself in the head.

"I would have heard—"

"It wasn't in the trades. I heard it from my—" She didn't know what to call Dan Womack. "I have a source who was close to him."

Again, the men stared at her in surprise until even Sally in her inebriated state grew self-conscious.

"Well," she said. "Okay, bye."

"If you change your mind about joining us, let me know," said Jordan.

She wandered away wondering where she was going. Then a sudden, urgent desire came over her. Something important that remained missing. Another part of her resume she had on her at all times. Her audition wasn't complete.

Sally stomped back to the hot tub. She clenched her fists against her cheeks.

And screamed.

A horror scream shrill and loud enough to tremble glass, assault eardrums, and terrify a future movie audience.

Sally screamed for all she was worth while Max goggled, Jordan regarded her with a little half smile, and the Saudis thrashed the water in pell-mell flight.

Then she bent to vomit all over the producer's redwood deck.

INSPIRATION

*The first monster that an audience
has to be scared of is the filmmaker.*

Wes Craven
Director, *A Nightmare on Elm Street*

FIVE

Max liked the angle and the morning light falling on the lovely woman sleeping on his pastel couch. He noted it for future adaptation. He didn't have a photographic memory, but he had a solid memory for photography.

"You've got a hell of a scream, Sally Priest," he said. "It's time to rise."

Curled up in his monogrammed terry-cloth bathrobe, she let out a cute little moan. Fiery red hair poured over the pillow. Her mouth puckered around a drool spot. She had what people called an overbite. This minor flaw only distinguished her even more from the competition.

Max's Pomeranian found her interesting too. Standing with paws resting against the side of the couch, the little rusty dog eyed Sally with distrust. Then glanced at Max as if to say, *Can I eat her now, Master?*

"Be nice, Suse," he warned.

At last, the woman's lips moved, as if running lines in her dreams. A little blush colored her cheeks.

Her eyes flashed open, bright green and bloodshot.

"It's alive," said Max.

Sally blinked at Susan, who pushed off the couch to puff out her chest and growl. Her bleary gaze shifted to Max standing over her still wearing his tux and then swept across his living room. The rounded brass coffee table, potted palms, Lucite lamps, tropical wallpapering, and framed Patrick Nagel neon noir prints.

"What the hell is going on?" she croaked.

"Everything's okay," Max said, and offered a mug of coffee. "You passed out before I could get your address, so I let you crash here."

She slowly reached out to accept the mug.

"Tell me what you meant," he said. "About horror only being horror when it's real."

She winced. "Oh. My. God."

"What's wrong?"

"It's all coming back to me. Sometimes, I take the whole Bad Girl experiment way too far."

"I'd like to know more about what you think," Max said.

Horror is only horror if it's real. Put as simply as this, it had struck him as an epiphany. More, an epiphany that forced him to challenge his assumptions.

He'd always seen fictional horror as a way to both avoid and safely process the horrors of reality. What if its purpose instead might be to do the opposite?

Feeding his chronic insomnia, this question had kept him awake along with his haunting memories of the off-kilter premiere. In the dark, quiet hours, he could hear *Jack*'s rowdy audience laughing in muted echoes, as if they'd been transported into his house's walls.

Sally sighed. "Mr. Maurey—"

"Call me Max."

"Max, I made a total fool out of myself in front of you and a major producer last night. I blew up my career before it's even started. I *hurled* on Mr. Lyman's deck. So I'm not sure what you want me to say."

"Jordan has seen it all," he assured her. "In terms of weirdness, I doubt you made a scratch. Actually, I think he found you amusing."

Brightening a little, she sat up. "Oh. Seriously?"

"One of his backers seemed quite taken with you, though. If I were you, I wouldn't answer your phone until they fly home. Unless, you know..."

He politely coughed into his fist and spread his hands. He didn't like the game and didn't play it, but he knew it existed.

"I don't do that to get ahead," she said.

"And I don't require it. Just so we're clear, my casting couch is used only for casting. And the occasional dignitary who needs to crash."

Sally threw a final suspicious glance his way.

"So let me get this straight. Last night, I got high, took off my clothes, and passed out. Then you brought me here so we could chat about horror."

He smiled, glad they were all caught up.

"Now explain what you meant," he said.

"Well, shit." Sally shrugged. "Okay, then."

Taking a moment to collect her thoughts, she offered her hand to Susan. The dog jumped back with dramatic indignance before padding forward to sniff the woman's fingers.

"Lady Susan likes you," said Max.

The Pomeranian glanced up at him. *Can I eat her now, please?*

He gave her a little shake of his head.

With a shudder, the dog allowed Sally to scratch her behind the ears, her suffering black eyes boring into Max's the entire time.

"She's nice," Sally said. "You have a lovely place."

"Thank you." With its bold eighties colors and gaudy materials, Max had never liked it. Flush with cash, he'd had an interior decorator put it all together and had signed off on it because he had a living room and needed stuff in it.

"Okay." The woman took her first sip of coffee and made an appreciative noise. "Horror can't be horrifying unless the audience believes it might be real, you know? But it can't only be *Faces of Death*, because that's just spectacle. Pure shock."

"There's no story," Max said.

"Right. Shock is not the same as drama. The same way sympathy is not empathy. That's what I think I meant when I said that last night."

"Are the two irreconcilable?"

"We do reconcile it. All the time. It's what horror movies are today. They're gross and they're creepy and they're fun."

"I mean *really* reconcile it. Reconcile it until they're the same thing."

"I'm not sure you'd want to. If it's too real—"

"It might not be fun," said Max. "I understand."

"And if it's not fun, very few people are going to want to sit through it."

"Does the horror in a horror film *have* to be fun? *Cannibal Holocaust* wasn't fun. It was raw and visceral."

Sally considered it. "Horror makes the rest of life more interesting. It's a foil for all the good things we take for granted. It shouldn't be an end in itself."

"I'm thinking of horror that makes you understand life as it really is. Horror is too fair. It's loaded with cop-outs."

"I'd say it has rules," she countered. "It's not about morality but safety. If you follow the rules, you won't die. The audience learns how to survive."

"But that's not real!" They were back at the beginning. "Real life isn't fair. Bad things happen to good people all the time. Horror should be unpredictable."

"Okay, but I don't think you want it to be cruel, either. Nihilism is a mega bummer." Sally thought a little more and added, "You know who does a terrific job at it is Dario Argento. His movies are like dreams. Horror is a feeling, not a genre, right? He captures it so well. The fear starts with creating discomfort, that weird sense that things are not what they seem."

Max grunted. He was after something blunter and less artsy.

Watching the accident reel and talking about horror's essence with Sally had brought him to the edge of a profound truth. He just didn't know what it was yet.

For him, the question was how one might bottle the *Mary's Birthday* accident's real, visceral horror in a story without actually murdering actors. Was it a matter of content or technique, or maybe both?

If he could lay his hands on the film again, he'd study it like the world's most puzzling koan. He'd catalog everything he saw and felt. He'd ghoulishly examine each of its nine thousand celluloid squares until he'd determined what made it so affecting and could re-create its emotional power on demand.

The answer was close. He knew it was close because he now asked the right question.

Max glanced at his watch. Almost noon. He was running out of time.

"Finish your coffee and then get dressed. I'll drive you wherever you need to go, but I have to make a stop first in North Hollywood." He squinted at her. "How did you know Arthur Golden had died?"

"My workshop teacher is Dan Womack."

Max sucked in his breath. Womack was one of the three survivors of *Mary's Birthday*. Make that two, seeing as Golden was no longer alive: Womack, who'd played the picture's loving but clueless dad, and Helga Frost, who'd played his daughter Mary, the heroine.

Another stroke of serendipity. The whole thing felt like fate.

This Sally Priest was getting more interesting by the minute. He made a note to reach out to Womack at some point. Today, however, he had bigger fish.

"Dan kept in touch with Arthur over the years," she added.

"What's this Womack like?"

"Cultured, smart, and kind of a basket case."

"Did you ever meet Golden himself before he died?"

She shook her head.

Max walked over to his dining table and scooped up a newspaper. He returned to drop it on her lap. "Well, his estate sale is today."

"Oh. That's where we're going?"

"That's right. If you want to come, that is."

Sally's green eyes flashed bright and alert at the prospect of something new.

"I'm always up for everything," she said.

Behind the wheel of his sleek little black MG, Max drove them onto LA's spaghettied arteries. A Michael Jackson hit played over the radio. He had the top down, the only time he enjoyed being exposed to direct sunshine, though he wore his bucket hat with its MORT'S SPORTING GOODS logo, a personal trademark on set. Among rushing glass and steel that was one collision away from turning into its own *Mary's Birthday*, he glanced over at Sally.

Cured by coffee, aspirin, and youth, her hangover had departed. Her suntanned face smiled behind sunglasses and wind-thrashed hair. He'd given her an old T-shirt, which she'd fitted with last night's skirt and suspenders into an outfit.

As for Max, he'd finally changed out of his tux into his usual uniform of a black suit worn with a band tee. Today, it was Devo's turn. He imagined they made quite a picture, veteran horror director and budding scream queen. His dark crashing against but utterly dependent on her bright light.

"Sally Priest," he said. "How did you come up with that as a stage name?"

"I wanted something that sounded sweet and pure but corruptible."

He had to chuckle at that. Yes, the lady was a scream queen at heart.

Then he growled as brake lights crowded the roadway ahead

like glowing demon eyes. Slowing, his MG joined the rear of a crawling parking lot, a visible reminder that wherever you hoped to go in this town, some malevolent god would try to stop you from getting there.

Sally said, "I already know where you got yours."

"Me?" he wondered, willing the traffic to either move or get out of his way. "You think I changed my name?"

Sally tilted her head to regard him over her shades. "Oh, come on." Gazing at his blank expression, she pushed them back onto the bridge of her nose. "Suit yourself. I guess it's a coincidence and you've never heard of the Grand Guignol."

But of course he had.

Modern splatter horror could trace its routes to Elizabethan revenge tragedies like Shakespeare's *Titus Andronicus* and even further back to the Roman playwright Lucius Seneca. Its first real flowering, however, occurred at the Grand Guignol. The Theater of the Great Puppet.

From 1897, this Paris theater specialized in nihilistic horror under the command of a French playwright named Max Maurey. The sensationalistic short plays served up realistic murder, torture, sex, and cannibalism.

"He's actually a distant relation," Max said. "From what I could learn."

Sally looked impressed. "I imagine he'd be quite proud of you."

"I'm not so sure about that."

He doubted anyone laughed in the Grand Guignol.

At last, the traffic unknotted enough for him to surge ahead to his exit. He steered his roadster into a lowbrow neighborhood of stuccoed fifties dingbats. Arthur Golden, it turned out, had been down and out and living on the cheap.

Under an overhang protruding from one of these old shoebox apartment buildings, Max parked the MG and cut the engine.

"I live in a building just like this," Sally noted.

Max grunted. Seething with anticipation, he marched inside, Sally in tow.

Aside from a little daylight and a single glaring fluorescent fixture, the vestibule was shrouded in shadows deep enough to hide creatures and maniacs. The air smelled musty. Ancient wallpaper bubbled and peeled.

Dim stairs led up into gloom.

"Very moody," Sally said.

"Yeah," said Max. "It's perfect."

They mounted the creaking stairs.

"I have a relation in the business too," Sally said. "My mother, in fact. She's Maude Turner."

Max grunted again. "I don't know that name."

"You wouldn't, though if you're a fan of old movies, no doubt you've seen her somewhere. She played a townswoman in *East of Eden* and a drunken brunette in *The Barefoot Contessa*. A dancer in *Houseboat*. All through the fifties, she got bit parts in some of the decade's best films."

"Why didn't she stick with it?"

"By the mid-sixties, she still hadn't hit stardom and had started to age out. So she quit, married rich, and had me."

"Well. I imagine she'd be quite proud of you too."

"Ha," said Sally.

"What?"

"I'm not sure about that either. I guess I'm still working on it."

Max shrugged. "Either way, what we do is in our blood."

He stopped in front of the door marked with the right number and knocked. It creaked open to reveal a mohawked Amazon in designer eyewear.

"Welcome to the castle," she said with a husky Irish accent. "I'm Clare."

The woman stood nearly as tall as Max, taller counting the bristling red mohawk that contrasted with her business suit.

"We're here for the sale," he said.

Sally said nothing, eyeing the Amazon with fascination. The estate sale agent gazed back at her with a different kind of appetite.

"Of course you are, love," Clare said.

Max went inside and looked around at the little living room and attached kitchen. With its stained walls and air that smelled like stale cigarette smoke and industrial cleaners, the dead director's abode struck a depressing scene.

Heartbreaking, in fact. Arthur Golden had poured most of his fortune into *Mary's Birthday* and hadn't worked since. Haunted by the tragedy, he'd shut himself off from the world he'd once sought to terrify.

Stacked everywhere, Golden's meager possessions were on full display, marked with yellow price tags and red SOLD stickers. The detritus of a man's sad life arranged as a liquidation sale.

Everything must go, the room announced.

"You're an actor?" Clare said to Sally. "I do a bit of it myself."

While they compared notes, Max zeroed in on a pair of book-shelves filled with VHS tapes. This turned out to be Golden's personal horror collection with a side of extreme German por-nography. All marked SOLD.

He didn't care. He'd come for *Mary's Birthday*.

Jordan had acquired a print of the accident reel. A surprise he had it in his collection at all. Contrary to the urban legends of the paranoid seventies, there was no cabal of rich perverts paying top dollar for snuff films.

The producer had nonetheless gotten his hands on it, which must have cost him a pretty penny. Enough to allow Golden to maintain his hermit lifestyle a few more years.

Which meant the original film had to be here somewhere.

Max spotted a closed door and gravitated toward it.

"I wouldn't go in there, love," Clare called to him. "They hav-en't yet properly scrubbed the, um, stains."

"Are there any film cans?" he asked.

"*Mary's Birthday* was sold," the Amazon enthused. "A collector snatched it up first thing and walked out with it."

He'd arrived too late. Glum, he picked his way through other yard sale stuff, most of which looked destined for donation or the garbage heap.

"Max," Sally said. "Check this out!"

She held a large, nasty-looking kitchen knife.

He grunted. "That's—"

Testing its point with her thumb, she plunged it into her heart. Her head dropped to the side, tongue lolling.

"Probably Mary's knife," Max finished.

Sally examined the collapsible prop. "I'm going to give it to Dan."

"It's a nice find."

"That isn't what I wanted to show you."

She'd discovered a film camera.

It rested on a bed of red velvet inside a teak trunk carved in a Gothic style, odd symbols surrounded by frolicking angels and demons.

Max recognized it as an Arriflex 35BL.

Introduced in 1972 at the Summer Olympics, the 35mm camera was terrific for its time. Small and portable, it proved versatile when one needed handheld and tight shots. The fixed butterfly reflex shutter offered a true representation of the captured image, with a footage counter modeled on an odometer.

"And it's quiet," Max lectured. "That's what the *BL* stands for, *blimped*. A lens blimp that reduces noise. The 35BL has had an enviable run. The industry used it to shoot *Taxi Driver, Barry Lyndon, Apocalypse Now...*"

Sally gave him an amused look. She was an acting geek, not a film geek. Still, she was enough of an overall nerd to appreciate his tech talk anyway. The same nerdiness that had made her excited to connect with this slice of genre history, however sad it looked arranged for sale.

"And *Mary's Birthday*," he added.

Its unblinking glass eye had witnessed the tragedy.

Max doubted anyone had ever cheered while watching it. No one thought it funny. No one munched popcorn they wouldn't be able to keep down. Perfect horror demanded one's full attention.

Inside the box, he found various lenses and accessories. And like the solution to a puzzle of *one of these things is not like the others*, an old blue Danish butter cookie tin rested on its red backdrop. Back in the fifties, Max's mother had used one like it to store her sewing kit.

He picked it up and gave it a quick shake, producing a satisfying rattle. His ears told him a stretch of film lay coiled within, a little mystery to explore.

"Are you a cinematographer?" Clare asked over his shoulder.

"Director," he said.

"He made the *Jack the Knife* series," Sally told her.

"Fucking A," said Clare. "I have a date to see the third one on Friday."

Max had stopped listening. He wrapped his hand around the pistol grip that Golden's photography director had attached to the camera.

The grip responded with a brief rippling vibration, as if it were alive.

He murmured, "Do you hear that?"

The camera seemed to hum.

A deep, pulsing bass at the edge of hearing, more felt than heard, like the Sensurround system developed to show the 1974 *Earthquake* movie.

Sally tilted her head. "Hear what?"

Max was certain the camera wanted to tell him something. He lifted the heavy apparatus out of the box and raised it to his ear.

The hum elevated into a flurry of enraged screams. Then they too stopped as Arthur Golden's apartment disappeared and the world turned black. The darkness almost tangible. Absolute.

Back in the real world, Sally said something, a muffled blur that cut off to silence. Max wondered if he was dead, what that meant.

Then the dark noticed his presence. It had something to show him.

A spark in the void. Max fell toward it. The spark became a fire. The fire a raging conflagration in which shadows flickered and danced.

"Max."

That's my name, he thought.

"Max."

It chose me—

A hand roughly shook him.

"Max!"

Then he was back in Golden's shabby apartment. Sally eyed him with her hands splayed to break his fall if he fainted.

"Is he okay?" Clare asked.

"Wow," said Max.

"He's an artist," Sally said, as if that explained everything.

He smiled at the camera in his hands.

"I need this," he added.

Sally cleared her throat. She pointed to the red sticker on the box.

He growled. "Damn it."

Max tightened his grip on the camera. This was the eye that bore mute witness to the *Mary's Birthday* tragedy and captured it in time. It *spoke* to him—a sleep-deprived hallucination, granted, but just the same. He had to have it.

Despite his nice house and car and housekeeper, he lived frugally. He had plenty of money. He'd contact the buyer and make an offer they couldn't refuse. He'd pay off Clare right now to look the other way. Max sized her up and wondered if he bolted how far he'd get before this Amazon tackled him.

Not far, he surmised.

As if sensing his thoughts, Clare stomped over in her combat boots to loom over the scene. Peeling off the sticker, she pressed it against her business card and handed it to Max.

"I'm an actor," she said.

Max mutely nodded his thanks at the giant with the beautiful face, linebacker shoulders, and bright red punk hairdo.

"I'll remember you, Clare." He meant it. He pocketed her card.

Completing the transaction, which included a fat tip, he and Sally hauled the entire cabinet of curiosities down the grungy stairs into the trunk of the MG.

Even there, it hummed for attention.

"What are you going to do it with it?" Sally asked.

"I'm going to make a motion picture," he said, realizing as he said it that yes, that's exactly what he'd do with it. "Something entirely new."

A grand film that would be remembered like *Mary's Birthday*. Now he understood his greatest work as an artist lay not in his past but in his future.

The *Jack* movies all had a purpose. They'd prepared him for this. He'd go to Jordan with a new concept, and this time, he'd get final cut on it. Realize his dream of becoming an auteur, controlling every aspect of production, every frame that went into the movie. A true Max Maurey production.

"Do you have an idea?"

"Not yet," he admitted. "All I have right now is inspiration. But sometimes, I feel like everything's been done."

"I have a movie pitch for you," Sally offered. "One you can't refuse."

"Oh?"

"Make the movie *you're* dying to see. One that scares *you*."

"I like it already." Max remembered his father's eyes flashing with panic as he died. The memory sent a shudder through him.

"Movies are like life, full of possibilities." She cast him a sly look. "So, are you thinking about casting Clare in it?"

"I probably should, and not only because of the favor. She really is striking."

With Golden's camera, Max felt fairly punk again himself. He regarded its acquisition as an omen from the movie gods.

Again, he felt chosen.

"I liked her too," said Sally. "She has a great energy."

He expected a catty follow-up from the actor, but she seemed genuinely happy that a woman she'd just met might get a lucky break.

You're a rare animal, Max thought.

"She's not Final Girl material, though." Then he winked.

SIX

Clad in white stucco and shaped like an inverted V, Max's Spanish-style home in Sherman Oaks confronted him like a straitjacket outstretched in a cheerful hug. He parked in the driveway and lugged the trunk inside.

Flush with residuals from the *Jack* franchise, he'd entered the housing market in search of something deliciously Gothic or at least Victorian. Not so easy to find in happy, sun-drenched Los Angeles—the city of angels, not demons. He'd settled on this house, as it at least offered a three-story, cone-capped turret built into the center like the pin in a giant door hinge.

Dazed from lack of sleep and excessive sunlight, Max hauled the ornate teak box to his dining room table. His home's decor gleamed in perfect orderliness; Mariel, his housekeeper, had swept through the place in his absence.

Susan swirled and panted around his legs.

Then she cocked her head to growl at the box.

"You hear it too, Lady Susan? Sometimes, it screams."

The dog barked at it.

He crouched to give her a scratch. "Maybe Golden put a demon in the camera. Wouldn't that be cool for Daddy?" He slipped into his baby-talk voice. "Yes, it would. Oh yes, it *would*."

Distracted by his pampering, the Pomeranian grinned, her little pom-pom tail windmilling so hard her bum seemed about to go aloft.

Max couldn't wait to take the camera out for a test drive. First, he needed a nap, which he knew would cure him of his auditory hallucinations. He'd stayed up all night seething with ideas as he had many times during his creative life, but he was hardly a young man anymore, brimming with midnight oil to burn.

In his upstairs bedroom, he gazed balefully at the bed and furnishings afire in bright California sunlight streaming through the window blinds. Mariel liked to lecture him about vitamin D and otherwise enjoyed telling him all the things he did wrong with his health and how he'd die from it. He closed the blinds she'd cranked open and let out a relieved sigh in the resulting gloom.

While cleaning, she'd discovered his discarded tux and hung it up. She'd also done his laundry and put it all away, folded with military precision.

On the bed, she'd left a pair of red panties.

Max picked them up and pictured the young beauty with the overbite who'd worn them. The whole afternoon, she'd gone around without wearing any underwear. Chuckling, he dropped the lacy garment into his dresser's sock drawer.

During the ride home, he'd asked Sally what truly scared her. *Not being good enough to survive in this business*, she'd answered. When his turn came, he didn't have to think about it. *People*. Though this wasn't true, not really.

What truly scared him, he'd buried somewhere deep.

Max had left the girl buzzing at the hint he might cast her as a Final Girl in his next movie. Well, let her buzz.

He'd seen her perform in *Mutant Dawn*. She'd overacted a bit, which might have been a lack of confidence, or maybe her sensing the movie wasn't working so she might as well play it on the campy side. Nonetheless, she alone had inhabited her role among a rookie ensemble that largely looked like they were reading lines.

Under his firm and deft direction, Sally would do better. She had the look, and the minute her talent caught up to it with the right director, he saw no limit to how far she might go. So, yes, he'd be happy to work with her. If nothing else, it'd make a refreshing change from babysitting Ashlee Gibson and her coke habit.

Max stretched out on the bed on top of its preppy mono-grammed linens. He closed his eyes and fidgeted until he'd reached a position approximating comfort.

His mind refused to relax. The *Jack* premiere. Jordan. Sally. Arthur Golden. The helicopter accident. The strange camera patiently waiting for him on the dining table.

The film in the cookie tin.

His brain still racing, he climbed out of bed and checked in at his home office. The answering machine blinked with recorded messages. His fax chattered opening-night reports detailing ticket sales along with breakouts per region and per-screen averages. So far, *Jack*'s third time out looked like a commercial success, eking out a respectable showing against the weekend's other opening films, including *Young Guns* and Martin Scorsese's latest, *The Last Tempta-tion of Christ*.

Which should have made him happy, only last night he'd stopped liking his own franchise. No doubt, one of the messages recorded on his machine was Jordan congratulating him for pro-ducing formulaic pap.

Susan padded over and looked up at him. *What's next, Master?*

"I want to make something that hasn't been made before," Max said.

At his tone, the little dog grinned.

He knew what he should do right now. What he should have done the minute he'd arrived home to this overbright house.

Returning to the dining room, he opened the box and removed the round metal cookie tin. Pried the lid with his thumbnail.

A stretch of developed film lay roughly coiled inside like a dor-mant and exotic parasitic worm. Under this work print, he found a magstripe, a length of blank film onto which a magnetic coating had been mounted with a sound recording. Despite their age, the uncomposited pair were in excellent condition. He guessed there was some two hundred feet in the can, about two minutes of footage.

On the back of the lid, Golden had scrawled a message in black marker.

Never use this camera, fellow traveler.

Max smirked. "Sorry, Arthur. That's not how it works."

He ascended the stairs to the top of the turret, where he kept the Moviola. If he were a mad scientist, this small circular room would be his laboratory.

Shutting the blinds to erase the spectacular neighborhood views, he settled onto the stool in front of his hulking apparatus. Constructed of smooth cast aluminum finished in gray-green enamel, the Moviola was a film- and sound-editing machine. The industry had moved on to flatbed editors but still used Moviolas to watch dailies, evaluate sizzle reels, and of course do a little editing.

Max enjoyed giving his own movies a last polish, as he liked having as much creative control as possible. Forsaking food and sleep, he'd disappear here for weeks—patiently slashing his slasher, littering the floor with bits of cut film—until the final product ran perfectly smooth and sharp where needed.

At his feet, Susan snuggled into her little plush bed and gazed up at him with quivering eyes. She let out a soft whine.

Max pulled on a pair of cotton gloves and threaded the film snug into the gate under the viewing scope. He inserted the sound on the left so it would run in sync. He levered the first picture frame until it appeared in full view on his bright scope, showing a woman leaning against a deck railing.

"Bonanza," Max breathed in the glow.

It was Helga Frost.

Mary's Birthday's lead and one of the only three people to survive its final day of shooting on a grassy field in Pennsylvania.

He stomped the pedal. Dragged forward by sprocket teeth biting through perforations, the ribbon of film chattered through the Moviola, which appeared to devour it as he fed the machine from his hands.

The picture came to life.

The scene is a deck overlooking a lush green slice of Laurel Canyon, where numerous flat and stilted homes were built along the hillsides during the sixties.

Helga Frost leans against the railing. Wearing a yellow housecoat, she raises a bare foot to idly scratch a spot on her other calf.

The view trembles a little. The scene is being shot as a handheld. As if following the action, the camera lurches into a voyeuristic zoom toward her legs but then pulls back.

She takes a drag on her cigarette and exhales a long stream of smoke before turning to the camera.

"Why did you bring that goddamn thing, Arthur?"

She speaks with a clipped German accent, which she altered during filming of Mary's Birthday *to fit the character of an all-American girl.*

"Because I want something to remember you," he answers. "I don't know when I'm going to see you again. You've shut yourself off from the world."

"What is wrong with that?"

"It's been months since the accident."

"And?"

"You're alive," Arthur replies. "You should live."

"Why?"

"I don't understand the question."

"It is a simple question. Everyone else died. Why do I get to live?"

"Ah. The question is about importance."

She turns away and takes another drag. "Go away, Arthur."

"We all die, Helga. Returning to the eternity before we were born. We're the only animal that knows it's coming. One way to accept the horror without losing our sanity is to try to transcend it. Do great deeds, have

*children, live a moral life, make powerful works of art. Anything that will
endure."*

*Sighing, Helga leans against the railing with both hands as if she
needs its support to stay on her feet. She appears mentally and physically
exhausted.*

*"I feel like I was supposed to die that day," she says. "That it is only a
matter of time before Death realizes he left someone behind."*

"Survivor's guilt. I'm trying to tell you you're important to me."

"Put the camera away. I am done acting."

"This isn't about making pictures. This is about me and you."

She turns her head toward him.

"What do you mean?"

"The truth is from the first time I saw you, I've loved—"

The railing cracks in her hands.

In an instant, she is gone.

"Holy mother," Max shouted, his face burning with a sudden
hot flash.

Arthur Golden cries out in anguish.

"HELGA—"

The image in the Moviola's scope lurched and then went blank
as the length of film disappeared. Susan lowered her head and
whimpered.

"Holy mother," Max said again, this time an awed whisper.

His face still felt hot. His heart pounded in his chest.

The camera failed to capture what happened next, but he could
easily guess. Max had seen the houses built along those hillsides.

Helga had plummeted headfirst to smash against the canyon's
rocky slope.

What caused it? Just before she tumbled over the edge, the deck
railing had appeared solid. Then it crumbled under her hands.

The only things that came to mind were faulty construction or
perhaps termites, but even then, the suddenness and bad luck of it
were uncanny.

Max played it again and hit the brake to freeze the image on a frame showing Helga's hands blurring through the splintering wood.

The surprised look on her face.

He advanced the frames one by one. The railing coming apart. Helga's slim body pitching forward. Her face morphing from surprise to animal terror—

And then, for a single final frame before she disappeared, what appeared to be poetic resignation. Simple acceptance of her fate. Understanding. Possibly even relief.

Maybe *Mary's Birthday* truly was cursed. Or Arthur Golden was.

He'd delivered a heartfelt thanks to the cast and crew of his dream project only to witness them being mowed down and incinerated in a rush of flame. He'd filmed Helga Frost because he loved her and wanted at least one more memory of her that would endure, and then he'd helplessly watched her fall to plummet onto the rocks.

In the end, not Frost but Golden became the recluse.

A man who no doubt had come to believe he lived under a curse.

Max plugged in his editing room's rotary phone. He dialed a number and waited through the long rings, leg jittering.

An answering machine picked up.

"Hey, you've reached Raph. Leave a message and I'll holler back. Thanks."

The machine beeped.

"Pick up, damn you," Max railed. "I know you're there."

Muffled clicks, followed by the phone clattering across the floor and a sighed obscenity at the other end of the line.

At last: "Maximillian, is that you?"

Max gripped the phone in his sweaty hand. "What are you doing right now?"

"Do you know how hungover I am today? I'm not doing *anything*, man."

"I need you to meet me at Lake Balboa Park in half an hour."

At the word *park*, Susan raised her head with frank hope. Max shook his head at her in apology. She couldn't come this time. She whined again.

"What's the matter with Lady Susan?" Raphael asked.

"I just told her she can't come."

"You sound manic. Have you been up all night again?"

Max declared, "I've made an important discovery."

"Oh, for the sake of all that's holy—"

"The picnic pavilions area. Okay?"

A long pause.

"You're lucky you're my favorite client, you bastard."

The man hung up.

Max replaced the phone in its cradle and unplugged it again. He returned the coils of film to the cookie tin. He turned off the Moviola editing machine.

Then he went downstairs.

And stood smiling down at the Arriflex 35BL in its carved box. Which once more sang to him.

Again, that feeling it tried to tell him something. Again, he wondered if he hallucinated from staying awake too long, or if something else was in play.

"It's time to take you out for a spin," Max said.

Lake Balboa Park sprawled lush and green in late afternoon sunshine. Stands of cherry blossom trees and distant oleander, lavender, and hyacinth produced a riot of pinks and violets. Geese and mallards quacked on the pristine lake. Butterflies fluttered past. And everywhere, Los Angelenos tossed Frisbees on the lawn or hung out on picnic benches in the shade of pavilions.

Even Max, who didn't know how to relax, considered this place a serene oasis. He tried to imagine something horrible happening. Nothing came to him, even as the shadows lengthened to herald the coming twilight. He had a hard time imagining the worst around cherry blossoms.

Max mounted the Arriflex 35BL on a tripod and aimed it at the lake.

Again the familiar voice behind him: "So you got a new toy?"

"Yep. I'm giving it a test drive."

Back at the house, he'd unscrewed the camera cover and wiped the film channel with a cotton swab and mild alcohol solution. Applied a high-grade, low-temperature oil to saturate the wicks in the cam shaft lubrication reservoir. Checked the drive belt for proper tension, replaced the power fuses, popped in a twelve-volt battery, and tested the signal lamps. Threaded a fresh roll of film until the sprocket teeth caught it and fitted the rest onto the magazine's supply core.

Then he'd found a battered old plastic case to house the Arriflex 35BL along with its lenses, filters, and accessories.

With all this finished, he'd driven the camera here to take it off its leash.

Wearing a leather jacket over a faded gray T-shirt, Raphael shambled up to him rubbing his forehead. "This is why you dragged my hungover ass out here? To test a new camera and drum up some slice-of-life inspiration for future shots?"

Max gave him an evil grin.

"It's not just any camera," he said.

"Christ, look at you. Did you get any sleep at all last night?"

"This is the camera that captured *Mary's Birthday.* And the tragedy."

"That's a fascinating bit of cinematic trivia." The special makeup effects artist plunked onto the ground and groaned.

Max kept grinning. "And then it witnessed Helga Frost's death."

"Wait." Raphael gazed up at him with bloodshot eyes. "What?"

"The camera came with a stretch of footage I loaded and watched on my Moviola. Golden filmed Helga while they talked about the accident. Right when he told her he loved her, *bam*! She fell through a railing."

"Holy crap." The man eyed the camera with a shiver. "That thing is bad juju."

"I have a theory that it somehow makes horror."

"What?"

"Or horror is drawn to it. I don't know."

"Maximillian."

"It was *singing* to me—"

"*Max*. Look at me, man. You need to get some shut-eye."

"I know."

"All right. Fine. It's just that sometimes you go a little nutty. Like, obsessive, man. Remember last year you couldn't find your keys and became convinced your house was haunted? We had a séance and everything—"

"It wasn't only the keys. It was other stuff. My office was freezing."

"Because your air-conditioning malfunctioned. Remember I fixed it?"

"Okay, okay. I'm probably being neurotic again."

"Well, good—"

"And yes, I'm enjoying it. Imagine being in your very own horror picture. Crazy or not, I'm mining these feelings for inspiration."

Max and the Arriflex had found each other at just the right time. Its horrible history fueled his creative juices. He could allow it to work again and fulfill its purpose. There was a movie here, lurking either inside the machine itself or in the feelings it produced in him.

It was all a game. A game of make-believe. He wanted to go on playing it.

"Well," said Raphael. "As long as I'm the one who survives."

Max evaluated his friend. "No, you're too nice. You're the one kind adult who tries to help the kids and then gets an axe in the face."

"Oh. Seriously?"

"Sorry, Raph."

"Jesus." The man shuddered. "Well, at least I'm nice." He sighed. "Okay, so what are we doing here? Waiting for magic hour?"

This was a period of time after sunrise or before sunset when the light turned warmer and softer than at midday. And the shadows were great. Ideal for shooting.

"You're half-right." Max hoped for magic. The hour didn't matter. "I just want to see what this thing can do. If anything weird happens, you're my witness."

Raphael waved at him. "Fine, fine. And then we grab a steak and a stiff drink somewhere. I think the only cure for me today is a little hair of the dog."

Max made a positive grunt as he positioned himself behind the eyepiece. He worked the zoom handle and brought a distant couple into both frame and focus. They dashed around the grass as they flung a Frisbee back and forth.

Aside from laughter and Frisbee throwing, nothing happened. Raphael prattled away about how wonderful the party was, narrating every detail of the skinny-dipping as if watching a movie in his head. In a reverent tone, he described Ashlee Gibson dancing in her glittering dress on the pool diving board. The man's long-standing crush on her had intensified to become religious.

Panning right, Max caught several kids trying to either skip pebbles across the lake or brain a duck, he wasn't sure. He kept panning. He loathed children and hated the current studio trend of ruining every interesting Hollywood franchise by sticking the precocious monsters into them.

The camera brought a family into frame. The tired and irritable dad hauled a cooler. Overloaded with bags and beach chairs, the mom trailed after him, a gaggle of kids in tow. Heading to the parking lot and home after a long day.

The father glared into the lens as if to say, *Get that thing out of my face.*

Max kept panning right.

The frame discovered two boys fooling around with lawn darts. If anything weird would happen, it'd be here. These darts had caused injuries and even a few deaths. Time passed as the camera consumed blank film. His four-hundred-foot roll offered roughly five minutes of shooting, and he'd already used up half that.

"What a gorgeous day," Raphael sighed. "This was actually a solid idea."

The man still sat on the ground resting on his elbows, head tilted to feel the sun on his face. He looked altogether too content for Max, who panned, fuming, across a large family setting up a meal at one of the picnic pavilions.

He finally settled on a smiling middle-aged man juggling for a pair of teenage girls, who pointedly ignored him. They lay on a blanket prodding and giggling at each other and shooting the man nasty looks.

Nothing to see here, but Max lingered anyway. The scene struck a chord in him.

There was meaning here. A story about a divorced father who missed most of his daughters' childhood. He used to be able to win their affection with weekends at Disneyland and trips to this park, but things are different now. The girls have reached an age where their parents aren't cool anymore. They chafe at being stuck here when they could be out with friends. So Dad learned juggling. Only the harder he tried, the more they scoffed, intent on punishing him for holding them hostage.

Behind the viewfinder, Max winced. The scene reminded him of his own father. Not a comparable memory, no. He had so few of those. No, it made him aware of the empty space where these memories should be.

When Max thought of his dad, he again faced that blank and sensed the black hole his father's death had punched through his soul. A tiny black hole behind which an infinite void stretched. A hole he'd spent his life stuffing with monsters that as a child he'd imagined lurking under his bed.

The girls' father gamely kept at it, tossing the red balls in the air in a blurred oval, face stretched in a pandering grin, dripping with flop sweat.

I know how you feel, guy, Max thought. *Every time I make a movie—*

A silver midsize sedan roared into the frame. He glimpsed a panicked driver fighting the wheel. The horn wailed.

The car swerved away from a group of running kids.

Straight toward the girls.

The tires narrowly missed thumping right over them—

The front fender instead striking the dad and plowing him into the grass.

The girls screamed as he disappeared under the left tire. The red balls plunked off the windshield. The body tumbled into the axle. The unyielding steel broke his bones with a sickening *crack*, loud as a gunshot.

A pale arm waved above the tire as the car kept going to crash against a cherry tree and almost topple it. Water vapor poured from the crumpled hood like horror movie fog.

"Holy mother," Max breathed.

He couldn't look. He couldn't look away.

Across the park, screams.

Raphael entered the frame and turned to deliver a disgusted glare.

"Are you still filming?"

An inhuman shriek passed overhead. He looked up as the shadow of a hawk crossed his face.

The red lawn dart came down right in his eye with a wet smack. Flinching, the man gently pawed at its length.

"Damn," he said. "I'm hit."

Max gawked at him. "Raph?"

Raphael took a few stumbling steps with the foot-long dart and its plastic fins protruding from his face.

"Medic," he mumbled.

"Raph, are you okay?"

The man's remaining eye fixed Max with a glazed stare.

"Why are you still—?"

He pitched forward onto the ground, where the dart disappeared into his brain.

Max's vision sparked and dimmed.

"Raph?"

Raphael's leg twitched as if it alone could get him back on his feet.

Max's brain couldn't process it, fighting against what his gaping eyes told him. People shouted nearby. Someone screamed. The sounds barely registered.

"You're okay, right? This isn't real."

At last, the leg quit trying.

Max understood the game he'd been playing wasn't make-believe after all.

SEVEN

When Max finally made it home, his office phone rang. Stumbling into the dark room, he answered it in a daze.

Jordan's flat baritone boomed over the line.

"Where the hell have you been? Sticking pins in dolls? Haunting attics?"

"I was at the—"

"I've been trying to reach you all day!"

"Park," Max mumbled, still utterly numb.

"I just got a call from a reporter telling me he heard from the LAPD that Raph Rodriguez died in the mother of freak accidents and that you were there. Also that some father of two teenage girls got run over right before it happened."

Suddenly, Max was back in the sunshine watching some poor slob tumble across the grass until his body broke apart in the runaway car's axle. The red balls thumped off the windshield. A disjointed arm waved from the tire.

A lawn dart quivering in his eye socket, Raphael flinched as if suffering a massive bloody sneeze—

And Max cringed, thinking, *Was this me? Did I do this?*

"Babe," Jordan yelled. "Are you still with me?"

"Sorry, what?"

"I said, can I hope and pray the starlet you left with last night is still breathing?"

"Sally?" He blinked, and then he was back in his office, a phone in his sweaty grip, wondering how he'd gotten here. "I assume she is. I drove her home."

"Thank God for small favors. What were you doing at that park anyhow?"

"Trying out a camera I bought at an estate sale."

A camera that made horror.

The police had questioned him at length after hearing his description of events. Which they'd found incredible if not unbelievable, especially after finding out he directed horror movies. After confiscating his film as evidence, they let him go with a mild scolding about shooting without a permit.

Max looked over at his office's open doorway and startled at a shadow that didn't belong. Tiny eyes burned in the darkness. His heart caught in his throat.

He switched on his desk lamp to discover Lady Susan still groggy from a long nap and glaring at him.

You left me alone, the dog seemed to say. *All night.*

Jordan exhaled a loud sigh. "Hell of a thing. Jesus. A lawn dart. What are the odds? How about you, Max? How are you holding up?"

"I'm not sure," Max said. Nothing made sense to him.

Susan huffed and took a few steps forward. Her tongue popped out to lick her own nose before retracting.

The plan, Master. You remember the night plan, yes?

Of course you do. The food. Then the walk. Then the snuggles.

"A good man," Jordan was saying. "One of the best in the business. Salt-of-the-earth type. Quiet and reliable. I'm hosting a little industry get-together at my place Tuesday night to pay our respects. Hope you can make it."

"Yes." Max swallowed hard. "Yes, I'll be there."

Another sigh from the producer.

"Well. If you need anything, let me know."

"Wait," said Max. "What were you calling me about?"

"What?"

"Earlier today. You called me."

"Oh, I wanted to go over the box office numbers with you. Seems inappropriate to say it now, but *Jack the Knife III* came out swinging and had a happy night. We've got two weeks to rake it in until *Nightmare on Elm Street 4* drops. Overall, the new *Jack* is shaping up to be a profitable addition to the franchise."

Jordan had an uncanny ability to look at the ticket sales on release day and accurately estimate what the film's total gross would be across the entire price discrimination strategy, from theaters to cable TV to *Jack* action figures.

"I'm starting on a new idea," Max heard himself say. "A new picture."

"Your friend just died, and you want to do a general?" Hollywood-speak for a meeting to talk background and projects.

"I'd like to know if you're up for scheduling a pitch meeting."

A metallic click on the line. The producer puffed on the cigar he'd lit.

"Well, babe, as you're asking, the answer is yes to the meeting, no to something new. *Jack* is looking to make a killing. So we're doing another *Jack*."

Max finally snapped out of his shock.

"We ended the trilogy!"

He could almost hear the producer's shrug.

"You're a creative guy," Jordan said. "You'll find a way to make it work."

"You always told me you wanted original material. I'm working on an idea that has never been done before. Something big, bold, and viscerally terrifying. It—"

"It sounds terrible already. So that's a firm no out of the gate."

Max sputtered. "What do you *mean*?"

"When I say I'm always looking for original material, I mean something already proven with a twist that keeps it fresh. You should know this by now."

He sadly did know it. Making a movie involved 10 percent inspiration, 90 percent bullshit. The hard part started now—convincing someone to hand over a small fortune so that he could turn inspiration into a finished feature film.

The problem was Hollywood loved bold new ideas, only no one wanted to be first to risk investing in them. If a new idea somehow got produced and proved successful, the cash spigots would open for highly profitable derivatives.

But what inspiration. This movie needed to happen. What he'd witnessed at the park...As reality, it was horrible. As cinema, it was beautiful. At last, Max had reconciled fiction and realism. As much as his brain needed to process and compartmentalize his experience, he wished to stay immersed in it. He wanted to internalize it until he understood it and could summon it on command.

Then he could share it with the world.

"Screw the risk," Max said. "This new picture is going to be terrifying. It'll scare the crap out of people and blow their minds."

"Yeah, that's another thing. You have this weird idea that the goal of a horror movie is to make people cry and shit themselves. Our goal is to sell tickets and popcorn, not send half the nation into therapy. It's called show *business*. Not show...experimental film that gives people freaking nervous breakdowns."

"It will make money. I know it will, on the notoriety alone. All I'm asking is to give me a chance."

"Look, there's still plenty of creative leeway in the slasher trend," Jordan said with grating patience. "The first half of the trend set up the rules. We're now in the second half, where we subvert expectations by bending them. You kinda tied off the story in the last *Jack* picture, but that's an opportunity to reinvent. How about changing up the Final Girl, make her the new monster? Or go meta for satire? Maybe do something bigger with the dog. Actually, I like that idea. A whole slasher flick from a dog's point of view."

Jack the Knife III's audience chortled in Max's ears.

"You can't be serious—"

"Carve a fresh path through familiar territory is what I'm telling you."

Max sulked. "I can't even give you a lousy elevator pitch."

The producer toked again on his cigar. "Oh, I'm sure it's a wonderful idea. And if you can find someone to finance it, go for it. Perhaps you'll follow in Roger Corman's footsteps and produce yourself. Either way, you'd have my earnest and sincere wishes for success. I can't wait to rip it off and make a killing on that too."

"In that case, I'll do that," Max threatened. "I'll shop the idea around—"

"That's all in the future. In the meantime, we have our inviolable contract."

"Contract?" He hadn't looked at it in years.

"Read the fine print," Jordan said. "You're on the hook for another *Jack* picture."

"I'm on the hook for *one* more picture. It can be anything I want it to be."

"Of course. But I have final say. And I say it's *Jack the Knife IV.*"

"Oh," said Max.

"That's the way the cookie crumbles, babe," the producer told him. "You'll thank me later when you're eating it."

Jordan had him boxed with the contract. Flush with *Jack the Knife*'s success, Max had eagerly signed. The terms promised him a three-movie deal—pay or play, meaning if Lyman Entertainments released him, he'd still get paid. Between that and the money he'd be making, it had all looked perfect to him.

But yes, the producer was most likely right about his having final say on what those three movies would be. Which meant Max was screwed.

"Come over," he blurted.

"Sure, sure." Jordan rustled some papers. "I'm available—"

"Come over now. We can talk about where to take *Jack*." Gritting his teeth, he added, "I like what you were saying about changing up the Final Girl. What if there were, I don't know, two Final Girls? Or two villains?"

"Right now? I don't see how it can't wait—"

"The truth is I'm still shaken up by what happened to Raph. I could sure use the company. To be honest, you're the only friend I've got right now."

Jordan sighed again, betraying what he thought of that notion, but he said, "All right, babe. I'll swing by for a quick nightcap."

"See you soon."

Max hung up, satisfied that his acting had worked. He was tired of being pushed around. This time, he refused to take no for an answer.

Susan glared and stomped her paw.

"Okay, okay," he growled.

He stormed off into the kitchen, trailed by the strutting little dog.

"Jordan thinks he owns my soul, Suse. I made him a lot of money. The least he can do is hear me out on a new concept."

Susan wagged her tail with joy. Max shook some Chuck Wagon into her bowl and mixed it with a little warm water.

He watched her scarf it down.

There's another option, friend, a voice said.

He wheeled. "Who's that?"

It's me, your old pal Arthur Golden, here with some free advice.

"Do you hear him too, Suse?"

The dog looked up to follow his gaze and then returned to her eating.

In its plastic case on the dining room table, the Arriflex 35BL sang, its throbbing hum even louder after his return from the park.

Max approached it with slow, cautious steps, worried about a jump scare, the camera popping out of its case like a jack-in-the-box and punching him in the face.

The voice hadn't come from here, however, but inside his head.

Again, he found himself teetering on a line between reality and fantasy. The game, it seemed, wasn't over. Again, a part of him liked it.

I'll play, he thought.

"What do you want?"

I'm trying to help you, the voice answered.

"I seriously doubt that," Max said. He knew how this worked.

Of course, if you'd prefer to spend the rest of your life basking in praise for making lukewarm, overcooked movies you end up hating—

"Okay! Jeez. Just tell me how you want to help me."

I hoped to make a perfect horror movie. I spent my fortune on it. I lived it. I suffered and eventually died for it. I understand need. I know obsession. I can relate to the hungry black hole that's eating you from the inside out.

I'm like you. You're like me. The million-dollar question, fellow traveler, is will you go as far as I did to get what you want?

"Jordan will hear me out," Max said. "I'll make him see things my way."

And if he doesn't? Because he won't? You're barking up the wrong tree.

"I'm not killing anybody for a movie."

You won't, though. That's the thing. The camera will do it all.

Max unlatched the case and inspected the old scarred machine. The pulsing hum stopped. The sudden silence alarmed him. He gave the case a little shake, but the camera didn't respond, lying still and lifeless.

I mean, accidents happen, right? Sometimes they happen to random strangers. Sometimes to trusted friends and colleagues.

Why not parasitic producers?

"Shut up, I'm thinking."

How far *would* he go? Was he all bark, or did he also have a bite?

A heart defect had killed his father. Max had the same defect. He pictured spending his remaining years producing drivel for Jordan.

"It's just a game," he said. "It's all just make-believe."

Drunk on lack of sleep and what happened at the park, Max was doing what he always did to process life's horror. He played out his own horror movie, forcing reality into sync with the dark things that lived in his head.

Yes, like a movie, Arthur said. *Aren't you dying to know what happens next?*

"Answer one question for me."

Of course, friend!

"Are you really here, or am I talking to myself?"

Does it matter?

"It kind of matters."

Just remember what ol' Wes Craven said. The first monster a director can use to scare his audience is himself.

"I'm not that kind of monster." Max frowned. "I'm not. Right?"

Either way, he found himself threading a fresh roll of film into the camera. He watched his hands mount the camera again on the sticks.

"It's not me doing this," he said.

The voice didn't answer.

Obeying the dark impulse, Max aimed the lens at the front door.

EIGHT

U nder a giant painting of Prometheus chained to a rock, Sally Priest stretched on the king-size four-poster in Dan Womack's bedroom. The morning sun glared through the closed blinds, its light exposing the imperfections of his crummy apartment while lending it a certain bohemian grace.

She'd woken to Dan's clumsy pacing around the room. Sitting up, she slid a blunt between her lips and scanned the side table for her lighter.

Noticing she'd awakened, he stopped.

"We can't do this anymore," he fretted. "It's not right."

"Mm," said Sally, focused on her search.

Back when he scored a speaking role as a major character in *Mary's Birthday*, Dan was a hunky thirtysomething sleeping with Angela Crispin, the fading actress who played Mary's mother and his on-screen wife. Nearing fifty, he was now still that handsome devil if the lighting was right, though his long hair had largely gone gray and he'd become as paunchy as marshmallow with age and too many bottles of fine Merlot. A big, shaggy bear of a man with a salt-and-pepper beard.

After surviving Arthur Golden's schlocky nightmare, Dan never acted in front of a camera again and performed instead in a wide range of stage plays. He'd earned his biggest accolades for playing Prometheus in *Prometheus Unbound*, the ancient Greek tragedy by

Aeschylus, at the Geffen. Between gigs, he taught a theater work-shop, where he educated scores of bright minds and, rumor had it, more than a few female bodies.

Sally's mother had told her to always level up by taking acting classes. The problem was that like any other creative field, Holly-wood was chock-full of charlatans and rip-off artists preying on the desperate young. Some acting teachers abused their students and treated them like children to foster emotional dependence and feed their own egos. Some demanded adherence to methods that involved breaking down actors' emotions in sadistic ways reminis-cent of a cult.

Anyway, Dan wasn't like that.

Okay, maybe he was a little. But he wasn't the worst of the bunch.

Sally allowed him to seduce her, as he seemed so worldly and erudite compared to the vain, gorgeous, and horny boys in her class. She'd never had a spring-fall relationship and thought it might offer an interesting experience, which proved out: Dan liked to cuddle, had an encyclopedic knowledge of American theater, and never made things too heavy, at least until now.

"Despite my strong feelings for you, this isn't right," Dan said.

Sally's hands clenched empty air. "Have you seen my lighter anywhere?"

Tonight, she had a rehearsal for a play the workshop would put on at the tiny community theater Dan rented out. She'd originally planned to read for the lead role of Zoey. Her mother had con-vinced her to instead play the smaller but more challenging role of Shana, a clingy, obsessive, and jealous young woman.

She found it hard work inhabiting a character that was so not her. Sally loved a challenge, but she wanted to get mellow before she stepped again into Shana's turbulent head today. A little weed would do the trick. A ginormous cup of coffee and a half-decent orgasm would be nice too, but neither seemed to be in the offing.

Dan, meanwhile, had gone back to his pacing.

"I'm your teacher," he moaned. "I'm supposed to be teaching you."

"Ha!" Sally spied the lighter behind the table lamp.

He wheeled. "What?"

She pulled on it only to end up gripping the prop knife she'd scored at Arthur Golden's sad little sale. She collapsed the blade against her palm and sighed.

"Look, it happens to everyone," Sally said. "Please don't sweat it, okay?"

She'd given him the production prop last night in the hope that he'd appreciate it as a keepsake, something with which to remember his long friendship with Arthur Golden. Instead, he'd become gloomily maudlin, swilled too much wine over dinner, and ended up with a limp noodle in bed.

"I don't know whatever you mean." Dan padded into the bathroom huffing, where he continued to lament their doomed romance.

Still no joy finding that lighter, which had turned into this scene's primary motivation. Sally thought about getting up to at least scavenge some coffee.

She didn't move, her paralysis a visible expression of the creative wall she'd been banging her head against all week.

Shana: I'm sick of trusting you with what's mine.

Tony: I don't know what you're talking about.

Shana: What I gave you is a gift, but it's still a part of me. You carry it like a condom in your wallet, something you can use and throw away, but even then it's a part of me. It's always a part of me. You're always a part of me.

Tony: You're acting crazy.

Shana: I'm not crazy. I just want you. I just want you.

Sally sighed.

Shana, Shana, Shana.

Where's the key that will let me inside to become you?

Probably hanging out with her lighter somewhere.

It's always a part of me.

It's *always* a part of me.

It's always a part of *me*.

Hoping to dissect what made the character tick.

What do you want, Shana? How can you expect that making Tony suffer is going to convince him to show you he loves you more? You're driving him straight to Zoey with your controlling behavior. You're destroying what you're trying to save.

It didn't help that Shana's dialogue sounded stilted, either.

Sally tried to imagine being this possessive about Dan Womack, which almost made her laugh out loud. The fact was she'd never been jealous in a romantic way about anyone. She knew what it looked like, having been on the receiving end, but she couldn't relate enough to harness it as hers. She could only produce a copy.

An odd thing, feeling angry at herself for not having been mauled by the full spectrum of ugly traumas and emotions that plagued the human race. Sally had led a relatively charmed life that in the world of acting could be inhibiting. Life had never really punched her in the face.

People who'd seen real shit, Sally envied them for their far deeper creative well. That was the kind of jealousy she could relate to. It was part of the mix that had attracted her to Dan. The man had experienced horror. Notable example: Sixteen years ago, he'd shown up on the *Mary's Birthday* set moments too late to hear the director's farewell speech but just in time to witness a slaughter.

"And that's why we can't go on like this," Dan now opined from the bathroom. "A relationship as wonderful as ours must progress. All relationships, in truth. They must move forward or die. But what do I have to give? I can teach you, yes. I can make you a star, if that's what you want. But what else, really? Think about it,

Sally. You will end up falling in love with me. What then? Should we get married?"

God, he was monologuing now, probably going at it full tilt in front of the mirror.

"I think I'm gonna take off," she called.

He immediately reappeared from stage left, shambling into the room with his junk dangling between his hairy thighs, tilting his head to fire up his own fatty.

Goddamnit! He had her lighter. He'd had it the whole time and didn't tell her, letting her search for it while he'd opined about them breaking up.

Wait—she could use this.

He had the lighter but didn't tell me.

She almost grasped the essence of it.

The lighter—

Something he treated casually but is important to me. Something I needed him to keep safe but that he could toss without a care if provoked, and then I'll never smoke a joint again and I'll fail as an actor.

Her whole career rested right there in his beefy paw, and he appeared scarcely aware of even holding it, ready to crush or drop as he pleased. It made her angry and helpless, which she continued to amplify.

Balling her fists, Sally tossed the sheets aside and rose to kneel on the bed. The vulnerability of her nakedness only fueled her desire.

"I'm sick of trusting you with what's mine," she snarled with caged fury.

Dan coughed on a cloud of pungent smoke. "What?"

"What I gave you is a gift, but it's still a part of me." Passive edging toward full-on aggressive, seething with a deep weakness presented as strength. "You carry it like it's a condom in your wallet, something you can use and throw away, but even then it's a *part of me.*" Livid now. "It's *always* a part of me." The first cracks appeared as she faced her vulnerability and realized she'd never be able to leave this person who could easily destroy her. "*You're* always a part of me."

"Oh my God, Sally, I'm so sorry—"

"I'm not crazy!" she screamed with anger approaching hate, though she directed it at herself now, the woman who fell in love and thought this time it'd be different. That this time a man would love her back the way she needed.

"What's wrong? Are you okay?"

Pleading: "I just want *you*." A hollow, petulant echo: "I just *want* you."

"Oh, Sally, I'm here—"

While he stumbled toward her with his arms outstretched, she flopped back onto the bed and exploded in a sigh. "I got it!" She laughed. "Fuck!"

Dan froze. "Wait—you were running lines, weren't you?"

She extended her fingers. He handed her the joint, and she took a deep drag and held in the hot smoke before sighing, "Yep. I just cracked that shit."

"Oh." His own hand disappeared into his thick graying mane to scratch the back of his head. "It was good."

"Maybe." Scowling, already doubting herself.

"I might be in love with you," Dan said, going off their own script.

"You're . . . ?"

"I'm sure that sounds ridiculous to you, but I think I might be."

Her heart melted. He looked so sad standing there, rubbing his bare rotund belly and hoping for reassurance. But she had to get back to work. Sally handed the joint back to him and rose to swipe her panties off the floor.

"Listen, it was totally thoughtless and stupid of me to bring you that prop," she said. "It obviously dredged up some horrible stuff." Another little pang of envy; she wished again against her better judgment that *she* had been there at that set and forever had to live in the traumatic echo. "I'm sorry about that, Dan. I really am."

"It's okay," he said, watching her nudity disappear with longing.

"And I'll tell Max Maurey that you want to be left in peace. I think you earned that much."

"Maurey?" Dan frowned.

"I met him at the *Jack the Knife* premiere party?"

"What?"

"We went to the estate sale together yesterday. I told you all this last night..." But he'd been distracted by his nightmare.

"Of course I wouldn't remember him," he huffed. "The man's a barely talented, overpaid hack."

Sally gave him a knowing look. "He's a pretty successful director."

"If you find that sort of thing attractive."

"I'm not interested in *dating* him, Dan."

He grunted, only half-mollified.

"He's a huge fan of *Mary's Birthday*, that's all," she added. "He wants to make a new movie using the camera he found at the sale. And he might cast *me* as—"

"Wait." Dan blanched. "What camera?"

"An Arriflex 35BL. Max said it was the one used to shoot your movie."

His face turned into an icy grimace.

"What's wrong?" she asked him.

"Evil," he whispered.

"What?"

"I thought Arthur destroyed it. That camera. It's the devil itself."

"Seriously, what are you talking about?"

"I, uh, changed my mind. I'd be happy to meet this Max Maurey."

"I thought you hated—"

"If you don't mind setting up a meeting." Dan swallowed hard.

"Are you kidding? He'd love it." Cocking an eye at him, Sally shimmied into her jeans and zipped. "Are you sure, though? You look pretty—"

He took a step forward to lay his hands on her shoulders. "Listen. I wanted to tell you I'm sorry too. Laying that guilt trip on you. I didn't mean any of it."

"It's fine, Dan." But Sally was still thinking about Max Maurey.

He gazed at her with his overgrown puppy eyes. "Are *you* sure?"

Turning it around on her, one of his little rhetorical tricks. This time, she decided give his inquiry a long, hard think.

Now that she'd cracked Shana's pretzeled brain, her mind already raced ahead to her next role. She hoped it would be in Max's new project.

Back in front of the camera, Sally would scream again.

Max had hinted he might cast her. Perhaps even as the lead.

With most men, in particular directors, she had an instinctive read on them. Nature or nurture had made Max Maurey a different animal. He acted like a monk whose self-flagellating religion was making horror movies. It was this singular passion that allowed her to connect with him on something close to a human level.

A strange guy, a bit spooky, in fact. Take a man like John Carpenter; you'd find him so personable you wouldn't guess he'd directed some of the era's most provocative horror movies. With Max Maurey, you likely wound up wondering how many bodies he had buried in his backyard.

The director seemed to know this but not care. Hell, he appeared to take a perverse pride in it. As egotistical as the best of 'em—the type who complained about how hard they had it when their PA brought them a cappuccino with insufficient foam—but his ego appeared to be narrowly focused on one thing: terrifying people using the medium of film.

On set, he had a reputation as a mad tyrant. He micromanaged production and sometimes fired crew for failing to translate the movie playing in his head. As a result, he had few loyalists who would drop everything and work for him. On the other hand, he knew what he wanted and could make decisions.

Max was an oddity for sure, but for once, an industry bigwig's interest in Sally had nothing to do with the dimensions of her chest. She'd screwed up by making herself so vulnerable at Lyman's party, but he'd been a total gentleman. She had to admit it was refreshing to be appreciated for her ideas.

This being Hollywood, Sally didn't trust the man, but still, a girl could hope.

A lead role. At last, she might be the Final Girl.

In the tarot deck of horror, the Final Girl stood out as strong, resourceful, and smart. Modest and responsible and kind. Out of all her peers, she acted the most grown-up and prosocial. She lived more or less chaste to fulfill the masculine idea of purity, but she proved no stereotyped helpless female. She had real agency. She got knocked on her ass over and over and always came back swinging. This made her the embodiment of both living terror and courage in the face of evil.

Overall, the Final Girl was empowering.

Sally had to make ready for the role, and do it now, always now. She was young and attractive in a town where these qualities were a dime a dozen. As her mother reminded her every chance she got, the biological clock was ticking. Hollywood worshipped feminine youth and beauty and hated wrinkles. Past thirty, major roles for women dried up. Past forty, they took a nosedive. Before Sally had even started professional acting, she'd been running out of time.

She needed lightning to strike. She needed to be the lightning.

Dan stared into her distracted eyes. "Are we okay, Sally?"

The Bad Girl was dead, along with all she entailed. Long live the Final Girl.

"I'm her now," she murmured, free and receptive to a different load.

"What?"

"I'm the Final Girl." Her voice firm.

"I don't know what that means," said Dan.

"The girl who makes it. The girl who defeats evil. The girl who's pure."

"Okay." He frowned. "I still don't understand what that means."

"It means you were right about one thing," Sally said.

He perked up. "Oh?"

"About it being time we ended things." She stood on her toes to give him a chaste peck on the cheek. "It's been lovely, Dan. I'll see you at rehearsal."

Living life to the fullest meant abandoning all regrets.

As for the lighter, he could keep it.

CONCEPT

Monsters in movies are us, always us, one way or the other. They're us with hats on.

John Carpenter
Director, *Halloween*

NINE

Among the backyard rosebushes, Max dug a grave with the gardener's shovel.

Then he'd sleep at last. Yes, he'd sleep like the dead.

The California sun beat down on him with an almost physical force. The heat soaked into his pale flesh. Colors sparked in his vision. He was no stranger to manual labor. He didn't mind getting his hands dirty. But aside from some catnapping he hadn't really slept since the premiere, and he wasn't a young man anymore.

How fitting it'd be to topple over into the deep hole he'd dug, dead of a heart attack like his dad. A fitting end. And possibly deserved for playing with taboo.

Instead, Max took a break. He leaned on his shovel and inspected the hole.

In the dark pit, he saw death.

Last night:

He'd aimed the Arriflex 35BL down the hall, across the foyer, and straight at the front door. A fresh roll in the magazine. The door unlocked and ready to open. The camera ready to shoot.

"It's not me," he murmured again behind the viewfinder. "It's the camera, and cameras aren't possessed by demons. Accidents happen."

And sometimes they happened to people who wanted to enslave him to make formulaic crowd-pleasers instead of pursuing his life's purpose.

He made a few zoom and pan adjustments to fix the door in frame. He worked the focus just so. Arthur Golden said nothing, knowing better than to interrupt a fellow creative while he was working.

Lady Susan proudly strutted into view with Roger Ebert in her jaws.

Max gasped. "No, Suse!"

Heart galloping on pure adrenaline, he jerked the camera in a quick pan.

At his tone, the Pomeranian tilted her head.

"Daddy's working," Max explained as he reached for the squeaky giraffe toy gripped in her clenched teeth. "I'm going to put you in the—"

Susan growled and backed away from him.

"I can't play with you right now, Lady Susan."

The puffy dog wagged her head. Snarling and chomping on the rubber toy, challenging him to take her rightful kill if he proved strong enough. He grabbed it and tugged hard, but she clamped down even harder.

"Come. On." He growled back at her. "It's. Just. For. A few. Minutes—"

Susan dug in her paws and refused to be budged.

Max sighed. "Then you give me no choice."

He crossed into the adjacent kitchen and retrieved a box of Milk-Bone biscuits from its cupboard. He shook it.

"Who wants a treat?"

Susan padded over, dropped the toy, and panted happily at him. The moment the biscuit hit the floor, she scarfed it down.

Taking advantage of her distraction, Max attached her leash to her collar and knotted the other end around the refrigerator handle. He tested the knot.

"Now, stay," he commanded. "Daddy won't be long."

The Milk-Bone cracked in her jaws, an unpleasant reminder of the park.

Max returned to the camera and framed the door again in its gaping lens. In the kitchen, Susan finished her crunching and now made Roger Ebert squeak. Minutes passed. He felt flushed and feverish again. He wiped sweat from his eyes.

Forget this, Raphael said in his head. *You need sleep, Maximillian.*

"It's just a creative experiment," Max muttered.

You aren't thinking straight. You're going to get somebody killed.

Max shrugged it off.

In fact, you aren't thinking at all—

"Come on, Jordan," he said. "Before I change my—"

A knock at the door. In the kitchen, Susan started yapping.

An evil grin peeled across Max's face. He set the camera to rolling.

"It's open," he called. "Come on in—"

The door swung wide to reveal Jordan dressed in a suit, no tie, his collared shirt unbuttoned to present a V of hairy chest. As always, regardless of the hour, the producer wore his mirrored shades.

He stepped inside and frowned.

"What are you—?"

A snarling shape blurred onto the scene.

Max's heart caught in his throat. It was Susan, charging in full guard-dog mode. The little dog bolted into view with the giraffe toy clamped in her jaws.

She took a flying leap—

And yanked to a sudden midair stop at the end of the leash.

YAK—

Roger Ebert kept going to flicker out of the frame.

With a sickening snap, the dog flopped to the floor.

Jordan gazed down for a long moment, then looked at Max.

"Christ," he said. "This just isn't your day, is it?"

TEN

Max laid the furry pink bed in the fresh pit. With a final kiss, he placed his beloved dog's body atop it. He pulled Roger Ebert out of his back pocket and set it next to her so she'd have something to play with in the afterlife.

This was a fitting place for her to rest. She'd always loved these rosebushes.

He rested his hands on the shovel and said a prayer.

"Lady Susan, you died fighting. You died for art. If there's a Valhalla for good girls, I know there's a bowl up there for you."

Max never killed animals in his movies. Too mean-spirited. It was something of a rule in the genre; animals were always innocent. In the kind of movies he made, the monster only killed the deserving.

He wiped his tears away with his palm.

"Goodbye, friend." The only friend he'd had left.

It robbed him of the happiness he should be feeling this morning. Last night, he'd won a major victory, only he couldn't enjoy it.

Last night:

Jordan parked on Max's pastel couch swirling a tumbler of scotch on his lap, a smoking cigar poised for his next drag. As always, the burly producer presented the very image of self-possession.

Max paced the carpet. "I was trying out the new camera again. I didn't want her to bump the sticks and knock it over, so I tied her up. When she heard the door, she bolted straight for it, and—"

"She was a good dog."

"The best." Max let out a sob. He wanted to pull his hair out.

"Look, if it's a bad time, we can meet at my office later this—"

He stopped pacing. "What? No. We're doing this. I'm going to pitch you something fresh, and you're going to listen."

Jordan sighed. "You tricked me. We've been through all this already."

"Right. You reminded me our job is to turn art into edible garbage for a profit."

"I had no idea the horror genre was so pure."

Max gazed fiercely at him. "It could be."

The words hung in the air with Jordan's cigar smoke. The producer twirled the cigar in his meaty lips and puffed, regarding Max coolly.

At last, he smirked. "Crazy eyes."

"What?"

"I said, okay. Let's hear it."

Max sucked in his breath. Beyond surrendering to Arthur Golden and the camera's dark influence, he hadn't thought tonight through. Still on his feet so long without sleep, lurching from one thing to the next, he hadn't really thought out any of it, even as his brain screamed on constant overdrive.

In short, he hadn't developed a pitch aside from what existed in his own mind, which was to make a horror movie that distilled the essence of what Arthur captured with his cursed camera.

Max glanced at the apparatus still on the tripod, which hummed again.

"I'm still refining it," he said.

"Look, I'm giving you a shot here. Show me what you got. Anything." Jordan pursed his lips. "First, sit the hell down. You're making me nervous."

Max did as he was told, though his knee jittered in a blur. He took a bracing sip from his own tumbler.

"Great," the producer said. "Now we can talk. What's your vision?"

As a movie director, Max found himself asked this question every day while shooting a movie. The talent, the director of photography, the assistant director, the soundman, the key grip, and the gaffer all asked it. His production assistant once absentmindedly threw it out when taking his coffee order. Hell, he often asked himself.

Everything led back to the all-important question.

My vision is to make something entirely new and frightening, but what?

He started with what his vision *wasn't*.

He *didn't* want to have to find new and interesting ways to kill off attractive and unlikable kids on culturally significant anniversaries.

He *didn't* want to glorify and then exact horrible justice against youthful narcissism. He wanted to avoid making kids societal scapegoats punished for the cardinal sins of sex, drugs, playing with dead things, walking off alone to investigate noises, and saying, *Stay here, I'll be right back!*

And he *didn't* want a villain who'd evolve into a cultural hero beloved for giving teens the sick vicarious thrill of having an awful amount of power. No laughing at his screenings. And certainly no cheering the monster.

"The vision is we subvert expectations," Max concluded. "Every single one."

The rest poured out of him. He'd put together a cast the audience cared about. The characters would be thinking young adults placed in a horrible situation where they do all the right things to survive but still don't make it. He'd trust his audience's imagination by refusing to reveal the monster until the last act, with no instant gratification. He'd take a cinema verité approach—no quick, flashy cuts for this MTV generation, maybe add some dialogue ad-libbing—which would make the whole thing look and feel gritty and real. Besides that, he'd refuse to run the race to push the boundaries toward bigger gross-outs and taboo. He'd shock with true suspense, wonder, and surprise as much as gore.

In short, he'd stop chasing the proven formula and return to foundational horror storytelling to make something new. He'd give moviegoers characters they could empathize with and then stimulate the hell out of their imaginations.

Panting, Max stopped his manic rant. The camera filled the silence with its hum. It seemed even louder and more urgent now, as if cheering him on.

"That's the vision," he rasped.

"God," said Jordan. "You're not going to do some Sundance art-house product, are you? No offense, Max, but you're no David Lynch or Roman Polanski."

"No, I—ouch." Max glared at him. "No, it's not an art film."

"Then let me get this straight." The man sipped his scotch. "You think the key to commercial success is to buck every one of the decade's trends proven to satisfy our primary market of teens and yuppies."

"Yes," said Max. "Because they're all going stale."

The producer replied with a thoughtful nod.

"What's the story?"

Max let out a long *um*, uttered as a placeholder for an intelligent thought he hoped would come to him. In truth, he had nothing. He'd been living and breathing *Jack the Knife* for eight years. He'd toyed with plenty of ideas in that time, but he never bothered developing any of them.

Fresh scripts crossed Jordan's desk all the time. Max could ask to see them. But then he'd have to pitch him all over again. Max had him on the hook, and he couldn't stop until he'd gained commitment.

"It starts with a town," Max said.

Yes, keep going, he told himself. *Worry about the consequences later.*

"A little girl walks along with her dad, who is prospecting with a metal detector. He digs up an ancient amulet. Amazed at his find, he gives it to his daughter and asks her to make a wish. She thinks the people in the town are too mean. She wishes for everyone to leave her alone—"

The producer stirred on the couch. *I'm already losing him.* Jordan regarded time as money, and right now Max was wasting it. The man looked down at his cigar, and Max realized he'd never had a meeting with him that lasted longer than it took him to smoke one all the way to the end.

Talk his language, Max. Think.

The innovative and experimental seventies were dead and buried. The big studios ran the show. Under their control, Hollywood had become hyper-focused on return on investment. The bean counters wanted blockbusters and accordingly green-lighted big-ticket crowd-pleasers they believed would fill theater seats. That meant major stars and dumbed-down formulaic scripts, endless sequels, jaw-dropping explosions and special effects, teen sex comedies and muscly action heroes.

It also meant a picture was more apt to win backing from a man like Jordan if it could be condensed into a logline—a single-sentence summary presenting the protagonist and central conflict with a strong emotional hook.

Something marketable. Compelling. High-concept.

The camera went on humming its white noise. How could Jordan not hear it?

He changed tack. "Seeking closure, a young woman returns with her friends to the empty hometown they'd left after almost everyone died. As her friends die one by one in horrifying ways, she must find a magical item so she can put an end to the wish that killed the town and now threatens the outside world. Basically, it's a modern and expansive retelling of the classic story 'The Monkey's Paw.'"

The producer grunted. "That's not terrible."

"It's gonna be the next big thing." More producer catnip. "It'll be so visceral they'll take it home with them. We'll be picketed by nuns."

"Okay." Accepting and dismissing Max's bragging.

"There's a strong but fragile female protagonist who must dig deep to—"

Jordan raised his hand. "I got the basic vision. It's a careful-what-you-wish-for Cinderella plot with a slasher element and the wish as the twist."

"So." Max was drenched in flop sweat. "What do you think?"

"I'm actually interested. I have to crunch the numbers, but off the top of my head, I'm thinking I could throw you half a million. Under certain conditions."

Max slurped his scotch, barely tasting it. His knee jumped a mile a minute. This was good news. Very good news.

But not great.

A half mil wouldn't be enough to do the movie he wanted to make. And there were conditions. There always were. Jordan rarely offered a clear green light. More often than not, financial backing pivoted on whether Max could meet this budget, hire some up-and-coming starlet the producer liked, whatever.

He braced himself for the anvils to drop.

Jordan counted them on his fingers. "One, you don't go a dime over budget. Getting picketed by nuns is terrific publicity, but we need actual distribution, so you will not screw with the censors. If we have to cut film, it goes on the floor. You won't have money for fancy reshoots. Got it?"

"Got it," Max grumbled.

"Two, you wrap principal photography by the end of the year."

He groaned, but Jordan still hadn't finished.

"And three, you sign a new contract with Lyman Entertainments."

He grimaced as it stacked up. He'd have to work miracles.

Then he blinked. "What new contract?"

"A new three-picture deal, my pick, and for the first, I pick *Jack the Knife IV.* Which I want to see concepts and a budget for on my desk first thing in January with minimal bitching attached."

"Then give me final cut on this one," Max said.

Final cut: final decision on every frame produced and placed in his movie.

The producer glanced again at his cigar. Almost done. He tapped ash into the little brass tray on the coffee table.

"I'll be happy to give you all the creative freedom you need."

A firm *no* to giving Max final say on everything, but a promise to stay out of his hair and not meddle with the story as much as possible.

Max didn't think highly of the producer's promises, but the camera roared its approval. Arthur Golden did a slow clap, mocking in its approval.

Jordan added, "Naturally, though, I'll want to see dailies and otherwise remain informed about the picture's progress."

"Should I sign it in blood?" Max asked.

The producer chuckled.

"I'll settle for your sweat, babe. We're going to do great things."

Yes, I am, thought Max.

Jordan's instincts detected that Max might be onto something, and he smelled profit. He also had his favorite horror director over a barrel. The deal wasn't perfect, but Max had his first green light. He could make his dream movie, and after, horror would never be the same. Now he just had to make it.

The only problem was the story he'd pitched Jordan didn't belong to him.

Max gazed into the little abyss he'd dug among Lady Susan's beloved rosebushes. The burial wasn't complete, not yet.

The camera rested next to him in its gray plastic case. He inspected the mundane aluminum alloy body, switches, and instruments. Nothing weird about it. Just a movie camera. A devil hiding in plain sight.

He picked it up to examine it from all angles. The compact machine weighed thirty pounds, though it seemed far heavier now, as if producing its own dark gravity. The gravity of guilt.

It still emitted its ominous pulsing hum loaded with want.

Why did the infernal thing take Susan and not Jordan? A question he'd puzzled over half the night, long after the producer packed up and went home.

You know why, Max, the camera said in Arthur Golden's voice.

The camera wasn't actually cursed. Whoever *used it* was cursed.

Bingo, said Golden.

Yes, it killed. Against all reason and sane expectation about how the world worked, Max had become convinced of this. It definitely, inevitably killed.

But it only murdered living things the filmmaker cared about. Things the filmmaker himself saw through the camera's evil eye.

No wonder the apparatus had killed the one man at the park Max had empathized with. Then his friend Raphael. And then his poor little dog.

No wonder it skipped right over Jordan—because Max hated his greedy guts.

He thought: *Arthur Golden, you genius freak.*

The rumors were true. You dabbled in the occult.

You loved horror. Truly loved it. So much that you dreamed of making the perfect horror picture. A picture that would shock an America jaded by war and the new crop of gross-out films.

You understood horror was only horror if it was real. Deranged by desire, you consorted with occult forces to make it so. Demons? Elementals? The Old Ones? Djinn? It doesn't matter. Whatever you called, it answered.

You empowered a camera to make horror. Horror created by the eye of the beholder. You thought you'd be the greatest director who ever lived.

Whether the rituals and spells you used were all a lark to you—a devilish attempt at fostering inspiration—or you believed with all your heart it was real, the result proved the same. Whatever you did, it worked.

Only you were a fool. Black magic always has a catch, buddy. Something you should have known as a horror fan. Something I should have known before fooling around with the camera last night. It's a venerable trope.

You thought the occult forces you drew into the Arriflex 35BL would serve your artistic vision. You were trying to paint with a scalpel, sculpt with a hand grenade. You made your picture without these magical effects, though you likely loved your own film enough to believe they had indeed been at work the whole time.

On the last day, while the crew prepped for the martini shot, you gathered the people you'd grown to love to thank them for contributing to your opus.

Then you witnessed the camera's power as it butchered them all in an improv horror short that made a mockery of your real work. Even then, you refused to blame the machine. So you filmed Helga Frost to capture the moment you confessed your love. And you killed her too.

Finally realizing what you'd done, you hid from the world.

Only you couldn't destroy the camera.

Because what if. Always what if. Words that themselves counted as a magic spell in Hollywood. The elixir of high concept. The prompt for a terrific story, a story that leaves everyone dying to know what happens next.

The occult apparatus always had so much potential to make something wonderfully terrifying, didn't it? Surely, it must have tempted you. You owned a machine that made real horror, but you couldn't use it. That was the real curse.

Unable to live with it, you at last wound up destroying yourself.

The curse now belonged to Max.

And the temptation.

You know, he heard Golden say, *you could still—*

No. He didn't need it anymore.

Max had Jordan's go-ahead to write a story treatment. He'd find a way to create the same visceral horror without the crutch. And, oh yeah, regardless of his scary pop-culture reputation, he didn't actually enjoy killing people, especially the scant few he actually cared about. He might be a misanthrope with a very morbid imagination and love of horror, but that didn't make him a psychopath.

This left him only one solution.

Max returned the camera to the case, latched it, and wrapped it in plastic. Then he placed it in the grave with as much remorse as he'd felt laying his dog to rest. He scooped dirt until he'd filled in his makeshift burial plot.

At last, the soil muted the machine's warbling song. Max greeted the silence with relief, though he already missed it. Another empty space. A new lack.

He finished by patting the dirt with the shovel. Wiping away fresh tears, he noticed Mariel gazing down at him like a guilty conscience from his bedroom window. Her face a mask of disapproval.

First, a bit of lady's lingerie discovered on the floor. A strange camera appearing in the living room. Now the dog was dead. All very suspicious. Her boss the horror movie director was clearly up to no good.

Hoisting the shovel onto his shoulder, Max exhaled a bitter chuckle.

Lady, you have no idea.

He returned the tool to the gardening shed and went into the house to buy a story from a science fiction writer named Frederick Munsch.

Time to start his own magnum opus.

Just before he entered the house, he turned to gaze longingly at the burial plot. Already feeling the black hole inside him reopen.

ELEVEN

Max told Mariel to take the day off. After she left muttering and making the sign of the cross, he had his house to himself again. Without Lady Susan's volumetric presence, however, his home felt empty.

"Time to buy a story," he mumbled.

One last thing to do before he could rest. He'd now been awake longer than his chronic insomnia had ever pushed him. His trembling body practically wept with hot flashes. He'd started to see double.

Max poured a fresh mug of coffee and sipped it at his home office desk. From a filing cabinet drawer, he dug out the *Twilight Zone* issue where he'd read Munsch's story, "If Wishes Were Horses." The title was the first part of the Scottish nursery rhyme *If wishes were horses, beggars would ride.* If wishes came true, even the poorest wretches would have everything they wanted.

"But they do come true," Max muttered. He was living proof.

Dialing the number for *The Twilight Zone*, he hoped his luck would hold. The receptionist put him through to the editor. The editor refused to divulge Frederick Munsch's contact information but would reach out to the author on his behalf.

Dropping the phone back on its cradle, Max reopened the magazine and checked the man's bio. No photo. He imagined a shifty-eyed bearded introvert smoking a pipe in a tweed jacket. Aside from discovering that Munsch's stories had been published in *The Twilight Zone*, *Asimov's Science Fiction*, and the *New Yorker*, he learned the man resided in the village of Big Bear Lake. A remote town in a forested wilderness about a hundred miles east of Los Angeles.

Max didn't have a phone book for San Bernardino County, so he dialed PacBell's directory assistance.

Munsch wasn't listed. He sighed and hung up again.

Nothing left now but to wait and hope the man reached out to him.

In the kitchen, he discovered a box of steel-cut oatmeal that Mariel had bought and set out for him like another nagging warning about his mortality. As an act of small mercy, she'd removed and disposed of all traces of the Milk-Bone and Chuck Wagon. He ignored the oatmeal to wolf down a Snickers from his secret stash under the sink. He chased it down with a glass of wholesome milk.

This done, he went upstairs to brush his teeth and enjoy a long hot shower. While giving himself a thorough scrub, he revisited the story he wanted to tell in his new movie, which he was already retitling.

Make a Wish Upon a Grave. Sticks and Stones. Soul Survivor.

Scratch all that. He'd call it *If Wishes Could Kill.*

In the remote town of Lonely Pines, a crying little girl trails her daddy while he prospects with a metal detector. A hobby of his, searching for little pieces of history left behind by the gold rush that built the town long ago.

"Everyone is mean," says the girl, whose name is Penny. "Everyone is so unfair to me." But he is not listening, his own way of being mean. He has found something. Digging, his muddy hand resurrects an old amulet.

Daddy smiles at the prize find.

She says, "Can I make a wish? It's for wishing." He answers, "If wishes were horses, beggars would ride." Penny does anyway. She makes a wish. She wishes for all the meanies to leave her alone.

Daddy drops the detector and starts marching back home.

The girl runs after him but fails to keep up. When she reaches the town, she sees everyone banging out of their front doors. They walk stiffly with eager smiles toward the lake, as if drawn by music they alone can hear.

Penny races to the shore in time to see her father disappear into the water. While her closest friends scream and pull at their family's arms and legs in a futile effort to stop them, she watches the entire town march into the lake.

Years later, the girl is all grown up and living in a city. She has a dead-end job and a relationship with a man who does not love her. When the man breaks her heart, Penny says, "I wish you'd leave me alone forever." And he does, straight into traffic. But it does not stop there. Soon, an epidemic of suicides plagues her neighborhood.

Her old wish appears to have caught up to her.

Then one of her old friends reaches out. A fellow survivor of the day Penny's town died. He is getting the old gang back together for a trip to the lake. They all saw their families and neighbors drown, and they all went through the foster care system. Now they are adults who want closure. Penny is reluctant at first. Plagued by strange memories, she feels somehow responsible for what happened. But the suicides go on, dozens, and she knows she must take action.

So, at last she agrees, and the band of survivors returns to their lakeside town to find it in ruins, the earth itself poisoned. Picking through their old homes, they catch up on each other's lives, resolving and expanding ancient alliances, feuds, and romantic interests. As for Penny, she has a different, very important mission. She needs to recover the amulet and make a new wish.

Time, however, is running out.

One by one, her friends start dying. Again, it might be her fault.

Even if it read more literary than sensational, the short story was built on a solid premise. For screen adaptation, it offered a complete emotional arc and limited shooting locations. Aside from the drowning town scene, the story required a small, intimate cast—

Max gasped as the temperature plummeted. He'd been in the

shower too long and drained the hot water supply. Rinsing his hair, he yanked the taps closed and dried himself off in the foggy bathroom. Feeling a bit more human, Max returned to his bedroom to dress in his silk pajamas and bathrobe that still retained the suggestion of Sally Priest's pleasantly female scent.

His bed now tempted him in a louder voice than the camera's. Any other day, he'd resist it; as a dedicated insomniac, he found sleep uncomfortably similar to dying, waking up a painful resurrection. If his insomnia had a voice, it would repeat an endless mantra, *Just one more thing*, but even it had hit the wall.

Max had hoped to wrap up a deal with Frederick Munsch before crashing, but fate had other plans. The world had faded to a confusing blur.

He needed the man's story. Of course, he could simply try to steal the idea in the tradition of all great artists, changing things around enough that it'd hold up in court. But that wasn't how Max did business. Even if his morals sometimes fluctuated around what was best for his movies, he'd always been ethical.

Sunlight streamed through the bedroom's open blinds in sheets of blinding liquid fire, more of Mariel's subversive handiwork. Max didn't have the energy to fight it. Collapsing onto the bed, he hugged a pillow over his head.

He thought, *I have to figure out how to show an entire town drowning in a lake on the cheap.*

Then he passed out.

Max awoke in the dark with a pounding headache. A glance at his alarm clock told him it was precisely 3:00 AM. The witching hour of folklore when demons, ghosts, and witches became most active. When the veil between the normal and the supernatural turned leaky and threadbare.

A warm glow flickered past the blinds. Still groggy, he slithered off the bed with a groan and peeked outside.

Under a bright, pregnant moon, the neighborhood stood silent and empty. Not a single window illuminated nor even a lone car prowling the road. The kind of silence that one couldn't help but notice. Silence that took on a tangible psychic volume that suddenly turned deafening.

In the distance, an orange light glowed with an eerie pulse, as if alive. It came from the nearby school. Someone had lit a bonfire in the playground.

The strangeness of it drew him out into the night to investigate. The warm air smelled like ash. The darkness blanketing the neighborhood thickened like a bad omen. It seemed to eat the light. Something ominous was out here, he could feel it.

Some vast ancient thing, watching him.

The same presence he'd felt when he first picked up Arthur Golden's camera.

Padding down the road on slippered feet, monogrammed bathrobe flapping around his pajamaed legs, Max understood he'd committed perhaps the worst sin in modern horror cinema: curiosity.

As he came closer, he spotted figures capering about the fire. Shrieks that may have been laughter or screams broke the silence. The darkness surrounding the streetlights and flames became ethereal with a thickening pall of smoke, like a fog. Crossing the lawn, he felt the intense heat on his face.

A man stood in front of the fire. He turned and flashed a bright smile under the fins of a lawn dart protruding from his eye.

"Maximillian! You came."

Raphael wore the same leather jacket, old gray tee, blue jeans, and boots he'd had on when he died. Max gaped at him before gazing in wide-eyed terror at the bodies writhing in the fire.

Stiff, charred shapes rose from the hellish flames.

"Am I dreaming?" He rubbed his eyes. "I'm dreaming, right?"

Shedding sparks, the smoking apparitions wandered off into the night.

"No. Yeah. Something like that. Think of it as astral travel."

"Astral...?"

"Your consciousness is here. Your body is not, though it'll probably end up following you if you didn't tie it down." The man shrugged.

"Then who are these people?"

Raphael chuckled. "Come on, man. Don't be insulting."

Max stared at the dart fins sprouting from his eye socket. "Does that hurt?"

"Yeah, but, you know..."

He waited. "I honestly don't know."

"It's better than nothing."

"Damn. I'm sorry, Raph."

"The dead see things different, man. We all got to go some-time, am I right? Anyway, I died doing what I loved. Remember when I told you I always wanted to make a practical effect of a dude with an arrow sticking out of his eye?" He tapped the fins and chuckled again. "Top this, Tom Savini."

"It deserved an Oscar," Max said. "You're missed."

"I doubt it. I never let people get close to me. Something you and me had in common. All that shit from 'Nam I carried around." He sighed. "To be honest, I had no idea how good I had it. It's funny how you only learn life's biggest lessons when it's too late to use them."

Another man shambled over. Or what remained of one. His legs labored to balance a torso wobbling on a broken spine, broken arms waving in zigzags.

"I'm gonna go see what my girls are up to," he said.

"Okay, Dave," said Raphael.

"Catch you later."

He turned to Max to stage-whisper, "Now, *that* deserves an Oscar."

"Is that the . . . ?" Sickened, Max watched the broken man lurch away.

"That's him," Raphael said.

"So these people really are the camera's victims."

"You are correct," a prim voice cut in.

The corpse sashayed over to Max and gazed up into his face from a jarring sideways angle. It was Helga Frost, blond hair matted with drying blood, head lolling on a snapped neck around her right shoulder.

Even in this morbid state, she was beautiful.

"Raphael informed me that you are the camera's new master," she added in her clipped native German accent. "You should know what is happening here. We are trapped. Alive and not alive. Unable to feel anything except the numb shock of our final moment, we roam and observe the living."

Helga tilted her body and rolled her eyes so she could look up at the sky, a whole other disconcerting effect. "And when the full moon rises, we are reborn together to do it again." Blinking, she pivoted to quickly survey the scenery. "Hmm. This is far more pleasant than North Hollywood."

Max said, "Is there anything I can do for you?"

"Obviously." The sideways eyes bored into his. "You can destroy the camera."

Behind her, a rust-red shape bolted past in an alarming blur.

"Or don't," Raphael said with high cheer. "Do you want to bet it all there's something after this, Helga? Heaven or nirvana or whatever? Bet your very existence? We may not be alive, but at least we *exist*."

"I have been here fifteen years," she deadpanned.

"I imagine it gets dull after that long." The special makeup effects artist pointed at the squirming pile of ash at the center of the still-blazing bonfire. "Probably no fun at all for those poor slobs."

"You have no idea. We do not eat. We do not sleep." Her eyes burned like embers from the grisly pyre. "We watch. That is all we do. We watch you all the time. The living are our movies. And you are so very *boring*."

Raphael glanced at Max, the dart in his eye giving him the unnerving illusion of winking. "Like I said, it's better than nothing, right? Sometimes, you just flip the channels and watch whatever's on."

Max didn't trust the man's easy grin. In fact, he was a little afraid of his old friend. Raphael didn't seem like himself anymore. Dying had changed him more than physically transforming him into a ghost. It had drained his personality by sucking all the enjoyment of life out of him.

The rusty shape zipped past again.

"All these years, I begged Arthur to destroy the camera and set us free," Helga told Max. "He refused. So stupid. In love with a spirit. He tried to make it kill *him* so he could join us. It wouldn't. He took his own life to remove the choice."

Rust blurred past once more.

"Okay," Max said in alarm. "What *is* that?"

"Oh, that's Lady Susan," Raphael said. "You don't have to fear *us*, man, but steer clear of her for a while. She smells the camera on you. And she's pissed."

"She—wait. *You* can hurt me?"

The man splayed his large hands. "Oh, I could shred you. I could rip your arms off and slap you into hamburger with them, stick them up your—"

"I get the picture," Max said, taking a step backward.

"But why would I do that? That'd be crazy!" The man chuckled. "I like it that you're here. It'll be nice to see a friendly face every full moon. We can hang out."

"Yeah." Max swallowed hard. "Hanging out is wonderful."

"Destroy the machine," Helga hissed. "Free us from this hell."

Max said, "I won't use it anymore. I promise. In fact, I buried it."

Though even now, even here, he missed it, as if the little black hole inside him had turned instead into its own ring of fire.

"Yeah, sure, okay, *or,*" Raphael went on, grinning, "you can dig it right back up and realize its purpose. Go all the way. You know you want to. All those gorgeous ladies in your movies. Kill 'em all, man. Starting with Ashlee Gibson."

Max goggled at him. "You want me to kill people?"

"Haunting houses is boss, but do you know what's super boss? Having more friendly faces around, people to hang with. Anyway, how else are you gonna make that perfect movie you were going on about?"

Max shook his head. "I can't do it. I mean, I let Arthur Golden make me use it once, but all I ended up doing was killing poor Susan. And you."

Helga and Raphael exchanged a glance.

"Arthur spoke to you?" she asked.

"Yes. He talked to me from the camera."

"You have a conflicted soul," she said. "Like Arthur. A man at war with himself. His heart and need pointed in opposite ways."

"What do you mean?"

Raphael snorted. "She's trying to say you were talking to yourself, brother."

"But—"

"The camera doesn't *talk*, man. It just is. Arthur's gone. And you're cuckoo."

"He's here. Something is, anyway." Max gestured toward the black sky. "I can feel it, all around us."

"That is not Arthur," Helga said.

"It's what he summoned," Raphael filled in. "We don't know

its name. We just know it's there. It's old. We call it the Beast. We watch the living. It watches us. Honestly, we simply ignore it."

Max gazed up at the dark sky and shivered. "Okay."

"Hey. Norman Bates. Look at me. You didn't kill me, man. I'm right here. The only real murder would be destroying the camera like ol' Helga here wants. If you destroy the camera, you'll put an end to us all."

"Mercy killing," she said.

Max felt sick. "I can't use it again, Raph. I'm sorry."

"Hey." Raphael's face became a ghoulish, lifeless mask. "You owe me. I died so you could learn what the camera can do. Don't tell me that's the end of it. You already went this far. Why not go a little further and see what happens?"

Max screamed.

Pain crunched through his bones. His leg buckled, and he went down hard. Still screaming, he gaped at his Pomeranian with her jaws clamped around his ankle.

Snarling ropey strands of drool, Lady Susan wagged her head in a fury.

"This is not helpful, pup," Helga scolded. "We were discussing—"

"Wait," Max howled as the dog dragged him toward the squirming pile of charred flesh at the bonfire's center. "What are you doing? No, no, *bad girl*—!"

"Bring me Ashlee," Raphael said. "Or next time, it might be me hurting you."

Max went flying into the roasting flames.

And awoke to find himself caged behind bars.

TWELVE

I got that motherfucker," a gruff voice said.

Heart pounding, Max lurched upright on a thin mattress. The bedframe squeaked. Rows of steel springs above his head. He was in a bunk bed.

What the hell? He looked around, processing what he saw.

Concrete walls framing a tiny room. Porcelain sink on the wall. Steel toilet in the corner. An iron-barred door. Empty and dim corridor outside.

A dungeon, the institutional kind.

With a gasp, he inspected his ankle. He still wore his bathrobe and pajamas and his foot was filthy, but his flesh remained intact. Not even a bite mark.

A dream, then. A horrible fever dream. His own fault too. He swore to himself that he'd never stay up that long again. The premiere and finding Arthur Golden's old camera had infected him with a sort of madness. He groaned as all the loony things he'd thought and done since then flooded his mind. Raphael, Lady Susan...God, he'd actually helped his evil camera try to kill his producer.

All of it culminating in the nightmare. Jeez, it had felt so real.

What about this place? Was this real?

Then he smiled, remembering Jordan granting him his green light.

"I got him good," the voice said from the neighboring cell.

"Hey," Max called out.

The loud muttering stopped.

"Hey, yourself," the man said.

"If you don't mind, can you tell me where I am?"

"Van Nuys pig station, man."

Max said nothing, and the man started up again on his guilty rant. Forcing himself onto his feet, he emptied his aching bladder into the toilet and gulped water at the sink's tap until he couldn't drink anymore. Wiping his mouth, he inspected his surroundings with a fresh eye.

From the looks of things, he was out of the fire and had landed in some sort of frying pan. He'd been arrested. But how? He'd gone to bed and experienced a bizarre and vivid nightmare that had him wondering what was real and what wasn't. And more important, *why* did the police arrest him?

All his memories since the premiere themselves felt like strange dreams.

"Hey," he ventured again.

"What."

"I heard you say you 'got' someone. Who was it?"

A snort. "Somebody who needed to get *got*."

"I'm assuming you mean you killed him," Max said.

"Something like that. Exactly like that, actually."

"How do you feel about it? What was it like?"

"Good, I guess." A pause. "Then bad."

"You must have known what would happen," he pressed. "That you'd end up here. That it'd cost you everything. Why did you do it?"

"Because some things need doing. They just have to be. You got no choice. And when you finally get to it, it's like scratching the biggest itch you ever had."

Max could relate. Feeling good, bad, the itch. All of it.

"But enough about me," the man added. "What are you in for?"

Max opened his mouth to say he didn't have a clue but then closed it. Did the police know about the camera's power? He doubted it.

"I'm not sure," he said. "I'm a horror director."

"Director? You mean like the movies?"

"Do you like horror pictures?"

"Naw, man. No offense."

"None taken."

Max meant it. He took a perverse pride in the rejection, like he belonged to an exclusive club. Meeting a *them* always intensified one's sense of an *us*.

"Not since *Cannibal Holocaust*, anyway," the man clarified. "That movie was all right. It scared the shit out of me."

Ruggero Deodato's 1980 film was so graphically violent that it resulted in the director's arrest for obscenity charges. Multiple countries banned it.

Max doubted the police had nabbed him on similar grounds. *Jack the Knife III* was about as offensive as a loud belch at McDonald's.

"What did you like about that movie?" he asked.

"It freaked me out that it actually happened. People can be real garbage."

The found-footage documentary format had also proved so effective in convincing people the film was real that Deodato had faced an additional charge of murder, based on a rumor the actors had been killed while on camera. Even the murderer in the next jail cell deemed it offensive.

"Yeah," Max said. "They can."

Footsteps pounded down the corridor. Wearing a short-sleeved black uniform bulging with massive arms, a square-jawed police officer stopped outside his cell. The cop glared through the bars.

"You're awake." The man looked familiar.

"Can you tell me what I'm doing in here?"

The cop unlocked and opened the metal door, offering Max a long look at him. Seemingly made of muscle and rope, the man appeared to spend his spare time shooting steroids and working out. He was no Arnold Schwarzenegger, but he looked well on his way.

"Let's go, Maurey," he said. "The chief wants a word with you."

Max's mind rolled back to red and blue lights flashing in a twilight park. A cop strung up yellow tape. Another questioned him.

He shuffled into the corridor, slippers slapping the floor. "I remember you. You were one of the police who came to the park."

"Where two people died while you were filming, yeah."

"Officer McDaniel, if I recall."

"I'm onto you, shitbird."

Max started. "You're onto *me*?"

"Nobody just films nothing at a park for fifteen minutes and then two people up and die all of a sudden. The same day, we pick you up wandering around like a zombie at a school playground in the middle of the night."

"It is weird," Max agreed.

"Then you slept in that cell for a whole day and night. You're into something, and I'm going to find out what. Some kind of *Peeping Tom* stuff, from the looks of it."

"*Peeping Tom*?"

"Is that what you're into, Maurey?"

"Are you calling me a literal Peeping Tom, or are you talking about the horror picture?" Made in 1960, it was about a serial killer with a film camera fitted with a knife that murdered women while documenting their terrified final moments.

The cop snarled. "You make snuff movies for rich sickos, is that it? You're already into a sick genre, and now you want to see how far you can take it?"

"Seriously, I'm impressed you know that film." Like *Mary's Birthday*, it was obscure but considered a progenitor for the modern slasher. "Hardly a model for a real-life crime spree in broad daylight, though."

"Go ahead and act cocky. I'll be keeping an eye on you, Maurey. And when I figure out what you're into, I'm going to put you away where you belong."

They'd reached an office and stopped in the doorway. Behind the desk, a paunchy cop with a bullet head bristling with cropped silver hair glared at them.

"For Chrissakes, climb off the man's back," the man growled. "Take a hike, McDaniel."

"Sure thing, Chief." The big policeman gave Max a final meaningful stare. "I'll be seeing you around, Maurey."

After the man stomped away, the police chief offered Max one of the visitor chairs. "Sorry about all that. John's a solid cop and usually has excellent instincts, but he sees conspiracies sometimes."

As Max parked himself, he asked, "Was I really asleep here for a whole day?" Twenty-four hours of preproduction time lost.

The man chuckled. "A few more hours, I was gonna send you over to the hospital. It must have been one hell of a party."

"Actually, I got involved in a new project right after the premiere of—"

"Wow, wow. Very exciting." The police chief's tone said the exact opposite. In this part of town, you tripped over people doing projects and attending premieres.

"And I stayed up too long working and I guess I wound up sleepwalking."

"Well, maybe tie yourself down. Whatever else you were doing, do less of it."

"Was I disturbing the peace? Do I have to pay a fine or something?"

"No, no. You're an important member of this community in

high standing, Mr. Maurey. We didn't want to see anything bad happen to you, that's all. You're free to go. There's a man outside who's been waiting for you."

"Jordan Lyman?" Max suppressed a groan. He'd hear no end of it.

"A guy named Womack. Said he's a friend of yours. He'll drive you home."

Blinking in the harsh sunlight, Max sank into the hot passenger seat of Dan Womack's cherry-red Chevy Camaro.

The actor filled the driver's side with his bulk. The door clunked shut. Taking his time, he put on calfskin driving gloves and a pair of mirrored shades. Then he started the car, which responded with a macho growl.

All of it conveyed the impression that this man was in control and had plans for him. Starting to sweat, Max stared at his shaggy profile and waited for the other shoe to drop. Again, he wondered if all this was real or not, whether he might be in a surprising double dream sequence like in *An American Werewolf in London*.

Womack shot him a glance, followed by a sheepish smile that broke character. He seemed just as anxious about their meeting, if not more.

Max smiled back, more practiced social reflex than genuine happiness, though he did feel a little less trepidatious now. Whatever was happening, this man wasn't sure of himself.

"How did you find out I was here?" he asked.

"Oh, you know, it's a small town," Womack told him. "In all the worst ways."

"What's the buzz?"

"You, uh, had some kind of mental freak-out about Raphael Rodriguez."

"Ah." It wasn't completely inaccurate.

Womack's face twisted into a bitter grimace.

"But we both know better, don't we?"

With that, he threw the car into reverse and stomped the gas, only to brake hard an instant later to avoid plowing into a cop walking into the station. He winced, his little dramatic moment ruined.

"Sorry, officer," he called out the window. Then he sighed. "Goddamnit."

"You seem stressed-out," Max said.

"You have no idea."

Max smiled again, the real kind this time. The cops had nothing on him. Officer McDaniel was all bark. As for Womack, he knew something about the camera, but he was just an aging actor feeling his way through an improv scene.

"I'm a huge fan," he said. "I'd love to ask you some questions about Arthur Golden and his picture sometime, if you don't mind."

Womack did mind. He grimaced and said nothing.

"So why are you here?" Max said. "Why did you pick me up?"

The man pulled out of the parking lot and took off onto Sylmar.

"I'm in the market for a movie camera," he said.

Then he blanched as Max started laughing.

"I don't have any equipment for sale," said Max.

"Sally Priest went to Arthur Golden's estate sale with you. She said you bought Arthur's old rig. It made me sentimental. I'd like to buy it from you."

"Sorry, but I'm going to keep it as a collector's item. Like I said: huge fan."

"Even after two men died at Lake Balboa?"

"Jeez Louise," Max said. "Word travels like a bullet in this town."

"I'm for real. Name your price."

"I told you it's not for sale." Acting on another dark impulse, he added, "I'm thinking about using it to make my next picture."

Turning a sickly pale, Womack gripped the wheel so hard that it creaked. The man's bearish frame appeared to deflate, and for an alarming moment Max worried he might crash the car.

At last, he spoke through gritted teeth. "You can't do that."

"If you're interested in getting back into film work and want to audition—"

"Destroy it," Womack said. "Or give it to me."

Max now had the full story. At first, he'd wondered if the man desired the camera's power at his own command. If nothing else, it was an instrument for the perfect crime. As a case in point, Max had pretty much killed two people with it in front of dozens of witnesses in broad daylight, and the only thing he'd suffered for it were the paranoid suspicions of one Officer John McDaniel.

But no, Womack's heart seemed purer than that. He wanted to end the curse. Only his idea of ending it was to destroy the camera. Max realized Raphael was right. If what he'd experienced in his long slumber was in some way real and not just a vivid dream, the camera was haunted by its victims. If Max destroyed the machine, he'd erase their existence, however unhappy it might be.

"Sally said you remained friends with Arthur over the years," he said.

"That's right. His soul was tortured by what happened."

"Yours too, from what I can see."

Womack gripped the wheel even harder. "That's right."

"Then you should know if Arthur wanted the camera destroyed, he would have given it to you before taking his life. And you should know why he didn't."

"And if *you* know about any of that, you know you should never use it!"

"I'm not going to," Max said.

"Wait. But you just said—"

"I was messing with you. I'm not going to use it."

"You will. You're just waiting for the right excuse."

"All I'm doing is keeping it safe. Turn left up here."

"At least leave Sally out of it," Womack pleaded. "She's innocent."

Max snorted. In Hollywood, no one was innocent. He suspected the actor had fallen in love with Sally. It wouldn't have surprised him if he had. The woman had been born to break hearts.

"That's my house," he said.

Womack parked the car in the driveway and sat trembling. "You can't do this."

"Let me ask you just one thing. Can I ask you something?"

"Go ahead, I'm listening."

"What was it like? When the helicopter—?"

"I don't talk about that."

"Well." Max didn't know what else to say. "Thanks for the ride."

"I won't let you hurt anyone else."

He looked over and gasped at the gleaming carving knife in the man's hand.

Then he chuckled right into the actor's sweaty, determined face.

"You'll have to kill me, I guess," he said.

The knife was the collapsible prop from *Mary's Birthday*.

With a cry that was equal parts despair and rage, Womack stabbed the dashboard. Max stared at the very real blade left wobbling where it had struck the hard plastic.

"Um," he said.

"Next time, I might stick it in you," Womack panted.

"For a second there, I thought *I* might be the bad guy," Max told him. "I'm heading inside to call the police. I suggest you be gone by the time they show up."

He stepped out of the Camaro and slammed the door. Just in time to avoid being dragged away, as Womack jerked the transmission into reverse and dramatically stomped the gas pedal.

Coming to a screeching halt, the man rolled down his window in a rage.

"Damn you, Maurey! That camera is a curse."

"Or a blessing," Max yelled back. "Depending on how you look at it."

"You won't get away with this!"

"And you need to stop overacting. Less is more, Dan."

Already cranking his window back up, the actor didn't hear him. With a final glare through the windshield, Womack swung the Camaro around, humped the lawn, and mowed down Max's mailbox before roaring down the road. The last Max saw of him was the silhouette of a hand raised to flip him the bird.

He growled. "Son of a…"

Then he laughed. Bubbling, maniacal, movie villain laughter that was mostly the catharsis of not being stabbed, though the whole thing really was comical. The clueless cop and the obsessed nemesis stood the test of time as venerable horror tropes, and now his personal horror movie had both.

Given these roles were played by the likes of Officer McDaniel and a washed-up actor named Dan Womack, Max suspected he didn't have much to worry about.

THIRTEEN

Sally Priest drove her clunker—a 1975 two-door Austin covered in colorful harlequin patches from an old accident—onto the Sunset Strip and parked near Spago, a favorite among Hollywood's celebrity caste.

Inside, the patrons lunched in bright white decor lit by track lights. The staff hustled around delivering food. The dining area smelled deliciously of Wolfgang Puck's gourmet pizzas.

On its far side, a curvy and stunning fiftysomething flirted with an aproned waiter at one of the tables. Always stylish, today she wore a short-sleeved, form-fitting party dress with puffed sleeves and bold eighties colors.

Sally hadn't seen her mother in three months. Last time, things hadn't gone all that well.

Still, she'd been happy to receive Maude Turner's phone call inviting her to lunch. It offered a perfect opportunity to test out her new Final Girl persona. Responsible, obedient, and always thinking of others regardless of the temptation to punch them in the nose. A girl who bought her mom holiday cards.

Sally wanted to inhabit the character archetype so fully that Max would believe she *was* the Final Girl. Directors considered acting a bunch of hooey and were always looking for talent that walked into an audition embodying the role. If Sally could convince her own mother, she could convince anyone.

Maude assessed Sally with a cursory once-over.

"Hello, darling," she said.

Sally slid into her white chair with all the grace of a surly teenager. Her next stop in her Final Girl transformation would be a new wardrobe. A prodigious hairspray perm and glam-trash fashion did not suit her new good-girl image.

"Hi, Mom—"

Maude had already turned away batting her eyelashes. "Do freshen up this drink if it's not too much trouble, Raul."

Flirting like a fading Doris Day, an image of robust female sexuality rendered as coy, dumb, and malleable. Sally hated it.

"At once, signora." The waiter retrieved her glass. "And for you?"

While considering her choice, Sally looked up at an angular face she found familiar. In her mother's loaded and domineering presence, Sally wanted a tall shot glass filled with tequila, but then she remembered herself.

"I'll have a ginger ale," she said.

"Of course, signora." Raul winked at her and left.

She blushed, recalling where she knew him from. An actor himself, he was a friend of Ashlee's who had witnessed her *Look at me, world* strip-show antics at the *Jack the Knife III* premiere party.

At least she'd blushed over it. She felt like a Final Girl already.

Maude looked around. "Well, this is pleasant enough."

"It's a very popular place. Swifty Lazar—he's a top agent?— holds an Oscar night party here every year."

"Of course I know Swifty. A lovely man."

"Well, celebrities come here all the time."

"I doubt the kind of men I worked with—Grant, Bogie— would hang out in a *pizza* joint. Maybe James Dean. Yes, I'd give you James Dean."

"It's *haute cuisine*, Mom. They make pizzas topped with smoked salmon and caviar here, for crying out loud."

Sally didn't know why she was arguing about it, but it felt familiar.

"At least it's not Gorky's again. Pierogies. So proletarian." Maude slipped into a charming smile. "So, Emily!" Using Sally's real name, the one she'd given her daughter. "I haven't seen you in ages. You look well."

"Thanks—"

"You've put on a pound or two. No, no, it looks ravishing on you. Anyway, your father sends all his love. Tell me what you've been doing. Do you need any money?"

"No, I've got some exciting news. I've—"

Raul returned with the drinks and offered to take their lunch order. With a final glance at the menu, Maude flirted her way toward a chicken salad. Sally felt a perverse desire to eat an entire large pizza on the motherly dime but remembered herself and demurely ordered a Cobb salad instead.

Raul assured them they'd made excellent choices.

Maude gave her an approving look as well. "That's probably for the best. The camera adds ten pounds, you know."

Sally did in fact know, as she'd heard it from her mom many times before. She laid out her latest progress in building an acting career. *Razor Lips* wrapping and the workshop with Dan Womack and his emphasis on Stella Adler's take on the Method. She finished with her hope to read for the lead role as the Final Girl in Max Maurey's next horror movie.

"Isn't that awesome?" she asked, fishing for approval.

"Well, if you think that's what's best for you, I'm happy for you, naturally."

"You don't *sound* happy, Mom."

"I think you can do better. There, I said it."

"Don't act—" Sally caught herself before she lectured her mother about pretending to find being critical anything close to a

difficult job. In that role, Maude's performances were quite uncon-
vincing. "It's the lead in a major feature."

"Yes, but it's *horror.*"

She sighed. They'd been through this many times.

Maude offered a rueful smile. "Such a dirty, distasteful genre.
Even sci-fi is more artistic." The way she said it, one would think
she was talking about the decline of Western civilization. "And so
misogynistic."

"No more than any other genre," Sally said. "It's all the same
bullshit idea of masculinity. The same male wish fulfillment, the
same hot girls. At least horror is honest. It's all out in the open."

"Well, I see you're still quite the little philosopher. You're
young and want to rebel. That's wonderful. You may regret it later
when you're typecast and find yourself stuck doing the same role the
rest of your career."

"Jamie Lee Curtis got her start with *Halloween*. It's not a black
hole."

Maude shrugged. "That's her. Tony Curtis and Janet Leigh's
little girl. She's practically royalty. As for you, well. Not so much.
You do what you think is best, of course. I just happen to think
very highly of you and that you can always do better. Which, as the
woman who brought you into this world, I am allowed."

Raul returned to present their salads with a flourish, and Sally
dug into hers fuming at her mom and sulking that she hadn't ordered
a signature pizza. Too late, she remembered Tom Hanks's first role
had been in *He Knows You're Alone*.

Damn, being the Final Girl was proving way harder than it
looked. No wonder the girl displayed so much warrior strength
when the maniac showed up with a chainsaw. She worked out on a
treadmill of family dynamics and carried a lifetime of grit and per-
severance built up layer by layer into a kind of medieval armor.

In comparison, playing the Bad Girl was a piece of cake.

"I have a suggestion about a move in your career that's far more vertical," Maude said. "I bumped into Chazz Morton."

"The producer." A top executive at one of the major studios, in fact.

"Lovely man. He's putting together a new picture around— well, some very big stars and a *very* hot director. It's all hush-hush right now, but he did let slip it's a lighthearted romantic comedy. Anyway, I pulled a few strings to wiggle you in to read for a minor speaking role."

"Mom, I just said I'm waiting for a phone call about being cast as a lead. What you're describing sounds like a step down, not up."

"But this gets you into a far bigger playing field. The major league."

"Maybe," Sally said, chewing on it. "How much speaking are we talking?"

"I was told it's an under-five."

Meaning she'd have fewer than five lines of dialogue. Well, she could do both movies as long as there were no scheduling conflicts. Work was work, though the idea of stepping outside horror's comfort zone worried her a little.

The more she thought about doing the under-five, though, the more it appealed. A blockbuster movie. Sharing a set with household names. A small step up into a whole new league. Today's memorable minor character might be tomorrow's leading star.

Yes, she could do it. She *would* do it.

"Chazz wants to meet you to talk about it," Maude added.

"Seriously?"

A top dog like Chazz didn't put in time for a no-name actor auditioning for an under-five. Sally didn't see that they had anything to talk about.

"It's your chance to make the right impression and swing a bigger supporting role. These things happen."

"Ha! Over dinner and a nightcap at his place, I'll bet."

Sally had heard stories. Word got around in this town. Who respected actors or treated them like cattle, who had a clear vision or was prone to change everything on the fly. Whom you could trust being alone with.

Or maybe he was only taking the meeting as a favor to an old friend.

Okay, she decided. She'd meet with him. It wasn't the kind of thing an actor refused. But she'd do it in a public place. He'd flirt, she'd playfully deflect, and perhaps between all the bullshit they could do business.

Maude shrugged. "It's the game."

"Well, I don't play that game."

"Everyone plays it, darling. One might as well play to win, right?"

Sally froze, lettuce forgotten on her fork. She had a creeping sensation this conversation had stopped being academic.

"Wait," she said. "What?"

"All I'm saying is he has his power, and you have yours. You can use yours to get what you want."

"He has a hell of a lot more power than me. What if *he* uses it?"

Another shrug as Maude stabbed at her salad again.

How far Sally wanted to take things was up to her.

She watched Mom take a demure bite. "Just so we're clear, acting in a horror movie is beneath me, right? But selling my soul is fine."

"Hollywood doesn't care about your soul, darling. It simply charges it as the price of admission and then throws it away."

"Now look who's the philosopher. My body, then. That at least appears to be worth a good deal." Sally winced as a thought struck. "Did *you*, Mom?"

"Did I what?" she muttered.

"Play the game to win?"

Maude refused to look at her. "I assure you I don't know whatever you're insinuating."

"How did it work out for you?"

Her mother smiled, though it turned into a bittersweet grimace.

"You know precisely how it worked out," she said. "You're here, aren't you?"

"See? Playing that game doesn't get you—wait. What?"

"It's not important. Water under the bridge, as they say."

"It *sounded* important, Mom."

"It's a chat for another day, darling. Now let's talk about something far more interesting." Maude raised her glass. "Like how you're going to take your first real step to becoming a movie star."

Sally scowled. "Fine."

Still unsettled, she couldn't shake the nagging sensation she'd missed some salient truth that lurked just outside the light.

What she did know: She had an opportunity. So, yeah, she'd take the meeting, risks and all. Life was full of risk. A life without it was one not fully lived.

Her story was only beginning, waiting to be written and bursting with potential. She couldn't waste a single page.

STORY

Everybody's a mad scientist, and life is their lab.
We're all trying to experiment to find a way to live,
to solve problems, to fend off madness and chaos.

David Cronenberg
Director, *Scanners*

FOURTEEN

Clad in black, Jordan Lyman's guests mingled in his vast living room, helping themselves to a buffet and professionally tended bar. Amid the hushed murmuring, a string quartet covered Pink Floyd's "Wish You Were Here" in front of windows filled with the amber glow of LA's golden hour.

The producer welcomed Max with a handshake.

"Glad you could make it, babe," he said. "This is important."

"I'd rather be working," Max grumbled. "Some of us have a new picture to make on a ridiculous schedule and budget."

"Which you get to make because I work my ass to the bone for you."

"You blab on the phone all day. Me, I'm the one working."

"Doing what, getting arrested in your PJs at school playgrounds?"

Max scowled and said nothing. Their customary small talk out of the way, Jordan got to business, his eyes as always inscrutable behind mirrored shades.

"I'll be curious to see your treatment," he added, referring to the pre-script document that summarized essential characters, scenes, and themes. "Swing by when it's ready, and I'll free up more money and start pulling together a crew."

"I'm working on it," said Max.

For his last two *Jack* pictures, he'd scheduled three months to write a ninety-page script, three for preproduction, and up to six weeks for principal photography shooting two to four pages a day.

For his new project, he faced doing all that and more in half the time and with a fraction of the budget.

Crew, equipment and facilities, craft services, permits, film stock, so many actors and extras at such and such a daily rate times so many shooting days—it all added up quick. To succeed, he'd have to get back to his roots. Lean, fast, and cheap. So cheap that everyone might be wearing more than one hat and he might be wearing his without pay.

Before any of that became relevant, he needed the rights to the story from one Frederick Munsch. The writer continued to prove elusive, which Max found annoying. Not even a single message on the answering machine. Who wouldn't want his short story adapted into a major motion picture?

Jordan shot a glance at the decorative fireplace across the room, where a blow-up photo of Raphael Rodriguez gazed beneficently from an easel. "I guess I'll need to find you a new special effects makeup artist."

"Maybe not," Max murmured, half to himself.

Jordan's bushy eyebrows lilted above his shades. "No?"

"For a while, I was, uh, playing around with a new experimental technique. It turned out to be nothing, though."

"Hey, if it does the job and it's cheap, I say have at it."

"Oh, there's a significant cost," Max said. "Just not the financial kind."

The producer had stopped listening, already moving off to greet another guest. Max crossed the room to the catered bar, where the bow-tied bartender poured a few fingers of scotch into a snifter for him.

Cupping the glass, he walked over to Raphael's portrait. There, he studied the man's dark eyes, which had rarely matched his warm smile.

The way Raphael had grabbed life with both hands had always impressed Max, though it often had a tired, dutiful quality to it. Even two decades after his tours in Vietnam, the man had fought to keep death at bay. Now haunting the camera, he'd lost any lust for life he might have had left, but he seemed almost relieved about it, as if he'd shed a massive burden.

Nicholas appeared next to Max, his cheeks set in a sourpuss expression. Gazing at Raphael's portrait, he let out a choking sob.

"Are you all right?" Max asked.

"He was an amazing dude. I spent a lot of time with him."

When Jack showed up in the films, half his face was charred and disfigured from his fiery car wreck back in the fifties. Nicholas had to sit in a chair while Raphael applied makeup burns from a blueprint, a process that could take hours. For actors, this was about as fun as a visit to the dentist.

Max nodded. "He was a great artist and friend. This one time—"

Ashlee Gibson popped up on his other side.

"A lawn dart! Can you believe it?"

Nicholas said, "When I'd complain about sitting still for so long, he'd set me straight by telling me stories about what he went through in 'Nam."

"That must have been horrible for you," Ashlee told Max. "Seeing it."

"It was horrible," Max admitted.

"He's in a better place. I feel like he's looking down on us right now."

He pictured Raphael gloating with his one dead eye in front of a human bonfire, and he shuddered.

"Raph was a major admirer of yours, actually."

"Ha! He could be such a flirt."

"I mean, that dude saw a lot of shit in the jungle," Nicholas went on.

"Yes, he did." Max recalled one particularly grim story. "He once told me how during the battle of Lai Khê, his platoon found a gold wedding band in a hut, and it turned out—"

Ashlee leaned into him until her breast grazed his arm. "If you need anything, a ready ear or a shoulder to cry on, let me know."

He inched away toward Nicholas. "Thank you."

"Excuse me." She dabbed at her moist eye with her knuckle and sniffed. "I should get a tissue."

"Okay."

"When I come back, maybe you'll tell me about this new project I hear you're working on. It might be a welcome distraction from your pain."

After Ashlee left, Max frowned. "What was I saying? Oh yeah, a gold wedding ring—"

Nicholas shook his head. "A *lawn dart*. Stupid. After everything he survived, what a way to go." He seemed to reconsider. "It sounds macabre to say, but given his love for makeup effects, I wonder if he would have approved of how it looked."

Max couldn't resist a morbid smile.

"Actually—"

A short, bespectacled man shouldered him aside to wedge his stout form between him and Nicholas. He burst with a loud sigh. "Poor old Raph. What a great guy. He was loved. What a tragic loss for the industry."

"Always live life to the fullest," said Nicholas. Tears rolled down his pudgy cheeks now. "You never know when it's going to be your time."

"Truer words, Nicky." The newcomer looked up at Max and ran his hand over his balding pate. "Oh, hi, Max. My condolences. Sincerely."

"Hello, Saul." He was Nicholas's talent agent. "Thanks for the thought—"

"Are you okay? How's everything? The ticket sales for *Jack III* are booming, I hope. A little glimmer of light on such a dark day. We've all got our fingers crossed for a fourth in the franchise. I think Raph would have wanted that."

Max gloomily sipped his scotch. "It'll probably happen."

"Terrific. But not soon, right?" The agent offered an encouraging smile. "I hear you've got something else in the pipeline? Some David Lynch type of thing?"

"It's still early days." Max gestured to Raphael's portrait. "At the moment, I'm—"

"Very interesting. Naturally, you'll want Nicky on board."

"We're not even close to casting."

"Not too far to talk to Sally Priest, if the little birdie who told me was correct."

"Goddamnit," Max said.

"Nicky has a bright future," Saul said. "With his credits and talent, the sky's the limit for this kid. Of course, you don't want him wandering. I receive a lot of calls, a lot of TV scripts. I always say, 'It's not the right time. Nicky is too loyal to ol' Max.' Which is a two-way street. You don't want to lose your star villain."

Max scowled. "I only have half a million to play with."

"That's between you and Lyman. Me, I'm looking out for my boy here."

Ashlee reappeared sneering on his other side. "That goes for me too, Max. Nicky and I are together. A package deal. Where he goes, I go."

Max sighed. Her nose-candy habit was her business, something he'd never been able to do anything about. When she overindulged, however, it transformed her into a raging, needy diva, a real-life case of Dr. Jekyll and Mr. Hyde.

He shot a look at Nicholas, who stared at Raphael's picture while blinking back more tears. "What Saul was saying. Is that how you feel about it?"

"Leave me out of all this," the actor said with pious irritation. "I'm here to pay my respects to Raphael Rodriguez as an artist and a friend."

"Sure," said Max.

If what the actor said was true, he wouldn't have brought his agent to a wake. While Saul worked him over, the kid played the righteous mourner.

"We could always talk to Mr. Lyman," Ashlee said in a grating singsong threat. "See how he feels about his two leads disappearing into the night."

Her transformation to diva was now complete. Trapped, Max gulped down the rest of his scotch and came up gasping.

"Max, Max. Chill." Saul offered an indulgent chuckle. "Take all this enthusiasm for your art as a compliment. Look, we understand you have constraints. Nobody's trying to break the bank here. We're all very reasonable people."

"I'm not done talking," Ashlee said. "Don't interrupt—"

Saul went on chuckling. "I think Nicky is looking at this project as a way to step outside type and do some terrific character work with bigger creative risks. You know how it goes with typecasting in this town. Nicky wants to expand his horizons. Show the world his extensive range and—"

"Can I freshen that up for you, Mr. Maurey?"

Max looked down to see another snifter of scotch on a silver tray, looked up to find a handsome bow-tied surfer dude staring hungrily back at him.

"It's me, Mr. Maurey. Johnny. Johnny Frampton. From the premiere party?"

Grateful for the brief reprieve, he set his empty glass on the tray and took the full one. "I remember you."

"I know how you hate to wait in line at the bar."

"I appreciate it."

"Is it true you're making a new movie? You said you'd consider me. Granny flipped when I told her. Should I just show up for the casting call, or what?"

Max growled.

"I'm not represented," Johnny went on. "How do you want to handle—?"

"Hold that thought," said Max. "I'll be right back."

He fled through the crowd, looking for a quiet place to perch for a while. Everyone shot him probing glances as he passed, their eyes shining with a predatory gleam. He felt like a prize lamb at a butchers' convention.

He didn't care if Nicholas and Ashlee moved on to fresh pastures. In fact, Max's first emotion would likely be gratitude. As a would-be auteur, he valued creative control above all, and actors getting too big for their britches made that even more difficult.

But it wasn't his call to make. It was Jordan's, and he knew what the producer would say. He wouldn't want anything to interfere with the future box office success of *Jack the Knife IV*. He'd tell Max to cast them and find the money for it.

Max didn't even have a script yet, and he was already being sabotaged.

You can always use the Arriflex, a jolly Raphael said in his head. *A quality movie camera with a sterling track record in the industry. Portable, silent, and loaded with features. And think of all the cash you'll save on practical effects!*

"I can't," he muttered.

Kill 'em all, his friend urged.

But Max truly couldn't. Even if he wanted to. Because he loathed these people. To feed them to the camera, he'd have to find a way to like them.

He wandered around the room, but nowhere seemed safe. The string quartet glided into a haunting rendition of "Goodbye Yellow Brick Road." Gripping his drink, he walked outside to the pool. The warm twilight air welcomed him.

On the far side, a heavyset woman sprawled in one of the poolside recliners. She wore sweatpants, tennis shoes, and a tight black

T-shirt emblazoned with a feral, snarling Mickey Mouse. Held in place by a headband made from colorful beads, thick braids lay draped over her sizable bosom like slumbering boas.

She greeted Max with a sly glance. "There you are."

"Me?"

"Yeah, you, honey. I came all the way to Hollyweird just to find you."

"What? Why?"

"Well, I hear you're looking for me."

He sighed. He'd come out here to escape. The last thing he needed right now was a freaky fan shouting lines from *Jack the Knife* and asking him why Jack and Tina never hooked up.

"I assure you I am not," he said.

"Come on, Max." She smiled. "Do you want my story or don't you?"

"Frederick Munsch, I presume," said Max.

"The name's Dorothy Williams. Fred is my snooty alter ego. Helps me compete as a Black woman in a man's literary world." The woman heaved upright to rest her arms on her knees. "Pleased to meet you, I'm well, thanks, blah blah. You wanted to talk to me, I'm here. Show me what you got."

He hedged. "I didn't mean for you to drive all this way. I was calling because I was curious if the property was optioned."

"Ha! When I heard from my editor, I thought you might be doing a little idle fishing, but I figured I'd come on down here and get the skinny. I hear you're working on a new movie. A movie that sounds an awful lot like my story."

"There are a few similarities—"

"I'm a writer. Communication is very important to me. What I'm trying to say is I've got you over a barrel." She stared at him. "In a legal sense." When he still didn't answer, she added, "Meaning I could stick my—"

"I'm interested in acquiring rights."

"Excellent!" Dorothy beamed at him. "So how about we eat this cake and skip all the shitty icing. If you want to acquire rights, start acquiring."

"Okay, okay. The problem is budget. I can only offer five thousand."

"That's all? Well..."

"I just don't—"

"You got yourself a deal, partner."

"Well, um. Great." Max couldn't believe his luck. He'd low-balled her. Writers, it seemed, were as desperate as their stereotype let on.

"Not quite yet, hon. Here's what I want. You hand over that fiver right now, and then I join your little production. I want in the club."

Max started. "You want me to give you a job?"

"Hell, I want you to give me *all* the jobs. Like I told you already, I'm a writer. I sit at a desk writing. That's all I do. It's a lonesome profession, let me tell you."

"I'm not sure you're qualified to do anything on set," Max said. "And we use a union crew for our productions."

"Not a problem." This woman was about as easy to deter as a gale. "How about I write the script for you, and you can work out getting me my guild card and whatnot. A sweet little screen credit. Otherwise, you can let me hang around. As a consultant, maybe. A fly on the wall, whatever. I want to see my story get made."

"I write my own scripts. You've produced some interesting speculative fiction, but I'm not sure you understand script writing or even horror."

"Ha! How hard can it be?"

"Well, it's harder than you might think. Before you start the script, you need to build a treatment, which is the story in summary form—"

"My son Carter loves your *Jack* movies. He thinks they're hilarious."

Max growled. "If you think horror is funny, you definitely don't understand it."

"What do *you* think horror is?" She raised her hand. "What I mean is, do you know where it lives in the brain? *Why* do we think something is horror?"

He had a solid answer for this one. He considered his average audience member as sentient meat that wanted to avoid death as long as possible to procreate in a hostile world controlled by larger forces it labeled good or evil. Sex and death, and its deep human drives of lust and fear, were older than taxes.

Horror was all about death and its contrast with life.

And out of all human fears, two topped the list: fear of the unknown and fear of something preying on them. But overall it was one, the fear of dying. A case of life's real horrors shaping the appetite for the fictional kind and inspiring its creators to give their fears names and faces.

Horror, meanwhile, had three aspects, to paraphrase Stephen King. Chills: You hear your wife calling out for help from somewhere in your house, and then the phone rings and you find out she died in an accident across town. Gross-outs: You see a man fall into a threshing machine and come out the other end as a rain of blood and bone. Revulsion: You run from a giant mosquito or a murderous man so grotesque in look and deed you instinctively find him repulsive.

All of it provoking horror, a human emotion.

Why would anyone want to suffer through this?

Max had an answer for that too. People watched horror pictures to gain a momentary, reassuring feeling of importance. They wanted to symbolically face death and vanquish it, experiencing a cathartic sense of immortality. *Poor old Joe kicked the bucket*, we think at the cellular level, *but I'm alive.*

"Well," he said, "it all began—"

"Wrong," Dorothy said. "It's grief."

"It's not, though." His mind flashed to his dad face-planting into his mashed potatoes, and he shuddered. "It's in the shock."

"You show people dying, but nobody gives a crap. There are no real consequences. Me, the story isn't a maniac hacking up teenagers with an axe. It's the struggle to go on afterward. The Final Girl, all the clueless moms and dads with murdered kids, they wind up the fiend's final victims trapped in a hell of despair, blame, and what-ifs. Their minds become broken. Haunted by ghosts. And all the while, they yearn for it all to mean something. Isn't that real horror?"

"Maybe," Max admitted. He looked around at the black-clad mourners and didn't see a single person laughing. "It just isn't very cinematic."

"Of course it is! It's drama, consequences. It's *story*. Horror has to be personal. Psychological horror with a splash of fear of the unknown is where it's at. This splatter-porn stuff is cheap. It does nothing for me."

"That splatter broke real artistic boundaries and is still doing it."

"And every time it reaches a new gross-out height, over time the kids get bored and laugh. Grief, though? Grief in your bones? That's eternally shocking."

Max now flashed to the years of eating dinner with an empty chair his father had once filled as he had the rest of Max's world. Memories didn't haunt him, the lack of them did. The only one that hadn't faded was Dad deadpanning a joke before he slumped over. Nonetheless, it had created a ghost.

"It's depressing," he said. "I'll give you ten thousand dollars, and then you go away."

"Nope. I want to see my work adapted right instead of rammed into some dumb splatter formula." The writer grinned. "Come on, Max. I heard you were an artist looking for something new and different."

Max scowled. She was right.

Dorothy scooped a wide-brimmed leather bolero hat adorned with an eagle feather and squared it on her head.

"We're wasting time here," she said. "Are we doing this, or what?"

Sighing, he pictured screaming matches about where to put the pinch points and fisticuffs over adverbs. As an artist who treasured creative control above all else, he didn't want any of it.

He also didn't have much of a choice.

As the writer quaintly phrased it, she had him over a barrel. Even if he wanted to steal her idea and bolt for the exit at this point, she'd come all this way to negotiate with him in person. In front of witnesses she could call in court.

"Fine," Max growled. "But I have final cut on the script."

"Ooh, 'final cut.' I'm having fun already." She thrust out her hand, and he grudgingly shook it to seal the deal. "Now let's make like a tree and motor."

"Right now?"

"No time like the present. It'll rescue you from this horrible wake, anyhow. Talk about depressing. We'll set up shop at your place."

Struck by a vision of beauty, Max barely heard her.

At the edge of the hill overlooking a gorge, Sally Priest stood against the sunset. Gone was the scampish Madonna look, shed like an old skin. She now wore a simple formfitting black suit, and she'd also dyed her hair platinum blond and fashioned it into a bun with swooped bangs.

Max could tell she was grieving.

"Lovely," he murmured while the writer nattered on.

Dorothy was right. Grief could be cinematic. He wished he had a camera to capture Sally in this moment. She looked stunning as a blonde. The striking combination of sadness and sex appeal made her stand out as some kind of archetypal helpless waif. The raw emotion on display was stirring.

She'd arrived with Nicholas. Why was she so upset? Had she and Raphael been friends, or maybe more?

This last idea gave him a surprising twinge of jealousy. No, if Raph ever had a thing with Sally Priest, Max would have heard about it and no end to it besides. Irritated, he dismissed the notion and focused on the image she presented.

Composition and color, angle and light.

What was she thinking right now?

Facing the wind and dying sun, she looked like a Final Girl. He simply had to cast her. Sally belonged in his new film.

"You have hella good taste, hon," Dorothy said. "That girl is smoking hot."

Max bristled. "Don't be perverse. It's not like that. Of course she's attractive. I just like the light and the angle, the way she's standing there."

The writer eyeballed him while wearing her goofy smile. "I imagine it's the same thing for you, huh?"

"What?"

"Fucking and filming. Worshipping beautiful women through the lens."

While he sputtered, she walked off toward the house. Max slouched and followed, ignoring the hungry looks and Johnny Frampton's frantic waving.

In the vestibule, Dorothy gripped the handle of a trunk plastered with Grateful Dead stickers. In her other hand, she hefted a typewriter case painted with a single graffiti message: THIS MACHINE KILLS FASCISTS.

Eyeing her with distaste, Max tried to reconcile this hippie with her brooding, emotionally complex stories of unsettling nightmare and cosmic terror.

"All set," she said with a happy grin. "Now let's go make some art."

FIFTEEN

Max liked living alone, and he hated waiting. For five days, he didn't get his way on either score.

Stretched out on his bed, he read the latest issue of *Variety*.

He cut his toenails over the wastebasket.

He wondered if he should get another dog.

The grating clack of a typewriter started up again downstairs, rattling like a machine gun over the muffled pounding of *Led Zeppelin IV*. Someone, at least, was having fun.

Every keystroke galled him. He'd always produced his own scripts. He used an electric typewriter. Dorothy wrote on the portable manual typewriter she'd brought, a cherry-red Olivetti Lettera 25.

Day and night, she typed while bourbon and takeout flowed like room service into his office. The main floor now smelled like buffalo wings, patchouli, and incense. Mariel gave him a daily affronted reminder that she couldn't *clean in there*, glaring as if expecting him to do something manly to defend himself against this home invasion.

Max concluded that being haunted by the living was worse than sharing a house with a restless ghost. Though confined to a single room, the writer made his home feel crowded with her outsize psychic footprint.

Downstairs, the bell dinged at the end of another line. *Led Zeppelin IV* climaxed and started again at the beginning.

Respect the creative process, he told himself.

The only problem was the process took time, and he didn't have it. Jordan wanted film in the can by January.

Setting aside *Variety*, Max left his bed to gravitate toward the window. He pried the blinds open enough to peer out. No light at the school playground, which remained shrouded in darkness.

He'd become convinced his macabre dream hadn't been a dream at all. In a few weeks, the full moon would rise again, and he'd have to face Raphael and Helga at the bonfire. Lady Susan too.

Maybe he shouldn't get another dog.

Something stirred in his peripheral vision, down the road.

At the edge of the pool of amber illumination cast by a street-light, a car had parked. Someone sat behind the wheel, as if waiting for something.

It gave him a bad feeling. In the past week, his life had gone beyond assuming odd events were pure coincidence.

Padding downstairs, he approached the office. Through the closed door, Robert Plant moaned about a stairway to heaven. He knocked.

"Fuck off," Dorothy screamed back at the top of her lungs. Still typing.

"Do you do any—?"

"*I'm in the zone!*" she howled again, and then: "What do you want?"

"I was wondering if you do any bird-watching."

"*Why?*"

"You strike me as the type."

The clacking stopped. The music cut off.

The door burst wide to reveal Dorothy wearing her feathered bolero, a pair of gym shorts, and nothing else. Her face wet with tears.

She took a ragged breath. "Hell, yeah. I love bird-watching."

"Are you okay?"

"I'm great!"

"You're crying…"

The writer blanched. "Poor Penny. It's all her fault. All of it." Lamenting her protagonist's flaws.

"So, the script is coming along?"

She swept her arm to present the typewriter surrounded by glasses, empty bottles of bourbon, and the latest plates of greasy chicken bones. A stack of paper rested next to it, far taller than needed to make a ninety-minute feature film. *If Wishes Could Kill*, in the process of its creative birth.

"Of course," Dorothy said.

"It's a script, not a novel, you know." He looked away. "Would you mind covering yourself?"

"I would mind," she replied. "Anything else, or can I go back to work?"

"I wanted to know if you have binoculars. You know, for bird-watching."

"What did you see? An owl?"

"An interloper," said Max.

"Roger that." The writer shuffled through the crumpled papers littering the floor to root through her oversize suitcase next to a rumpled sleeping bag. At last, she produced a pair of spyglasses and handed them over.

"If you spot a nightjar, let me know," she said. "They're beautiful birds."

"Thanks. So, when do you think you'll finish—?"

The door slammed in his face. Robert Plant sang again. After a throaty, frustrated growl that didn't sound quite human, the clacking resumed.

Max returned to his bedroom to peer once more into the night. The car remained parked at the edge of the light. He switched off the lamps in the room and aimed the binoculars, adjusting the focus knob until he gained a clear image.

Officer John McDaniel sat behind the wheel of his police cruiser, eyeing Max's house with the patient gaze of a basilisk. He sipped from a thermos.

Well, well, Max thought. *Maybe you are an interesting nemesis.*

McDaniel no doubt pictured himself the hero in a cop drama. A thriller where the tough, no-nonsense maverick obeys his instincts first and his excitable police chief second if ever. He bucks the system and its confining and self-defeating bleeding-heart rules about civil rights. Doing it his way—even if it costs him his badge—as the main thing he values is justice.

In the end, the lawman nails the bad guy, proving he was right all along.

Max chuckled. The cop didn't know it, but this was no police drama. Rather, he was in one of the horror movies he held in such high disdain. The bumbling deputy trope. The head-scratching cop who always shows up too late to do anything except bear solemn and gawking witness to the gory aftermath.

A part of Max wanted to invite the muscle-bound cop inside for some decent coffee. They'd talk about movies and maybe laugh the whole thing off. A part of him wanted to confess, get caught, show McDaniel where he'd buried the camera.

Another enjoyed the game. His nemeses had always been Jordan, needy actors, crew mistakes, the MPAA censors. A movie director was supposed to be a god while on set, but he wasn't. In the end, he enjoyed very little control, a glorified puppet on strings. Golden's apparatus changed that dynamic.

Not that he needed it. His movie had the potential to be powerful without his little deus ex machina. With a strong enough story and deft direction giving it the right documentarian feel, he thought he had a real crack at making his perfect horror movie, and it wouldn't involve killing anyone.

But he *could* use it. You know, if he *wanted.*

All he had to do was dig it up.

Knowing this gave him a heady sense of power. The power over life and death. For the first time, he truly understood how Jack felt. What his teen audience likely felt too while watching the latest *Jack the Knife* movie.

McDaniel posed minimal threat, but Max didn't need any plot complications. Returning downstairs, he knocked again on the office door.

"Leave me *alone*," the writer shrieked.

"Wrap it up tonight," Max called back.

"You're breaking my flow!"

"We're taking a road trip in the morning."

The typing stopped. Dorothy flung the door open again, breasts akimbo.

"Where?"

"We're going to do some location scouting."

A proposition to which she agreed, but only after he promised to bring her a fresh bottle of bourbon to water her demons.

Surrounded by empty dirt and patches of scrub, the I-10 highway cut the desert in its endless pursuit of the horizon. Flying down the road with the top down, Max downshifted to swing southbound onto route 86.

He wasn't the sort to be truly happy about anything, but the desolation satisfied him. No meddling producers, wheedling agents, or one Officer McDaniel acting out his police procedural fantasies in nocturnal stakeouts. Just blue sky, speed, and free thoughts. Reading his notes on the script, even Dorothy remained quiet and still for the ride.

Then the writer ruined it by shouting into the wind.

"What do you mean, I need a *pinch* point?"

She held a sheaf of paper splayed like a losing poker hand. Max glanced over and saw his red scribble marring her neatly typed scenes.

"Script writing is different than writing fiction," he reminded her.

"No shit, Sherlock! Want to hear a saying among us writers? In publishing, you hear constant nos until you finally get a yes. In Hollywood, it works the other way around."

"A scriptwriter needs to follow a very tight story structure," Max lectured.

He explained how the character changed through conflict punctuated as a series of story beats organized in four acts: the normal, the protagonist reacts, the protagonist attacks, the protagonist goes all in.

Desire thwarted by opposition, followed by catharsis. Flaw, change, the hero becomes whole. Inciting incident, rising obstacles, climax, denouement.

Every scene building the story bit by bit, while the theme slowly manifested in the viewer's mind until it burst.

"That still doesn't answer my—" The wind whipped a page out of Dorothy's hand and whisked it away onto the road behind. "Oh, fudge."

Max turned the wheel again to hop onto route 111. Following the telephone poles, he passed palm trees and a long train of boxcars standing in the hot sun.

"Between each act is a turning point, a catalyst that changes everything," he explained. "The pinch points have a different purpose. They're at around a third and two-thirds into the script. These are scenes where the antagonist's power is displayed. The audience should feel the pain."

"You mean like when the Grand Moff blows the hell out of Alderaan right in front of Princess Leia in *Star Wars*?"

"That would be a fine example of a pinch," said Max.

The writer frowned at the bundle of paper in her lap. "Connect the dots. I'm not sure if this is easier or harder than it looks. It feels rigid with rules."

He said, "You give the director, actors, and the rest of the team scenes and dialogue as a simple blueprint. Then you trust them to build it."

Dorothy scowled to let him know what she thought of that. A solitary creative animal, she didn't trust anyone. A would-be auteur and a misanthrope to boot, Max empathized. But motion pictures weren't made in a vacuum.

Despite the difficulties of working with a team, the process often delivered unexpected and beautiful results. A keen-eyed director of photography who captures the perfect light. A skilled prop master who transforms an Oldsmobile into a 1957 Corvette. An inventive actor who delivers a poignant interpretation of a minor character.

Or, in this case, a talented writer. Max had to admit Dorothy brought something to the table. Her dialogue proved natural and character-revealing. She just had to follow the rules or at least know them well enough to break them with intent. They were trying to make a movie, not win a literary award.

"Can it be a flashback?" she wondered.

Eyes on the road, he nodded.

The writer reached down to pull her portable typewriter onto her lap. Threading a sheet of paper onto the platen with the roller knob, she levered the carriage until she had the guide positioned. Then she started banging the keys, which responded with a staccato series of clunks.

The bell dinged, and she slammed the carriage return to start a new line. "This movie business is art by committee, isn't it? High pressure, constant change, giving up control to other people." She blinked in surprise. "I'm actually having fun."

"Maybe we should trade places," he said dryly. "You haven't seen the worst of it yet. Working with others means giving up a lot of yourself."

"Ha!" Dorothy held up another sheet of paper marred in red. "There's no way I'm cutting this line of dialogue. It marks a major change in Penny's thinking."

Max glanced at the page and sighed. Case in point. But she was right.

"Fine," he growled. "But we're going to end up with a six-hour movie."

He swung the MG onto a cracked road leading off into empty dirt and scrub. A solitary sign greeted him: WELCOME TO BOMBAY BEACH.

He'd read about this place. He'd always been curious about it.

Max believed it might be a perfect location for his horror movie.

What a disgusting place. But also beautiful.

The largest lake in California had formed by accident. The Salton Sea did not exist a century before. In 1905, flooding overwhelmed irrigation channels cut into the Colorado River. The river dumped itself into a basin to form a new inland sea.

Around fifty years later, a carefree resort town appeared on the eastern shore: Bombay Beach, built on the southern tip of the San Andreas Fault.

Through the sixties, the town boomed as a destination for water skiers, anglers, yachters, and the likes of Frank Sinatra. But the lake, fed by irrigation runoff from farmland, was already dying.

The contamination from the runoff spread disease among birds. The skyrocketing salinity produced waves of dead fish amid massive algal blooms.

In the seventies, two tropical cyclones flooded the town and sank part of it. Most of the population fled, leaving a handful living in small homes and trailers on dusty lots. A third of the town closest to the beach remained abandoned, a bleached and rusty wasteland surrendered to the tides.

A perfect movie set, depending on the movie.

Max parked near the Ski Inn, the town's single watering hole. Resetting his old bucket hat on his head, he strode down a gravel road into ruins baking in the desert heat. He wore a Fuji camera looped over his neck and a satchel stuffed with pencils and drawing paper in case the inspiration to do some storyboarding called. He carried a tape recorder and microphone slung over his shoulder.

A good old-fashioned location scout.

Dorothy remained in the car, still clacking on her Olivetti, oblivious to the Atomic Age ghost town sprawling around her.

The smell hit him first. Salt, chemicals with a gasoline tang, and fishy rot. Nothing he could do about that. He could hear the actors and crew bitching already, but that was show business.

Singular derelict buildings stood like structures washed ashore by some ancient supernatural storm. Pelicans and egrets perched on rusting shacks and the odd tilting telephone pole, sickened to lethargy by cholera and botulism. Though filled with tetanus hazards, these structures offered terrific shooting locations. A small hotel. A mobile home half-sunk in drying mud.

The rancid breeze brought a canine bark, which made him flinch.

Bad girl, Max thought in rising panic.

Only it wasn't Lady Susan. Another bark replied, setting off a cluster of howls. He recalled hearing that feral dogs roamed the area, yet another hazard.

It was all so perfect.

Mopping sweat from his brow, Max pressed record and raised the microphone to his lips.

"There's a little drive-in," he said. "A handful of old cars were abandoned here. You can imagine ghosts waiting an eternity for the picture to start."

He took a few snaps with the Fuji, but the sea called to him. Past the humped sea wall, it sprawled green in the sun. Not an emerald green, but a darker shade far more sickly and algal. More Linda Blair and *Exorcist* than the fabled city of Oz. The green of sludge. It glistened at the water's edge like crud on a zombie's teeth.

As Max approached the sea, the stink grew stronger. In happier times, beachgoers once packed the shore, swimming and sunbathing. A thick salted crust clumped with dead and dying tilapia now blighted it.

Max narrated everything he saw into the recorder and captured more images. The sand crunched under his footfalls. Only it wasn't sand.

This place just got better and better.

"Bones," Max cried with delight into the mic. "Millions of them."

They crackled under his tennis shoes.

"The beach is coated in bleached bird and fish bones. When the water laps the beach, they shift around and make this terrific sound..."

He'd always been a solid believer in using audio as a way to create texture and identity, build dread, and deliver shock. For him, a surprise scare depended as much on a sudden wall of sound as on its visual aspect.

He closed his eyes to let the morbid rustling wash over him. He'd tell his soundman to record the tiny bones shifting in the lapping water and use it as a constant unnerving background noise, like crickets on a summer night. An audio bridge across the whole second half of the movie.

Bit by bit ramping up in volume toward the climax—

An aerosol roar intruded. He frowned up at a passenger jet still climbing to full altitude on its daily journey from LAX to Tucson, Houston, or some other southern city. The Salton Sea, it appeared, straddled a flight path. Something to note during shooting, a bit of diegetic sound his crew would have to work around.

Max explored the shoreline further, cataloging fresh discoveries. Graffitied and windowless ranch homes stood surrounded by broken furniture, one reduced by the elements to a skeletal wooden frame. Salt-encrusted posts stuck out of the water like rotten, chipped teeth.

So deliciously moody. He went inside a few of the buildings to explore and took plenty of photos for future storyboarding.

I can see it now, he thought.

It was all starting to come together in his head, where his film would exist waiting to be shot and edited.

For the monster, he'd use *Jaws* as a model. In Steven Spielberg's movie, the shark wasn't visible until near the end, and even then for only a sum total of four minutes of screen time. Before then, it existed largely in the audience's mind and scared the crap out of them. For Max's new movie, he'd use an eye. The all-seeing eye of a god. Penny's wish awakens it. Its very gaze kills.

Dorothy had proposed shooting the opening scenes at her hometown of Big Bear Lake, a village standing at about seven thousand feet above sea level and no stranger to Hollywood productions. Most recently, *War Games* and *Better Off Dead* had been shot there. Beautiful greenery surrounded it. Yes, this was where the wholesome folks of Lonely Pines would march into a lake.

In his mind's eye, a slugline appeared:

EXT. NATURAL SCENERY—DAY.

A sleepy main street in the pale light of dawn. Log houses, clean and orderly yards. A small park where children play. A sign: WELCOME TO LONELY PINES. Mist drifts across a lake calm as polished glass. Trees stand like silent sentinels in a dark and brooding forest. Ferns drip with dew. Feet plod through a meadow. The bare legs of a young girl, blue jeans worn by a man.

PENNY'S FATHER frowns in concentration as he walks. His metal detector sweeps the tall grass. Following, PENNY stares at his moving feet. This outing was supposed to be time spent together, though she feels alone.

She asks: "Why are people mean to each other, Daddy?"
He does not answer her, his own gaze locked on the ground.
"Why are they mean to me?"
The detector beeps with a find. PENNY's disappointment turns to hope.

The story kept playing in Max's mind. Once little Penny makes her wish to be left alone, the screen goes black, and then the eye flashes open, just a teasing glimpse. Then back to Lonely Pines, which we now see from its stalking point of view. To show this, he'd switch to a Panaglide gyroscopic body mount that John Carpenter's opening sequence in *Halloween* had popularized for the slasher genre.

Suddenly, the eye has agency.

Some critics hated the trope of showing the killer's point of view, lamenting that audiences wound up rooting for the villain. Max would make it scary again. The Panaglide-mounted camera would take a long walk through the forest straight up to Penny's daddy, who breaks into a lunatic grin right at the lens; Max would speed up the tracking shot in editing like in *The Evil Dead*.

A leitmotif sound effect next accompanies quick, tight shots of a crowd in fog, bodies packed and surging in tumult, disappearing into the water. The whole sequence slightly overexposed to show it as taking place in a past, dreamlike time.

After that, a few scenes, shot on a soundstage in LA, would present the surviving children now living their separate unhappy lives as adults. Destined to reunite and one day return to their old, dead town to finally say goodbye.

Then *bang*, Bombay Beach gets its turn.

EXT. DESERT RUINS—DAY.

A dead bird rolls in the toxic surf among millions of tiny bones and other strange sights. Salt-crusted posts in the water. Houses reduced to leaning skeletons. A half-buried ancient TV set. A drive-in screen slowly crumbling. Desert all around. A desolate world revealed in lurid colors.

A sign: WELCOME TO LONELY PINES.

Extreme close-up on a pair of eyes taking it all in with regret. The camera sluggishly pulls back to reveal PENNY and her childhood friends, fellow survivors of the day their town walked into the lake.

They have come to open old wounds that never healed. Discover truths that should not be known. Confront the burden of living after so many died.

To finally say goodbye.

This done, they will die next as PENNY's wish reawakens.

Dorothy's story of grief and sought redemption, coupled with Max's grisly slasher layer. The film now played complete in his mind, awaiting its construction.

If the story wasn't real, it was the director's job to make it so.

SIXTEEN

As things went in Hollywood, Chazz Morton's people called Sally's people, and she went to dine at another gourmet restaurant where she couldn't allow herself to eat anything.

Right off the bat, her alarms pinged.

The restaurant was attached to the posh Hollywood Palace Hotel. The gaunt and foppish maître d' informed her that *monsieur* was running behind due to business and that she should go up to his suite for their meeting.

"Screw that," replied Sally. "I mean, I'll wait for him here."

The maître d' smirked, as if she were being stubborn.

"Monsieur Morton said—"

"I heard you, sir. But I'll wait."

"Of course, madame. Follow me this way, if you please."

The man seated Sally in one of the plush chairs. She had on the black suit jacket and skirt she'd worn to Raphael's wake, serious but shapely. She'd styled her hair the same way, professional yet playful. A few tourists at a nearby table shot her searching glances, on the lookout for someone they might recognize. She ordered a glass of wine and sipped it while perusing the menu for the most filling and least socially compromising salad.

A business lunch, nothing more or less. Win the part, get out. And maybe do a little fishing. Maude and Chazz knew each other from the old days. Something Maude had said. Two simple sentences that burrowed into Sally's brain and wouldn't stop itching. She'd been brooding about it off and on ever since.

Sally: How did it work out for you?

Maude: You know precisely how it worked out. You're here, aren't you?

"Sally Priest," said a gruff voice. "Great name. Hello, sugar."

She looked up at the man. "Hi, Mr. Morton."

"Chazz, please. Sorry to keep you waiting. I got held up."

As if summoned by dark arts, a waiter appeared at the side of their table to be of service. The studio executive ordered for both of them—fancy salad for Sally—while grinning at her the whole time like a man who'd bought a prize horse and couldn't wait to see her strong legs run.

Sally appraised him right back as sixtyish and homely but well-dressed and flush with the kind of confidence that came with having obscene amounts of money, success, and power.

Hollywood was a people town—which explained why everyone was nice to the point where *nice* didn't mean anything—but Chazz's word carried real weight. That myth about girls being discovered in malt shops and becoming movie stars? Men like Chazz did the discovering.

He said, "When I heard Maude Turner's little girl was all grown up and in the business, I checked out *Mutant Dawn*. Let's say I was impressed. Seeing you in the flesh, even better. You look great as a blonde."

"Well, it's an honor to meet you."

"When I watched that picture, I told myself this is a girl who likes to have fun."

"Yes, well. That was my character, Chazz."

"Oh? What's the real Sally Priest like? This I have to hear."

"I'm more like the Final Girl."

"I'm afraid I don't know what that is, sugar."

"It's a horror trope. Do you like horror?"

"Not so much. No, I can't say I like it a lot."

"Well, the Final Girl beats the monster by following the rules."

"I have no interest in the low-budget gross-outs that pass for horror these days," Chazz went on as if he hadn't heard her. "Enormous waste of funds and crackerjack talent, if you ask me. A load of crud. No, I am interested in blockbusters that fill theaters and make history. Romance, comedies, they endure. They make people feel good. Everybody loves 'em."

Sally pounced on the chance to segue into the main topic. "Like your new project. What can you tell me about it?"

The food arrived. She idly stabbed at her lettuce while he wolfed down the steak she wished she'd ordered for herself. The man had a prodigious appetite. As he chewed, he talked about the movie he planned to make. Big budget, colossal stars, hot director, major promotion plan, the works. A family vacation goes wrong and then right for a single dad. They'd shoot it in Maui.

The more he talked, the more she wanted a piece of it, no matter how small. It sounded like the kind of film where even a bit part could open doors.

"So, what were you thinking for me?" she asked.

Chazz clipped the end off a cigar and lit it. "We need a siren at the hotel pool who tempts the single dad until he realizes he's meant to be with someone else."

An eye-candy role, but at least she'd have a few lines.

"That's very kind. I appreciate the opportunity."

"We'll go up to the suite after lunch," he said. "We can look at the script."

Sally regarded his loaded stare.

"I'm very comfortable right here," she said.

"I'm happy Maude reached out. This is a town where it can be rough going it alone. People need to take care of each other. Give each other a hand. I'd be willing to consider you a special friend."

"A special friend," Sally echoed.

She wondered if Mom had been someone's special friend, selling herself to be a dancer in *Houseboat*.

"Sure," said Chazz behind a cloud of silver cigar smoke. He reached to plant his large hand on hers. He squeezed. "Everybody needs friends, right?"

Oh, shit, she thought. *This is happening.*

She'd thought she could control the meeting. She'd been wrong.

He had all the power. Not only to put her in a major feature film, but to keep her from ever working in one of his studio's productions.

"A girl like you needs a mentor," he added. "Someone to guide you."

One of the things Sally loved about horror was how simple it was. The monster wore a mask and wielded a machete. Here, the monster smiled in a business suit and offered you everything you wanted, confident you'd sign your name in blood and tears. He didn't threaten you outright because he didn't need to.

The Final Girl would walk away now on principle. The Bad Girl, the party girl who screwed for fun but never as a career shortcut, would toss her drink in his face. After that, she'd laugh at him for presuming to buy what wasn't for sale.

Sally did neither. Her fear of failure kept her pinned to her seat. It crushed her like a sudden and horrible form of gravity.

This was a mistake. Everything had been so clear before she'd shown up here.

"I guess," she heard herself saying. Her brain had scrambled.

"Then it's settled." Chazz signaled for the check. "A quick elevator ride up to the suite, and we can take a look at that script. We can figure out where you might fit."

Everyone plays the game, darling. One might as well play it to win, right?

Sally wasn't her mother.

And no, the Final Girl wouldn't simply walk out. She isn't perfect. She is flawed and tested and beaten to a pulp. What makes her special is she never surrenders. She fights, and she survives alone on her own merits.

Sally tapped into this Final Girl energy and decided she wasn't going anywhere with Chazz Morton.

You know precisely how it worked out. You're here, aren't you?

She said, "Did you know my father?"

"I don't think I've ever met Ben Corn."

"I mean my father."

The studio executive regarded her with an unreadable expression. He took a thoughtful puff on his cigar. His face softened into a slight smile.

"Maude finally spilled the beans, huh?"

"Yes," Sally lied. "I was wondering if you could tell me who—"

"I don't rat on my friends, sugar."

She stared at him as it all sank in.

"Eww," she blurted.

The waiter materialized again as if by magic. Chazz signed the slip. The remnant of his cigar plumed in the ashtray. Then he stood.

"Sorry, but I just remembered I have an important call to make."

"What about the part?"

"My people will call yours."

As things went in Hollywood...

People made promises all the time they didn't have to keep.

Sally returned behind the wheel of her rumbling Austin. She had a hazy memory of leaving the restaurant and walking back to the car. With a phlegmy cough, it sped into traffic and joined the constant flow of motion.

Los Angeles. People in cars, always, everywhere, fleeing their demons and chasing their dreams. Sally was one of them.

She drove past the turnoff for the tiny apartment she shared with Monica, another hungry actor. She kept going east, all the way to the city limits, and then beyond even that.

Her Austin knew where she needed to go, through Pomona, where she swore she saw Max Maurey's roadster flash by going the other way. After San Bernardino, civilization began to thin, and the old Wild West asserted itself.

Dry grass, power lines, and eucalyptus trees swept past under sparse fan-shaped clouds. Only twenty more miles of hot asphalt to Joshua Tree park. When at last she arrived, she parked on the usual patch of dirt.

Rummaging around the mess in the backseat, Sally scavenged a pair of Chuck Taylors, ratty army surplus shorts, and the T-shirt Max had given her. She changed out of her formal outfit into this comfortable if gamey ensemble, feeling a little more like herself again. Then she exited the car into hundred-degree air.

Taking a deep breath, she inspected the dry earth and rock, rippling with heat waves radiating off the baking landscape. She spotted the trail she wanted and started hiking. She'd come here before, many times. Her special place. She liked the barren space, the quiet. A woman could think here. Really think.

Sally had plenty to think about.

Maude had planted the acting bug in her from an early age. Instead of Goldilocks and Snow White, her bedtime stories were about Hollywood. To Sally, it was a mythical but real place where girls went from malt shops to movie premieres, their faces shining on the cover of every magazine in America. Disneyland for grown-ups.

As Sally grew older, she fell in love, if not with Hollywood then with its product. Wonder, dreams, imagination. Hollywood existed largely in the brain, itself a projected image, an illusion. What religion did for thousands of years, the magic of cinema usurped, providing myths and meaning, moral lessons, gods to worship.

How could one not be romantic about it? Not want to be a part of it if she had a chance—even a slim half a chance?

Maude's dream for Sally was for her to become a big star, an actress so successful that she didn't have to put up with any shit. Once she fought her way to the top, she could be anything she wanted. And until that day, she should do whatever it took to get there and settle for nothing less.

I played to win, Maude once said. *But I made mistakes along the way.*

And one of those mistakes, apparently, had been Sally.

Some Hollywood mogul likely promised old Maude she'd be the next Marilyn Monroe and instead put a bun in her oven. She'd married Benjamin Corn, the rich, kindly bank executive Sally would end up calling Dad her whole life.

After the baby was born, Maude's Hollywood dreams were over, and she'd forever know whose fault it was. She also knew who owed her what for it. Ever since, they'd all played the roles they'd been assigned in life's script.

Sally spotted her favorite point, a tall boulder pile looming over the desert. After crossing a stretch of sandy gravel, she gazed up toward the summit.

The sun's glare half blinded her. The heat dried her sweat to a crust. She noticed her growing thirst. Taking her first step past prickly pear and clumps of juniper, she began to climb the bare hot rock.

The climb itself another meditation.

Her entire life, Sally shared Maude's vision. School, competitions, internships, waitressing, workshops, running lines on rooftops by moonlight, flubbed auditions. And networking, always networking in a town that spoke in cheerful code and sometimes felt like a giant Amway convention. Actors, she learned, were like beautiful zombies that fed on hope instead of brains.

Then her lucky break came. A speaking role in *Mutant Dawn*. Dashing around sand dunes half-naked, chased by radioactive mutants craving human flesh.

God, that was fun. The whole production rolled out like one long party. The energy was terrific. They were making popcorn post-apoc horror, and they knew it.

Out in that desert, Sally had gained so much. She'd cut her teeth on professional acting and didn't flop. She'd embraced her inner Bad Girl and finally ditched her virginity for a hunky, gentle stuntman. She'd not only solidified her love of acting but found something of a home for her talent.

In horror, the roles weren't particularly challenging, being somewhat flat, but the genre was edgy, playful, and accessible. In *Mutant Dawn*, she'd screamed a lot, flashed her boobs, and died with a wink. The audience loved her for it.

Her mother did not approve. Not because of the nudity but because of the lowbrow genre and bare-bones production quality. It was the start of a rift that widened in time, her first clue Maude didn't want her to live her life on her own terms.

Climbing the rocky hill, Sally realized how much pressure she'd been under all along, now that it was all out in the open. Pressure that extended even to Maude willing to see her daughter consider making the same mistakes, because that was how Hollywood worked, it was all she knew. Any pride Sally felt about protecting herself from Chazz Morton was ruined by this understanding of how hard things were, how having principles might preserve your self-respect but otherwise won you zip. And her inner critic chided her for not going along to get ahead, saying, *Whatever mistakes she made, Mom is always right in the end.*

Parched and gasping, Sally clawed the final distance to mount the summit. By the end, she wept hot tears that evaporated in the thirsty air. Standing atop the bare hill, she gazed out across a desolate flatland populated by Joshua trees, twisted and bristling creatures with leaves like knives. Sucking in a deep breath, she took a moment to admire its harsh and deadly beauty.

And then she screamed.

Throaty. Bloodcurdling. Full blast.

A solid practice horror-movie scream, trying out a whole new pitch she hoped to incorporate into her craft. But as always, it proved therapeutic. This time, she screamed to frighten not an audience but her own demons.

Sally screamed—

At her mother, who'd pressured and lied to her over her entire life and may have regarded her as a mistake that put the final nail in her dreams' coffin, and the lie Sally had lived her entire life regarding where she had come from—

At the brutal and hungry predators that lurked behind Hollywood's glittering veil, starting with the first jerk who tried to grope her back when she was an intern reading scripts in an office the size of an outhouse—

At the rigid and rampant typecasting and how some genres were considered a smart career move and others a black hole—

At her fear of all the wasted minutes that might become wasted years, the prospect of ending up bitter like old Maude, whose life and youth had been lived in a single decade, her remaining years spent mourning their loss—

At the resulting perfectionism that both helped and hurt her—

And the new emotion she'd added to her acting toolbox, which was a deep sense of shame she didn't deserve.

Life had never punched her in the face. Careful what you wish for, right?

The twisty Joshua trees appeared as human figures in racing flight, bolting in mute terror from her banshee screams.

Sally screamed until she didn't have any left in her.

The next time she did this for a camera, it would be the real thing.

PREPRODUCTION

Horror by definition is the emotion of
pure revulsion. Terror, of the same standard,
is that of fearful anticipation.

Dario Argento
Director, *Suspiria*

SEVENTEEN

Max returned to Los Angeles buzzing with a solid treatment, the script in progress, and two perfect shooting locations. Besides that, the passenger seat was blissfully empty, as he'd left Dorothy at her house in Big Bear Lake to finish the script without him. He entered Sherman Oaks in triumph.

And discovered a police cruiser in his driveway.

"What the hell now?" Max stormed into his house.

Officer McDaniel greeted him with a nasty grin. "What are you into, Maurey?"

The place was a mess.

Someone had broken in and ransacked it. In the living room, the invader had toppled furniture and gutted the couch of its cushions. In the kitchen, every cupboard stood open, and cans and pasta boxes littered the floor.

Mariel went on yelling a litany of complaints in her native Spanish. No doubt filling in the LAPD on her employer's dark artistic appetites, crass houseguest, one dead dog, and a starlet's panties.

"Care to explain all this?" the cop pressed.

Max stared at him. "Are you serious?"

"They were in every room," Mariel said. "They took your teak box."

That left only one candidate for who'd done the breaking and entering. He nodded with sympathy, as if it were her home that had been invaded.

"Thank you, Mariel. You can go. Take the day off. I'll handle all this."

The housekeeper left muttering, relieved to be free of the house and its owner.

"It's just you and me now, Maurey," said McDaniel. "Where were you, exactly? Anything you'd like to share? What's in the box?"

"Share? Jeez, I don't know, officer. My house was broken into and you should find and arrest the guy who did it?"

"It's not enough for you to corrupt the minds of America's kids. Turn the whole country into the *Class of 1984*, a bunch of effeminate entitled pussies—"

Max grunted. "Another interesting film."

"The point is I don't like you, Maurey. I don't like your movies or your ghoul face. And I know you're into something. I'm taking you to the station."

"You're arresting *me*? For what?"

"That's what I'm going to find out by asking you some questions."

"You were spying on my house every night for the past week," Max shouted back. "Where the hell were you while I was being robbed?"

The nasty grin evaporated.

"Um, no, I wasn't—"

"I'm pretty sure that was you parked down the road."

The cop scowled, refusing to budge.

"I *saw* you." Max kept at it. "With a pair of binoculars."

"You went out of town," McDaniel mumbled. "So I took a few nights off."

"Okay, I'm ready to make a confession."

"Good—"

"I'm going to tell the chief how you've been stalking me like a psychotic fan."

The cop blanched. "We don't need to do that."

"Then how about instead you go do your job and solve the crime of who broke into my house. If you want a lead, I'd look into a guy named Dan Womack. He's an actor who's obsessed with me. A real freak. A very violent guy. Dangerous."

"Womack? What's his beef with you?"

"You'd have to ask him."

Another smile crossed the cop's face, one far more calculating.

"I'll do that," he said.

"He broke into my house," Max reminded him. "Which is a crime."

"I'll see you around, Maurey. We'll be in touch."

Grinning again, Officer McDaniel stomped out, and Max wondered if he'd made a mistake connecting his archnemeses.

Finally alone, he sighed with relief. He'd take care of the mess later. Wheeling, he rushed to the sliding door at the rear of the house. It was unlocked, a bad sign.

He yanked it open.

His backyard appeared the same as it always did, manicured to perfection by professional gardeners. The door to the toolshed remained shut. The burial plot in the rosebushes didn't seem to be disturbed.

Getting down on his knees, Max pressed his ear to the dirt.

Nothing.

He was sweating now. He'd chosen not to use the camera, but the idea of not having the choice panicked him. Maybe he should dig it up and check on it. He should definitely move it to a safer place.

If he did that, however, he knew he might never bury it again.

As if sensing his presence, the Arriflex stirred to life in its grave to welcome him with its fuzzy babbling.

"Yes," Max hissed. The camera was safe.

Like a father who knows his baby's cries, Max could tell it was hungry. Furious at the home invasion, he was feeling fairly hungry himself. Womack might be a larger problem than he'd first surmised. Max wondered if Raphael would mind if he sent a washed-up actor his way instead of Ashlee Gibson.

But first, he had to deliver a script treatment to his producer.

Max stormed back inside to his office, now a bona fide disaster zone between Womack's frantic ransacking and the detritus of Dorothy's writing marathon. Ignoring the mess, he stuffed the three-page treatment for *If Wishes Could Kill* into his fax machine. He punched Jordan's number and waited.

With painstaking slowness, the device sucked the pages and digested their contents into electronic signals. After, Max stared at the phone on his desk and willed it to ring. He had so many things to do and not enough time to do them, but whether they needed to be done hinged on a final green light from the producer.

The phone remained silent. After a while, Max spent his nervous energy on restoring his house to proper condition, fuming the whole time.

A few hours later, he called Jordan. His secretary answered.

"Mr. Lyman isn't available," she said. "He went to his club."

Max ground his teeth. "Did he receive my treatment?"

"He read it right before he left. Shall I have him call—?"

"Thanks!" He hung up and hustled back to his roadster.

One last yes, a real yes, and he'd have everything.

Back behind the wheel of his MG, he followed Bellagio Road's serpentine circuit to Jordan's country club. Another palace in the producer's world that reminded Max how badly he was being ripped off.

The course consisted of eighteen holes among canyons over-looked by modern mansions, some of the holes so separated in topography that golfers accessed them via tunnels and elevators. The key to all this magnificence was the posh clubhouse. After parking, however, he found entering it more difficult than barging onto a studio set to yell *Hi, Mom* into the camera lens.

He finally gained approval after Jordan agreed by phone to treat Max as a guest, though they made him wear his Dead Kennedys T-shirt inside out and tuck it into his pants. A giant in golf shirt and khakis walked him to the twenty-tee driving range, where he deposited Max with a final glare warning him to behave himself.

Walking past the rich and powerful practicing their drives, Max found Jordan stretching his quads and hamstrings in knickers and a red plaid sweater vest.

He eyed the producer. "You look like an over-the-hill Scotsman limbering up for his next big porn scene."

Jordan shot a baleful glance back at him.

"And you look like an undertaker who ran out of bodies."

"So, this is where you moguls do all your deals," said Max. "Out there on the links."

His warm-up over, the producer selected his favorite driver and tested its feel and weight with a little swing.

"Not really," he said. "But you can learn a lot about somebody. His temperament, whether you want to do business with him."

"Then I don't have to learn the game." Max had never understood its appeal.

"Listen, babe. I came here to blow off steam. I have a tee time at three to play a round with Jack Nicholson. This can wait until tomorrow, yes? I'm sure it can."

"I was hoping to—wait. Jack Nicholson? Seriously?"

"I'd ask you to join us, but I think all the sun and fresh air might physically harm you."

Max ignored the barb, though he now thought maybe he should learn to golf at some point.

"Give me a few minutes to talk about *If Wishes Could Kill*."

Jordan plucked a ball from the bucket and set it on the tee. "Yup."

"The script is coming along."

"Uh-huh."

"The short story writer is putting it together for me."

"Right."

Max started to sweat.

"We're really subverting expectations on this one," he said.

"You sure are." Jordan ran a few practice swings toward the ball. "I'm flushing your postmodern turd."

Max exploded. "You promised me you wouldn't meddle!"

"I did." Jordan swung the club, which connected with a satisfying click and sent the ball zooming downrange. "I did not promise to stand idly by while you light half a million on fire."

"But the core idea is to do something original—"

"It baffles me that you persist in seeing me as some kind of art-house incubator. You want to subvert genre, that's awesome. You want to throw the entire rulebook out the window, that's not awesome. *Awesome* being defined as earning the highest return on capital for our investors. Being a moviemaker today means serving the market. The auteur years are over, and good riddance."

"People can't buy into something new if we never—"

"Sure, you've still got your Martin Scorseses out there, but they're holdouts from a dead era. And no offense, babe, but you're no Scorsese."

"If we never—*ouch*."

Jordan snorted. "Hell, you're not even—"

"I get it," Max growled. "You don't have to rub my face in it."

"I'm glad we understand each other."

He glared at the producer. "You think I'm a pretentious hack, don't you?"

"I think you're a very fine director, Max."

In Max's ears, *Jack the Knife III*'s audience burst into laughter.

"A hack," he said. "The real director is some pimply teen haunting a small-town cineplex. He's the one calling all the shots. You should hire him to make your movies."

"Welcome to the industry," Jordan said. "Where as long as seats are filled and profit is maximized, everything is as it should be."

Max watched him line up his next drive and knock it flying into the greenery. He didn't know what to say. He was a motion picture director. An artist. This simple descriptor was how he defined himself. It had always been both his identity and his aspiration.

If all this time he'd been a hack, a second-rate imitator of better directors and films—then he wasn't just a hack. He was nothing.

Jordan resumed a driving stance.

"Your project is red-lighted," he said. "You know, I'm glad you came by. This has been a productive meeting. Was there anything else on your mind?"

On my mind, Max thought.

Where something snapped, so clear he actually heard it.

It was the sound of his self-image fracturing like a mirror in a jump scare. The sound of whatever relationship he had with the producer finally breaking.

The sound of an idea. Hearing it brought him a strange, dark relief.

"You're right, Jordan," he heard himself say.

"Yeah?" The next ball clicked and disappeared. "About what?"

"Everything. All of it. In the end, art has to serve business or it can't stand on its own. I admit I got sucked into the writer's vision instead of making it mine. It could be more commercial."

"Well. That's very mature of you."

"So, can I have another crack at it?"

Jordan swung again. The ball sailed away in a white blur.

"Show me what you've got, baby."

"I'll do right by you." Swallowing what little pride he had left.

"Now I know you want it bad. You're actually being humble. It's even more impressive than crazy eyes." Jordan paused from his practice shots to lean on his club and regard Max with a cool stare. "I've got goose bumps over here. Go forth and create."

Max's eyes narrowed to serpent slits. "Oh, I will."

He already had a new plan.

EIGHTEEN

ax returned home to the sound of his office phone's grating
ring. When he picked up, Dorothy's voice barked at him
from the other end.

"Did you hear from Lyman?"

It was one thing they had in common: a loathing for small talk.

"He loved it," Max said. "He was practically raving. He's fully
on board."

A lie, but that was Hollywood. Everyone lied, all the time. In its
pantheon of sins, lying barely registered and could even be regarded
as a virtue.

"Groovy," said Dorothy.

"Hold tight," he said. "I'll be back in touch soon."

He hung up and got to work. The keys on his electric typewriter rattled out a new treatment. Under his fingers, *If Wishes
Could Kill* became a commercial product.

Poor Penny.

*Shy, smart, and extremely beautiful though she does not know it. Just
your average teen about to tangle with supernatural forces she unwittingly
unleashes by playing with things best left buried.*

*Penny is the responsible member of an unlikely group of friends rep-
resenting a cross section of today's college stereotypes now home for summer
break in a small town. On a dare, she spends the night with them in a
haunted house.*

The local crank warned them to avoid the place, but they laughed at the old wino and his stories about the town's bloody past. What could go wrong?

Entering the derelict mansion, Penny wonders if he might be right, but she does not care. The town is full of mundane cruelty—her divorcing parents who ignore her, the man she babysits for always flirting, the mean girls in town playing cruel pranks. This is her chance to rebel.

They split up to explore the house. A cat jumps out of a cupboard to provide the early false scare. Inside, Penny discovers the amulet and makes her wish that the meanies go away and leave her alone.

After Penny rejoins her friends, they all pass around vodka and play spin the bottle. The booze emboldens Penny to kiss Michael, her long-standing crush. Despite all the randy teen fun, she greets the morning's sunlight with relief.

The next day, they go to the local restaurant for lunch. There, Penny watches in horror as one of the local mean girls chokes on a cheeseburger after giving her the stink eye. Soon, people all over town start croaking in random and gruesome ways, starting with those who wronged her in some way.

When even her friends begin to die at the hands of an implacable entity, Penny realizes this is all her fault. It is her wish, and she must find a way to reverse it.

Max spiced the tale with unlikable youth stereotypes, a nude hot tub scene, a titillating sex scene. A dumbed-down emotional hurdle to give the Final Girl the bare bones of a character arc. The killer's victims arranged in grisly tableaux in the climax. Plenty more dumb decisions plus a final shocker at the end.

To top it off, he added a visible monster that embodied the wish itself: an unkillable naked man without a face, hair, or genitals, his body painted white. Every character who dies on-screen made an offhand wish earlier in the story—*I wish I could quit eating these fattening burgers, I wish Mom and Dad would shut up, I wish the baby would stop crying.* The creature efficiently delivers on each in morbidly creative ways like visual one-liners, sometimes with a little pantomime routine.

The familiar, presented with a twist.

By the time Max finished, he'd laid on the tropes so thick that the story had reached the edge of satire, or at least trying way too hard. He actually kind of liked it. It would certainly be entertaining. But it didn't terrify from the balls up, and it didn't add anything new.

It wasn't horror, not how he understood it.

Inspired, he put one more cherry on top. A suggestion to do the whole thing in 3D—if the producer gave him a larger budget to play with.

"Last chance, Jordan," Max muttered while the new treatment printed.

After faxing it over to his producer's office, he placed another call to Sally Priest, the final key to his plan. Her roommate told him she'd caught a ride to the community playhouse Dan Womack rented. They were doing their show tonight.

"Hold on a second," the woman said. "You're *the* Max Maurey?"

"Yes."

"Like, *Jack the Knife*?"

"Yes, that's my picture."

"That shit is epic! I'm Monica, and I'm an actor too. I'd love it if I could have just, like, five minutes to pick your brain—"

He hung up.

"It looks like I'm going to the theater," he said.

A pleasant evening out. First, he had to retrieve his property.

In the backyard, he found the shovel in the toolshed. He crossed back to the rosebushes where he'd buried the Arriflex 35BL.

The blade entered the black soil with a satisfying thud. After carefully removing a foot of dirt, he flung the shovel aside to finish the job with his bare hands. A creepy centipede scrambled out of the cascading dirt in panicked flight; Max ignored it. His scraping at last revealed the camera case wrapped in plastic.

He unraveled it like a Christmas present. Opened the case's lid—

Arthur Golden's camera cried out with joy. Max choked back tears. With loving care, he flicked a dirt crumb off its gleaming black enamel.

"I missed you too," he said.

Womack's playhouse stood sandwiched between a pawn shop and a New Age bookstore. Max bought a ticket and entered the theater's front of house, which offered around two hundred seats on the raked main floor.

There was something about entering a live theater that felt similar to going to the movies, and both were a little like going to church. The large space, cool air, soft seating, and dim mood lighting all contributed to the atmospheric charm. But mostly, it was the raw anticipation to see a show that made you believe you were someone and somewhere else for a couple of hours.

An experience shared with total strangers as a community. The modern version of cavemen gathering around the campfire to hear stories. Some in the industry worried VHS would transfer motion pictures into the home. The boob tube, however, could never match the movie theater in terms of overall experience. And if Max was being honest, neither could match the immediacy of live theater.

Lugging his camera in its plastic case, he found a seat in the back and waited while the rest filled up with friends, family, theater addicts, and neighborhood locals. He leafed through the program until he discovered Sally's smiling headshot. She was playing the role of Shana.

A stunningly regal woman occupied the seat next to his with a sigh.

"Well, this should be stimulating." She glanced down at the gray mass at his feet. "What have you got there?"

"A film camera." He caught a whiff of lavender on her perfume.

"I thought it might be. Are you in the industry?"

"I'm a director. I'd like to cast one of the play's actors in my next picture."

She wrinkled her nose. "You're Max Maurey. Emily told me about you."

"Maude Turner, I presume. Sally mentioned you as well. It's an honor. Shouldn't you be in the front row?"

"I'd only make her nervous," said Maude. "Em tries too hard because she thinks too hard about failing. Then she imagines I'm to blame."

Max let out a surprised chuckle. He was accustomed to mothers posing as living resumes for their actor kids, not critiquing them in front of movie directors.

"I know she's talented and needs the right director," he said.

"It's not a matter of who her director is. Go make your horror picture. Once she realizes she's wasting her time, I'll be here, ready to steer her onto the right path."

"Because it's horror," he said sourly.

"No real actor would choose it as a home," said Sally's mother. "No offense, Mr. Maurey, but it shows me she lacks confidence in herself. The fact is the longer she stays in that genre, the harder it will be for her to build a career outside it."

"Why would she want to?"

"Because it's horror," she said with grating patience.

Game on, thought Max.

"Can I ask why you think horror isn't worthwhile as a genre?"

"Where do I begin?" Maude laughed. "All your slasher films do is contribute to violence."

"You mean like James Bond?"

"What do you mean?"

"There were forty-two kills in the last James Bond picture. Worse, the Bond films make killing look clean and bloodless, something that can be done without remorse. In my pictures, you see the reality of it."

Maude stared at him. "So by showing beautiful women murdered while taking a shower, you're actually doing a public service."

"Your words." This rote criticism was child's play to him. "As for the shower, of course. Sleeping, napping, having sex—those are times we're most vulnerable. It amps up the fear factor, which you kind of need for a scary picture."

"Certainly, Mr. Maurey, you'd admit people become desensitized to violence through overexposure. In particular, violence toward women, as I doubt you see many naked men getting hacked up while showering. You make the victim responsible for their violence."

"Desensitized through overexposure," Max echoed. "You mean the way watching musicals leads to Americans breaking into song as a way to cope with their problems?"

Maude shrugged. "Fine. Have it your way. It's at least outside the realm of decent taste."

And that, Max guessed, was the crux of it, despite all the intellectual posturing.

Another grave nod. "Absolutely."

The room dimmed to darkness. The room quieted.

Max added, "If you'll permit me, Mrs. Turner, I'd like to give you a live demonstration of exactly how powerful my genre can be."

The audience offered polite applause as Dan Womack took the stage in a tight black turtleneck. He stood grinning and glowing in the bright lights. This was his big night, the terminus of a lot of love and hard work.

Max decided it was time to put in a little work himself.

Shifting into the aisle, he flipped the case's worn latches and opened it. With delicate care, he hefted Arthur Golden's camera and mounted it on a tripod.

"Welcome to the Womack Workshop's presentation of Jaimie Brewer's *The Heart Stop Diaries*," Dan's voice boomed.

Max brought the man in frame for a medium knee shot.

"A play about how when it comes to affairs of the heart, it's dangerous to want what we should never have."

Max adjusted the focus.

"And a story that teaches us that in pursuit of our heart's desire, sometimes, sadly, our only true adversary is ourselves."

Max pressed the start switch. The camera purred in response.

"I've been blessed with a wonderful workshop class full of talented students this season, and..."

Camera speeding. Film rolling.

"And...I, uh..."

The man froze, turning pale in the hot light. In the ensuing silence, the camera's whir filled the room.

The camera loves you, baby, Max thought.

Squinting into the glare, Womack's eyes suddenly widened.

"I'm..."

Max gave him a little wave from behind the viewfinder.

"I'm very sorry," Womack stammered. "But tonight's show is canceled—"

Ducking down, the actor wheeled and dove at the curtains, which billowed around him in crimson waves. Crying out, he thrashed as if drowning, all the while emitting a high-pitched scream that sounded part terror, part frustration.

At last, he found the seam and disappeared from the stage.

You're lucky I don't.

The audience broke into confused babble. The house lights brightened. Max packed the Arriflex 35BL back into its case.

Then he grinned at Maude, feeling more powerful than Jack ever did.

"Horror deserves respect," said Max. "In a way, it's the perfect crime."

Words to live by. A fitting epithet for his gravestone. A short and sweet manifesto with which he'd soon educate Jordan. After him, all of America.

This parting message delivered, he went outside and leaned against his roadster to wait for Sally to emerge from the stage doors.

Max needed her to teach him the secret of acting.

NINETEEN

When Max learned script writing, he'd read a lot of Joseph Campbell, whose work documented the story beats in the enduring narrative archetype known as the hero's journey. According to Campbell, this journey through change involves the hero refusing the call to action, followed by him accepting it.

After a long, sleepless night of pacing his empty house, Max had fully committed to his own path of change in a world of supernatural wonder.

He'd always mined inspiration from real life by imagining the absolute worst happening. Blood dripping from the ceiling onto a child's birthday cake. A smiling woman reaching into a Christmas present only to withdraw a squirting stump. A mall scuffle between shoppers over Cabbage Patch Kids escalating into genocide.

He now had the means to never have to rely on imagination again. The chance to live a life of horror rather than make it in his head.

At noon, Max drove his MG downtown to realize his plan's final act.

What's your vision, Max?

To make the perfect horror movie.

He found a parking space and fed coins into the meter. Then he unlocked the trunk. Inside, the Arriflex throbbed against the walls of its plastic cage.

The time had come to take it off its leash for real.

• • •

Max knew Jordan's routine. The producer was an early riser. He worked out in his home gym, followed by a breakfast of coffee, bagel, and hard-boiled egg. Then he drove to his office, where he'd be at his desk by nine sharp.

Drinking cup after cup of coffee, Max had stared at his phone and fax.

At ten, the phone rang.

"I didn't know you had it in you," Jordan said. "It turns out you can teach an old dog new tricks. This new treatment for *Wishes* is the best work you've ever given me. Congratulations."

Max forced a smile. "I guess I needed a little motivation."

"This movie, it's what the people want. Smart, funny, scary, relatable. And making it 3D, that is a bona fide stroke of genius. You know, sometimes, it's actually a pleasure doing business with you."

"We're funded?" he asked.

"Right after this call, I'll authorize the bank to transfer the rest of the money. You might notice a more substantial amount than promised, which should handle the 3D aspect and more. I'm upping my investment to seven fifty."

Max swallowed his first pang of regret. "Thank you, Jordan."

"I was right to trust you. This is gonna be a big one, baby. Stupendous. Janet will fax you when the transfer is done."

"How about we go out for lunch to celebrate?"

"What, today? I've got—"

"We can talk out the treatment and make changes. Punch up its mainstream appeal even more. Think big and go all out."

"You know what? You're on," the producer said. "I have lots of ideas."

They'd agreed on a place and time. The fax machine coughed out a slick sheet of thermal paper confirming his new picture had full funding. Max spent the next few hours drinking coffee and staring at the clock.

Then he prepped his machine and drove downtown.

What's your vision, Max?

To achieve perfection at any cost.

Pedestrians hustled past, ignoring Max as he removed Arthur Golden's occult camera from its case. Cars rumbled on the road. Arguing over how to handle their unruly teen, a couple entered a nearby bakery. A truck rolled out of a parking garage a few doors down.

Showtime.

Planting the sticks, he mounted the camera and took a few deep breaths, forcing air into his lungs. His legs had started shaking.

Then he aimed the Arriflex down the street toward the office building that stood near the end of the block on the west side.

Cars snarled up and down the road. Across the street from the office building, a mid-rise was being renovated in an echoing cacophony of drills, hammers, and heavy construction materials hauled around and banged into place.

The world's full of hazards, Max thought. *As the kids say, shit happens.*

Shit happened all the time. Acts of God.

You look up at the wrong time, and a lawn dart plops into your eye. You tell a joke at the dinner table, and your heart breaks.

A young couple glanced at him standing behind his camera but really didn't care what he was doing. This was Los Angeles. A movie camera on a sidewalk provided a subject of curiosity but was ultimately no great shakes.

Still, it made him nervous, being watched, like a version of stage fright.

So did the prospect of what he intended. His entire body trembled in its own private earthquake. Sweat trickled from under his bucket hat.

He had the desire to do this. Did he have the will?

The first time Max had used the camera with any intention, he'd been driven by a dark impulse he'd imagined as Arthur Golden directing him. A part of him still hadn't believed it did anything. The whole event had played out like another experiment in imagination. In his ear, he'd heard Raphael scolding him, telling him to quit before anyone got hurt.

This time, he knew exactly what the camera could do.

As for Raphael, Max now heard his old friend chuckling with satisfaction. Arthur giving him another slow clap.

He'd given Jordan a chance. He'd offered a clear and simple choice of two movies, one the usual profitable drivel and the other a bold and original vision. The producer had failed the test, but he'd fund the right movie in the end.

If only you'd given me a green light on the movie I wanted to do, Jordan . . .

Instead, the producer had enslaved Max to do four scary movies that wouldn't scare anyone. Another decade Max would spend doomed to work his ass off toward a definition of success he considered failure.

His creative life wasted making commercial swill. His producer on his back like a fattening parasite, controlling his every decision and draining his essence drop by drop. Devouring what was left of his life. An entirely different but just as brutal form of murder.

Didn't he have a right to defend himself?

What Max planned to do wasn't murder. It didn't really count as self-defense either. No, this was horror movie justice, and he was its agent. Jordan had challenged dark forces beyond his comprehension, and now he'd pay the price.

What's your vision, Max?

To remove anyone who stands in my way.

The only thing that could stop him now was love.

Specifically, a lack of it.

• • •

Last night, he'd waved at Sally as she came out the playhouse's stage doors. He'd offered her a ride. Still amped for her aborted performance as Shana, the actor had expressed a dire craving for ice cream.

In a Dairy Queen parking lot, they spooned Blizzards while leaning against the warm hood of his car. Traffic zipped past on the nearby roadway.

"That was so weird," she said. "Dan banged straight out the back exit."

"Very weird," Max said.

"Not out, really. More like *through* it."

"He doesn't strike me as emotionally stable."

"Oh, he's a freaking basket case," she agreed. "I've just never seen it affect his work. He totally freaked out. Arthur's death threw him for a loop."

Max again thought about his father's passing. "Trauma affects you in ways you don't know until they come to the surface."

"I'm sorry you didn't get to meet him. You being such a huge fan. I was going to try to connect you two."

He smiled. "I'll catch up with him another time."

"Anyway, we all have our issues," Sally said. "My mom came tonight. I saw her on the way out."

"I sat next to her. She gave me an earful about my chosen genre."

"She's pissed at me at the moment."

"For the same reason?"

"Let's just say I'm pissed at her too, and I'm not really speaking to her right now." Sally cocked her head and regarded him. "You know, she said the oddest thing about you before I banged out the door myself."

"Oh? What's that?"

"That she thinks you're dangerous."

Max chuckled. "It sounds like she's learning to appreciate my genre."

"I kinda doubt that. So what did you want to talk to me about?"

"I'm hoping to get some advice," he said. "An acting hypothetical."

"Oh." Her face transformed into steely determination. "Let me have it."

He asked his questions. She answered.

Thus Max learned how to unlock the occult camera's true artistic potential.

Max spotted Jordan walking out of his building.

The producer always parked his Cadillac in the garage across the street. He'd stroll down the sidewalk a bit and pause to light one of his foul cigars. Then he'd jaywalk to complete his own daily hero's journey to his car.

Standing on the hot concrete, Max felt light-headed. Giddy, excited, and nauseous. What he intended to do should not be allowed. It certainly shouldn't be this easy. He wouldn't suffer so much as a parking ticket. His brain had coughed up a sketchy plan in a fit of rejection, and all the pieces had fallen into place.

All he had to do now was cry *action* and roll.

He zoomed onto his producer and punched the start switch.

Camera speeding. Film rolling.

What a great guy, he thought. *He gave me my first real break. No, this isn't me, it's someone I need to be. I'm a director looking for a father figure. I'm—*

Max could lie to people like Jordan easily enough, but not to himself. Not willfully, anyway. Otherwise, people lied to themselves all the time.

What was acting, if not lying so convincingly you ended up fooling an audience who showed up knowing they were being lied to? So perfectly that you even fooled yourself?

He'd needed to learn the secret.

"How would you handle a scene where you had to love some guy, but in reality, you can't stand him?" he'd posed to Sally in the Dairy Queen parking lot.

"You have to master the magic what-if," she'd answered.

"What do you mean?"

"What would you do if this person told you he suffered from a terminal disease? If he apologized for being a horrible person and said he behaved badly because you intimidate him? If he asked you straight to your face to be his friend?"

"I see," said Max.

"Run through the what-ifs and pick the one that resonates. Then lean into it. Draw on experiential memory to re-create a feeling. Imagination and experience, working together. That's how I'd do it."

"You've done this before? Told a lie so real it convinced you?"

"My entire life," Sally said sourly. "You could say it started the day I was born."

He gave her a questioning look, but she shook her head. Whatever she'd alluded to, she didn't care to elaborate.

Instead, she added, "The thing is, once you become aware of one big lie, you start to notice all the little ones."

Max nodded. That last sentence described his recent experience with Hollywood perfectly.

Sally went on. "If the what-if isn't enough, get to know the other person. Ask them questions and find out about their life. In real life, everyone seems like a flat, secondary character until you get to know them. Once you do, they become a complex character. And even if you hate someone, there is something about them you would probably connect with and like. Find it, and again, lean into it..."

As she went on talking, he glanced at her and found it impossible to look away. Leaning against the hood of his car, she lectured about acting while digging through the remains of her Blizzard. So effortlessly beautiful.

For the first time in his life, the black hole in his soul faded.

Then flared back to life.

I can't cast you as the Final Girl, he realized.

Sally's mother had been right about him.

I forgive you, Max thought as he tracked Jordan with the camera. *I'm so sorry you have only six months to live. Bone cancer, how awful.*

He'd spent half the night practicing Sally's techniques. It wasn't working now, however. Jordan reached the point where he would cross the street. Per his habit, he paused to prep a cigar and light it first.

Face glued to the coaxial viewfinder, Max kept at it.

Oh, you want to will me all your money to produce my new picture, and give me final cut? It's superb of you to recognize my—

After taking a few puffs from his cigar, the producer glanced both ways and stepped onto the road.

I love you. I love you, I love you—

Pouring sweat, Max sucked in his breath. If anything was going to happen, it'd be here and now. A truck roaring with failed brakes. A steel beam tumbling from a dizzy height. A decapitating pane of glass like in *The Omen*.

I freaking love you, brother—

Nothing.

Not a car in sight. The renovating mid-rise too far away. Even the usually busy lunchtime pedestrian traffic had dwindled to nothing. The whole block seemed eerily deserted.

The perfect chance. But still nothing happened.

Max was starting to develop a whole new respect for actors. How did they do it? Dig deep enough to become someone else so authentically? Pretend so convincingly they fooled themselves?

I'm a horror director with a camera that creates horror, and I can't use it. Christ, maybe Jordan's right: I am a hack.

Even now, he heard the audience chortling in his ear, rolling over him like canned TV studio laughter.

He let out a disgusted snort. This wasn't going to happen.

Honestly, it was probably for the best. The whole plan had been crazy from the get-go. A part of him now actually rooted for the man to safely cross the road.

Screw it, he thought.

The new *If Wishes Could Kill* wouldn't be the worst thing ever to hit the silver screen, and Jordan wasn't evil for liking it. It wouldn't realize the genre's true potential or Max's original vision, but it'd be fun.

He'd direct it, and then he'd direct *Jack the Knife IV.* He'd go on directing movies, and he'd go on fighting Jordan over creative decisions.

It was how things worked and how they'd always worked. It was how they were meant to be. It was the machine of Hollywood, wicked but charming, something one fought and subverted but never actually caused harm.

Or perhaps this presented a sign for Max to throw in the towel altogether. If the game proved so rigged the only way to play it right required resorting to actual murder, maybe it wasn't worth playing at all.

Perhaps he'd start up his own theater company. If he liked it real, well, it didn't get any realer than live theater, tears and sweat poured out on stage every night.

Max Maurey presents the return of the Grand Guignol, blood and madness five nights a week, a doctor in the house at all hours in case anyone faints.

You can make it, Jordan—

A muffled roar. The ground moved.

The earth jolted under his feet.

The same instant, the manhole cover under the producer's feet exploded upward in a gust of smoke like a vertical cannon shot.

Two hundred fifty pounds of solid cast iron rocketed into the sky along with another two hundred pounds of Hollywood producer. Both defied gravity in three hundred feet of rapid ascent.

Jordan had vanished as if he'd never been there.

Staggering from the tremor, Max tumbled onto his back. High above him, a human-size rag doll flew between the buildings along with a black dot that might have been a shoe or maybe a pair of mirrored shades.

He didn't need to see the man come back down to know how it turned out.

He gasped, "Never call me a hack."

No one laughed now. The audience haunting his head had at last been shocked into an awed hush. They didn't even breathe.

And as for Max, he felt—

Remorse and triumph.

Good then bad.

The biggest itch he'd ever had. Oh, he'd scratched it.

If only to reach the even bigger itch underneath.

Yes, he'd go all the way now. In for a penny, in for all of it.

The moment he'd cradled Arthur Golden's infernal camera in his arms and learned how it fed, a part of him knew it would come to this. It had always been a question of time before he answered its siren call. A matter of fate, really.

After all, they proved a match made in hell. The camera's need joined to his creative ambition, both of them free at last to realize their true potential. And he would, because he knew he could never bury the camera again. If he was damned, damnation offered a distinct upside in that it freed him to follow his desires. Like Al Capone said, if you're gonna steal, steal big.

Regardless of his conflicted feelings, Max had higher powers to serve, namely, horror and art and his image of himself as a horror artist. With this occult machine, he had the power to break the ultimate boundary and set a new standard for what was possible in filmmaking. The artistic equivalent of being the first man to smash the sound barrier or step onto the moon.

He owned a camera that produced its own spectacular real effects. With it, he could make the perfect horror motion picture. A film not only seen but experienced. Not only experienced but studied. Not only studied but feared as physically dangerous. A film that would forever endure.

As for the cast he'd feed to the machine as human sacrifice, well, this was Hollywood, a dog-eat-dog town, a world of predator and prey. From a utilitarian perspective, one might argue a handful of actors sacrificed to make a perfect film offered a net moral positive. And as the camera pretty much guaranteed an afterlife, it's not like they were really dying anyway.

Hell, they should *thank* him for the opportunity he was about to give them. With this film, their names were destined to live on forever, and they too would live forever to enjoy their posthumous celebrity.

In any case, the cast wouldn't suffer alone. Max would share in their sacrifice. Once the bodies were carried off the set, he'd face manslaughter if not murder charges. The victims' families would probably hit him with a lawsuit. At a minimum, he'd be kicked out of the Directors Guild and never work as a movie director again, a creative if not physical death. And the censors at the Motion Picture Association of America ratings board, already prejudiced against the less moneyed indies, would refuse to rate the film, limiting distribution.

Max would do his part and welcome it all. He'd happily suffer too.

Better to make one perfect movie than a lifetime of schlock. One perfect terrifying film instead of a slew of movies about as

frightening as costumed children trick-or-treating on Halloween.
A beautiful swan song for an enviable career. A film that would
make the mouth of the most jaded horror fan, the pimply kid who
thinks he's seen it all and giggles through it, drop open like a Venus
flytrap. A horror movie that would imprint itself on the American
psyche.

And if no one ever watched the movie except him, Max would
still know he'd created it. Like Sally said, make the movie you alone
are dying to see.

I'm proud of you, Arthur Golden said.

"Thank you," Max said.

*You're a real artist now, answerable to no one but your vision. But even
now, even after going all the way, you're still willing to compromise.*

"I can't cast Sally."

Not as the Final Girl, at least. It'd be hard enough to convince
himself he carried tender feelings in his bosom about five needy
actors without also forcing himself not to care about Sally.

Because he did care about her. More than he ever had about
anyone. He wouldn't shoot the Final Girl with the cursed camera,
but having Sally anywhere near it was too great a risk.

*You should cast her. I was right about Jordan, wasn't I? I'm right about
this too. She of all people will understand. If you really do have feelings for
her, you'll give her this shot at fame. She'll live forever. You owe her that.
She wants it.*

"No," said Max.

Not as the Final Girl. Not in any other role. He'd invite her to
the casting call, and then he'd find a way to let her down with as
little harm as possible.

Keep her as far from *If Wishes Could Kill* as possible.

Good art requires suffering. Great art demands sacrifice.

"Don't ask again," he growled. "I'm the director, not you."

The voice went silent.

At the distant howl of police sirens, he sat up. A pall of smoke and dust hung over the road. He wondered if he should say any final words for Jordan Lyman. Something appropriate. Then it came to him.

Max said, "Now, *that* is how you make a killing, baby."

Arthur Golden cackled along with him.

TWENTY

Sally Priest had always believed acting was a dangerous profession.

In the end, every actor was a survivor.

Acting involved willingly tearing down her ego and instinctive psychological safeguards. True, in one sense, she simply pretended to be someone else. In another, it was like emotionally stripping bare in front of strangers.

Besides that, even with a solid performance, the actor almost never had any control over the final product. The most she could hope was for the director to grant another take if time, budget, and his whim allowed, and then hope the edited composite of takes and angles captured her at her best. She didn't have a say in whether that one perfect scene ended up in the film or on the cutting-room floor.

But Sally didn't think about any of that as her taxi stopped in front of Max Maurey's house. She thought what made acting most dangerous was people.

Yet another glance at her watch. Six minutes late now.

To an *audition*.

Sally forked over rolls of pennies to pay the driver and bolted toward the house. On the long drive home from screaming at the Joshua trees, her Austin had developed a coughing problem that led to a visit to the shop. Nicholas had promised a ride, but he'd never showed. She'd run back upstairs to her apartment to call a taxi, only to find the phone ringing for a heavy-breather call.

The casting brief that Louise, her talent agent, had messengered over read:

IF WISHES COULD KILL, horror feature film, shooting 11/3– 11/30, Lyman Entertainments, Max Maurey directing, Los Angeles, Big Bear Lake, and Bombay Beach.

A young woman and her friends return to their dead town to resolve childhood traumas and lift a deadly curse that threatens to claim them one by one.

PENNY, major character, early twenties, no accent. Penny is the woman who launched the curse. Haunted by vague guilt and suppressed memories, she is sweet and pure of heart but fragile and prone to paranoia.

Major character? Damn, Penny was the lead! Horror's newest incarnation of the Final Girl, a perfect fit for the right scream queen.

People could say what they wanted about Max Maurey, but the man proved a rarity in that he wasn't filled with hot air. And for once, Sally had laid eyes on a female character profile that didn't say *super sexy but isn't aware of it.*

"Break a leg," Louise had told her. "Make us proud, Sally."

Her agent didn't have to add, *And be on time.* A guideline so sacred it was practically a commandment. You showed up early, you waited somewhere between ten minutes and all day, and then you went in and gave your all.

Seven minutes late now, and she had a gnawing doubt her watch ran slow.

Steeling herself with a deep breath, Sally entered the house where weeks earlier she'd woken up from a major drug trip to discover a director who wanted to engage her in a theoretical chat about horror over gourmet coffee. A horror director with a prissy little dog. Only in Hollywood.

Judging by the number of cars parked outside, she guessed only a few people had been invited to the casting call. This at least proved accurate. They sat on Max's furniture in nervous silence, as if waiting their turn to see the doctor and find out whether they were going to live or not.

Nicholas flushed scarlet at the sight of her, while Ashlee, nestled against him on Max's sprawling couch, offered a look of smug condolence.

"I'm so sorry, Sal," he said. "I totally spaced out."

"After he picked me up, we kind of got distracted." Ashlee giggled.

Megalomaniacal directors, misogynistic cameramen, casting directors trying to get in her pants, Sally considered these all common and recognizable hazards in her profession. She'd learned to navigate them to avoid being used without blacklisting herself.

Sometimes, however, other actors were the worst. Sally would rather piss off the Mafia than find herself on an actress's shit list. Because that actress came at you sideways. You ended up like the hunky dude in the horror movie who offers the Final Girl a confident smile assuring her he'll protect her with his life. A moment later, his head topples off his spurting neck, already dead but unaware of it.

Anyway, she had only herself to blame for trusting Nicholas, who was out for himself and worked in mysterious ways that would make even the Lord wonder at his cunning. Sally had always considered herself immune to the games he played, as they weren't competitors.

Ashlee held his hand in a tight grip on her lap. They'd taken their publicity romance one step closer to a real marriage of convenience. According to the grapevine, Nicholas's agent strong-armed Max for a role, and Ashlee now clung to the actor to hitch her own ride. The vine also reported that Max favored Sally for the Final Girl, a part to which Ashlee no doubt felt entitled.

Everything fell into place. Today, she had to work hard at

embodying sweet and pure of heart to portray Penny. The paranoia, however, came easily.

Sally glared at Nicholas. "Very disappointing."

He shrugged.

Ashlee said, "I could be wrong, darling, but I think they called your name right before you came in. They're all in Max's office."

Sally stomped off toward where she remembered the office being located, passing other actors who sat around in anxious contemplation.

From the other side of the closed door, she heard voices. She gripped the doorknob and twisted. Then she froze.

Ashlee was messing with her.

Or maybe not. Maybe Sally really was just being paranoid.

She imagined barging into the room and interrupting an actor in the middle of a scene. Not only would she announce herself as late, she'd mess up an actor's audition, another cardinal sin.

Perhaps she should knock instead—

Damn it.

Retreating back to the living room, Sally stood fuming with hot energy. Some of the actors offered her a curt nod; she thought *sweet and pure of heart* and forced a smile. One of the men gave her a warm, genuine smile back, which he could afford as they weren't competing for the same role.

She'd run through her final vocal warm-up exercises in the back of the cab, where she'd left the Jack Ketchum paperback she'd brought to browse while waiting her turn to audition. Nothing to do now but wait to face the music.

Use the time, Sally told herself. *Pull it together.*

Bracing her feet with her body straight but relaxed, she placed her hands on her stomach and breathed in for a count of four seconds and out for another four.

"*Sssss*," she hissed like a deflating balloon.

Then breathed in again for four and out this time for six.

"Mmmmm—"

"Why am I even auditioning?" Ashlee wondered. "He's never seen me act?"

Nicholas patted her knee.

"He wants to make sure you get the best role for you, Ash."

She sniffed. "I already know what the best role is, and it's not Wanda."

He turned to Sally. "Some budget that old Max pulled together for this little art project, huh? Casting out of his house. This is indie even for an indie."

Sally concluded her exercise with a final sigh.

"Maybe he's being cautious," she said.

"What do you mean?"

"You know, with Jordan passing."

"You think the financing is in jeopardy."

"I don't think anything," Sally said with a sense of déjà vu, feeling like she'd quoted Nicholas back to him from some past conversation. "I'm here to act."

"Who are you reading for?" Ashlee asked her.

Sally lifted her chin. "Penny."

"Cool beans. I'll bet Maude is mega excited."

"I couldn't ask for a better cheerleader. She's always praying for me."

"I mean, damn. A lead in a horror movie! It's an ace step up for your career. I'll bet she's really rooting for you."

Sally glowered, regretting ever introducing Maude to Ashlee at some minor celebrity fundraiser for kids with cancer. No doubt Maude had dished about her many disappointments in her rebellious progeny while couching it all as high praise. The two women certainly had one thing in common, which was the ability to sniff out someone's weak spot. If Ashlee and Maude had been around in the days of Homer, they would have sized up and ended the invincible Achilles in a matter of minutes.

Then Sally regretted glowering. For a gal who considered herself dedicated to the craft of acting, she still had a hard time faking certain things. While she'd worked in Hollywood long enough to understand its hidden language of bullshit, innuendo, and smiling delivery of verbal paper cuts, she didn't speak it fluently. She had two general modes: being nice and, when confronted by naked threat, going to war. Passive-aggressive remained a subtle art she'd never mastered.

As a result, nothing came to mind to shoot back that didn't make her sound like the asshole. In any case, Ashlee had already triumphed; if her goal had been to worm into Sally's head before her audition, she'd succeeded.

Nicholas patted the woman's hand again, as if to say this time, *That's enough, Ash, she's bleeding.*

Ashlee said, "I think you have something in your teeth."

Sally resisted the urge to run to the bathroom. It was just another head game.

"There's about to be something in *your* teeth," she said. "My—"

The office door opened. Braids dangling, a heavyset woman popped her head out, glanced at her clipboard, and bawled, "Sally Priest, batter up!"

"Break a leg in there," Ashlee said, sounding sincere.

"You really are a good actor," Sally said.

She returned to the office to find a giant mohawked beauty blocking the doorway. The woman smiled down at her.

"Look at you, Sally Priest!"

With only a handful of seconds before Sally had to go in, they whispered a rapid exchange in passing.

"Hi, Clare! Who were you reading for?"

"I read for Katie, love. The smart-aleck comic relief. Can you believe it? Must be the jaunty Irish accent and all, though they made me drop it for a second read."

"I hope it went well for you."

"I'm just glad Max gave me a chance. I'll wait for you. Break a leg!"

"Wait! Do I have something in my teeth?"

Clare had already stomped away in combat boots. After running her tongue over her teeth one last time, Sally walked into Max's office wearing a confident smile she hoped wasn't marred by a slab of lettuce.

She could do this. She *had* to do this.

Actors excelled at willing suspension of disbelief.

The director's desk had been moved and converted into a table. Behind it, three people sat on chairs swiped from the dining room. Max, the director in his usual black suit and New Wave band tee, his wild hair now sporting a few more streaks of silver since she last saw him; a sullen boy who looked barely out of high school and who perked up with sexual interest at the sight of her; and the heavyset woman who looked familiar and whom Sally guessed was the casting director. Another kid stood behind a video camera mounted on a tripod.

Despite the room having the air of a military tribunal, Sally offered a little wave. "Hi, everyone."

"Hey, yourself," said the kid behind the camera. "I'm Donovan."

Max scowled at him before mustering a smile for Sally. "Hello."

It wasn't a happy smile. He appeared distracted.

Be confident but not cocky, she thought. *These people are on the clock. Respect their time. Make one little point of connection and move on.*

"Thank you for inviting me to read," she said. "Where's the puppy today?"

The director's face darkened as if a storm cloud crossed over it.

"Lady Susan passed away quite unexpectedly."

Flustered, Sally blurted, "Like Mr. Lyman."

Max let out a bitter cackle.

"Exactly like Jordan," he said.

"I'm sorry to hear that." Jesus, this day was such a disaster. Every time she tried to stand up, the ground moved under her. She was like a walking earthquake.

"My name is Dorothy," said the woman with the braids. "I understand you're already acquainted with Max. And this is Carter, who will be reading with you. You know the drill, right?"

"Oh, I know you. You're—"

Sally shut up before she set off another tremor for the Richter scale. But she did know this woman.

At the little industry wake for Raphael Rodriguez at Jordan Lyman's Bel Air mansion, she'd wandered off to gaze at the sunset and brood over Maude's jarring pronouncement at lunch: *You know precisely how it worked out.*

She'd turned to spot Max following this woman into the house. The mysterious outsider had caused a rolling wave of gossip across the party. *A writer*, the vine informed. *A real hoot. Max Maurey is buying her story for his new project.*

Now here sat Dorothy in a tie-dyed shirt and Native American headband, presenting like a Grateful Dead fan posing as a casting director. Nicholas appeared to be dead right about the budget. Or maybe her guess had been correct that Lyman's death had frozen the accounts. Or perhaps something else, that Max wanted total control of casting and Dorothy was here as window dressing. Or maybe cover so he could avoid promises he'd made to certain people.

Most of it wasn't good. None of it mattered now. Max and Dorothy had created a character and wanted someone who inhabited it in reality while also being able to perform. It was time to give them the real Penny.

"Yes, I know the drill," Sally said.

She took two strides to stand on a little slice of blue tape on the carpet, then faced the camera to do the slate. The kid behind the camera raised his thumb to signal he'd started recording.

"I'm Sally Priest, reading for the role of Penny. My agent is Louise Berkman."

"Anytime you're ready," said Dorothy.

Sally closed her eyes, reminding herself this was for all the marbles. Then she also remembered: This is the fun part. The thing she loved doing more than anything in the world.

She'd reviewed her *sides*—the two-page scene she'd perform, typical as most scenes in movies were two or three minutes long—and had run the lines with Monica so many times that she'd internalized them. In this scene, Penny is exploring the ruins of her old house with Michael, a man who still carries a childhood crush on her. Sally had it nailed.

Sweet. Pure of heart. Fragile. Prone to paranoia.

For weeks, Dan Womack had taught her his approach to acting, applicable to screen work but with a major theater bent. Regardless of medium, the entire history of performance was to make it more natural to engage the audience with empathy.

In theater, actors performed live across space. They projected, playing to the back row, feeding on the audience's active energy. Performing for a camera proved a whole other ball of wax. The audience came after the fact, and you acted while ignoring a hyper-focused crew. The camera eliminated the stage and its distance to make the viewing experience cozy, even voyeuristic. For the camera, you weren't really performing at all, you were *living*.

Softening her gaze, Sally settled her focus on a framed "Fear Favorite" award Max had received from *Fearmonger* magazine and mounted on his wall.

She entered the zone.

"You know, I don't really remember my dad," she said.

She waited. Dorothy, who'd silently mouthed Sally's line along with her like an anxious parent watching her daughter do a school play, nudged Carter with her elbow.

"What do you remember?" the kid read in a monotone.

Sally shot him a quick, distrustful glance. Then she raised the back of her hand for a brief inspection.

"Hands," she said with grim certainty.

"That's it? Hands?"

By the time he finished his first question, she'd already nodded in response. Acting wasn't only waiting to talk, it involved listening, responding. Engaging with the other actor in a real conversation.

"Hammering nails into wood," she said. "Whittling. Sweeping his old metal detector. Pointing where he wanted me to go. Gripping my arm. Pulling an amulet out of the dirt."

"I think it's healthy to remember."

"Even if it's not worth remembering?"

"It's always worth it," Carter read. "I remember—"

He stopped with a little choking sound. Dorothy glanced at the script and muttered, "Oh, for Pete's sake, boy. Just say it."

She spoke to him with a familiar intimacy. The way a mother did to a son. Talk about low budget. The casting director was the scriptwriter, and the reader appeared to be the scriptwriter's kid.

"I remember being in love with you back then." The boy grimaced. The kid behind the camera snickered. Probably a friend of Carter's from high school.

Sally struggled to stay in the zone.

"I've never been in love," she said. "Not the real kind."

You have shit in your teeth, Ashlee said.

Heat flared in Sally's chest. She fought it back down and finished the scene well enough, but the heat had already torched Penny's fragility and replaced it with a steely anger. She didn't perform the scene so much as conquer it.

Acting was dangerous.

Max tilted his head. He'd noticed the change as well and now eyed her as if she were a beautiful puzzle with a critical piece missing.

"I'd be happy to do it again," she said hopefully.

"No, it was very good." His hands steepled under his nose. "Sally..."

She waited.

"I can't...I need to know..."

She kept holding her breath.

He asked, "How bad do you want to be in this movie?"

"I want this role more than anything." The only answer she could give, as it was true. "Max, I think this is going to be a once-in-a-lifetime movie."

"Even if it cost you everything?"

Well, that sounded weird, but she took it in stride. Actors had a reputation for being drama llamas, but directors had their own penchant for dramatic flair, especially when it came to discussing commitment to a passion project.

"I want to be in this movie," Sally said, repeating, "more than anything. And I will give it everything I have."

Max bowed his head behind his hands and grimaced. She had no idea where all this was going, but it didn't look good. The man appeared to be in actual physical pain.

At last, he sighed and nodded to Dorothy, who looked more than a little confused herself. The writer–slash–casting director turned to Sally.

"We'll be in touch, honey," she said.

Sally left in a daze. Back in the living room, Nicholas offered a sympathetic smile from the couch, where he now sat alone.

"It went great," she said before he asked.

"That bad, huh?"

"Where's Ashlee?"

"Feeding her olfactory muse."

"I hope *she* breaks a leg." Her tone betraying the wish as literal.

"It isn't personal with her, Sal. It's just business." He reconsidered. "Though for Ash, it's probably the same thing. Do you need a ride home?"

"I'll take her," Clare said as she entered the room with a glass of Max's wine.

Sally eyed it thirstily. "Can I have a sip of that?"

"I poured it for you, love."

She chugged the entire glass and came up gasping. Then she stretched her mouth in a chimpanzee grin. "Do I have something in my teeth or not?"

"All I see are pearly whites," Clare said.

The woman drove her home nattering about Hollywood and how you could still be discovered, if not in a malt shop then at an estate sale for a dead director. Still brooding, Sally grunted at her cues.

Returning to her little shared apartment in her crummy building, she inhaled the familiar homey scents of pot, stale beer, and chip dip. Monica chilled on the couch with her bong, wearing a wool winter hat despite the stifling heat.

"How'd your thing go?" her roommate asked.

"Fantastic," Sally growled, and went to her room for a good cry.

This done, she went to the bathroom to inspect her teeth while drawing a warm bubble bath. At some point, she'd find whatever had gotten stuck in there. Instead, she ended up once again hating her overbite. Then she found herself in the cooling tub with only a hazy recollection of how long she'd been soaking.

Reaching over the edge, she swiped her bottle of white zinfandel and poured another sloppy glass. The bottle was almost empty.

"I've never been in love," she said. "Not the real kind."

The line came out slurred, but it sounded utterly natural.

Of course it did, as it was true. Acting had always come first. Which was a shame, because Sally had so much love to give.

Instead, she'd sacrificed romantic love along with so many hours and gallons of sweat. Which was fine, if it all helped her reach her dreams of living the life she wanted. Dreams like getting into this movie. She'd meant what she'd told Max. More than anything, she wanted to be in *If Wishes Could Kill*, which, just from the sides she'd read, promised to be something special.

And then she'd flubbed it. Sally had discovered a razor-edged nuance for her character only to let all the shit get in her head and come out as blunt anger. She wanted to blame Ashlee, the teens, Max, and even her mom, but a real pro rolled with the pressure and always delivered on point. Looking back, she fretted she'd over-acted, a cardinal sin when playing a deep character in a complex drama. In one way, acting was like murder; it only succeeded if no one caught you doing it.

Actors flubbed auditions all the time. It was part of the trade. One more thing to roll with. You dusted yourself off and moved on to the next. This time, she'd allow herself to sulk first. She'd really wanted to be the Final Girl.

The telephone rang in the living room. Sally sank deeper into the bubbles.

Screw it. She'd never leave this tub.

But it kept ringing. And as disappointed as she was in herself and life right now, she couldn't let go the eternal hope that the next incoming call might be the one that answered her dreams.

Wrapping herself in a towel, Sally hustled dripping out of the bathroom and shot a glare at Monica, who hadn't moved an inch.

She picked up the phone. "Hello?"

Heavy breathing on the line.

She slammed it back into place. Jesus, what a day.

The phone rang again.

"Son of—" Sally wrenched it off the hook. "Don't call this number again, you jerk! No one wants to hear you wasting oxygen."

Silence. She basked in this dark day's single moment of triumph.

"Uh, Sally? It's Louise."

Her agent! "Oh, hi, Louise, I'm so sorry, I thought—"

"Right, right." As if Sally's shouting at her had filled up their obligatory quota of small talk. "I heard from Lyman's people. I have some good news and not-so-good news."

Sally's heart pounded. "What's the good news?"

"Your audition apparently went very well. We already got an offer, and it's above guild scale for a production of this size."

This announcement struck her like lightning.

"Oh. My. God," she said.

Louise said nothing. The silence stretched, more ominous than the heavy breathing.

"Um," Sally added. "So, what's the not-so-good news?"

"The offer is for a different part. They want you for the role of Wanda."

Wanda, the Bad Girl.

PRINCIPAL PHOTOGRAPHY

*It's not a big trick to chop somebody's
head off on-screen; it's a big trick to make
the audience care about it.*

Sean S. Cunningham
Director, *Friday the 13th*

TWENTY-ONE

Max awoke to the crackling roar of flames.

No was his first thought.

Please. Not again.

His ankle itched where Lady Susan had clamped on it last time with her sharp teeth. He'd hoped the grisly resurrection he'd witnessed thirty nights ago had been a mere nightmare, but no, this was happening.

He sensed the dead stirring into dismal existence.

The red glare writhed around the motel window's blinds. The alarm clock's angry numbers declared the witching hour had begun. Groaning, Max pulled the blanket over his head and cowered.

He knew what awaited him at the bonfire.

For a while, he lay shivering. The room filled with the stench of burning aviation gasoline and barbecued flesh.

The shrieks of the damned reached him soon after.

Of course, he had to see.

Pushing the blanket off him, he shrugged his bathrobe over his silk pajamas and stepped into his slippers. For the first time, Max understood why dumb teenagers in horror pictures hear a bump in the night and declare, *You stay here, I'm gonna go check it out.* It was always better to try to identify what hunted you than wait for it to show up.

In his case, it was more than that. Max had achieved his own wish of living in a horror movie. Whatever instinctive revulsion the dead provoked in him, he couldn't hide from it. Besides, a horror movie had conventions and rules. The protagonist accepting the invitation to play ranked near the top of the list.

Early in the day, he'd arrived at Big Bear Lake to start shooting *If Wishes Could Kill*'s prologue and childhood flashback scenes. Arthur Golden's occult apparatus had come with him, though a camera of the normal, non-cursed variety—a Panaflex Gold II—was being used to shoot these forest and lakeside scenes. Max had no wish to accidentally kill his townsfolk extras or the actors he'd hired for these parts. Not even the annoyingly precocious children he'd cast as the younger versions of the major characters, hired as sets of twins to ensure he could film as long as he needed without breaking child labor laws.

Accompanied by a small crew, he'd roamed the woods filming establishing shots of trees, water, and sky while recording the natural soundtrack on magnetic tape. Meanwhile, trailers loaded with equipment arrived for tomorrow's intense shooting.

He had four scenes to work through for the prologue—the young Penny with her father, townsfolk bursting from their houses to march to the lake, bodies disappearing into the water, a few washed up on the shore. Then another ten scenes of the kids interacting with each other and their parents for the flashbacks. He had to do every take just right because he was never coming back.

In five days, he'd return to Los Angeles to get the rest of act one in the can, and then soon after he'd start shooting in the desert at the Salton Sea, where the real fun would begin. Weeks of fourteen-hour days playing whack-a-mole, pampering egos, and explaining his vision over and over; just thinking about it drained him. Directing, he'd started to believe, might be a young man's game.

Padding across the carpet to the window, Max pulled the motel room's blinds. Bracing for a cheap jump scare, he peered out into the firelight. Down the gentle slope in the pines fronting Big Bear Lake's stony edge, the cast and crew of Arthur Golden's doomed film rose from the flames.

This was their ritual, the infernal clock that regulated the world of the dead. Every full moon, the camera's victims awoke in pain in the fiery afterbirth of Harry Stinson's crashed Bell 47 chopper. They roamed unseen among the living until the next lunar cycle, when the process started all over again. On these nights, the camera's owner visited them long enough to witness the suffering he'd caused.

Even without his calendar, Max should have known this was coming.

Yesterday, he had hosted a read-through with the principal cast at his house. He'd kicked things off by sharing his vision to make something new and authentic, dramatic and viscerally frightening. Reading from copies of Dorothy's script bound with brass fasteners, the actors tried hard to make it sound like the real thing while holding back from going all the way. After endless haggling and editing with the writer, the final script had come in at a hundred and five pages. That equaled around an hour and forty-five minutes of screen time. By the end of the day, they'd done three read-throughs, leaving everyone exhausted.

All the while, the Arriflex 35BL shrieked where he'd hidden it in the wall safe behind a Patrick Nagel print, demanding its release louder than ever. Building up to the worlds of the living and the dead overlapping again.

Quivering in his motel room, Max flinched as a demonic howl struck the night all the way up to the bright moon's frozen stare. It turned into a jackal's harsh laughter. Remembering to breathe, he gasped, his heart still pounding.

The infernal sound had come from Lady Susan, now the ferocious predator she'd imagined herself in life. *Well played, scary camera. Jump scare achieved, cheap but effective.* Max had always wanted to live in a horror movie, but man, he found the real thing even more stressful than directing.

For a few minutes, he spied on the silhouettes of the dead stumbling past the bonfire's amber glow. Smoke wafted into the dark pines.

Then something big began to trudge up toward the motel.

A grotesque and humpbacked creature. Large as a horse, it swayed on four thick legs that seemed to glide across the rough ground.

Coming for *him*.

His bowels liquefied at the sight of it.

The thing let out a soft lowing moan. Max realized the sound had come from somewhere deep in his own throat.

Despite all the talk among the dead about the Beast that possessed the camera, he'd begun to doubt it was an actual entity. In the end, he'd decided the camera was simply bewitched to operate following occult mechanics. An otherworldly algorithm. A machine with rules. It killed whoever you loved who fell under its malevolent gaze, and then it forced you to witness their death on repeat.

He'd been wrong.

A monster lived in the camera, and it had decided to make itself known.

Max yanked the blinds shut. Crouching below the sill, he crawled to the door and put his back against it.

"Holy mother," he breathed.

Hugging his ribs, he clenched his eyes closed and willed himself to wake up. It didn't work. Then he prayed the thing wouldn't find him. That it would sniff around until it lurched somewhere else in search of easier prey.

Wishful thinking. In a horror movie, the monster always found you. The game must be played. Otherwise, there was no story.

But nothing happened.

Max opened his eyes and released the breath he'd been holding. He chuckled. "Sometimes, my imagination—"

Pounding shook the door on its hinges.

The Beast was *here*. Demanding entry.

He told himself he remained safe. Arthur Golden had owned the camera for many years, and the only thing that had succeeded in killing him was a night with a bottle of whiskey and a .38 Special.

But that didn't mean anything, not really. He'd entered uncharted paranormal territory. But one thing seemed certain: He had broken an inviolable rule.

It's coming for me because of what I did to Jordan, Max thought.

He'd intentionally killed his producer for his own gain. Now he would pay for it. Another horror rule. In horror, justice stood paramount. The prohibitions against social taboos must be reinforced. You make a mistake, and dark forces punish your transgression with brutal karma. Simple Grand Guignol mechanics. The camera wasn't supposed to serve him—he was supposed to serve the camera.

The door trembled at a fresh round of pounding.

He'd grown so obsessed with his project that he'd redefined good and evil as anything that helped or hindered him. He'd thought that as long as he sacrificed people only for his movie, there was a certain morality to it.

But there existed supreme moral laws innate in humanity, laws that might even come from a supreme being, and one that stood out among the most sacred was *Thou shalt not kill*. Even if he wasn't doing the actual killing.

I'm sorry. I'm so, so sorry—

In the movies, contrition might be demonstrated, but it never worked. He wondered how the monster would kill him, for once cursing his fertile imagination. But kill him, it would. He was screwed. The mantle of protagonist would pass on to another, someone with the moral fiber to handle the challenge and resist the camera. And then the story would go on without him.

The pounding stopped.

The silence stretched. He held his breath.

"Max," a familiar voice called out. "Are you gonna let me in or what?"

TWENTY-TWO

Max blinked in surprise. "Jordan?"

"Who else?"

No monster, though this was bad enough.

"What do you want?"

"I was wondering if you were up for a general."

Max sat against the door in stunned silence.

"Um," he said. "Sure. Okay."

No Beast. No vengeful spirits. He found this strangely disappointing.

Rising to his feet, he opened the door.

It *was* Jordan—a torso propped upright on shattered legs, the whole grotesque heap piled atop a litter borne by four charred, roughly humanoid mannequins. Sparks fluttered like fireflies around the walking corpses.

The producer leaned to light a cigar from the embers glowing in one's shoulder. He smirked behind his mirrored shades while he puffed.

"Even dead, I look healthier than you. You're in over your head, Max."

"The camera is offering—"

"I'm not talking about the camera. I am talking about your movie."

The faceless corpses shuffled forward with the crude litter they'd lashed together out of pine saplings, bones, and rags. Bits of burnt flesh crumbled like charcoal onto the carpet as they all squeezed through the doorway and perched the producer on the dinette table. Then they shambled back out into the dark.

Even among the dead, Jordan ran the show.

"I honestly thought you'd hate my guts," said Max. "You know, for, um..."

"Having me murdered?"

"Yes." He swallowed with an audible gulp.

Jordan shrugged with his one working shoulder.

"Yeah, that's something the genre gets all wrong," he said. "When you're dead, you just don't care. It's liberating not to be consumed by want."

"Sounds wonderful." Max shivered.

"I highly recommend it. I think you'd like it yourself. In a lot of ways, you're more like us than you are them."

He frowned. "What's that supposed to—?"

"Anyway, I wouldn't have guessed you'd have the balls to take me out like that. I actually admire the will it took. Maybe you aren't a hack after all. I hope you drained the account before my creditors froze it."

"I did." All the funds were now committed to the project.

"Any trouble with that?"

"I've got lawyers on it. Otherwise, there's this maniac cop who's onto me. He hassled me about your death, but he's nothing I can't handle."

Jordan's face twisted into an ugly grin. "So, the camera. Am I correct in assuming you're going to use it in your new movie?"

"That's the plan," Max replied. "A horror picture that ends with real horror."

"Terrific vision."

"Oh." He'd never heard Jordan so quickly excited about a pitch and was equally surprised at the warm glow it gave him. "I'm happy you think so."

"Even with the original script treatment you sent me, which I'm sure you're using. The end result will be a perfect blend of commercial and art. It's gonna change everything."

"It'll get me arrested. I'll never work as a director again. And the picture won't see the light of day. The MPAA won't rate it, New Line will disavow it, no self-respecting theater will show it. At best, it'll wind up an underground video nasty. We'll be lucky to earn our money back on residual—"

"It's gonna be huge." The producer chuckled.

Max stared at him. "The entire principal cast will *die*. *On-screen*."

"Well, yes, except the one that gets away, of course."

"The Final Girl. Right."

"Let me tell—who do you have for it, by the way?"

"Ashlee Gibson."

God help him. If there were any justice in real horror, she'd be the first to shuck her mortal coil and join the camera's witching-hour family. If such justice existed, Sally would be the Final Girl, surviving to face any sequel, just as he'd planned before the camera changed everything.

"Good choice. Now let me tell you about a little picture called *Noah's Ark*." Jordan toked again on his burning cigar. "One of the first silent pictures with some talkie scenes. Came out in 1928. One of John Wayne's first gigs; he played an extra. For the biblical flood, the filmmakers pumped six hundred thousand gallons of water onto the set to make it real. Three extras drowned. Others suffered broken bones, one so bad his leg wound up amputated. Dozens of ambulances hauled away the injured. The picture grossed two million—fifteen in today's dollars. Fatalities happen, Max. Indie video, porn theaters, private collectors: Who cares where your movie goes to earn out? Plenty of people will hunt it down and pay you anything to see it. The country's full of jaded sickos who can't not look. America is ready for this. What I'm saying is this is going to be a landmark film."

"Well." Max waved away Jordan's smoke cloud. "Either way, I'm committed to this picture. But you're right, I'm in over my head producing as well as directing. I'm running myself ragged, and we only just started shooting."

Starting tomorrow, things would *really* get rough. Weeks in the woods, a soundstage in Burbank, and finally the desert, where he planned to hunt his cast among the ruins of Bombay Beach.

The producer smirked again. "It was almost worth dying just to see you realize I actually worked for a living. Who have you got?"

He told Jordan he'd hired as director of photography Spence MacDougal, who was talented if unreliable, being an irascible alcoholic. The round, cheerful, and perpetually sweaty Frank Boston as his soundman. The list went on: first assistant director, production designer, wardrobe, prop master, key grip, gaffer. None of them the best but certainly the best he could recruit on short notice.

From there, he talked schedule, budget, permits. The more Max detailed the production, the more excited he became, until he felt a little light-headed. Sharing all these mundane details aloud gave his new project substance and form.

His movie was happening. His dream movie, his perfect horror movie.

Yes, it did show *terrific vision.*

Inspecting his dwindling cigar with growing impatience, Jordan responded with a vague grunt. He may have died by exploding manhole, but some things hadn't changed. When Max finished talking, the producer recommended experienced line producers to help with the hiring, contracts, and other particulars, and then he got to what he really wanted to talk about.

"The whole project hinges on you being able to use the camera," Jordan added. "Nobody would ever call you a touchy-feely kind of guy, babe. You're not exactly brimming with brotherly love. It's making us nervous."

"Us?"

"All of us here. Well, most of us." Judging by his irritated tone, he'd met Helga Frost. "We're interested to see some fresh faces around the campfire, so to speak. The only thing the dead truly want is company."

"I learned some acting techniques to foster empathy," Max said. "Will that be enough?"

"Well, it more or less worked with, um, you."

Jordan stabbed the air with his cigar. "You have to be absolutely sure. I suggest looking into yoga techniques designed to inspire universal love. Hypnosis, maybe. Get to know your cast on a personal level and develop some real empathy—outside your wheelhouse, I know, but you need to make the effort."

Max frowned again. "Hey—"

"What I'm telling you is go full spectrum. Explore. Hollywood is filled with cranks and cults loaded with brainwashing expertise. Find the best that works for you. And then run another test before the big night at Bombay Beach."

"Another test?" The prospect had Max blanching, caught between loving the idea of making a horror movie with real death but still revolted by real murder.

"Pick an actor you deem particularly annoying and tell him you want to do a screen test for another project coming up after *Wishes* wraps," the producer told him. "Then see how good you are at using the camera. Don't focus on the result, only the caring. Learn how to love your fellow man. The camera will do the rest."

Max thought maybe he should visit Dan Womack again.

"I might have someone in mind," he said.

"How about Sally Priest?" Jordan smacked his lips. "A very lively lady."

"No."

"No?"

"She deserves her chance to be on-screen first. I owe her that much."

Max had planned it all out—keeping his promise by inviting Sally to the audition for the role she wanted, after which Dorothy would drop the hammer that she wasn't busty or tall enough for the role, whatever worked. He'd give the cast to the camera, she'd go on living, everyone would win.

Then he'd watched her perform her scene. At first, it was satisfying enough—she'd grown quite a bit as an actor since *Mutant Dawn*—but then near the end, she appeared to dig deep and bring real fire to the lines.

I want to be in this movie, she'd said. *More than anything.*

He simply couldn't say no to her.

"You like her, don't you," Jordan said.

"She's special," Max blustered.

"What I mean is if you like her, you can save her for later. Pick someone you hate and don't mind replacing. Knowing you, that should be a sizable pool to choose from. Then get it done, and quick, or you'll have to do reshoots. *Wishes* is gonna be a blockbuster. Then we make it a franchise, baby. A whole new art form."

We're gonna make a killing, Max expected him to add, but he didn't. Instead, the producer whistled. The meeting was over.

"Where are you off to in such a hurry?" Max asked.

"I'm gonna go haunt MGM," said Jordan. "Oh, before I take off, I should mention you have one more thing to track."

"What's that?" Even dead, Jordan imposed his conditions.

"I sold a product placement contract with Frito-Lay. You owe them a scene where their new Italian Cheese Potato Chips are displayed in a prominent way. If you could make the character an Italian American stereotype, that'd be terrific."

Shedding ash everywhere, the scorched crew shuffled back into the room and hoisted the producer's litter onto their crumbling shoulders.

"Best of luck, babe."

Then he was gone, leaving the cigar stub still pluming in a motel coffee mug.

Max breathed relief. Jordan held no grudge against him. He wanted to help. Despite his grating personality, the producer knew all the right people and how to twist their arms. With his invaluable knowledge, Max would get *If Wishes Could Kill* shot, cut, and even distributed.

He frowned, irritated at the gnawing idea that he still worked for the man. And now doubly annoyed he had to put goddamn potato chips in his movie.

The door pounded again. The hinges cracked.

Max rose from the bed.

"Okay, okay," he groused. "You know, you can just knock like a normal—"

Loud as a gunshot, the door popped off the frame to fly across the room. Raphael stomped inside in leather jacket and boots, his square ghoulish face a mask of fury, the lawn dart bristling in his eye socket.

"I am very disappointed with you, Maximillian."

Max cowered on the mattress. "What the hell, Raph?"

"All month, I went to parties and watched. I watched people do enough drugs to kill elephants, I watched an orgy, I watched an actress accidentally murder this dude, and then I drove out to the desert with her to watch her bury the body."

"Okay—"

"Then I went to the movies and saw everything that's out now."

"Okay," Max repeated.

"Actually, it wasn't that different than when I was alive."

"That's good, right?"

"I had nobody to share it with. Nobody cool. Have you seen the mopes out there? Being dead is lonesome, man. Even more lonesome than living."

"I'm sorry, but—"

"You promised me companionship. You said you'd give me Ashlee Gibson."

"I can't," Max said. "I'm sorry! I had to cast her as the Final Girl."

Raphael stared at him with his undamaged eye.

"Why would you do something like that, Maximillian?"

"Because after working with her on three *Jack* pictures, I honestly can't stand her—"

Max yelped as the special makeup effects artist gripped the front of his robe and hauled him upright as easily as hefting one of the lowbrow beers he'd favored while alive. In death, Raphael had superhuman strength. The puckered wound around the dart leaked a dollop of bloody jelly that slid down his stubbled cheek.

Corn syrup, cocoa powder, and food coloring, Max's brain blurted. Only this wasn't fake, it was grossly all too real.

"You owe me, you son of a bitch," his old friend growled inches from Max's face, which froze in a silent scream. The man's breath smelled rank as an open grave. "That wasn't a Hollywood promise you gave me, it was a real one. I don't care if you hate her guts. Figure it out. Fall in love with her the way you did with Sally Priest—"

Max gasped, "I'm not in love with Sally."

"Yeah? Then why didn't you cast *her* as the Final Girl?"

"It's complicated."

"Remember what I said I could do to you? What I could tear off, and where I might shove it?"

"Please don't," Max said.

Raphael dropped him back onto the bed and patted his shoulders, smoothing out the wrinkles he'd made in the bathrobe. "Take it easy. I won't hurt you, Maximillian. You're the only real friend I got."

"Thank you. I'll figure something out. I swear to God."

The man already had begun walking back to the door. Pausing, he said softly over his shoulder, "I know. I know you will. In a town of liars and phonies and frauds, Max Maurey stands alone as a man of his word."

He vanished into the night, where he let out a piercing whistle. A bestial growl filled the air, loud as Jack's Corvette.

"Oh no," Max groaned.

A furry rust-colored shape bolted into the room and blurred toward him, its flapping head emitting a bloodcurdling snarl.

"*No*, Suse! Bad, *bad* girl—"

He screamed as teeth sharp as razors chomped into his ankle and dragged him bouncing and flying through the night and past the pines straight into the flames.

TWENTY-THREE

Sally had arrived at Clare Byrne's Oakwood apartment intending to spend a relaxing afternoon of sun and surf at nearby Venice Beach. They never made it out the door.

Now they lay on their bellies on the queen-size bed, Sally brooding with her chin resting on bridged hands, Clare sighing.

"Well, it was good for *me*," the woman said.

The first line in the scene they'd been rehearsing all day. Sally looked around the bedroom, which seemed to be themed toward an odd but workable juxtaposition of black hard-core punk and pink Hello Kitty. A decorative representation of Clare's duality. The apartment was small but pleasant, far nicer than the messy shoebox Sally shared with her stoner roommate.

Her eyes settled on a little TV and boxy VCR, on which rested a few rentals from West Coast Video in their clamshell boxes. *Dirty Dancing*, *RoboCop*, and a strange little movie called *Repo Man*.

"No, no, it was great," Sally insisted.

"What's wrong?"

"Well, I'm worried about her."

"People all over the neighborhood are dying in freak accidents, and she thinks it's all her fault. There's a word for that."

"But what if—"

"*Narcissistic* comes to mind. *Paranoid*—"

"What if she's right is what I'm saying."

"Weird stuff happens all the time," Clare said. "Sometimes all at once. That doesn't mean there's some genie or god involved. You start theorizing about random chance, you're on a slippery slope."

"Life is a slippery slope."

"You want to go back to Lonely Pines, don't you?"

Simply hearing the name of their dead hometown flooded Sally with denial, dread, and a strange longing.

"Paranoid or not, it's a good excuse to face some things I'm frankly tired of running from," she said. "And it gets me out of this place for a while."

She stood and mimed getting dressed, quick movements showing a sense of determination. As if steeling herself to leave for Lonely Pines, where her childhood ended in horror.

The situation fake but the emotions real.

"We could always hang out here," Clare said. "Stay in bed all day."

"I'm supposed to meet Brad. I'm already late."

"Yeah. You wouldn't want him to figure out what we've been doing."

"He doesn't own me."

"That's right."

"You don't either."

Clare winced, holding back tears. "It doesn't mean anything to you, does it?"

Focused on listening, Sally reacted by letting her emotions speak for themselves on her face. In a movie, solid reaction shots—where you acted without talking—were a film editor's gold, ensuring you received more screen time.

When Clare finished talking, she allowed a moment of not speaking, what actors called a thought pause. Dismay, reluctant agreement, and then hardness crossed her face.

"Actually, it means a lot," Sally replied. "Every time I fuck, I feel alive." A grin peeled across her face. "And *scene*. That was awesome!"

Clare rolled onto her back and stared at the ceiling. "How many times do we have to run lines?"

"Until we internalize our characters so well that we can step in and out of them whenever we need," Sally answered. "Until playing them is effortless."

"I thought we were going to have fun at the beach today." The woman still wore a bikini top and colorful Jams shorts. "I was going to show off my bodacious hacky-sack skills."

Sally smiled at hearing *bodacious* said in the Irish accent Clare had temporarily switched to American during the scene. *Bo-DAY-shuss.*

"Well, it was good for *me*," she said, echoing Katie's line.

Delicious, in fact. The dialogue flowed with a pleasing rhythm. Besides that, Wanda proved to be no cookie-cutter, horror-nerd-fantasy Bad Girl.

The character showed quite a bit of complexity. Every good time she chased and caught wasn't about serving herself for fun. She did it to avoid something real that haunted her. And while she carried no regrets about her reckless hedonism, it fed a bigger, deeper well of shame.

Sally's interpretation: Wanda existed as a creature of need. A small-town girl acclimated to the rough big city, her only family the fellow survivors of a horrific childhood tragedy, wishing for anonymity but lonely. She's ready to go back to Lonely Pines not because she wants to but because delaying it is exhausting.

Out of all the major characters in *If Wishes Could Kill*, Wanda knew merely surviving was not really living.

Sally had let that inner vulnerability come out in her performance.

"It worked," Clare agreed. "But I think it'd be even better if we were actually topless under the sheet like we'll be on set."

"Uh-huh," said Sally. "I'm sure it would. We'd slip right into character."

"Can't blame a dog for trying." Clare grinned.

Sally stiffened, wondering for the first time if her phone breather might be a woman. Was Ashlee Gibson still messing with her? She had another flash of regret she hadn't been cast as Penny; she had the paranoia down pat.

"I'm just not into girls," she said. "Sorry."

"And I'm not trying to make you switch teams, love. I just thought you might want to fool around a bit. I'm horny, and you're so uptight."

"I'm not uptight!"

Now it was Clare's turn to say, "Uh-huh."

"Okay, I am a little. This is a solid role. It's not the lead, but damn, I'm going to bring it everything I've got."

Besides transcending stereotype, Wanda delivered a decent number of scenes with real meat on the dramatic bones. Playing her, Sally could show range. The type of role that could open doors to bigger and better things.

So yeah, she did feel a little uptight.

Make that a lot, and the looming shoot wasn't the only reason. The breather calls hadn't stopped.

Disturbing, of course, though hardly a rarity in Los Angeles, where creeps worked the phones around the clock to get off. What made the whole thing eerie was this creep knew Sally's name. On the rare occasions Monica shifted her ass off the couch to pick up the phone, he'd ask her to hand it over to Sally. Then he'd breathe into her ear, as only hers would do. Once he heard her voice, he'd remain on the line for a scant few seconds before hanging up, but it made its point.

Sally had a stalker.

Getting one's own freak was something of an unhappy merit badge among professional actors. It sometimes came with the game.

In fact, the whole experience could be useful to her as a horror actor; creepy telephone calls remained a genre staple. Nonetheless, she hated the vague and constant sense of threat it imposed on every minute of her day. It felt like being under siege.

Sally wanted to live her life her way. She'd begun to understand that fame carried a price. And she wondered if she didn't want to go out today because of this man.

Her mind flashed to Jim Foster, the actor Max cast as Brad, another of Penny's childhood friends and Wanda's jealous quasi-boyfriend. She'd first seen him at the audition, where he'd given her a warm, genuine smile.

At the table reading at Max's house, however, he'd shown up a different person, eyeballing Sally with a loaded, unsettling stare. She couldn't remember how she'd responded to him at the audition; maybe he considered her stuck-up.

Or maybe he was a creep.

"Not a single funny line for me in that scene," Clare complained. "I'm supposed to be the witty comic relief."

Sally snapped out of her worries. "You're not, though, and you should be grateful for that. We all get to play complex characters."

The whole movie was complex, in fact, a highbrow drama with a lowbrow gory horror payoff, the kind of high-concept hybrid that could only happen in Hollywood but also *never* happen. *The Big Chill* meets *The Evil Dead*.

On the downside, Dorothy had a tendency to overwrite, particularly with parentheticals telling the actors how to deliver lines. Sally ignored these.

"Yeah, I have to say it's cool to play a woman who happens to be a lesbian instead of a gay stereotype," Clare said. "It's rare to see that on a screen."

"Are you up for doing it again?"

"Hell, no. Bitch, we're going out. We'll grab some tacos and catch a concert."

"Are you sure? We're in the booking window."

They might receive a call from an assistant director at any time telling them to report to set the next morning.

"You have your way of preparing," Clare said. "I have mine. And it involves living my life and blowing off steam. It's been six months since my last gig—a walk-on in a dumb soap—and I've been managing estate sales the whole time. I don't need any more stress. I'm going out and having fun."

Sally sized up the woman in her bikini top and garish shorts. Clare didn't have the linebacker shoulders she'd first imagined. The woman looked quite shapely, in fact. But solidly built. And very tall.

Yes, Clare would keep her safe.

"So, who's playing?"

"Scrape Nuts."

Sally laughed. "You're joking."

"They're awesome. And they're playing at the Palladium tonight."

"I have one more little problem, you know, being a full-time actor..."

The woman sighed. "I've got money."

"Then I'm all yours."

As if picturing this in the literal sense, a sly grin washed over Clare's face.

"Girls' night out!" she said. "But first, let's do a punk makeover."

No joke; the marquee of the Hollywood Palladium did indeed boast that a hard-core punk band called Scrape Nuts was playing. Inside, the concert space filled with restless youth sporting black leather, band tees, ripped jeans, and safety pins, all of it looking like it had been rescued from a dumpster tucked behind some apocalyptic warehouse. Jittery with energy, the kids checked each other out while they chain-smoked. The room carried the tart stink of an enormous amount of hairspray.

Accepting a plastic cup full of foamy beer, Sally looked around in wide-eyed wonder at the wild mix of neon hair, razor-edged irony, and tribal norms—this odd crowd of *them* who came here to be an *us*.

"So teach me punk rock," she said.

Clare laughed. "That has to be the most un-punk thing I ever heard."

"Well, come on. It's like a weird club that's majorly mad about everything."

The woman wore a black leather jacket bristling with spikes and pins. As for Sally, she'd dressed in the team colors of black and white and more black. Over this glam-trash outfit, she'd ripped the crotch and feet in a pair of Clare's nylons and fitted them over her arms. While the Ramones crowed about Sheena being a punk rocker on Clare's record player, the woman completed Sally's transformation into a living goth doll with black lipstick, mascara, and pigtails. Even her hair was no longer blond but very dark now, having already received a fresh and rigorous dye job for *If Wishes Could Kill* to follow the brute casting principle that female principals should have different hair colors.

Despite looking the part, Sally showed up at the Palladium feeling like an impostor. Here, she was the *them*.

"It's more like an attitude," Clare said. "Fuck everything."

"Okay."

"You know, you're more punk than most of these posers."

"I am?" Sally didn't know if she should be flattered.

"You're fearless."

"I'm not sure about that either."

"You're committed to acting, aren't you, though? Totally committed. Me, I'm too scared to quit my day job and take a leap of faith. Anyway, there isn't much to learn. Do as the Romans, and you'll do fine."

"Teach me how to dance to it, at least," said Sally.

"Oh, I don't think I should. Things can get quite physical in the mosh pit."

"The what?"

Clare explained the pogo, skanking, windmilling, slam dancing. The chaos of the mosh pit. The major ideologies: straight edge, goth, skinhead, and so on.

"Punk has a lot of rules," Sally noted.

"Yeah. That's sadly true."

Strutting past, a punk with a bristling crew cut and suspenders paused to give Sally a leering once-over. "Who's your lady friend, Clare?"

"Nazi punks, fuck off," Clare said.

He laughed and flashed her the backward peace sign that conveyed a very British piss-off. Eyeing Sally, he waggled his tongue between his fingers.

"Yup." Sally glared as the kid walked away chuckling. "Going out tonight was a perfect call. No stress here."

"And here I was thinking you were a student of experience."

"Not when I'm in the booking win—ah, screw it." She reminded herself she was again the Bad Girl, for whom *do as the Romans* was practically a motto. "Hey, you!"

The punk smirked at her over his shoulder. "Yeah?"

Sally flipped him the bird with both hands. "Fuckity-bye!"

Cackling, he waved her off.

Clare laughed too. "Feels awesome, don't it?"

Sally clenched her fists. "Fuck everything!"

As if in response, the crowd burst into hoots and cheers. On the stage, Scrape Nuts had finished prepping, and the shirtless, heavily tattooed singer walked out to glare at them all from the microphone.

"We're a shit band," he announced as if bragging. "And now we're going to play you a selection of our shitty songs."

The crowd roared.

He added, "This first one's for all of you in the ear-bleed section."

The drummer: "*One-two-three-four!*"

The stacked speakers exploded in a wall of sound that struck Sally like an almost physical force. The musicians bashed out the first song as if they were in a race to get it over with, sacrificing complexity for raw intensity and tempo. Eyes wide as if witnessing a car cash, the singer shouted his lyrics seemingly straight into her face, the only part of it she caught being *You suck too! You suck too!*

And Sally thought, *Yeah, it does suck! Society, Reagan America, Hollywood, Chazz Morton and his blockbuster, all of it!* She'd never thought like this, always the picture of optimism and determination. Hell, her idea of teenage rebellion had been to piss off Maude by telling her she preferred Lee Strasberg's take on the Stanislavski Method over Stella Adler's, when secretly she favored Meisner's.

In short, it felt pretty righteous to say *screw everything.* She gave herself to the rage as something primal and cathartic, encompassing Ashlee Gibson and her stalker and Nazi punks too. Though, really, any handy target would do right now, not dissimilar to her performative hilltop scream therapy for the Joshua trees.

The first song ended, the few seconds of ear-ringing quiet offering Sally a moment of pure relief, and then they lunged into the second.

One-two-three-four!

Some fool in a T-shirt with a flannel tied around his waist skanked across the stage in combat boots before diving into the crowd. The audience boiled over into an all-out riot, thrashing at each other in an expanding fleshly whirlpool near the stage. But no, they were *dancing.* This was the mosh pit Clare described. Howling over the din, the mohawked woman waded into the throng like a warrior joyously greeting battle, all shoulders and elbows and flipping the bird with both barrels. Then she dove right into this human meat grinder, skanking during the buildups and slamming with the best of 'em at the dizzying crescendos.

It all struck Sally like one of the drugs she'd sampled, an audible cocktail of pure adrenaline rush. The air moistened with the smells of sweat, wet leather, and melting hairspray. The atmosphere splintered into a pell-mell sensation of living out of control. Her body trembled, itching now to throw itself into that vortex of aggression and pound the ironic smirks off some faces. Relishing the prospect of simulated violence as a form of personal expression, this perverse desire to not create for once but destroy and then destroy some more, because why not.

Don't even think about it, she told herself. Sally thrived on new experiences, but now wasn't the time to be taking risks. She pictured showing up on set with a black eye and a missing tooth.

Instead, she tossed back her foamy beer and returned to the bar for more to dull the edge the music kept sharpening. There, she watched Clare take a swan leap off the stage and disappear in the storm of bodies ricocheting like pinballs.

She's more fearless than she thinks, thought Sally, who appreciated anyone who lived for the day. *She's a badass.*

The unrelenting sound lulled her into a kind of angry trance of pent-up energy, and then the band stormed off the stage and the house lights came up. In the dazed aftermath, the slammers stood around blinking and drained in relative quiet that fell on Sally's eardrums like ice on an oven burn.

Clare appeared dripping and grinning, her mohawk wilting like a spent sex organ. Sally laughed, barely hearing it over the deafening ringing in her ears.

"God, you're a mess," she said.

"Right you are, love, but I'm a happy mess. I blew off a lot of steam." Whether due to happiness or exhaustion, her accent had thickened.

"So what happens now?"

"Now we try to escape in one piece," Clare said.

They followed the crowd toward the outside doors, lit up in colorful strobing light. As if they hadn't had enough, many people had started an impromptu mosh pit out on the street.

Oh, wait, Sally thought. *That's an actual riot.*

"The friggin' cops," Clare said. "They come after the shows sometimes to keep an eye on things and end up beating up on the kids."

"So what do we do?"

"We do a runner and hopefully don't get whacked by riot control."

Doc Martens crunching glass from the shattered doors, the punks poured out of the building and scattered, shouting and laughing. In the street, a knot of police officers fought a pack of kids in leather jackets, the entire scene made even more surreal by the flashing lights on the parked cruisers.

A van screeched into view and unloaded more police in riot gear.

Clare grabbed Sally's hand and yanked.

"Now's the running part, love!"

Dodging maniac cops, Sally bolted down the sidewalk. She ran both scared and elated, happy to burn off the show's energy and the soaring buzz the cheap beer had given her.

She stopped. Alone. Somehow, she'd lost Clare.

The woman caught up huffing.

"You're fast," she gasped.

"Now I know why you parked so far from the Palladium."

They walked arm in arm down Sunset. Clare gave her a little tug.

"So what do you think of punk now?"

"It's insane," said Sally. "Like visiting a different planet. You can be a different person there. Create a character and improv it."

"Actually, it's the one place where I can be the real me. Christ, love, even when you're having fun, you're working. Don't look at it as a new experience or a fresh crack at character. Experience isn't living. Living is living. It's an experience in itself. You don't have to force it."

"You were wrong. What you said before."

"About what? I'm not arguing, I just want to know."

"I am scared. I'm scared all the time. Everything you see is an act." Her playing Sally Priest, her alter ego.

"Well, you had me fooled," said Clare. "What are you so scared of?"

"Mostly? That I'm not going to make it as an actor and I'm wasting my life."

"Come on! You're about to do a major part in a horror movie."

"My mom says even if I succeed in horror, I'm still failing. To her, it's almost the same as becoming a porn star."

"That's her age talking. The lady is out of touch. Genre is huge now. Respected, even. It's added pressure you don't need. I wouldn't pay her any mind."

"Look, she can be overbearing, but she may not be wrong."

"Well, you can't do both," Clare said.

"What do you mean?"

"You can't win her approval and your own. You'll have to—what's the matter?"

Sally had stopped listening. Her body stiffened in instinctive alarm. Something didn't feel right. She glanced behind her.

Half a block back, a presence matched their pace. The bearish figure passed under a bright sodium streetlight, revealing a burly man in a hooded sweatshirt, his face a black oval of shadow.

It's him, her mind blurted. *The Breather.*

Sally had always considered Los Angeles too sunny, colorful, and cheerful for supernatural horror. The human kind, however, it packed aplenty.

She tightened her grip on Clare's bicep. "It could be my imagination, but there's a—"

"Why are we whispering?"

"Don't look, but I think that man is following us."

Clare shot a glare over her shoulder. "Him?"

"There's this guy who's been calling me and hanging up."

"You think he's the one?"

"Maybe," said Sally. "I've got a bad feeling."

"All I'm hearing, love, is this dude is bothering you."

"Well, yeah, a little—"

"It's nice to make things simple." Clare wheeled. "Oi! Mate!"

The man froze.

Clare now stomped toward him with fists clenched like sledgehammers.

"I said, oi, you creepy shit—"

Backpedaling, he turned and bolted back down the road.

"That's right, run," she called after him.

The woman nattered all the way back to Oakwood. Sally barely heard her. Her ears still rang from the blasting music, or maybe it was her blood singing. The night's adrenaline had burned the beer out of her system and left something coiled in her chest, making her amped and restless with nowhere to put it.

Back in Clare's apartment, the punk went into her bedroom to check the answering machine, leaving Sally blinking in the dark living room and wondering why they were here. She wanted to party all night and dance these feelings out of her. She wanted to explode.

"You were right!" Clare called out.

Sally walked in. "What?"

"They need us on set tomorrow morning. Call time is nine sharp."

That changed things. It left only one option.

"We should go to bed then," she said.

"Yeah, you're right about that too—"

Sally stepped forward and planted a wet kiss on her mouth. It tasted salty.

Coming up for air, Clare said, "Yeah?"

"Fuck, yeah," Sally breathed.

They tumbled onto the bed. She hadn't planned this, but she'd faced violence tonight and her body demanded proof of life. Before her mind blanked out in bliss, her brain came up with the thought that the pure and chaste Final Girl probably didn't remain a virgin very long after confronting the masked, machete-wielding maniac. Horror wasn't always about the battle between good and evil, but it was always about life and death. After surviving the night, the Final Girl likely grabbed the first clueless deputy who showed up and screwed his badge off.

Clare absorbed Sally's assault until its ferocity wore itself out and the act became gentle and tender. Sally had never done this before, but mechanically it all worked the same, and she trusted this woman and felt safe with her. She pictured Nicholas in the role of Michael down there licking and nibbling, and then for a single perverse moment he morphed into Max Maurey.

Right then, she went over the edge, the orgasm exploding between her thighs and at last purging her mind and body of everything.

Sally giggled in the aftermath. She was definitely alive. Long live Sally Priest. Another chuckle. Max Maurey! She really was a Bad Girl at heart.

Maybe she *was* a little punk rock.

TWENTY-FOUR

The next morning, Clare drove them up to the soundstage Max Maurey had rented in Burbank for filming. Marked LYMAN SET, yellow signs arrowed them toward an impromptu village of trailers.

There, a production assistant waved them to where they should park.

"Oh. My. Jesus," Clare swore.

Sally stiffened in her seat. "What?"

"That young man there just told me where to *park*."

"Um, I know."

"On a *movie* set. Where I'm going to *act*."

"Ah." Sally smiled.

"Doing my first real *role*. In a *horror movie*."

Clare kept gushing as they walked to the trailers. "*And* I'm going to be working with Ashlee Gibson. I've had a crush on that girl since the first *Jack the Knife*. Pinch me. I've died and gone to heaven."

Sally winced. "She's a fine actress."

A horrible person, but she'd grant the lady had talent.

"I saw her holding hands with Nicholas Moody at the audition. They came out as a couple in the press! They're lovely together, don't you think?"

"For sure," said Sally, in full acting mode now.

They entered the trailer village. Few people were about. The rest worked in the nearby soundstage building, a cavernous metal box housing film sets built for the production. Flies nibbled stale bagels on the craft services table. A cool wind rustled over it. The sky appeared overcast, threatening a storm.

"So what now?" Clare wondered.

Sally led her to the production office. "We try to find someone who knows what they're doing."

Dorothy Williams found them first, stomping across the circus in her feathered hat and boots. She gripped a handheld radio.

"Hi," Sally said. "We're looking for the second AD."

The second assistant director, who'd show them around.

"That's me," the writer–slash–casting director said. "Let's roll."

"You wear a lot of hats on this movie," Sally observed.

"So, this is what a movie production looks like," Clare said. "Cool to the max."

"I know, right?" Dorothy replied to both statements, beaming.

"Everything's going well so far, I hope."

"Right on. It's all happening!"

She showed them the wardrobe trailer. As Clare went in, Sally hung back.

"Okay, now tell me how it's really going."

She hoped to gain a sense of the production's vibe. Every set had its own character, depending on the people. *Mutant Dawn* had splattered across the desert like one long party, while *Razor Lips* clacked to its finish like a cold machine.

Apparently delighted to dish, Dorothy laughed. "The first day was a shit show."

Nothing surprising, in other words. The first day of principal photography often came together in a chaotic mess. Sally nodded, waiting for more.

"Since then, old Ashlee has been driving Max up a river of his own tears," Dorothy told her. "Demanding another take when he's happy with a shot and refusing when he wants her to do it again. She *is* good. Where she gets her energy, I have no clue. We spent the whole day shooting yesterday, and I didn't see her eat a thing."

Sally had an excellent idea where Ashlee got her energy but kept it to herself.

"Thanks," she said instead.

"You should know I heard her arguing with Max. She tried to grab one of your scenes for herself, but he wouldn't have it."

Her eyes narrowed to fuming slits. "You don't say."

Wardrobe involved Sally trying on the outfit she would put on at the end of her scene and then taking it off again. Dressed in bathrobes, they padded to the hair and makeup trailer, where Bert, the makeup artist, did Clare's first.

"Relax," the man said. "I'm gonna take great care of you girls."

"I'm just so excited," Clare said.

"Of course you are, honey. You're in the movie business."

"When we're on set, it might feel weird," Sally told her friend. "There will be a lot of men staring at us. Sometimes, one of them can get a little handsy."

Her mind flashed back to *Razor Lips*. The directors were Hans and Greta, twentysomething West German twins who ran an efficient if frosty production. For that movie, Sally did her first sex scene, awkward to begin with but artistically stylized to the point of being borderline embarrassing. Afterward, Hans congratulated her in that German way that sounded like he was mocking her, and then he gave her bare ass a slap loud enough to be heard across the set.

Startled, Sally had looked around at the crew, who stared back at her and did nothing. Greta even smirked, completing the humiliation.

"Anyone tries that with me, I'll knock his teeth in," Clare said. "Anyone tries that with you too. Watch me."

"Now I'm kind of hoping they do try it."

"If she won't, I'm sure Jim will step up," said Bert. He read Sally's puzzled expression. "Isn't Jim Foster your boyfriend?"

"Only in the movie. He plays Brad."

"Oh, uh…"

"I only met him twice. At the audition and then the table reading."

"Well, when he sat in that very chair you're in this morning, he talked the whole time about your relationship. I thought it was romantic."

She gaped. "Our what?"

Clare cocked an eyebrow. "Problem?"

Sally again wondered if he might be the Breather.

"I sincerely hope not," she said.

Clare closed her eyes to bask in the makeup artist's focused attention.

"Let me know if it is."

The trailer door flung open. Ashlee filled the room like a burst of sunshine.

"Hi," she called out. "It's me!"

The actor beamed a sparkling smile at them, as if her announcement was a source of hilarious excitement.

Then she dropped into the third empty chair facing the mirrors. "I hope you guys don't mind, but I am in desperate need of a touch-up."

"Which you should get on set," Sally said.

"I don't mind," said Clare.

"We're on call. I do mind."

"Pretty please, Sal. I need my Bert." Ashlee batted her eyelashes.

They stared at each other while Bert hung back with his hands in mock surrender. Sally pure stubborn, Ashlee dripping with honey-eyed venom.

Clare grinned. "I'm trying to be cool, but I am such a big fan of yours."

Ashlee's smile ceased being performative. "That's very kind of you."

Taking advantage of the sudden cease-fire, Bert got to work. Sally put on her Sony Walkman and started a mixtape of old disco songs that fed her wellspring of emotional energy.

"No, I mean it," said Clare. "You're a bit of a role model for me."

Sally glanced away to hide her wince. Her friend had made a severe mistake exposing her belly to a predator like Ashlee.

Or maybe Ashlee was about to make one if she messed with Clare.

"This is your first role?" she asked.

Clare nodded. "My first movie role. I'm so nervous."

"I'm sure you'll do great," said Ashlee. "If in doubt, remember Max picked you for a reason. He saw something in you."

Clare smiled at her reflection, as if seeing something special there for the first time. Sally softened a little. She and Ashlee might not be on friendly terms after the audition at Max's house, but that didn't make her a terrible person.

"Can I ask you for some career advice?" Clare asked.

"Of course!"

"When it comes to film versus TV, which is—"

"Drop the punk thing," Ashlee said.

"You mean . . . ?" She frowned. "It's not a thing. It's *me*."

"So you're playing yourself. You'll end up typecast for a role that almost never comes up. If you're happy with that, then no, I don't have any advice at all."

Clare no longer smiled at her reflection but instead regarded it as a beloved pet that might require euthanasia. Sally winced again.

Never meet your heroes, she thought.

Ashlee might have been right, but it was the kind of truth Clare needed to arrive at on her own, depending on how much she wanted to commit to acting.

Out in the real world, the tough punk had no qualms about

using her fists when required. In this world, she didn't know how to fight. This time, it was Sally's turn to defend a friend. Because, yeah, in fact, Ashlee *was* a terrible person.

"That's what makes you such a terrific actor," Sally told Ashlee.

"Oh, thank—"

"Because the real you is an evil bitch."

Ashlee laughed as if she'd heard the world's funniest joke.

"And done!" cried Bert, drenched in sweat. "You look wonderful, sweetie."

Taking her time, she inspected her face from various angles. Then she put on a smile—that trademark mischievous smirk that inspired her teen fans to want her.

If only *they* knew the real Ashlee Gibson...Who was Sally kidding? They wouldn't care. Movies, after all, were all about fantasy.

"Break a leg, guys." Still chuckling, Ashlee left the trailer.

"You too," Sally said sweetly. "Unless I break it—" No point in finishing the thought; Ashlee was gone. She turned to Clare. "You're in a movie. Don't let her get in your head."

The punk replied with a glum nod. As strong as she appeared on the outside, her heart was far more fragile.

"I won't," she said, though she still looked a little stunned.

"You are beautiful just the way you are, honey," Bert contributed.

Sally said, "Whatever you're feeling, use it for your character."

Dorothy returned to bring them to the set. She handed them umbrellas. Powerful winds flexed in the skies over Burbank, now darkened into a false twilight by black clouds. The atmosphere turned swollen and electric. The wind mussed Sally's hair, but she didn't mind as the scene called for it.

As for the storm, it hadn't broken yet, but it was coming.

The soundstage consisted of ten thousand square feet of sound-proofed metal structure with a grid of lights and catwalks mounted twenty feet over the concrete floor. Here, the carpenters had built multiple sets, including the bedroom for Clare and Sally's scene, where the cameras set up.

Colored electrical cables snaked along the floor to power various machines. Operators positioned the hulking dolly. Wearing headphones, the soundman checked room tone. Electricians placed lights and scrims. The first assistant director sweated over the schedule. The director of photography measured foot-candles. The grips and prop master stood ready to chip in when needed.

And there was Max in his trademark black suit and ratty bucket hat, surrounded by crew asking what his vision had to say about every detail. Ashlee Gibson's antics had put him in a mood as stormy as the one threatening to burst outside. As usual, under his jacket, he wore a band tee, this one showing the grinning Patrick Nagel girl from Duran Duran's *Rio* album cover.

He'd grown even gaunter than the last time Sally had seen him, his eyes hollow. Max appeared to be pouring his very life force into this film. *Every genius*, Sally guessed, *must be a little crazy.* And she did consider him a genius, this director who wanted to make a highbrow horror movie in the eighties.

Her mind flashed to last night's wild little fling, Clare morphing into his ghoulish visage between her thighs. The memory made her laugh out loud, and she wondered if maybe she had a bit of a macabre fetish.

"What do we do?" Clare asked. "They're all ignoring us."

"We wait," Sally told her. "Don't worry, this is normal."

She led her friend to a cluster of director's chairs scattered atop a rubber mat. She sat, unwrapped a granola bar, and stared at her scene card.

Then she looked up to find Jim Foster frowning down at her.

"And here she is," he said.

"Oh, hi, Jim." Giving him a questioning stare that asked: *Are we cool?*

"Who's Jim?"

"Um. You—?"

"A friend of yours?"

"What?"

"You know what my name is, Wanda."

Sally went on staring.

"Hi, Brad?"

"Where have you been?"

"Me? I've—"

"I'm a Wanda," he sang bitterly. "I'm a Wanda. I get awound, awound, awound, awound, awound."

God, he was in *character*.

She'd heard some actors did this. They went so deep into the Method that they lived and breathed their character day and night during the whole production. She did it herself, though in a general sense. When she played the Bad Girl, she was more likely to play one in real life to inform the role with experience.

Embodying the actual character nonstop the way Jim did, however, was different. It took a hell of a lot of discipline.

It could also be draining for the other actors.

"Listen," she said, "I admire your commitment to craft—"

"Thank you."

"But can we please not do this right now? I'm about to go on set."

"I've been missing you." His tone now pleading. "I miss your body. Your smell. Your laugh. Everything. Can we have some alone time soon?"

"Oi. Mate," Clare growled. "Piss off so we can work, all right?"

Jim regarded Sally with a loaded stare. "Sure. See you awound, Wanda."

"Hey," Sally called after him. "Uh, Brad."

He turned with a hopeful look. "Yeah, babe?"

"Have you been calling me at odd hours and hanging up?"

"You mean like checking up on you?"

"Yeah, something like that."

"Maybe I should," he said.

Across the soundstage, the first assistant director summoned them. Walking onto the set, Sally and Clare shed their robes and stood in panties, producing a shocked, rippled pause across the crew like a heart skipping a beat. Ignoring it, they climbed onto the bed and lay on their bellies, propped on their elbows.

"You were right," Clare whispered.

"About what?"

"Everyone staring. This is so weird."

"You got this," Sally said. "This is your shot."

"Yeah." Her friend seemed unable to shake her gloominess.

"Nazi punks, fuck off, right?"

Clare grinned. "Right."

The focus operator stretched a cloth measuring tape from their faces to the camera lens. The director of photography called for more key light. Satisfied with what he was seeing, Max rose from his director's chair, plunked into the seat next to the camera, and asked for a rehearsal. Which they did, with Sally ending the scene on her final blocking cue, an X in blue tape on the floor.

Where she smiled, suppressing a fist pump. The soundman asked Clare to speak up a tad on her quieter lines, but the rehearsal had gone well. Then she noticed Jim standing next to the director. In full Brad mode, he'd reacted to the scene with a deep, horrified sense of betrayal, as if he'd actually caught his girlfriend in the act of cheating.

"Goddamnit," she muttered.

"Okay," Max said, "let's do a take—"

"LAST LOOKS," the first assistant director screamed.

Sally got back onto the bed. A makeup artist rushed onto the set to give her and Clare a final once-over. Tongue sticking out in concentration, she repositioned a single lock of Sally's hair and then as quickly fled.

"PICTURE UP," the first assistant director howled next. For such a small man, Sally wondered how he produced so much volume.

"Camera ready," the camera operator said.

"QUIET ON THE SET."

Various crew echoed the call until the clamor dwindled away to utter silence. The transformation appeared nothing short of magical. The first time Sally had done film, she'd regarded the frantic activity as random flailing and banging. Then the camera had started rolling, and she saw how it all had a grand logic, its chaos grinding toward a common purpose like a Lovecraftian machine built by a madman.

"ROLL SOUND."

"Sound speeding," the soundman answered.

Here it comes, she thought.

The sublime joy, the exquisite agony, the raking doubt, all of it. She couldn't imagine doing anything else.

"ROLL IT."

"Camera speeding," the camera operator said.

"ROLLING." Another call the crew echoed across the building.

Dorothy walked onto the set and held the clapboard inches from Sally's face. "Eleven, take one. Mark!"

Wearing professionally sullen if slightly leering expressions, the crew sat or stood only a few feet from the bed. The soundman raised his shotgun microphone to hang over her head. Max rubbed his chin under his ridiculous hat, as if having second thoughts about something.

Next to him, Jim kept glaring, his eyes searching out Sally's as if demanding she do an improv romantic makeup scene with him instead of this one.

Gritting her teeth, she willed him to disappear.

Max read Sally's face and then cast a sidelong glance at Jim.

The clapper shut with a gentle click.

Put him out of your mind, she thought. *Focus on what Wanda cares about.*

"Camera set," the camera operator said.

This incantation brought the standard ritual for summoning a movie scene to the trigger point. Only a single word remained, the most powerful of all.

Sally went into the zone.

Camera and crew faded away. A whole different reality materialized around her, a new physical and emotional landscape.

I love you, Jim mouthed.

Picturing him breathing the words into a phone, she glared back at him.

As if waiting for this cue, Max said, "Action."

Sally got ready to deliver her first line.

Then the anger came flooding back, and she flubbed it.

TWENTY-FIVE

C ut!" Max gave the assistant director a thumbs-up for a good
take.

Next to him, Rodney screamed, "MOVING ON."

Max cocked an irritated eye at the first assistant director before
remembering this was why he'd hired him. To give the crew someone to hate so he could get his own job done.

"Coming in," the crew called out as they started to reset the
camera and lights.

Max told MacDougal, his suffering director of photography,
where he wanted the camera for the next shot and what lens should
be used. Then he told his annoying assistant director to take five.

"Happy to, boss," Rodney said.

The man stiffened his spine and pluckily raised his hand with
the palm facing out. Max regarded him with a baleful stare.

"I didn't ask you to give me five," he grated. "I asked you to
take five. What I'm trying to say is go somewhere else so I can
think."

While the assistant director walked off sulking, Sally and Clare
wrapped themselves in their bathrobes and returned to the waiting
area. Judging by her self-flagellating scowl, Max could tell Sally dis-
liked her performance.

He did like it. In fact, it had delighted him.

He'd hoped to see the hot steel she'd shown near the end of her audition. A ferociousness that brought Wanda to life. Something about Jim Foster pulled it out of her.

Max eyed the sandy-haired young man but couldn't figure what about him got Sally boiling. Visually, he was striking but not overly attractive. Max wanted regular people in his movie instead of the usual Hollywood Ken and Barbie dolls. Good-looking but not models. In fact, among the cast, only Sally and Ashlee were what one might consider beautiful in a movie-star sense.

He caught sight of Nicholas and Bill Farmstead, whom he'd cast in the other male roles, standing around ogling like this was a free peep show. Nicholas leaned to whisper something in Jim's ear. The man's face darkened to despair.

"Get lost," Max said. "There's no need for you to stand around gawking."

"Oh, sorry," Bill told him. "It was a hell of a scene."

"Yeah." Nicholas wore the impish smile he put on after he'd stirred up trouble. "Sorry about that."

Jim sagged. "I guess I'll—"

"Not you," Max said. "You can stay."

"No, thanks. I think I need to be alone a while."

"But I'm curious about you. Tell me about yourself."

"Well, I love acting, I've got a little corgi named Niro, my girl-friend Wanda and I have been talking about getting hitched, I—"

"Nero? You mean like the Roman emperor?"

The actor started to perk up. "It's short for De Niro."

"And when you say Wanda, you mean…"

Jim pointed. "Wanda, right over there. She's my girl. Soon, my fiancée, if she'll have me." His eyes took on a wistful glaze. "We just need time to work some things out—"

"You're talking about Sally, right?"

"Who's Sally?"

Max stared at him.

"You're deep into the Method, aren't you?"

"I'm pretty strict about it, yes." The young man chuckled. "I read this article about how Dustin Hoffman does it. I admired the commitment."

Max went on staring. "You're perfect."

"Wow. Thank you, Max."

"Where do you live? I mean, what part of town?"

"Malibu. You know how it is, still living with the 'rents, but that's the career I picked. After this movie, though, I'm hoping to get my own place." He eyed Sally with a hopeful smile. "Maybe one that's big enough for two."

"You got any plans after we wrap?"

"None at all, so if you need—"

"You should go straight home afterward and rest up. Big day tomorrow."

"Okay, I'll do that."

"Great. Let me get back to work. But stick around for the coverage."

Jim beamed at all the attention. "Anything you say."

MacDougal's growly voice intruded. "If you want emotion in this film, it wouldn't kill us to try doing a few close-ups."

This said, the squirrelly bearded man nipped from his flask. Max's director of photography reeked of whiskey. As the cinematographer, his job didn't involve capturing images but *how* they were captured. The film's overall look and feel based on the director's vision.

MacDougal squinted at the rumpled bed, quietly calculating the emotional sum of composition, color, and exposure.

"We'll do them when we need them," Max said. "Not because we can."

A movie was typically shot on a single camera. A scene often started with a wide master shot in one or two takes, followed by coverage, or doing it again and again with multiple angles and close-ups. As for Max, he'd always held to a classical if workhorse style of filmmaking.

No showing off, no following the latest trends like blasting sets with light and garish color. Just a simple playbook of shot/counter-shot with the one-eighty rule. Bare-bones filmmaking using an anamorphic camera lens for a widescreen visual field and an epic feel. It had always worked for him.

"It's an intimate scene," the man grumbled. "We need intimacy."

Max cast a sly, private look at Jim.

"Dorothy!"

She appeared at his side. "You rang?"

"Shot list, if you please."

She handed it over, and he scanned the remaining shots sched-uled for the day. After Sally and Clare's scene, he had an important scene to shoot with the whole cast. Ashlee's games had thrown him off schedule, but he now no longer needed to do this last scene.

He'd do it tomorrow. Which meant he could afford to indulge MacDougal a little.

"Okay, Spence," he said. "You can have your close-ups."

The director of photography returned the flask to his back pocket. "I'll take what I can get from you. Every meager little crumb."

Dorothy looked around beaming. "You know, usually, I think most things in my life make a better story than when they actually happened."

Max grunted. He had a similar point of view. He didn't think any real-life event that wouldn't happen on camera was truly memorable.

"But this," she added. "You take it for granted, but for me, this is all like a dream. I feel like I'm behind the curtain meeting the Wizard."

"I'm sure it'll make a good story too."

"It's weird how all this started with a story. And your vision."

"Seven hundred fifty thousand dollars buys quite a bit of vision."

Dorothy took in the whole operation again. "It sure as shit does!" Then she frowned. "Though now I have to wonder what would happen if that money had gone to something like curing cancer. Making people's lives better in some way."

"We are making people's lives better," Max said. "We're making a movie."

The crew signaled their readiness to shoot coverage. Sally and Clare returned to set, disrobed again, and got back on the bed. Sally still fuming. The endless tweaking of angle, light, and focus began. Seeing Jim still hanging around, her eyes sizzled. Max took a look through the viewfinder, now filled with her face, and let out a little gasp as his heart thumped and stirred in its cage.

So lovely, it mesmerized him.

Sally elevated his film to art. She was the *Mona Lisa* in motion, warm vitality and hot steel captured in twenty-four frames per second, demanding patient study. She brought so much life to his film about death, in particular this scene with its no-nonsense, mundane eroticism. Yes, they'd shoot close-ups today, and he'd order them sent to the film lab for overnight developing to make dailies.

She'll understand, Max thought.

The drive to perfection. The willingness to do whatever that took.

It was in their blood.

Sally might even applaud him. Either way, he'd make her immortal.

Raphael had been right about him. He was falling for her—had in fact already done so. Maybe Dorothy had been right too, and these emotions came through the voyeuristic lens. Jordan, meanwhile, had expressed a certain truth Max couldn't escape. That his very feelings for Sally had compelled him to cast her in the movie while also making her an ideal candidate for the human sacrifice necessary to bring his magnum opus to life. Maybe the critics had it right as well, that horror embodied a perverse desire to worship youth and beauty and then see it destroyed. To live and love is to invite the wrath of the gods.

Rodney screamed orders. The cadence of call and response wound down to the critical moment, all the moving parts of production falling into place.

And when it was all over, when every take that tied off this beautiful scene had completed, Max felt a rare and precious moment of contentment.

He said, "Cut! Print it. That's a wrap."

Scattered cheers broke out across the set, the long-haired and mustached film crew already picturing themselves kicking back with ice-cold bottles of beer.

They were done for the day, though not Max. He had work to do.

One more important task for his movie. Something he didn't want to do but must. Something he couldn't put off.

Call it a demonstration of commitment. A proof of concept.

And if he didn't do it now, he'd be stuck doing a ton of reshoots. If he didn't do it at all, he might have no last act.

Max had no choice but to keep going.

As always, the show must go on.

TWENTY-SIX

The storm clouds burst over Los Angeles. No mere storm but a real gale. The rain fell in slanting sheets. Gusting winds bent the palms and sent the stands of oaks along Ventura Freeway into a shuddering frenzy.

In the westbound lanes, Max's roadster growled among glaring brake lights.

"I've still got him," Sally said behind the wheel.

She'd begun to wonder exactly what she'd gotten herself into. The rain lashed the windshield, barely kept at bay by the frantic wipers.

Next to her, Max muttered to himself and hugged his old movie camera. She recognized it as the Arriflex he'd picked up at Arthur Golden's estate sale. His hand petted the machine as if it were his old dog.

He'd taken off his bucket hat with its MORT'S SPORTING GOODS logo. Instead of a single streak of silver in his dark hair running up like a skunk stripe, he now had two radiating from his temples like the bride of Frankenstein. The rain had turned his naturally spiky hair into a pair of thick, curved horns.

"I can do this, Arthur," he mumbled.

A cokehead diva, a Method actor who'd stopped distinguishing between reality and script, an Irish punk rocker, and a horror director who wasted away by the day and might be losing his marbles. This production had it all.

After the wrap, Max asked if she were up for a little adventure. He hoped to acquire footage of a car driving. The kind of thing the second camera unit handled, but he wanted it done right now. The storm being perfect and all.

He'd decided to shoot it himself, but he needed someone to drive his MG.

Could you play chauffeur and help me out? he'd asked her.

Sally had replied with her Bad Girl smile.

I'm always up for everything.

She was starting to regret it this time.

When it came to a fresh weird experience, she was usually the girl who couldn't say no. If horror movies—where dumb decisions always proved fatal—were real, she'd already be dead a hundred times over.

"I'll show you what I can do," the director muttered.

He seemed to be talking to the camera. The old Arriflex unsettled her. She couldn't pin why. Probably because it made her think of the *Mary's Birthday* massacre, though she suspected something deeper. Then she remembered what Dan said when they'd broken up.

That camera. It's the devil itself.

As for the director, Sally found him disturbing too and for a much clearer reason. Max was acting manic, unpredictable, off the hook.

She shot him a worried glance, and he put on a sheepish smile.

"My apologies," he said. "When I'm really tired, my brain gets too close to my mouth, if you know what I mean. I end up thinking out loud."

Sally reset her gaze on Jim Foster's Chevy Vega, easy to track even in this weather with its bright orange paint job. From what she could tell, Jim had no idea Max was filming him. She found the irony striking, how right now she stalked the man who might be her stalker.

"Sure," she said.

"You know, I was going to get rid of him. Order him off the set."

Her hands tightened on the leather-bound wheel.

"Why didn't you?"

"Because you were nailing it," he said.

"You mean the camera rehearsal. I had it perfect before we started shooting."

"No," said Max. "I mean the take. Wanda is broken, but she doesn't have to be the Final Girl to prove she's a survivor. She already survived. Every day, she survives."

Sally bit her lip, mentally chewing what he'd told her.

"You wanted a quiet anger," she said.

"I wanted passion. And you, Sally Priest, have a lot of fire to give. The same fire you showed me at the end of your reading. It's why I cast you."

"But not as the Final Girl."

"That's a whole different story, one I'll have to tell you later. If I shared it with you now, you wouldn't believe a word."

Sally sighed, accepting what he'd said at face value. Max was both directing and producing this movie on a lean budget and tight schedule. He had his own pressures, and frankly, they were none of her business.

"You know, you can just ask me next time. I thought I'd had it perfect."

"I think the more you chase the idea of perfect," Max said, "the easier it is for one little thing to derail it. The harder it is to enjoy what you actually accomplish. Do you think that's accurate?"

"Maybe," Sally conceded.

"You need to be willing to do bad to do good."

"What's that supposed to mean?" Surely, he didn't mean she should be willing to fail, because she couldn't imagine ever abiding that.

"It means reach for the stars and grab the moon. Anyway, you can't control the outcome. You have to trust yourself you'll get it right." Max shrugged. "In the end, what's ultimately good or bad isn't in your control anyway. It's up to the director, who you also have to trust, and the audience."

All true, though Sally didn't like hearing it.

"Is that how you see things?" she asked him. "When you make a movie?"

She already knew the answer to that. The director didn't believe his own sage advice. He was notorious as a raging perfectionist.

Judging by his smile, Max knew it too.

"It's different for me," he said. "It's personal."

"How so?"

Max pointed. "He's exiting for Topanga."

"I got him." Sally followed the orange Vega onto the ramp, driving south toward the canyon and the coastal highway that would bring them to Malibu.

Following the twisty two-lane road, they entered the dark hills.

"I'll tell you something I've never told anyone," Max murmured. "Not any actor, not Jordan either. Not even Raph, the closest thing I had to a friend in this town besides my dog."

She waited for him to go on. The wipers clacked as they swept the rain.

"When I was six years old, my dad died right in front of my eyes."

"Oh my God," Sally said.

"He told a joke at the dinner table. A second later, he was dead. There he was, the biggest thing in my world, and then poof, he

died and the world stopping making sense. He was so big and inde-
structible, and then there was just empty space. A few unreliable
memories. A long lack. I've spent a lifetime processing it. Studying
and trying to understand it. How unfair it was. How it could be
possible. I mean, since then, I found out about it. Heart attack. A
defect he'd been born with had finally caught up to him. I have the
same defect. Every day might be my last. Borrowed time. But I've
still never understood how it was possible."

She didn't know what to say. "I'm so sorry, Max."

It certainly explained the shadow that seemed to follow him
around.

"Horror is what you feel when it happens," the director went
on. "But Dorothy's right; it's also what you feel when you ask why
it happened, and you have no answer. It's a shock that nags to be
repeated until it's either understood or loses its power. When I
make a horror picture, I revisit that night again and again. When I
strive for perfection, I'm trying to replicate that feeling for everyone. Every day, I look around and see America living in a comfortable dream. I want to wake people up, make them understand. The
horror is always there, and it demands respect."

"Wow," Sally said. "That's a hell of a personal drive."

Though she shuddered instinctively against it. She'd always
shied away from dwelling on the truth of human mortality. Even at
Raphael's wake, she'd strayed from Jordan's house as far as possible
while still officially attending.

Max had his art, but she suspected what he really needed was a
therapist.

"Tell me yours," Max said.

"Oh, it'll sound silly compared—"

"I'd honestly like to know."

"Okay, well, for me, acting is life."

Sally shot him a sharp look as if he'd already made fun of her.
Max, however, said nothing. Waiting for more.

"Every time I perform, it feels more real than my actual life. And in my real life, I live to the fullest so I have a full range of experience to draw on. I've done hang gliding, bungee jumping, water skiing, and cross-country racing on a BMX. Last night, I almost dove headfirst into a mosh pit at a punk concert. Tons of odd jobs. I've acted my way into and out of more weird scenes and jams than you can count. Someone like Jim, he uses the Method to become someone else. Me, my goal is to use it so I can be anyone at any time."

Like creative reincarnation, as an actor she lived many lives playing out in overall communion with the creative everything. And if she proved talented enough to become a star, she might live forever.

Barring that, she'd at least live life as her fullest self.

Max said nothing. Sally pursed her lips. The traffic started to clear, and the MG resumed its steady pursuit of Jim Foster.

"I told you it's dumb," she said.

"Not at all," said Max.

What she'd said wasn't enough, though. She decided to spill all of it.

"I recently found out my dad isn't my biological father. My biological dad is most likely some Hollywood executive from the golden era. My mom lied to me my whole life and expects me to be someone I'm not so she can be a star through me. When it comes to my family, I've been playing a role since I came out of the womb. When I got into the industry, I took on a whole new role." She released a bitter little laugh. "Sometimes, I think the one role I can't play is the real me."

One of the only true things she'd said all day.

"We're quite different, you and me," Max observed.

Sally snorted. "Yeah, you could say that."

Though she appreciated the intimacy, enjoyed getting to know this eccentric man who'd worked his way up to become something of a titan on the horror scene.

"We're also alike in some ways. And one big way. What we do is who we are."

"It's in the blood," she said.

The same drive to win. The same passion.

"In the blood," he agreed. "Ah. Yes. Perfect."

The road snaked between slanting canyon walls, mottled brown and tan sandstone furred with scrub and chapparal. A lightning strike bleached the scene to white. The thunder's boom arrived seconds later, startling even though she expected it. The wind roared down the canyon like an angry and powerful spirit.

Max raised the Arriflex and peered into the eyepiece.

The camera whirred to life.

"Get home safe," he murmured. "Little Niro is waiting for you."

"What?" asked Sally.

Get home safe. She looked for hazards and spotted more than a few. On the right, the canyon sloped up. On the left, the northbound lane was protected against a sudden drop into a rocky ravine by a guardrail. The road curved into menacing blind spots. Rain and wind blasted the scene, which had suddenly and eerily emptied of traffic, like a setup in a horror movie.

She wondered what kind of footage Max was getting. A lot of out-of-focus raindrops and sweeps of the wipers, probably. Geniuses didn't always make sense.

Max whispered, "I have a little dog too. Her name is Lady Susan."

Sally shot him another anxious glance. He ignored it this time, talking to himself again, appearing at the edge of tears.

"She loves to play," he said. "Her favorite is a toy giraffe named Roger Ebert."

The orange Vega fishtailed.

Sally gaped through the windshield at Jim fighting for control of his car, which either hydroplaned or swerved along an oil patch.

"Holy—"

At last, Jim stomped the brakes and skidded to a halt. She did the same.

Max kept filming, muttering something like an incantation.

Sally finally breathed. "Oh, thank God, he's okay—"

The hill above the Vega bulged with a wave of mud that rolled down the rocky slope to slam into the car.

The metal frame shuddered at the impact and traveled sideways to the other side of the road, as if floating. Straight toward the guardrail.

Where the old Chevy slid until it bumped the rail and stopped.

The mud thinned as it flowed around the tires.

Sally sucked air into arrested lungs.

Jim's hazard lights blinked on.

"Yes. He's okay." As if double-checking.

The actor opened the passenger side of his car and leaned out to inspect the muddy carpet oozing across the road.

Another flash of lightning. In its sudden burst of light, Sally spotted the boulder come hurtling down with the rain.

Pried loose by the mud, the massive rock had slid down the hill, sailed off the nearby cliff, and now plummeted toward the road like a meteor.

Again unable to breathe, she followed its progress.

Then closed her eyes. Pressed her hands against them just to be sure.

Sally could still hear it, though, the sickening metallic crunch.

After a few moments, she found her voice. It came out a child-like whimper.

"Is he okay?"

"Actually, he is," Max said.

He sounded strangely disappointed.

Peeling her hands away from her face, she saw the boulder had nearly caved in the Vega's roof before rolling off.

She almost laughed. She couldn't believe this man's luck, both good and bad.

The guardrail had cracked. The heavy vehicle slowly drifted through it. Steadily sliding in the mud until the left-hand tires left the incline and touched space.

"Oh, shit," she yelled.

Jim tumbled out onto the muddy road as the Vega disappeared.

Sally gawked at the scene.

"What the hell...?"

"Oh, come on," said Max, still filming the whole thing.

"I'm going to offer him a ride."

The director frowned. He let out a resigned sigh.

"Fine—"

Yellow light haloed at the bend.

Jim picked himself up and frantically waved his arms.

Oh, thank God, Sally thought. *Someone is stopping to help.*

Horn bleating, the truck smashed into him with a nerve-shattering *BANG*.

The impact sent the body flying in a cartwheeling arc. It flickered in Sally's peripheral vision to land somewhere on the road behind her. Still honking, the truck howled past to brake in a long, slippery stop and sat idling.

Right before it finally slid to a halt, the tires thumped over something.

The film snapped in the camera.

If this were a movie set, the operator would yell, *Roll, out!* Signaling he needed time to load a fresh roll.

But this wasn't a movie. This actually happened.

She'd just witnessed Jim Foster getting run over by a speeding vehicle.

"Maybe he's…"

Max gazed out the back window.

"No." His voice sad and even more resigned. "This time, he most definitely is not."

Sally gripped the wheel as if to anchor herself.

"HOLY SHIT, MAX."

"I know." Max inspected his camera with something like awe.

"SERIOUSLY."

"I said, I know, Sally. You're okay."

"THIS IS NOT OKAY."

He reached over to squeeze her knee hard.

"Ow!" She slapped his hand away. "What the hell are you doing?"

"You were in shock," he said.

"Fine! Just don't be creepy about it." She sucked in a long, shuddering breath and let it out slow. "So what do we do now?"

"Keep driving," Max told her.

Sally stayed frozen. Irrational thoughts flew through her head. She'd somehow caused the accident, and she was in hot water with the entire state of California. If she started driving, she might be picked off next by a random and violent universe.

She asked, "Shouldn't we call someone?"

"We need to find a phone to do that."

"So, we find a pay phone, and we—"

"No," Max said. "We drop you home, and then I'll handle it. Unless you want to see your name in the gossip rags along with plenty of speculation as to what you were doing driving around these hills with your director."

"Oh." He was right. She had far more rational things to fear at the moment.

"They'll destroy you," he warned.

"Okay! You take the wheel, though. Right now, I don't trust…anything."

They traded seats. Sally buckled up and let out a shriek as something tapped the rain-streaked window next to her.

A pale face appeared in the dark. The man rapped again with his knuckles and mimed rolling down the window.

"Are you guys okay?" he shouted.

"It's the truck driver," Sally said. "I'm going to—"

Max upshifted and floored it, leaving the man in a spray of mud. They drove in silence for a while. Then the director spoke.

"I never thanked you, Sally."

"Huh? For what?"

"For teaching me the secret of acting. It really does work."

Sally shrugged, her mind on heftier things. Things like seeing Jim Foster mowed down by a truck and left as roadkill.

That horror Max had talked about, he hadn't been kidding.

Shocking, sickening, and grotesquely absurd. A powerful event, though it hadn't been cinematic. Instead, it had looked sadly mundane.

"I'm glad if something I said helped," she said in a daze.

"Oh, it helped," the director said. "It's making all this possible. It's helping me realize my dream. We're all serving something far bigger than ourselves."

How, exactly, he refused to elaborate.

It pissed her off to hear him talk like this. That he could drive the speed limit, go back to talking shop, and otherwise act like this was any another day. She regarded him and his horrible camera with a sudden and intense loathing.

"Jim is *dead*, Max."

"You're wondering what it means."

"Something like that." In any case, she struggled to process it.

He chuckled. "In the big scheme, it doesn't mean anything."

"Ugh." She clapped her hands over her ears. "Please stop."

"Now you know horror like I do."

If it was horror, it wasn't the fun kind.

"The kind of horror you live with," she said. "It doesn't belong in a movie."

"Which," said Max, "is precisely why it does. Whether we like it or not."

Sally stared at the director's satisfied profile, and for the first time, she suspected that deep down, he might not just play the monster but actually be one.

TWENTY-SEVEN

The next morning, Sally returned to the rented soundstage in Burbank. Max welcomed her with hardly a nod of recognition, as if they'd taken a simple leisurely drive that hadn't ended in vehicular manslaughter. She met Johnny Frampton, whom Max had cast as the new Brad sometime in the night and who showed up eager and clueless at the hair and makeup trailer.

The day passed in a haze as she continued to process the shock of Jim's sudden and violent death. No longer living her dream but floating in a nightmare. Still riding the roller coaster of terror and relief until the final horror. Struck by something Dorothy said over sandwiches at the craft services table: *Horror provides its own sequel.* A little afraid of her director, who shared her love of horror but saw it so differently.

Sally viewed it as a sexy little outfit hung on a moral hook that you wore for a fun if punishing night out. Max regarded it more like a heavy, soul-crushing blanket of nihilism and shock that didn't let you climb out of bed.

Mad scientist, indeed. That was Max. Instead of a laboratory, he used the medium of film to conquer death. Though what Sally wondered, what made her afraid, was whether he didn't want to fight death at all but worship it, and the silver screen gave him an altar.

While waiting to walk on set, she conserved her energy more than usual, like a dozing cheetah awaiting prey to transform into the world's fastest animal. When the call came, she played Wanda with a ferocity that silenced her inner critic and surprised even her director.

Of course she'd give it her all. She'd seen something so horrible the earth had dropped out from under her feet, but she was an actor. Reagan and Gorbachev could push the button and drop the bomb, and even that wouldn't stop her from performing. Acting might not save the world, but it could save her from the same darkness that resided in Max.

Besides, she had a lot of self-loathing to purge. Her inner critic suggesting maybe Jim's accident was all her fault, an idea that crawled like biting ants across her psyche. If only she'd done something—maybe yelled at him to get off the road the same way she'd yelled at characters making bad decisions during the horror movies she loved—anything except sitting there gawking. If only his death hadn't felt so inevitable, as if the universe itself wanted to murder him. If only a part of her hadn't wished he'd piss off for good before the universe did exactly that.

If only, if only.

If something like it ever happened again, she'd do something. She'd act.

It all worked beautifully for her character.

Firing on all cylinders under the hot lights. Possession and ecstasy. Bringing all these heavy feelings onto the set, where her body adjusted on its own and acted naturally in the role. Playing Wanda demanded everything Sally had in her, and she was grateful for it. Wanda helped Sally heal while Sally brought her damaged but empowered alter ego to life.

On the sets built on the Burbank soundstage, the story unfolded.

• • •

One cool, foggy morning, the entire population of Lonely Pines walked into the lake and disappeared into its murky waters.

Wanda still dreams of it. Grinning folks, hundreds of them, all marching to some invisible pied piper, eagerly stumbling into the water and mud. Moms carrying babies that were conspicuously quiet as if they too obeyed the dark command. Nothing about it making sense—this is a dream after all—but it also happened exactly like this.

A few stragglers went in last. A flurry of bubbles, and then there were only the screams of the handful of children left behind.

In her waking hours, Wanda believes that with enough effort, you can outrun even your own past. In that sense, she already ran a marathon, though she never made it very far. Years later, she now lives in an enormous dirty city less than thirty miles from where she grew up on the lake's crystal shores. Looking at it another way, she moved to another world.

Bucked through the foster system, she abides as a solitary animal. Even at its most crowded, the city seems empty, occupied by dream people. Only her old friends, the fellow survivors of that terrifying day, appear substantial to her. In this world, she does what she wants without regret. She feeds Brad dribs and drabs, just enough of herself to prevent him from breaking. She keeps the rest.

Michael wants the gang to go back to Lonely Pines. They left as children without understanding or even the chance to say goodbye, and only years later do they realize how bad they need it. Yes, horror provides its own sequel, living on in never-ending grief. This horror needs an ending. But they must all go together.

Katie is skeptical that it will make any difference, but she will go if the others agree—particularly Wanda, with whom she carries on an illicit affair. Brad of course will go for the same reason. Jerry, the only one of them who appears content and successful, agrees as well—in his case as an old debt paid to Michael.

As for Penny, she has convinced herself she is to blame for all this. The strange epidemic of suicides in the city, their town's grisly and efficient *self-murder. The most steadfast against going has become the most eager, as the plan to return to Lonely Pines changes from optional to necessary.*

That leaves Wanda, Penny's childhood best friend. They work together as servers at the same restaurant. Of course she will join the trip. She will go because it makes no difference to her. And Penny's wild theories about why their families died are as good as any.

Wanda can be bad, but she is no Bad Girl. Authority holds little power for this woman who already feels punished. Despite the futility of her existence, she stubbornly lives. She lives for the day, and she lives to the fullest. And despite believing she lives in a world where God himself died in the lake with all the others, she has the strength to say: I'm going to do the right thing even if it costs me everything; I'll go home with you.

Wanda might not be the Final Girl, no. But she is special.

After the last wrap, Sally drove her clunker home from Burbank for the final time and discovered her mom waiting in front of her building.

As always, the senior actress created a scene. The sky bright but cloudy, the air mild but heavy with humidity. Spitting raindrops. Maude a picturesque beauty in raincoat and umbrella, hair perfectly wind-tossed as if Mother Nature had styled it. Watching Sally park, she struck a pose as if expecting someone to yell, *Action!*

Sally slammed the door and crossed her arms.

"Hi, Mom." Spoken like a question.

"Oh, hello, darling."

"What are you doing here?" The question a challenge.

Here it comes, she thought. More controlling head games—

"I came to apologize to you," Maude said.

"Because if you—wait, what?"

"I'm sorry. About everything."

Lying about Sally's parentage, maneuvering her into Chazz Morton's path, trying to control her career, all of it.

Not good enough.

The apologies came *after* catharsis. They didn't preempt it.

"I can have any life I want," Sally said. "You want me to redo yours so you can have another crack at stardom. Right down to making the same mistakes. Do you see how that's like burying me alive?"

"Yes. I do. All of it. I see it now. I'm sorry."

She opened her mouth, closed it. If her mother had come all the way down here to make a scene, she'd failed, as there was no conflict.

Unaccustomed to such easy surrender, Sally wondered which was more important, winning or the fighting itself.

"Well, okay," she said.

"Wonderful. Now please stop shutting me out of your life."

Maude's worst nightmare wasn't failing but being ignored. Sally had a chance to learn the truth. Demand to know everything. Find out the identity of her biological father and how it all happened.

Now that she had this chance, she no longer felt sure she wanted to know. She loved Ben Corn and considered him her dad in every way that mattered. What she truly wanted—what she still desired even after everything—was her mom's simple approval. Then Clare's words returned to her like falling bricks.

You can't win her approval and your own.

And trying to have both wasn't Maude's fault.

Why was it so important that her mother believe in her choices so she could truly believe in them herself? It maddened her.

Mom was Mom. Despite being on her best behavior at the moment, she'd never change. But perhaps Sally could.

If she truly wanted to live her own life, she could start taking sole responsibility for it.

"I have a movie to finish," she said. "We'll talk when I get back. I promise."

They'd wrapped for the last time at the Burbank soundstage. *If Wishes Could Kill* made ready for its next stage of production. Bombay Beach, here we come.

Out in the desert, Sally would scream again.

Maude pulled her into a quick hug that surprised her with its warmth.

"Phone me when you're back home," she said. "I love you, Em."

"I love you too, Mom."

For a moment, nothing else mattered.

Maude smiled. "You've grown even feistier. I quite like it."

"I've been learning from a punk rocker."

"Just be careful." Maude reached to touch Sally's cheek. "You're all I've got."

"I'll call you, I promise."

Sally returned to her apartment to find Monica and her friend Kayley sitting cross-legged on the sofa. Smoky vapor hung in drifts. The air reeked of ganja.

They burst into laughter at the sight of her.

"There she is," Monica said.

"What's up?" Sally asked.

"What's up is we need chips," Kayley said.

"We could slaughter some chips," Monica confirmed.

"I'm so hungry, I almost ate your roommate."

Monica grinned. "The world's first cannibal was no doubt high as fuck."

She lit her bong. The thick, bitter smell intensified.

Sally crossed the room to open the window.

"I don't have any snacks for you," she said.

Down in the street, Maude sat behind the wheel of her Audi parked on the far side of the road. She touched up her makeup in her rearview.

Wait until you see this movie, Mom. You might just like it despite yourself.

Even now, hoping for approval.

Or maybe Sally would change her own tune regarding horror. Max's unsettling vision of it and seeing Jim die so randomly had gotten into her head. She suspected that the next time she watched Jack kill Tina's unlucky friends on-screen, its grip would feel pretty weak, the spell its artifice created unable to affect her.

Or maybe she'd end up feeling too much. She didn't know yet.

Sally gasped, electrified.

It's him, she thought.

In the alley by the convenience store across the street, a man stared at Maude.

"That's a bummer," her roommate finally responded through a cloud of smoke.

"I'd settle for barbecue," Kayley said. "Salt and vinegar, cheddar—"

It was the hoodie man Sally had encountered after the concert.

The Breather.

Sally was sure of it.

No, it hadn't been Jim after all.

"Sour cream and onion," Monica put in. "Sour cream and freaking *onion*."

"Hell, even the plain salty kind with a lovely herb dip—"

The man wore the same gray hooded sweatshirt, though this time he carried an umbrella. It seemed discordant—Sally's imagination regarding stalkers and serial killers did not involve them fussing over staying dry during a drizzle—but he exuded a silent menace.

The man spied on Maude while she finished touching up.

Frozen with terror, Sally could only watch too.

"Do you see any chips out there?" Monica called from the couch.

Not this time, Sally thought.

She wasn't going to just watch.

She wheeled and bolted for the door.

"Call the police!"

"That's the spirit," Kayley said. "This is an emergency."

"Bring back, like, a variety," Monica yelled after her.

Sally slammed down the stairs, raced past the mailboxes, burst outside—

"Mom!"

The Audi pulled away, taking Maude to safety. The Breather stepped onto the sidewalk to peer after her.

He gave a little bye-bye wave.

Stomping into the street with fists balled for violence, Sally pulled up short.

"Oh, for Pete's sake," she said. "It's you."

"Hi, Sally," the Breather said.

Dan Womack wasn't looking so hot.

He'd lost weight since he fled the stage on the opening night of his own production. The neatly trimmed beard had gone shaggy. His eyes appeared crazed. His deterioration struck her as a mirror reflection of Max's own decline.

"You," she said again. "You're the one who's been calling me and hanging up. You followed me and Clare after that concert."

"I followed you other places too."

For God's sake! He was bragging about it.

Sally glared at him. "Why?"

"Because I'm worried about you. I've been trying to protect—"

"Again: *Why?*"

"Because Max Maurey is planning to kill you."

She balled her fists again. "I'm gonna kill *you* for being such a creep. The only person I've been scared of is you."

"Oh." Dan blanched. "In all honesty, I hadn't thought—"

"You freaked me out!"

"I'm sorry. I truly am."

"Our relationship had its fun, but it's *over.*"

"This isn't about that, dear Sally. This is about life and death."

She frowned at his dramatic, erudite flair, which she'd once found charming but now grated in her ears.

"Just tell me what the hell you're talking about," she said, "and how I can get you to stop stalking me like a psycho."

He handed her a book. "This time, I came to warn you."

She accepted it with instant regret. The large, heavy tome had been bound in some type of leather embossed with strange sigils. The thing felt greasy in her hands.

Overcoming her repulsion, Sally opened it to inspect hand-writing in an archaic language and what appeared to be blueprints for grotesque and unearthly machines. She settled on a spread from which a malevolent eldritch eye glared. Along the margins, someone had stamped matching columns of bloody thumbprints.

It all looked like gibberish to her.

"What does this creepy prop have to do with anything?" she asked.

"It's no prop," Dan said. "This is the spell book Arthur used."

"Uh-huh."

"The occult was all the rage back then. Arthur was about to give birth to his magnum opus."

"Uh-huh, and?"

"He cast the very spell you're looking at on his movie camera—"

"Max's Arriflex?"

Dan nodded, clearly annoyed at his delivery being interrupted. His important speech had been rehearsed.

"The very same. Arthur bought the book at a garage sale, of all places. His movie production wasn't going as well as he'd imagined, and he was hunting for fresh inspiration. The book seemed to call out to him. He thought the spell he cast would empower his camera to make the images it captured more horrifying to the audience. Honestly, he didn't think much at all. Arthur *dabbled* in the occult. He didn't qualify as a witch or anything. That drawing of the eye looked cool to him. Made him think of the camera lens, the medium is the message and all that. Something to get the creative horror juices flowing."

Sally let out an impatient sigh. He took his cue to reach a point.

"After Helga died, at last he figured it out. Finally found an expert who told him how badly he'd screwed up. In some cultures, people wear amulets that ward off the evil eye, right? Well, this spell turns it into the evil eye itself. You cast it on the amulet, and it destroys instead of protects what its wearer sees. You see, Arthur hoped to create art but only ended up hexing himself."

"Oh, Dan..." The man was off his nut.

Taking her sympathetic tone as encouragement, he nodded again.

"For years, I begged him to destroy the infernal machine. He couldn't—he said something about Helga's soul being inside it. In any case, he wouldn't. A few weeks before he took his life, he gave me the book and told me he'd decided to finally end the curse. I thought that meant he intended to destroy the camera, but I was wrong."

"He destroyed himself," Sally said.

"Yes."

"And then Max bought the camera."

"Maurey knows what it can do. It took me a while to figure out his plan for it, but I've got it now. He's going to kill all of you as his movie's last act. To him, it's not a curse but a blessing. A revolutionary new technique. He thinks if he can repeat what happened in Wilkes-Barre as part of the story, he'll make history by fusing reality with cinematic experience."

"Dan," she said patiently. "Listen to me. Do you know how this sounds?"

His eyes took on a vacant glint.

"That day in Pennsylvania," he murmured. "That sunny, mild day, I was running late. Arthur wanted to thank everyone on camera, but I didn't care, too caught up in my ego and doubts about my life. I hated the movie. Pure schlock. I don't even like horror as a genre. I studied Shakespeare..."

Sally crossed her arms and waited. Dan was monologuing again, but she allowed it. He'd earned this one.

He shook his head to clear it, only for his eyes to glaze over again.

"I arrived just in time to see the helicopter fall, lurching out of the sky, the blades scything through the cast. The blades weren't sharp, no. They didn't cut so much as smash. *Thunk, thunk...* A crowd of people turned into a bouncing pink cloud of arms and legs and faces. *Thunk, thunk, thunk.*"

Sally let out a little moan, picturing it despite herself.

"The fire was worse. The guys rushing in to help. The helicopter exploding, the flames dancing along the ground to engulf the cast and crew. The bodies flailing blindly to escape the fire that was everywhere, that was on their clothes and skin and hair. All the while, I stood there like an idiot, utterly frozen, unable to look away. I can't unsee it..." He shook his shaggy head again, and this time his eyes remained clear. "I swore I'd never stand by and watch again."

It all sounded so similar to the oath that had surged through Sally's mind when she thought her mother was in danger.

"Dan." She collected her thoughts. "I'm so sorry that—"

"Thank you."

"But you have to admit, what you're telling me is way off the deep end."

Though her mind flashed to Max saying, *I'll show you what I can do*, not long before aiming the camera to film Jim Foster getting pulverized by a truck.

Raphael Rodriguez, Jordan Lyman, and then Jim Foster. All dead in the past few months. Not to mention Max's indignant little dog.

All starting the day Max acquired the movie camera.

Sally frowned again, this time at herself. Her inner critic had tried to sabotage her before, but never like this. The whole idea struck her as ridiculous. Curses didn't come true, and cameras didn't murder human beings. Dan's theory sounded like the kind of crazy that was just audacious enough to be contagious.

She said, "I can't quit in the middle of an important production because you believe Arthur's camera has a black-magic spell on it. I have to finish the movie."

"I figured you'd feel that way," Dan said.

He reached into his hoodie pocket and handed over a bulky handheld radio.

"What do I do with this?" she asked.

"I'm working with a very large, tough-as-nails cop who knows what I know. While you're out at Bombay Beach, we'll be nearby at all times. The minute something bad happens, day or night, call us and we'll come running to get you out."

Accepting the walkie-talkie, she resisted the urge to laugh. Ridiculous.

Then she remembered Max saying, *Now you know horror like I do.* Like she'd received a wonderful gift deserving a high five. Like she'd joined a special club.

Sally didn't need Dan's dire warnings to feel more than a little honest fright where her director was concerned.

"I'll hold on to this," she said. "On one condition."

"Name it, my dear."

"You don't show up unless I call asking for help. Got it?"

He raised one hand and placed the other over his chest.

"We'll lurk in the shadows," he swore. "You have my solemn word."

Looking at her bedraggled former workshop teacher who'd quite possibly lost his marbles, Sally wondered how much his solemn word might be worth.

"I mean it," she warned.

"Scout's honor." He offered one of his most potent rakish grins. "So how have you been otherwise, babe? You're looking good."

"It's time to exit stage left, Dan. And no more stalking, or I'll hurt you."

"Okay, okay."

He shambled off, leaving Sally holding the radio and the ugly old book, which were either props for one man's private movie madness or instruments of salvation and evil. Watching the old actor go, she couldn't help but feel a little sorry for him. Mostly, though, she felt relief. At last, she was alone.

No loaded motherly visit. No more stalking by a possibly deranged ex-lover.

Soon, she'd be in the desert, performing in the ruins of Bombay Beach. Until then, she had a few days to relax, rest, and run lines.

And soak in that warm bath she'd been looking forward to all day.

First, she had one more thing to do. Something that had to be done if she wanted true peace, both the inner and outer kind. Another cross to bear.

Sally headed to the convenience store to buy potato chips.

MARTINI SHOT

That's what heroic stories do for us.
They show us the way. They remind us
of the good we are capable of.

Sam Raimi
Director, *The Evil Dead*

TWENTY-EIGHT

The mad circus was coming.

Max awaited its arrival, gazing west into the night while the sun burned the horizon behind him. He'd come early, driving his rented Winnebago through LA's bright arteries until they unclogged and dropped him into the desert's lonesome void. Always the same view, a pool of cooling asphalt in a dull yellow glare, the center lines winking in and out of existence in an endless cycle of light and dark, like film flicker. The same mesmerizing view that inspired him to create *Jack the Knife* during an insomniac drive all those years ago.

He'd come back to the Salton Sea and parked at a campground west of the old Atomic Age town built on its dead shores. Stepping out of the camper van, he caught a whiff of the chemical fog drifting off the sea. The moon had set. Wild dogs barked on the breeze. The bones carpeting the beach clicked on the shifting tide. An eastbound flight out of LAX passed in a soft roar overhead. The air had a chilly bite. The day would raise the temperature back above eighty despite it being mid-November, nearing the terminus of *If Wishes Could Kill*'s runway.

Max had arrived first, and for the moment, he basked, if not happy, then content. The dark reminded him of his childhood, all the late-night hours he'd spent glued to the TV with Dracula and the Wolf Man. Time lost in singular solitude, though he'd never felt quite alone with his monsters and imagination as company, and he'd always felt safe with things he could predict and control. Anyway, it paid for the director to be first on location and welcome everyone. It showed proper form and set the tone. If the director was a god on set, Max wanted them all to know he was an all-seeing god who kept score.

He spotted a glimmer of headlights on the highway. Then another, and more, blobs of lights in chained pairs, a luminous Morse message spelling *I, I, I, I*—

The rumble of heavy engines carried like a herald on the wind. A vast convoy approached Bombay Beach like an invading army. Though this was no army, of course, but the madcap circus, its players driving out of the dying night to greet the new day and make the impossible true. The first vehicles turned off onto Avenue A, the expanding lights glaring in Max's eyes, the engine snarl drawing the locals out of their beds to peer pale and wondering from their windows.

And what they saw—

Hollywood had come in all its saccharine, cheerful, and fevered glory. It arrived with its beautiful people and dream machines and tinseled illusion. It landed ready to deposit irritable technicians, needy talent, a deep hierarchy of sycophants, and a wide assortment of abused and sundry gofers. The circus had come to town to put on a show for all the world to see. The trucks and cars exited the cracked road one by one until the entire triumphal parade lay coiled in a cloud of dust across the campground like a vast broken serpent.

In the Winnebago, Arthur Golden's camera roared, though it didn't sound angry and demanding this time. It now radiated waves of a dark and hungry glee. Like Max, the occult apparatus had a trailblazing vision for this movie's third act. Like every camera, it emitted a psychic call to its owner to go forth and create.

As if scorched by the rising sun, the trailers stood fiery and glaring in stark contrast against pronounced leaning shadows. The last engine expired with a final puff of exhaust carried away on the desert breeze. Rodney screamed into his megaphone to get it done, they were burning daylight. The key grip and gaffer cracked their whips, and the great unpacking began.

Light stands, sun reflectors, and boxes of clamps collected in small mountains. Dorothy blessed the production with some hippie sage-burning ritual while the script supervisor chased a flurry of pages scattered by the wind. The crafties flung tables onto a patch of dirt and loaded them with bagels, muffins, and hot coffee. The honey wagons got set up downwind for when cast and crew needed to relieve themselves, not that the place's constant whiff of fishy rot could get much worse.

Max pulled his bucket hat over his thorny head. Time to work.

The first assistant director appeared in his path and raised a clipboard.

"Do you want to review the schedule, boss?"

"No," said Max. "I—"

"Shot list for the day?" Rodney produced another clipboard.

Max gave him the stink eye.

"Is everyone here?" he asked.

"All present and accounted for. What's your vision?"

"Call the troops together. It's time for a pep talk."

The assistant director's lips pursed in a barely suppressed smile. He expected this "pep talk" to involve a thorough ass chewing about efficiency. The clipboards disappeared to be replaced by a megaphone.

"ALL CAST AND CREW, REPORT HERE ON THE DOUBLE."

The crew shrugged, dropped whatever they were doing, and ambled over. The cast left their trailers. A crowd formed around the Winnebago.

"HOP TO IT, PEOPLE—"

Max swiped the megaphone out of the man's hand.

"Take five, Rodney," he said.

He stepped onto the Winnebago's front bumper and clambered up to the roof, where the whole production could see him. He hoisted the megaphone.

"Good morning, and welcome to Bombay Beach," he said. "We're at the midpoint now. In these ruins, our heroes will face old demons before they meet their maker. As for us, this will be our post until principal photography wraps. Our home for the next few weeks. Our hill to die on, so to speak. No doubt, the first thing you noticed about it is the smell."

Some crew members laughed. Heads bobbed in sour nods.

"If you're talent, I suggest you use it for your characters, as this is an unhappy place for them. As for the rest of us, well, we'll handle it like pros. Honestly, it's the least of our worries. This area has real hazards. Unstable buildings filled with rusty nails, mud, even feral dogs. Be careful. Do not horse around, go swimming, pet any dogs, or wander off by yourself. If you receive *any* injury, no matter how small, see your supervisor so you can get first aid."

His next sentence reached for gravitas only to come out a morbid chuckle.

"Safety first." He cleared his throat. "That's all I've got right now."

He handed the megaphone down to Rodney, who bawled, "If you have *any* questions, please see me! Remember, there are no stupid questions!" He seemed to consider, then added, "There are questions, however, that waste time on set!"

The crowd scowled back. Max brought his hands together in a loud clap.

"Back to work, everyone," he said. "Let's bring our masterpiece home."

Remaining on his perch, he watched the operation start up again. The second camera unit marshaled to score a few establishing shots in the morning sun. The prop master supervised the unloading of the same massive WELCOME TO LONELY PINES sign that Max had shot in Big Bear Lake. Unspooling cable, the juicers set up the genny to power the circus. Spence MacDougal ambled off to tour the ruins near the sea, judging angles and available light and where he could direct the viewer's eye. From atop the berm, soundman Frank Boston surveyed the shoreline and grinned at the natural soundtrack. A team of carpenters moved off to inspect the distant decaying buildings for basic repairs and supports to ensure they wouldn't collapse on the talent's heads.

Then Max spotted Sally returning to her trailer and suffered a sudden strange and unfamiliar longing.

He chafed to get on with the show.

This has to work, he thought.

For weeks, he'd dreaded reaching this stage of production as much as he'd longed for it. Because yes, it *had* to work. The killing of five cast members in a single night without anyone getting wise.

Until then, the wait was killing *him*.

He now had the will to complete his vision. He still wasn't sure he had the nerve. In this situation, success would be all or nothing. Any number of things could go wrong. The actors might not hold their marks, might flee, might even resist. A major technical failure with the lights, camera, or wireless microphones could cost him invaluable picture and sound. He might not have the stamina to empathize with all five actors. Just lugging around the gear by himself would be exhausting.

Believe in yourself, Arthur Golden told him every night. *Stay true to your vision. I was right about Jordan. I was right about Sally. I'm right about this.*

Even so, nothing felt certain, despite all his planning.

In his mind, his perfect movie continued to unfold, demanding to be finished, regardless of what it cost his sanity and health. It loomed far bigger than himself, bigger than all of them, a dark god whose birth required a grisly sacrifice.

As for the last night, it would arrive soon enough.

TWENTY-NINE

E*stablishing shots:*
The flat, empty sea. Bleached bones and dead fish heaped along the shoreline. A pile of tires, an ancient TV set, a boat half-buried in sand. Salt-crusted docks surrounded by seagulls. The empty drive-in. Decaying houses and rusting trailers, several shot using a Dutch or canted angle.

All of it slightly tinged with a sickly and unhappy yellow, the result of a color filter added to the camera lens. Even without it, this land has obviously been cursed. Some rapid environmental catastrophe, maybe. Biological apocalypse. Or perhaps something supernatural.

A sign planted in desert dirt: WELCOME TO LONELY PINES.

The last time we saw it, it had been set among a lush forest thick with evergreens leading up to a happy community built along a crystalline lake.

Now it stands corroding amid desolation.

Something eating the world.

Next to the welcome sign, another displays a skull and crossbones against a bright yellow field with the words CONDEMNED. WARNING. KEEP OUT.

Extreme close-up on a pair of feminine blue eyes wide with dread. The camera lingers before a pullback to reveal PENNY, played by Ashlee Gibson. Her face shines in the morning sun's key light. A single tear courses down her cheek. Her jaw quivers as she holds back far more than this.

The slow pullback continues, bringing MICHAEL, played by Nicholas Moody, into the frame. The gang's old leader. It was his idea to come here. Judging by his scowl, he appears to be having second thoughts.

Next, we see KATIE, played by Clare Byrne, and BRAD, played by Johnny Frampton, who gape in confusion at the wasteland. And finally JERRY, played by Bill Farmstead, and WANDA, played by Sally Priest.

Brad holds Wanda's hand, though she does not reciprocate its pressure. Unlike the others, she does not appear horrified, saddened, or confused. Her face is a mask of indifference, as if she expected this nightmare.

Her eyes, however, betray a cold, hateful fury at whatever did this.

They have come home to revisit the moment their world broke and they were flung into a far different one. They have all dreamed of it, their beautiful little village and the carefree childhood it offered. Now that they are here, Lonely Pines is still a dream, insubstantial and dissolving, recalled primarily as a feeling.

Today, they will dream again.

And become a part of the dream. Making it real until they realize all the years lived after this place had been the real mirage.

Here, they will sift through the detritus of their skeletal homes and favorite spots, discovering old toys and books and photos that ignite childhood memories witnessed as flashbacks. Together, they will revisit old crushes and feuds. Michael will try to force them to face their demons, only to be rejected as controlling and discover that he himself is broken. After telling Wanda he can fix her, Brad will admit he loves and accepts her as she is. Wanda will learn she is not alone and that sometimes, you go on simply to avoid making others suffer. Jerry will confess his life is not as happy as it looks, that he is struggling with suicidal ideation, and that he returned to Lonely Pines to destroy himself. And Katie will give up on Wanda and finally learn to put herself first as Wanda does.

In the dead ruins, a miracle will occur. They will never learn why their town marched into the lake to die, or why the land around it appears cursed. Still, these old friends will rediscover themselves and each other as adults, renew and reinvent their relationships, open old wounds, and heal.

Putting the worst of it behind them to make room for new dreams.

Leaving only Penny.

While her friends find closure and become complete, she refuses to participate. Racked by shame, she knows there is only one way to make this right. A singular path to redemption. Seeing herself as irrevocably damned and unfixable, she wants instead to fix the world. If she makes things right for all, she might accomplish the same for herself.

At last, she will reclaim the amulet in the dirt.

The ancient eye once again will flash open. It will swivel to see all.

As always, it will obey its master.

THIRTY

The director invited the cast to join him for dinner at the local Ski Inn so he could make a significant announcement.

Sally entered the restaurant buzzing.

On top of the world.

The cast and select crew grinned at her arrival. Even the grumpy MacDougal smiled. Sally looked for Max, but he hadn't arrived yet.

The restaurant had a campy visual flavor with its dollar bills plastered all over the walls, but it felt homey in its way, and in fact it was by now something of a home. She'd eaten here often over the past few weeks, as aside from the production's cafeteria-style catering tent there was nowhere else to go, with the next nearest restaurant being a twenty-mile drive. In many ways, Bombay Beach seemed like an isolated outpost on a desert planet far from galactic civilization.

Clare waved Sally to the empty seat she'd saved.

"I can't believe it's almost over."

"You did so great," Sally said. "You should be proud."

The server arrived to take her drink order. Sally skipped the usual Diet Coke and asked for a beer, whatever they had on draft.

Tonight, she felt like celebrating a little.

After four intense weeks of shooting, including eleven days so far in this desert, they all did. Their little low-budget horror flick had something special. Commercial but heavy on real drama and art-house vibes. An underlying integrity, a sense of confidence about being different from the standard fare. A lot of critics would likely hate it because it defied an easy narrative. A lot of viewers would likely hate it as it didn't spoon-feed to satisfy audience expectations.

Honestly, as a horror fan herself, Sally wasn't even sure it was *her* thing. But she felt mega proud of it. She'd given her best to this role, the kind of breakout performance that built reputations and opened doors to bigger and better things.

Not perfect, but really, really good. For all his flaws, Max had taught her that perfect wasn't an achievable goal. It was an idea that kept you fighting.

The moviemaking marathon had entered its home stretch. All Sally had left to shoot was her death scene, and then she could kick back. Despite Ashlee's roller coaster of sunny and stormy days and Max's erratic behavior, the production had run smoothly, combining the fun atmosphere of *Mutant Dawn* with the unified efficiency of *Razor Lips*. No union strikes, no flooding or earthquakes wiping out the sets, no actors booted from the cast, no producers responding to dailies by demanding massive script changes.

The cast had enjoyed the day off while the crew hauled gear and cabling into the ruins. The final scenes would be filmed soon, they'd put the martini shot in the can, and the production would wrap on schedule, knock wood.

"I hate to see the party end," Clare said.

Sally's beer arrived, and she took her first foamy sip. Perfect.

"Me too."

"I love you, you know. No joke. I've learned so much from you."

Sally smiled. "I love you too, Clare. You've taught me a thing or two as well."

"I love all these people, actually. Like, a lot. I'm gonna hella miss all this."

Sally understood that too. Every production ended this way for her. Weeks of intense tribal collaboration and zero-to-sixty intimacy, artificial but oh so real while it lasted, resulting in a lonely sense of hangover when it all finished.

"I know what you mean," she said.

"How do I go back to estate sales after *this*?"

"Maybe it's time to think about taking that leap of faith."

Clare laughed. "Perhaps it is."

Sally's eyes swept across the rest of the people drinking at the joined tables. Dorothy cackling over MacDougal's dry if sour humor. The key grip and gaffer, leathery crew veterans, playing it cool to let everyone know that even if they all believed this was Oscar material, it was just another movie to them. Ashlee flashing a flirty private smile at Nicholas, suggesting maybe she really did like him. Nicholas wearing his own impish smile that said he liked her too but liked himself more and reserved the right to play with fire just to watch something burn. The very cute Johnny Frampton, as always appearing lost but grateful to be alive and acting. And Bill Farmstead, the hunk exuding a calm confidence, who cast a warm, smiling glance at Sally that seemed to whisper, *Hi. I see you.*

That look made her tingle.

"Anyway, it's not over yet," she said. "So enjoy it while it lasts."

"What's next for you?" Clare asked.

"Another workshop to detox and level up, probably. Possibly a theater gig. Or maybe I'll jump straight into another film. It depends on what Louise has for me."

"I should get represented."

"You totally should. Is that what's next for you?"

"Yeah." Clare set her jaw in a determined scowl. "Hell, yeah. I will. Maybe change my look a bit to net a wider range of roles, new headshots, the works. But I was thinking, well…" Suddenly flustered, just as surprising.

Sally finished her beer, signaled for another. "What's up?"

"I'm hoping we can stay friends, that's all. Hang out. Tell each other about it when things are good. Have each other's backs when shit gets bad."

Sally grinned. "It's a deal."

A real promise. And not a contact, either, but a real friend.

She shot her own glance at Bill Farmstead.

I see you too. Hi, back.

He didn't react, but she could tell he'd noticed. They'd been playing this game ever since the production moved to the desert. Only looking. A little observing. Allowing the lovely tension to build bit by bit to some delicious future potential. It was all so much like her courtship with Hank, the gentle stuntman from *Mutant Dawn* she'd taken as her first lover.

Maybe she'd be bringing something home with her besides a new friendship and a solid film credit. She loved this part, where anything was possible.

For a moment, nothing else mattered.

Then the spell broke as the food arrived, and they all tucked into burgers and patty melts. At last, Max showed up gaunt and clad as usual in black, the T-shirt under his suit jacket declaring, I WANT MY MTV.

The production had continued to take a toll on him. His hair appeared even whiter than yesterday. The man looked like a vampire had been visiting him nightly. On set, he acted manic, the very atmosphere around him appearing to vibrate. Sally once caught him having a shouting match with his creepy camera.

Everyone noticed it, though they didn't seem to care. They were all invested in finishing the film. When Sally shared her worries with Clare, her friend shrugged and said Max acted exactly how she expected horror movie directors to be. Her agent, Louise, told her to focus on herself, shut up, and act like a pro. Johnny proved outright defensive, raving how Max gave him a chance and had showed a huge amount of interest in his grandmother. Only Nicholas proved a willing audience, devilishly suggesting she make a tell-all call to the *Hollywood Reporter*.

Tonight, however, the director appeared a changed man. He seemed to have reached a state of inner peace. Sitting at the table, he bit into his own burger.

"*Vampyros Lesbos*," Clare called out.

The hubbub faded to silence. Heads swiveled to the head of the table, where Max had seated himself. He chewed, took a sip of his Coke, and swallowed. He raised his napkin to dab his lips. Then he smiled at her challenge.

"Seen it," he said.

Someone had started this game the first night in the desert, and it had gone on ever since. Trying to stump the world's most hard-core horror cineaste by naming a film he hadn't seen.

Soon, everyone called out titles while Max whack-a-moled them.

"*Eyes without a Face*—"

"*Magic*—"

"*The Brood*—"

"*Multiple Maniacs!*"

"Child's play," said Max. "Is that all you got?"

The group broke into easy laughter. Showing off his encyclopedic knowledge of the genre, for each film, he identified the director, year of release, prominent actors, and a few interesting facts and bits of gossip about the production. Then, of course, he couldn't resist postscripting this information with his own critique.

Despite her worries, Sally couldn't help but smile along. Then she noticed a bit of ketchup on his jacket's lapel. It reminded her oddly of blood. Struck by an unsettling premonition, she shot a look at the door. Somewhere out there in the growing dark, she suddenly remembered, Dan and his cop sidekick kept their silent vigil.

If Dan is right about Max, she thought, *it will happen soon.*

The only scenes left to film were the death scenes.

Sally gazed again at the director. The red spot had turned back into ketchup. The banality of evil? She didn't think so. Max was a weirdo and leaned into his death fetish, and for weeks he'd appeared to teeter at the precipice of a nervous breakdown, but he hardly struck her as a killer. The bark may have been unsettling enough to keep you awake at night, but there was no bite.

"Now that I have your attention," Max began, and they all laughed again. "Seriously, I've seen every horror picture you could name. So many, it's convinced me there are no new horror pictures. Yup. It's all been done. Until now."

They listened, waiting for him to explain.

"If the dailies are any clue, this film is perfect. You're all perfect. I don't say this very often—and when I do I generally don't mean it—but this time I will and I do: *Thank you.* I could not have made this picture without you. I'm grateful to you. We aren't just making a motion picture. We're making movie history."

"Aww," said Ashlee.

Lighting a cigarette, Nicholas turned to Bill and murmured, "Call the cops. Somebody kidnapped Max Maurey and replaced him with his happy twin."

Dorothy clapped her hand over her mouth, holding back tears.

"Tonight, I have a challenge for you," Max went on. "A very interesting game we can play. Consider it a creative experiment."

He scanned their faces and appeared to like what he saw. They were up for anything.

"We're going to shoot the death scenes. Dorothy?"

The second assistant director handed out scene cards while Max went on.

"You may have noticed the crew running equipment into the ruins all day. The riggers set up a ton of lights, so many we had to crank up another genny. Now the crew is all leaving." He smiled at his crew leaders. "I struck a deal with these fine gentlemen that for one night, I'll shoot the death scenes handheld myself, with Dorothy holding the sound gear. A neorealist experiment I made time and set aside some film stock for. A shift into a documentarian feel."

MacDougal shook his head ruefully, showing what he thought of directors fooling around. No doubt, he regarded as it an expensive exercise in ego.

"What do you need us to do?" Bill asked.

"You'll all be wired for sound and placed at the bonfire in the ruins. Be on your mark at the appointed time, I'll shoot your death scene, and then you go straight to your trailer. My challenge to you is that you always be in character, even when you're off camera."

The actors chuckled as they pictured it. Sally frowned.

"Follow the scene card, particularly the blocking," he went on. "Stick to the lighted areas and stay in frame. Otherwise, play. Ad-lib as you need and give me your raw, uncensored feelings. This is a chance to immerse yourself in the film as an experience."

"What about me?" Ashlee asked. "I'm not dying."

"You can play too. We'll get some reaction shots at the end of the night."

"Goddamn straight I'm playing, Max. You're not leaving me out of this."

Sally said, "If we're 'dying' tonight, where is the special effects crew?"

Max replied with a patient smile reflecting his newfound inner peace. She'd never seen this jittery and uncomfortable artist displaying such contentment.

"I'm going to let you all in on a secret. The monster will be animated." While the cast guffawed, he said, "That's right, we're going to paint the monster by hand as shifting gray and black smears straight onto the film. Don't worry, it won't be cartoony. It'll look muddy, like living shadows. At sunup, the crew will return, and Bruce Candy is coming out from LA to do some terrific gruesome effects to polish off the death scenes. I'm sure you know his excellent reputation, how realistic his effects are. We'll do pickups then too, whatever doesn't work out tonight."

MacDougal drained his whiskey. "My prediction is none of it is going to work out. I have to admit, though, I'm curious to see the footage."

"I might just surprise you," Max answered. "Anyway, between reshoots and the effects, I figure we're only two days from wrapping principal photography."

Nicholas nodded. "Cool."

"Cool?" Clare clasped her cheeks in her hands. "This is going to rooooock."

The director gave Sally a knowing look. "The key is to have fun. Don't try to be perfect out there. Don't be afraid to make mistakes. Dig deep. Tonight is a night of artistic freedom and wild creativity. This is *your* night." He smiled again. "I want you all to act like your lives depended on it."

The cast erupted in whoops and cheers.

"Aww," Ashlee said again, sour this time. "I wish *I* was dying."

Nicholas patted her hand. "Bad luck, Ash."

Bill cast Sally a wink, suggesting tonight also might be the perfect opportunity to do their own improv scene in the ruins, after the shooting ended.

Something she could look forward to as a woman. As an actor, the whole game sounded like a perfect night of play. Max's vision struck her as ambitious but rational. Still, she balked again, as it didn't quite feel right.

"Max," Sally said in a quiet voice.

His eyebrows lifted.

She asked, "What camera are you planning to use for this?"

The director chuckled.

"I'm glad you asked," he said.

THIRTY-ONE

Night has fallen on Lonely Pines, appearing to erase it.

At the campfire, old friends face and share final truths. Words are spoken. Wounds open. Others heal. Anger, love, forgiveness. A few wander off for private thoughts or conversations or kisses, and then they start dying.

One, two, three.

Panicking, the survivors try again and again to escape. They use reason and emotion, their bodies and their minds. They stick together and then split up. None of it matters. The eye sees all, and being seen brings doom.

For these people, there is nothing to appease or outsmart, no revelation that offers redemption, no riddle to unravel to achieve salvation. The story has only one ending for them all. The dream has become a nightmare with just one exit.

But there remains a chance, however slim.

Penny unlocks a final memory and bolts into the night. With feverish desperation, she ransacks the ruins. On all fours, she scrabbles at the dirt.

And unearths the amulet.

Clasping it to her heart, she makes her wish.

It is too late.

She screams their names, which echo back on the wind.

The dead town lies quiet. Her friends are gone, claimed by the dark.

And she realizes it was her all along. Her shame killed her friends. The idea that she does not deserve love and redemption. The survivor's guilt—the deep feeling that she should not have survived—that she projected onto them.

Producing fresh anger at herself that she flings back to the whole world. Her wish has gone global.

Close-up on Penny's weeping face, which gradually twists into a menacing frown. The frown slowly, oh so slowly morphing into a hungry grin.

In the void, the eye flashes open, blazing with its own terrible light.

Music. Roll credits.

All this was supposed to happen. But the story is about to change.

THIRTY-TWO

The convoy crept down the road on rumbling engines and grinding gears, dust rising in a gentle boil. MacDougal nipped from his flask and wandered away muttering. Frank Boston exchanged a feverish kiss with Dorothy that almost toppled them over. The actors walked into the night, laughing and excited.

Max watched them go. Sally lingered long enough to toss him a scowl.

"Okay, Sally?"

She replied with a slow, thoughtful nod.

"Okay, Max."

Like an implied challenge being issued and accepted.

The next time he saw her, he intended to kill her.

The next time she saw him, she might not let him.

"Remember what I taught you, cuddlebug," the soundman told Dorothy.

The writer answered with another over-the-top kiss that made Max wince. When he turned back to Sally, she'd already gone. He'd see her again soon.

"I'll be fine." Dorothy grinned. "Now, get lost before I jump your bones."

Chuckling, Boston hustled off to catch his ride out of base camp. The vehicles rolled past in whiffs of exhaust. The last truck ground into the dark until a single pair of brake lights remained like the burning eyes of some nocturnal beast. Then they too were gone.

Max heard the distant bark of feral dogs chasing the convoy, snapping at the wheels. At last, the rumbling train swung onto the highway heading west, where a stroke of lightning flashed on the horizon.

The mad circus vanished.

And with its departure, the night of reckoning arrived.

Max cackled, giddy and terrified about what this meant.

"Are you okay, buddy?" Dorothy said.

His smile shifted to become his usual directorial scowl.

"Yes, of course. Never better."

Max did feel content. Free and at peace. Soon, the camera would reveal its power by giving him a private horror show. Tonight, like a miracle, his movie would begin making itself. For the first time in his career, he felt like he didn't have to control everything, or even want to. He could trust in the process, and by the end, he'd touch perfection, the closest he'd come to seeing the face of God.

The biggest thing he felt was pure relief. The biggest itch he ever scratched. Some tools call to be used, some things must be done, and until it happens, the world remains off-kilter and incomplete. He could now envision the finished movie playing in the theater of his mind, fully edited and scored.

So darkly beautiful.

Dorothy eyed him. "Okay. I think I've just never seen you, well, happy."

"Soon, you'll see why."

"Trust me, I already know. I get like this too when a story I'm writing is racing to the finish. The best high that money can buy."

They set out down the road. The moon hung low over the quiet, resting town. In a few nights, it would fatten to full again, and Max would return to the land of the dead. He'd explain every-thing to Sally, and she'd understand. He'd love his goddess of death, and she'd never leave him. Jordan would at last acknowledge him as an auteur, a genius of his craft.

And after, so too would all of Hollywood. Make that the world.

They reached the Winnebago, where he unlocked the trunk in which he'd stashed the Arriflex 35BL. The camera already packed a magazine loaded with a thousand-foot film roll, which would deliver a little over eleven minutes of shooting. The anamorphic lens and eyepiece adapter were also attached. He'd cached fresh film at each of the night's shooting locations along with spare batteries, fuses, and lubricant, which had cost him a pretty penny but would prove worth every cent.

The camera sang in his hands.

"Back in," Max murmured. "Moving on."

Dorothy appeared draped in sound gear and toting a boom.

"You're good to go?" he asked her.

"I am woman," she answered. "I can do anything."

"What's next for you when this is over? Back to fiction, I guess?"

"Ha! I don't know if that'll do it for me anymore, Max. I've got the bug. As a matter of fact, I've never had this much fun in my life. It looks like it shouldn't work, but it does. I even met a hot guy. I might just stay in the movie business."

"I'll write a letter of recommendation," he offered.

"You'd do that for me?"

"Dorothy, again, I know I don't say it often, but here it is: Thank you. You're a hell of a writer. It's been an honor bringing your story to life."

Beaming, the writer followed him into the dark. Aside from the actors' trailers, the campground stood empty again. No guitars plucking around the bonfires, no classic rock wailing on transistor radios, no roaring laughter as old hands told stories about various production disasters. Tonight, there was only the moan of the wind and the faint roar of a jumbo jet still climbing out of Los Angeles.

Lights blazed in the ruins fronting the beach. Thick sheafs of electrical cables snaked along the ground to feed power to the tripod-mounted Mole and bell lights at the locations Max had designated for the death scenes. The gaffer had wrestled an enormous quantity of amps to get it all running.

And here came Johnny Frampton, right on time.

To the actor's credit, he didn't acknowledge the camera but kept walking. Similarly, Max didn't speak, didn't yell *action*. He simply pressed the camera's start switch, producing a clicking whir.

Camera speeding. Sound speeding.

"Wanda," Johnny called out. "Wanda!"

He carried a family-size bag of Lay's Italian Cheese Potato Chips. Max wondered what Frito-Lay would make of their paid product placement after this movie released. His smile turned into a worried frown as he pictured the camera making Johnny choke on a snack.

Job done and all, but it'd be kinda anticlimactic.

"Wanda, are you here?"

The camera's motor hummed. The 35mm film clicked along the sprocket gears to enter the exposure chamber. The shutter opened, exposing an image, and closed, producing a single still photograph. A mechanical claw yanked the film forward, feeding the exposed length into the rear magazine. This process repeated at dizzying speed, the quartz-crystal control keeping the film running at a constant twenty-four frames per second.

A mirror shunted some of the light entering the lens into the viewfinder, where Max watched Johnny poke into the ruins of a house, stripped by time and the elements to a shabbily dressed wooden skeleton. Concealed bell lights illuminated the scene.

Wanda's childhood home. Brad had hoped he'd find her here.

Max spotted a few shards of broken glass still stuck to the window frames that winked in the light. A wood shard sticking out of the back wall. A jagged, skinny plank angling down from the ceiling. So many hazards...

His gaze landed on a nasty, thick shard of wood thrusting more than a foot out of the floor.

That's the one, he thought.

Johnny walked straight for it. Max held his breath.

The actor veered around the shard to stop by a tattered old sofa chair in the middle of the house.

"Wanda? Come on, baby, where are you?"

Max suppressed a grunt as he hauled the camera along to track the action. The Arriflex 35BL was marketed as a lightweight camera, and it was indeed relative to its blimped competitors, but it still weighed about thirty pounds.

"Wanda, I, uh..."

Johnny shot a nervous glance at the lens. He wasn't used to improvising and appeared afraid of saying the wrong thing. Max gestured at him to continue, say whatever, let it rip. He couldn't kill his actors in the middle of them flopping. It wouldn't serve the movie, but more than that, he owed them their crack at excellence. He wanted them to die at their best, doing what they loved most.

The least he could do. After all, they were giving their lives for this movie.

Johnny dipped his hand into the bag, produced a chip, and briefly studied it before popping it in his mouth. His teeth crunched down. Prior to *If Wishes Could Kill*, he'd done a few TV commercials, so this was familiar ground for him.

"Mm," he said reflexively.

Then his chewing slowed. He forced himself to swallow. As if the Italian Cheese potato chip served as a metaphorical stand-in for his selfishness toward the woman he said he loved, turning it into a bitter pill.

Then he did choke, only he choked back tears.

"I'm sorry," he whispered.

He lowered the bag and looked around, again realizing he was alone.

"Wanda. Goddamnit. Wanda! WANDA." His rage spent, he broke into another choking sob. "I don't think I can do this without you."

Raw emotion poured out of him. Johnny Frampton gave the performance of a lifetime. Max had no clue that all along, the kid had this in him.

I feel sorry for you, he thought.

Johnny often came across as vapid, but this didn't make him a bad person. In fact, the young actor was one of the most selfless people Max had bothered to get to know.

Every day, you care for your ailing granny, the woman who raised you. You work catering jobs to support you both, but it's barely sufficient. And she isn't getting any younger, is she? Every year, you told me, she needs more help. You can't afford to place her in a home. So you do your best. You wake up and give life your best shot and hope it's enough.

Surely, a tiny evil voice must whisper that things would be better if your granny were dead. But not in your case. The voice tells you that you'll be lost without her.

All the while, you keep yourself sane by believing that one day you'll win your lucky break. Then one day, it arrives like a stray bullet. A horror director making a movie. He tells you a cast member kicked the bucket and wants to know if you're available. He even offers to pay for a nurse to care for Granny during the shooting. Your dream is coming true, God at last answering a lifetime of prayer.

Who will look after your grandmother tomorrow, when you're gone?

"Ow!" Johnny cried. "What the hell?"

He gingerly raised his foot to expose an inch of rusty nail jutting from the floor. Hopping on the other, he leaned against the window frame to inspect the damage.

Straight onto a shard of glass, which sliced into his flesh.

"Jesus Christ, oh God," he howled.

Yanking his hand off the sharp glass, he backed into the wood shard jutting from the wall, which jabbed him in the ribs. The room seemed to be shrinking, crowding him with hazards. Blood poured out of his shredded hand.

"What? *Why?*"

Crying, he wrenched himself off the shard. Tripped on the nail.

And stumbled straight into the splintered end of the plank that angled down from the broken ceiling.

It entered his throat above the collarbone with a meaty crunch. For several agonizing seconds, he struggled with the shard of wood, which appeared unwilling to come out of him.

Johnny coughed a gout of blood. The room seemed to expand back to its original size. With a final shudder, the actor grew still, frozen in a standing position, arms slumped at his sides.

The camera lingered on him, soaking up the imagery.

"Whoa," Max murmured.

He was about to cut the scene when the actor stirred. Gripping the slim shank of wood, Johnny gently extricated it from his throat. He turned to Max and tried to talk, only to produce a gargle that came out in a bloody spray.

Pale, eyes rolling, he stumbled drunkenly backward.

Oh no, thought Max.

Johnny losing his balance—

No, not that, oh please—

The actor's legs gave out and he flopped onto his ass next to his chip bag.

Right on top of the nasty foot-long shard of wood Max had spotted earlier.

To his relief, it missed Johnny's rectum, though that didn't make the result any less horrifying. The splinter ripped through the actor's pelvic floor and popped out his abdomen, freeing a springy loop of intestine.

Johnny's face bulged in a rictus of agony. His high-pitched scream seemed to burst through his nose, eyes, even his ears. His body jerked and spasmed.

Then, at last, he stopped moving.

"Holy mother," Max breathed.

The horror of it. The real horror.

He'd finally bottled it in a movie, captured in ten thousand images imprinted on celluloid frames.

His technique had worked beautifully, just as it had with the Jim Foster screen test. He owed this success to Sally, who'd taught him how to fake empathy until enough of a glimmer of the genuine article bled through.

Funny, how it took him learning to kill with his cursed camera to get to know his actors as human beings instead of as varying combinations of annoying traits. Tonight, he saw them all as real people, people with real problems, neither all good nor all bad but a mix of the two and distinctly, beautifully human.

More, he regarded them as eager collaborators. Fellow travelers on an amazing journey into the unknown.

"And cut," he said.

Still holding the boom mic, Dorothy wheezed out a chuckle.

Max gritted his teeth. "What's so funny?"

"You scared the shit out of me!"

He didn't know what to say. "Well. Yeah."

"You said you weren't doing any special effects tonight. You had *me* fooled!"

"You were just surprised. You didn't actually think it was funny, right?"

"Well, for sure, it was powerful as pure spectacle," Dorothy said. "But just a little slapstick, though, don't you think?"

"Slapstick?"

"And the way he died with the potato chip bag right next to him. It's like a TV commercial from hell." She let out another grating wheeze.

"I'll fix that in post," he growled.

"It sure as shit looked real, I'll give you that! You're a magician, Max."

Someone called out from the dark: *Johnny?*

The voice belonged to Bill Farmstead.

Johnny, that sounded real. Are you okay? Holler back, buddy!

Dorothy handed Max the boom and entered the shack.

"What are you doing?" he asked.

She raised the clapboard.

"Don't you want to shoot end sticks to mark the scene?"

Then she looked down at Johnny.

I'm gonna come and check on you just in case!

Max scowled. Bill was leaving his mark. The wind picked up a little. Lightning flashed again. He had to keep moving. A storm would ruin everything. It looked like it would pass by Bombay Beach far to the south, but it concerned him.

Dorothy lifted her head to gaze at Max with wide, watery eyes.

"I don't understand," she said in a small voice.

"All along, you were hoping to see behind the curtain. You wanted to meet the Wizard."

He'd planned for her to carry the sound equipment through at least a few of the scenes, but he didn't mind taking on the burden early. In fact, he welcomed it. This part of the journey was one he'd always known he would take alone.

"I think he's dead, Max. Really dead."

Hang tight, Johnny. I'm coming!

"This is as much your movie as mine," he said. "We did this together."

"But he's..."

"I owe you for that. Now, drop the sound gear."

Understanding seemed to fall on Dorothy like gravity. She sagged under the weight of this dawning horror.

"Okay."

"You're finally going to find out where real horror lives, Dorothy. The shock or the grief."

"Please, don't..."

Max smiled at the camera and gave its enamel skin a gentle pat. Then he swiveled his burning gaze back to the writer.

"You'd better go now," he said. "And never stop running."

THIRTY-THREE

Nicholas flung an armful of wood onto the bonfire, answered by a bright whoosh of sparks and a bloodcurdling scream from the dark.

Sitting on her log, Sally blanched as it sank into her gut and twisted.

Clare said, "Whoa. That was Brad."

"Yeah," Sally murmured.

"I thought you cared about him."

"I do," she said, like a machine.

Struggling to process what was happening.

Another scream of pure agony crossed the night. This time, it landed in her gullet. She leaned forward, hugging her ribs to fight past a sudden urge to be sick.

"Jesus," Clare said. "What's going on over there?"

"Bullshit is going on," Ashlee said. "I scream better than that."

Nicholas sighed. "Come on, Ash."

"What?"

"Please stay in character. You're ruining the fun."

She sniffed. "Yeah, you want me to do all the work to warm you up for your big death."

Sally shot her a quick glare. Ashlee was about as supportive as a wet blanket. When she wasn't sneaking mental wedgies on her castmates before they walked on set, she worked the director to try to steal their scenes. During her scene partner's close-ups, she delivered her lines with the emotional heft of a robot.

In Sally's view, she offered the closest thing this movie had to an actual monster. To make things worse, judging by the sniffing, she'd inhaled a prodigious quantity of cocaine before coming to the bonfire.

Another sigh from Nicholas.

"We're supposed to be helping—"

"'Oh, please, Ash,'" she mimicked. "'Gimme a quick handy, I'm about to go on set—'"

His face turned red in the firelight.

"Seriously, I—"

A final scream, the loudest yet. The anguish so real it defied acting.

Sally looked toward the town proper, where a handful of windows were still lit up, their occupants awake. Surely, they'd heard it. But they'd do nothing. The locals had been warned that they'd hear screams all night.

"Oh." Ashlee's sneer evaporated. "He's actually really good."

Sally said, "Guys, I think he might be hurt for real."

If only Max hadn't told his cast he'd be shooting their death scenes with the very camera that witnessed the *Mary's Birthday* massacre. The same camera that filmed Jim Foster getting pulverized by a truck.

If it'd been any other camera, Sally could dismiss Dan Womack's breathless warnings as the ravings of a damaged middle-aged actor. She'd be playing right now instead of worrying about people dying.

A camera that kills people in freak accidents. A director using it during a horror movie. Actors happily walking to their marks to die one by one.

It all added up to the perfect massacre.

Written by Dorothy, Sally's scene card read:

WANDA, congratulations on reaching the end of your journey! BRAD walked off to find you in the ruins of your childhood home. He needs you way more than he lets on. You might just need him too—if you'd allowed it. Fate, however, has other plans tonight. Things that are out of your control, as much as you hate that!

Goal: After MICHAEL sets out to prove his leadership and determine BRAD and JERRY's fate, go to the DOCKS by the lake (near base camp) to let fate know what you think of it. How you reject its permanent imprint on you. How you will be the master of your own fate from now on.

Fate hears you, my love. It does. Only it has other plans…

No victory: The shadow will descend upon you and end your life. In the lighted area, you will find two rocks. Stay between them and give us your best death! Max and the camera will take care of the rest!!!

"Something doesn't feel right," she added.

"Nothing about this trip feels right," Clare told her, still in character. "But I'm sure Brad's okay."

"I'd better go check it out," Nicholas announced.

Jaw set in steely resolve, he stood. Then checked his watch.

"Crap." He wasn't due on his mark for a while yet.

Someone called out in the ruins. A male voice yelling to Johnny. Nicholas blew a sigh of relief.

"Jerry's got this. He'll find out what's—"

"Stop," Sally shouted.

They all stared at her.

"I'm not kidding. I think Johnny is actually hurt, maybe even dying."

"Brad," Clare softly corrected her.

"That's our Wanda," Nicholas chuckled. "Can't remember what man—"

"Quit acting!" Sally said. "I'm saying this is not a movie anymore!"

"Boring," Ashlee said.

Clare leaned toward Sally to hiss, "What's going on with you?"

"I just told you!"

"I mean you breaking character. Come on, play with me. It's all coming to an end. I want to go out having as much fun as possible."

Ashlee stood. "Screw this. I'm gonna go talk to Max."

Sally nodded. "Yes. Thank you. We should all go—"

"I feel like I'm at a birthday party where everyone is celebrating their birthday except me. I'm the star of this movie, and I should get to do something. All I'm doing is sitting around watching you guys have all the fun."

"Ashlee, don't," Sally said.

Ashlee laughed. In the distance, Bill shouted again.

"Look at you overacting," she said.

"What we should do is find Bill right now and get out of here. We're all in real danger."

"There it is. Can't act your way out of a paper bag. You're lucky the director is in love with you."

"We need—" Sally gaped. "Wait, what?"

"Even if you really believed what you're saying, *I* wouldn't," Ashlee told her. "Because nothing about you is convincing."

The actors gasped and fell silent. Even the snapping fire became subdued.

Sally fought back tears. Her vision turned red. What Ashlee said was the most hurtful thing anyone had ever said to her, strong enough to make her forget Max's murder spree for a moment.

"I'll leave you to your games," Ashlee said. "I'm going to go work."

Clare stood and cracked her knuckles.

"You'd better," she growled. "Before I beat your skinny—"

"Don't care," the actor called over her shoulder.

Sally stared after her until she disappeared in the dark, caught between wanting to save the woman and strangle her before Max had his chance.

Screw it, she decided. She'd tried. Ashlee could save herself.

Lightning flashed in the distance. Its faint blue light glimmered along the empty patch of ground where she'd last seen the woman.

"Are you okay, love?" Clare asked her.

"What?"

Nicholas eyed her with concern. "I'm so sorry, Sal. She didn't mean what she said." He considered. "Though that's half the problem."

Stop, Sally thought. *Just stop talking.*

She didn't care about any of this.

"I think Max is planning to kill us," she said.

Nicholas snorted. "Uh, yeah. We know. It's the whole idea."

"No. Please listen to what I'm saying. I mean, *really* kill us."

Clare reached to clasp her hand.

"You wouldn't be pulling a Jim Foster on us, would you, love?"

"What?"

Both she and Nicholas regarded her with another sympathetic look. They believed she'd run too far into the Method. They thought she couldn't distinguish fiction from the real and was maybe suffering a psychic break.

Were they right? Was she confusing this movie with reality? Which was more probable, that or Max had decided to kill off his actors with a cursed camera?

"No, I am not pulling a Jim Foster on you," Sally said. "I am dead serious."

In the distance, Bill roared in pain. The jarring sound wafted over the ruins like an animal roar of defiance, horror, and rage.

Then cut off with a sharp metallic clang.

In the ensuing silence, Clare and Nicholas slowly swiveled their heads to exchange wide-eyed stares. The truth apparently dawning on them.

Yes, Sally thought. *Now you see.*

"Whoa," said Clare.

"Yeah."

"I mean...Yeah. Whoa."

"That was really good," he admitted.

"Even better than Johnny's. The two of them set the bar right high, mate."

Sally groaned. Nicholas glanced at his watch.

"I'm up next," he said. "You just wait. You ain't seen nothing yet."

THIRTY-FOUR

At night, the old Bombay Beach drive-in looked even scarier than the horror movies it once played. Empty but for a few rusting wrecks facing a silver screen that hadn't shown a flick in decades, it *brooded*.

So patient, as if waiting for the movie to begin.

And if it awakened, carnival music would sound again from pole-mounted speakers while cartoon hot dogs and popcorn boxes leered from the screen. A psychedelic pattern heralding coming attractions.

And the winding countdown would start.

Five, four, three, two, *one*—

Letting his imagination roam free, Max finished mounting Arthur Golden's occult machine on a tripod. He aimed it at the grounds, whistling a happy tune. This space wasn't on his shot list, but he'd hauled over and jury-rigged a few bell lights to create an illuminated area near the tattered silver screen. He hadn't intended for this scene to happen at all, but fate had other plans, and with Frampton and Farmstead already in the can, he enjoyed being ahead of schedule.

He also hadn't intended to put the camera on sticks tonight, but lugging the machine around along with the sound gear had grown tiring. Otherwise, he liked shooting handheld. Sure, the result would look shaky and amateurish on a big screen, but so what. This was guerrilla filmmaking, gritty and raw, a home movie that turns into horror. He could picture a whole genre based on it.

And here comes my leading lady, Max thought.

"Action," he said softly.

Penny enters the frame, body trembling with electric terror, ready to bolt at the slightest threat. In the moonlight, her face glows beautiful and pale as it swivels in search of both enemy and sanctuary.

Like the silver screen, the surrounding darkness, emptiness, and stillness serve as a blank slate for what she fears.

The screaming stopped minutes ago.

She arrived here an angry young woman determined to fix her horrible mistake and make the world right again. The night stripped all that away. Now she is an animal being hunted.

Because the hungry thing she unleashed wants them all.

"Brad?" In a stronger voice: "Jerry?"

She winces at the sound she made. A classic horror movie error, calling out for your friends. Letting the monster know exactly where it can find you.

Still, she does not want to be alone.

Behind the viewfinder, Max watched, spellbound. He'd resolved to shoot these death scenes with the actors working at peak performance, and Ashlee Gibson did not disappoint. She was giving it everything she had and then some.

Oh, the plans I had for you, he thought.

After sacrificing the cast to the camera, Max had intended for Ashlee to join him on a grand tour of the mutilated bodies to score some juicy Final Girl reaction shots. After that, he'd have no choice but to creatively partner with her to gain her buy-in on finishing the film.

He'd pictured her sobbing to the police how the actors had disregarded the safety rules. How Nicholas had forced Max to keep shooting.

A perfect acting role for her, really, covering up a massacre.

Then Ashlee changed the script. She'd caught him by surprise while he loaded fresh film, calling out, *Max!*

Her voice electrified him with panic. Hands on her hips, the actor had glared at him from the doorway of the ramshackle ruin.

His eyes darted to Frampton's and Farmstead's corpses. Hers followed his gaze, narrowing as they took in the grisly scene.

With a disgusted huff, she demanded he shoot a scene with her.

Max stared at her. "You want what?"

"A scene, Max." Enunciating as if he were hard of hearing or stupid. "You're the director. I'm the lead. I want to do a scene."

"But you're not dying tonight," he told her. "We'll get reaction shots later."

"I'm sick of watching everyone else work while I do nothing!"

"Believe me, you don't—"

"We'll shoot now. I don't care what it is. We shoot now or I walk."

After a few quick mental calculations, Max smiled. It morphed into a fit of laughter.

"You're the star. Whatever you say, my dear."

This solved all the problems that had nagged at him throughout principal photography. With this elegant solution, he no longer had to sacrifice Sally. Last on the kill list, she would realize her dream of becoming a Final Girl, as long as he could keep her away from the lens.

It didn't hurt that he'd also escape Raphael Rodriguez's wrath.

"Good." Ashlee again regarded the corpses with disgust. "I thought we weren't doing makeup tonight."

"It was part of the surprise."

"You want a reaction shot while they're here? That shouldn't be hard."

"No, no," Max said. "I have something else in mind."

Ashlee aimed her trademark mischievous smile at him. "What's your vision?"

Penny's voice becomes a strangled whisper: "Anyone?"

Only the wind blowing off the lake answers her with its briny stink of dead things.

She says, "It wants us too. It won't let us go."

The terrible screams came from behind. She considers going that way to help, but the amulet lies in the opposite direction. Her face hardens with resolve as she digs deep, past the anger she always relies on, and finds an even deeper spring of strength she never knew she had.

Someone might have died out there at the end of that final scream. They all might be dead, leaving Penny alone with the thing that is hunting them.

But not her. She is not dying, not tonight. She is going to make it.

She is not charismatic like Michael, pure like Katie, strong like Wanda, or smart like Jerry. But she is tough. Tough as nails.

Fists clenched and unafraid, Penny marches off through the rusting hulks straight onto a moonlit patch of earth near the big screen—

"Cut," Ashlee called out. "Let's do it again."

Behind the viewfinder, Max blanched in a flash of white-hot fury that virtually blinded him. He stopped the camera.

"What's wrong?" he yelled back.

Ashlee pointed up at the sky, now filling with the faint aerosol roar of a commercial passenger jet clawing to full altitude out of LAX.

None of it mattered to him. This was the type of moviemaking where you mitigated what you captured as best as possible in post-production or you learned to live with it. That included ambient sounds.

No one yells "cut" except the director, he raged.

He said, "It's fine. Pick it up anytime!"

"Not 'pick it up,'" she shouted back. "I said I want to do it again!"

"Just pick it—"

"I'm doing it again! From the top!"

Camera rolling.

Ashlee Gibson is evil. She also isn't.

The whole thing is an act, actually, though over time the cocaine changed that. Over the years, her nasty habit consumed her until the act took over her identity. Deep down, however, she still has the same good heart.

It's all a very sad story, one he'd finally learned after weeks of patient probing into what makes Ashlee Gibson tick.

Years ago, doctors diagnosed her little brother with cancer. They warned the family he had perhaps months to live. Back then, Ashlee was just another hungry nobody, soon to win her lucky break in a lead role in an upcoming indie horror movie about a vengeful spirit named Jack.

She found herself facing a choice of doing the movie or spending time with her brother. A choice of changing her life or supporting someone she dearly loved as his own life rushed to its end.

Ashlee chose her career.

And she never truly forgave herself for it.

Now she sponsors cancer charities and gives as much money as she can. Ashlee Gibson might be a vicious player in the game of Hollywood, and Max and plenty of actors came to hate her guts. But to a whole lot of kids, she matters.

To them, she's a star.

The camera whirred on the sticks, eating film. Hands clenched at her sides, Ashlee stood in the light, a little off to the right so that the composition followed the rule of thirds, with the drive-in screen in the background.

"Max! Hey, I'm talking to you!"

"What?" he called back, stalling.

"I said we're shooting until it's perfect! All night if we have to!"

All the children will be crying when you're gone—

A flash in the ether, followed a moment later by a single cosmic boom.

Max assumed it was more lightning, but it wasn't. Some colossal thing in the sky ripped the air in its descent, producing a heavy *whoosh*.

He glanced up from the viewfinder to catch a spinning arc of fire and sucked in his breath in anticipation, knowing something wicked this way came but not what form it would take.

From the sound alone, he knew it'd be superb.

Ashlee pointed up into the dark.

"Hey! Max! What is that—"

He saw it tumble out of the black.

His mind blurting: *This is going to kill it in the movie trailer.*

The burning turbofan plane engine hurtled down like a meteor.

In an instant, the silver screen disappeared in a cloud of high-speed confetti. A moment later, the engine crashed into the earth with a heart-stopping *WHUMP* and skidded in a dusty avalanche straight into the screaming actor.

The camera jumped a foot off the ground. Ashlee splintered and vanished in the impact with two tons of fast-moving sizzling metal.

Then the engine kept going, rolling past to demolish a chain-link fence and cinder-block shack until at last it slid to a stop atop an exposed foundation.

Stones sheeted down in a crashing, crackling rain.

His heart still stuck in his throat, Max remembered to breathe.

Holy mother, he thought. Unable to say it out loud.

He got it on film. The whole thing.

Overhead, the passenger plane veered to either crash or make an emergency landing back at LAX.

Then the vast brown cloud surged over him.

Coughing on dust, Max said, "Cut!"

THIRTY-FIVE

The impact sent a tremor through the earth. The lights around the drive-in went dark. Like an evil portent, the moon dimmed and shifted to a murky red.

At the bonfire, the actors gaped as the sky rained dust and gravel.

"Um," Nicholas said. "What's going on?"

"Ashlee went that way," Clare pointed out. "Where that thing hit the ground."

"Ashlee's dead," Sally said.

No one spoke for a while. Then she told them everything.

Max wanting to make a perfect horror movie. His need to confront death based on the trauma of witnessing his father's fatal collapse at the dinner table. His obsession with the *Mary's Birthday* accident, which he'd hoped to study and whose impact he wanted to replicate. Finding the camera at the estate sale.

As she talked, the facts cohered into a grisly narrative. The people around Max dying in freak accidents. The camera filming the universe killing Jim Foster like a cat playing with a mouse before biting its head off. Dan Womack's warning.

The director isolating his cast tonight for the final death scenes.

The all-too-real screams in the ruins.

She left out Max thanking her for making it all possible. Sally still didn't understand that part, why she was so important.

Nicholas said, "Again, you're basically describing this movie."

"Yes," said Sally. "And the camera is providing the special effects."

He pinched the bridge of his nose and sighed. "A horror movie in a horror movie. First off, it's so freaking derivative."

Clare laughed.

"You're messing with me," he said. "This is payback for all the times I was a shit disturber."

"That is the simplest explanation," Sally said. "It's also not true."

"Or Max is trying out a new surprise special effects technique that went wrong. For all we know, some movie magic went south and Max and Ashlee are hurt."

"Another rational explanation," Sally said. "Also not—"

"All *right*. I believe you believe it. It's just hard for *me* to believe it, okay?"

She let him have that. She didn't believe it herself until only tonight.

"If the others are alive, they should be in their trailers now," Clare put in.

"If Max is after us, we'd never make it," Sally said.

"He's one man."

"All he has to do is aim the camera at you. That's how it works."

Clare let out a loud sigh at how ridiculous that sounded. Then raised her hand to prevent Sally from any more explanations.

"I believe you," she said. "What do we do?"

Sally tried to think. Instead, she pictured a horror movie audience shouting at her through the screen, telling her what obvious step she should take.

Nothing felt obvious to her.

One option was to ditch her companions. She could run into town and bang on doors or hide until the crew returned in the morning. Another horror rule: The game ends when the sun rises and there are plenty of witnesses around.

Sally couldn't leave Clare, though. Nicholas either.

Sticking together guaranteed safety, according to the rules. Only she didn't think the well-worn maxim applied in this case. No, she couldn't abandon them because she didn't want them to die. She'd fight for their survival as well as hers.

"I know what to do," Sally said.

"Yes," Clare said with an encouraging hiss.

"First off, we get some distance from this fire. Max knows we're here, and we need to give our eyes a chance to adjust to the dark."

"Lovely. Then we stomp his ass?"

"Then we wait," Sally said. "If I'm right, Max doesn't just want to kill us. He wants to kill us *on our marks* so it works in the movie. Nicholas, you're up next. If Max calls out to you to do your scene, then we *know* we have a problem."

"We'll also know where he is," Nicholas said. "So we can check the trailers."

And even when they found no one there, he'd still doubt. Sally let him have that too.

"Yeah," said Clare. "Or like I said, we stomp his ass."

"Are you nuts? You girls are going to get me blacklisted."

Max's voice reached from the ruins.

"Nicholas!"

"Let's move away from the fire," Sally said. "Now."

They hustled into the dark to huddle behind the rusted hulk of a trailer half-buried in dried mud. And waited.

"Nicholas, you're not on your mark!"

"Okay, that's weird," he whispered.

"Don't do it," Clare told him.

Even now, he edged toward the sound of Max's voice.

"Maybe he's just really dedicated," Nicholas said.

"She's right," Sally warned. "Don't."

"I won't," he said. "It's just...I was nothing when he discovered me. I was living in a van. You don't understand. I owe him everything."

"I owe him too," Clare said. "But I'm not dying for a movie."

"Fine. Whatever. So now what?"

"We get the hell out of here," Sally said. "Make a run for it."

"Our best bet is to separate him from his camera," Clare insisted.

Sally shook her head. It sounded far too risky.

"If you're right about all this, what else can we do?" the punk asked her. "There's one road out of here, and it leads to a single highway. There's one car left here, his Winnebago, and I'm pretty sure he has the keys on him. All he has to do is check every building and then drive along the road until he finds us."

"The crew won't be back until tomorrow," Nicholas said. "He has all night."

Sally had a solution.

"Dan Womack said he'd be camping close by," she remembered. "The radio is in my trailer. If we can make it there, I can call for help."

"What is some old guy going to do?"

"He said he's working with a cop. A very large cop."

Nicholas nodded. "That could work. Let the cop be the bad guy. We can find out what's going on and see if this is all a weird misunderstanding."

"You go," Clare told Sally. "Get help. Nick and me, we'll take care of Max."

"Um," he said.

"I'm with him," Sally said. "It's way too dangerous."

"We know where he is," said Clare. "He also doesn't know that we're onto him. This is our best shot at taking him out. Nick will show up and distract him. Max won't kill him right away. He'll give him time to get on his mark. Then I'll jump him, and we can get all this sorted."

Sally sighed. "Then I'm coming too."

"Goddamnit," said Nicholas. He clearly hated this plan.

Max called out again.

"I am very disappointed, Nicholas! Last chance. Back in or moving on!"

"Yell something back to him," Clare said.

"Like what?"

"Tell him you're on the way or something, I don't know. Improv, mate!"

Nicholas cupped his hands. "Max! Max, are you there?"

"I'm here, waiting for you!"

"What was that loud noise we heard?"

"Nothing to worry about! Get on your mark!"

"Sorry, I got lost! I'm heading over to you now."

Impressed with his acting, Clare raised her eyebrows in approval. Then she extended her long arms to crack her knuckles.

"Let's get her done," the punk said.

Clare had become the new leader of their little group. Sally had zero objections to handing over the responsibility. When it came to fearlessly confronting a bully and punching him out, Clare stood as the group's sole expert.

She pointed. "Sally, go right and get behind him. I'll go left. Nick, you walk straight up to him. Go slow. Keep him talking if you can."

A simple plan, the product of not having enough time to make one. Nicholas's pudgy cheeks pursed in a scowl as he lit a cigarette, scarfed a few quick drags, and flicked it into the dirt.

"You'd better be on your marks before I reach mine, or I'm dead."

"Don't worry." Clare grinned. "We'll be on him like a ton of bricks."

"Make sure you don't hurt him. Just get the camera away from him." He eyed Sally with distrust. "In case this is all a bad practical joke."

"I agree," said Sally. "Also, don't hold back."

They split up, breaking a horror rule while satisfying one of the genre's most venerable tropes, but Clare was right, it offered the only way to go on the offensive.

As Sally saw it, the camera had two key weaknesses. One, its single eye restricted its view. And anamorphic lens or no, it lacked peripheral vision. Besides that, it was operated by a director who could be fooled or distracted.

She crept into the dark, orienting herself using the blobs of light illuminating patches of ground and several of the derelict structures. Nicholas yelled at Max from the darkness somewhere on her left.

Sweat trickled down her back, following the wire she wore for the lavalier mic clipped to her blouse. She'd forgotten she was still wired for sound, ensuring her assault on her director would be recorded for posterity.

Another yell. Max answered, sounding closer now. Nicholas was walking too fast. She had less than a minute to circle around her maniac director.

Breaking into a sprint, she found herself behind the remains of a house, which stood in a dangerous lean close to final collapse.

I'm in position, she thought with a delicious thrill. It turned into crippling nausea as she understood what this meant.

If I survive this, I'll never look at stage fright the same again.

Stage fright was nothing compared to what she felt at this moment.

She wanted a weapon. The house offered her one in the form of a wood slat protruding from its splintery skin. A lath, a flimsy four-foot slab.

Sally wrenched it free and gave it a test swing. The stick would likely break on impact, but it'd make a painful statement.

And if it breaks, I'll stab the pointy end through his heart.

Wait, what?

Would she actually kill?

Sally was angry. This was the anger talking. Better anger than fear, though. If her fear found its voice, she'd end up paralyzed, and her friends would die. Either way, she felt far safer holding a weapon.

"Okay, Max, I see you," Nicholas shouted. "I'm here!"

The director said something, but Sally couldn't hear it.

She tensed to spring. Then she realized what was wrong. Both men sounded too far away.

Sally had run too far and stood behind the wrong house.

"All right, girls," Nicholas cried in the distance. "Now!"

As she rushed toward the sound, she heard the pounding of receding footsteps.

What the hell? He was *bolting.*

"Wait," Clare yelled. She also hadn't gotten into position.

"Ah, Clare," said Max. "So wonderful of you to join us."

By the time Sally reached the house, they were gone.

THIRTY-SIX

Sally did not like being alone.

Not because she'd be any safer with the others, but because their presence prevented her from succumbing to terror altogether and losing her mind.

The plan had failed miserably. The plan they'd reasoned out as their best option. Simple, only it also happened to be very dumb. Again, Sally felt like she was living one of her horror movies, where people made dumb decisions all the time. She could now appreciate why they did—because they were young people filled with existential terror and not highly trained Special Forces operatives.

Think, she told herself. *Take a—*

A crashing sound near the sea made her jump. Sally took a step toward it, opening her mouth to call out for Clare but stopping herself in time.

No, she thought. *Take a moment and think.*

Being alone offered one advantage: a broad latitude of options. The only problem was they all sucked. She did know not to rush around blindly.

Think of it like a scene.

Goal: She wanted to help Clare and survive the night.

Obstacle: Max would be waiting for her.

No victory: The director would hit her with the world's biggest jump scare, and the last thing she ever saw would be the gaping lens of Arthur Golden's camera.

Okay, now change the script.

The Final Girl triumphed when she stopped seeing herself as prey and transformed into predator. That idea had already flopped, but the main thing was to avoid playing Max's game and play her own.

Then play to win or die trying.

Wheeling, she ran toward the trailers standing dark at the campground. She'd radio Dan and his cop friend for help. That was the best way to save her friends.

Passing a ruined house, she froze midstride.

Did a double take.

And forced back a horrified scream.

In a grisly tableau, Johnny Frampton sat slouched with his legs spread in front of him, as if some precariously balanced force kept him sitting upright. His head slumped with his chin resting on his chest, and for a moment she pictured him raising his head to grin at her with glowing eyes.

But Johnny wasn't about to do anything. Surrounded by a veritable lake of dark, congealing blood, he remained still as a statue, stone dead. A glistening loop of intestine peeked from below his oddly bulging shirt. A bag of potato chips rested upright near his left foot, placed like a midnight snack offering to anyone who might swing by.

Sally took an instinctive step back, fighting the urge to retch. Out of the corner of her eye, she spotted someone staring at her.

Bill!

She swung toward him. "You're alive—"

What she saw didn't make sense. He seemed to be in two places at once, and her similarly fracturing mind couldn't put it together.

His body lay on the floor.

While his head stares at me from a dusty old sofa chair.

Eyes like cold blue marbles.

Staring and staring but forever unseeing.

Eyes that had seen her as a woman only hours earlier over dinner. Eyes that had brimmed with life and flashed with youth. Eyes with which her own had exchanged glances loaded with meaning and exciting potential.

Now they saw nothing but eternal darkness.

"Not me," Sally said, and blanked out.

She revived to the sound of shouting in the ruins. Another crash. Clare and Max were fighting an all-out battle.

I have to do something.

She couldn't remember what it was. Her mind teetered on the precipice of flooding. If it did, she'd turn inside out, living entirely in her head.

While in the real world, she'd be paralyzed and helpless. Easy prey.

It's not me, Sally thought. *It's not me—*

The scenery changed. The trailers appeared around her. She shambled along, dragging her feet one step at a time like a zombie, propelled by this mantra.

Not me, not me, not me—

Wake up, girl.

"Goal," she mumbled. "See if the Winnebago has keys."

Maybe Max left them in the visor, and she'd get lucky. She could drive out of here. Floor it all the way to her apartment, where she'd hide under her blankets for as long as it took to process the horror she'd witnessed.

Not without Clare and Nicholas, though. She had to figure out a way to find them before Max killed them both.

She reached the Winnebago and opened the door.

No victory. That left the radio.

Dan, you'd better answer the goddamn phone.

She mounted the short steps and yanked open her trailer's door.

An apparition raised a pair of scissors to strike—

Sally smacked it in the face with the stick she still held in a tight grip.

"Ow!" Nicholas rubbed his cheek. "What the hell?"

She hit him again.

"Ow! Ow! Quit it, Sal! I'm on your side!"

About to whack him again, Sally lowered the stick. It had felt satisfying to rediscover her anger, so much healthier than terror's numbing toxins.

"What are you doing in here?" she said.

Smoking up her trailer, from the smell of it.

"If Max killed you, I didn't think he'd look for me here. I couldn't lock the door, though. It's busted."

Max had thought of everything.

"Why?" she demanded.

Nicholas glared back. "I like living. I don't know if you saw Johnny and Bill on the way here, but I don't want to end up like them."

She tightened her grip on the stick. "That's not a real answer."

"Fine! If Ashlee's dead, one of us would wind up being the Final Person. I figured if you and Clare got him, then mission accomplished. If he got you instead, I'd still win."

"It's the Final *Girl*, Nicholas."

"Don't be sexist, Sal," he scolded. "Anyway, while I walked over to meet him, I kept thinking what a dumb plan it was. I mean, you and Clare didn't take him out, right? If I hadn't made a run for it, I'd be dead now."

Sally opened her mouth to shoot him down but closed it.

Because he wasn't wrong.

"There is no final anything," she said. "He might be planning to subvert audience expectations by killing us all. Did you think of that?"

"Well, then we should stick together, don't you think?"

"Why? So you can push me in front of the camera and make a getaway?"

"Of course not." Nicholas huffed with indignance.

His performance was so convincing, though the calculating glint in his eyes betrayed him. Even if he hadn't planned to use her as a human insurance policy, he sure as hell imagined its wonderful possibilities now.

Sally eyed him with a quiet, seething fury. She thought about whacking him a few more times with the stick just because it felt good, but she had things to do.

"Break a leg, Nicholas," she said.

"Wait! You're leaving me here? What are you going to do?"

She reached into the closet and yanked the lid off a shoebox to expose the handheld radio. "I'm calling for help. Don't touch my shit while I'm gone."

Returning to the brisk desert night, Sally let the door slam behind her. She switched on the radio and mashed the talk button.

"Uh, Dan? Dan, are you there?"

White noise.

"Dan, answer me, please."

Nothing.

She slowly lowered the radio. "Oh."

They were on their own.

The radio burst to life.

"Sally!" Dan's voice. "Sally, is that you?"

Relief and terror poured out of her in a tearful flood.

"Dan, he's killing everyone, I'm so scared, you were right, I need help!"

"What's your ten-twenty?"

"I'm at the trailers! The campground west of town, by the beach."

"Hold tight, my love," said Dan Womack. "The cavalry is on the way. McDaniel and I are coming to rescue you. It's all going to be over soon."

THIRTY-SEVEN

Stay put.

That's all Sally had to do now to survive. Help mere minutes away.

A piercing scream electrified her.

"Clare," she breathed.

The sound had come from an abandoned house on the beach, not far from the docks where Max had slated Sally to die.

She knew if *she'd* been the one screaming, Clare wouldn't think twice. The punk would charge in swinging her fists. But Sally wasn't her.

She also wasn't Nicholas. Her life may have been of paramount importance, but so was all life, and Clare's stood near the top of the list.

It's pointless, she thought, hearing again the voice of her inner critic, which she hadn't heard from in weeks. *You already let her down.*

If Clare screamed, she was already dying.

It didn't matter.

Without another thought, Sally raced toward the sound. She stuck to the dark, her sneakers pounding the sand. The house glowed with portable lights.

No sign of Max.

Sally heard a groan. She stopped in her tracks, her eyes flooding with tears.

"Oh no…"

The woman sat wincing on the floor, transfixed by steel rods.

Against all odds, she lived.

Sally sank to her knees and took her hand.

"Clare? Clare, it's me, Sally. I'm here."

Her friend grimaced as she lifted her head, as if even this much effort imposed an agonizing cost.

"Almost got him," Clare gasped.

Already pale, her face had turned a ghostly white, breath cycling in shallow gulps. The glistening rods appeared like unnatural growths, a part of her. The bloodstains on the shirt under her leather jacket expanded.

"You're going to be okay," Sally said. "Dan is on his way."

Clare winced again. "Just run."

"I'm staying here with you until help comes."

No one should die alone.

"He's…"

"You got him," Sally said. "You messed him up good."

Calling on all her acting skills. Wasn't this what one did, according to the movies? Tell comforting lies to ease the pain of departure?

She added, "Max won't be able to hurt anyone ever again. You'll get help, and everything is going to work out."

"No, listen—"

"We're going to stay friends. Isn't that what we agreed? Maybe we'll find a place together. I'll help you run lines, we'll share everything, and we'll climb the ladder together until we can see it all. We'll go to the top of the world. We'll be stars."

None of it a lie. She meant every word. Easing her own pain as well as Clare's.

The woman gaped at her. "He's…he's…"

"Shhh," said Sally. "Don't talk."

"Behind you."

"Action," said Max.

She wheeled to see the director lurch into the light, a creature no longer quite human but a chimera of camera, tripod, boom mic, and recording devices.

She looked back at Clare. The woman's head rested slumped to the side. A trickle of blood spilled from her lips.

Springing to her feet, Sally ran for her life.

The movie camera whirred.

Then a whooshing roar filled the house, the angel of death.

Oh my God, holy shit—

Nowhere to go. She'd trapped herself.

She darted toward the back of the house, where a partition wall stood despite all that nature and time had thrown at it. A door set in the wall promised sanctuary. Gripping the knob, she pulled, only it didn't budge.

Sally hurled her body against it. The door toppled over in a crash, and she tumbled down with it.

Scrambling behind the wall, she huddled quaking on the floor.

If the camera can't see me, it can't kill me—

More nonsensical movie logic, but it was all she had.

Only, the wall dissolved, sections of it punched wide open in sprays of plaster, revealing Max leering maniacally over the viewfinder.

The door. Standing, she raised it to shield herself as something heavy cracked against it. Digging in her heels, she held fast.

A hail of objects pelted it in jarring thuds. Inches from her face, the points of nails peeked through the wood. She whimpered as they began to wiggle like worms, fighting to free themselves and penetrate her flesh.

Sally staggered back under the constant assault.

Even the floor appeared to be moving. Something rustled at her feet. She looked down in blind terror and revulsion to discover the earth seething.

Oh, she thought. *Oh no, oh God*—

Dozens of scorpions and snakes carpeted the ground, scampering and slithering in a heap that heaved across the dirt and scrap, spilling toward her—

The camera. It could see her *feet.*

Sally slammed the door down, producing a wet crunch.

The machine still wanted her dead. Sheets of dust cascaded from the crackling ceiling as its hungry gaze searched for her. A wood lath struck her arm and left a stinging echo of splinters. Another fell against her shoulder, only this one carried a nail that dug in and opened her flesh like a zipper. Something heavy raked down her back in a fiery trail of pain.

The house itself had begun collapsing on her. The boards and slats pounded down like repeated blows from a baseball bat. Gritting her teeth, she fought the pain with everything she had as her body crumpled into a quaking ball.

This is the end, no way out—

"NO," she cried. "STOP, MAX. PLEASE STOP."

Like a miracle, he did.

The destruction came to a sudden, palpable, gorgeous end. Sally lay trembling in the wreckage. Her body battered, her mind worse off, flooded with terror and suffering so acute that she could barely think straight. She struggled even to breathe.

"The story needs a Final Girl," Max said.

Sally didn't answer, too scared to call attention to herself, willing her very body to disappear. Her mind turned inward, a landscape of pretty swirling colors.

He added, "But a Final Boy would do."

Boy? What is he talking about?

"A nice subversion of audience expectations," the director said. "In the end, we see Michael, the leader the group rejected. He couldn't save his old friends. But he discovers the amulet, ends the curse, and wins redemption."

"Nicholas," Sally managed.

"That's right."

"I don't understand."

Max sighed.

"I'm offering a choice of him or you."

"But he's in the trailer," Sally heard herself say.

"Which one?"

She shook her head in confusion and said nothing, certain she'd made some crucial mistake.

Max chuckled. "Honestly? A part of me prefers a Final Boy. I couldn't find a single thing I actually liked about Nicholas Moody, and believe me, I dug deep. The kid is a born survivor because it's uncertain a real Nicholas even exists."

None of this made sense to Sally.

Don't do it, her scrambling brain blurted. *Don't tell him anything.*

"That's okay," said the director. "I'll track him down. Stay here, and then I'll come back and we can shoot the coda. With a different camera, of course. Don't worry about that." Another chuckle. "Wanda, the Bad Girl, the survivor. The girl who lived. The fighter who became a Final Girl."

"You can't hurt him," she said. "He loves you. He was living in a van when you cast him. You gave him a life."

"I had no idea. That's very useful. Thank you for me telling me, Sally."

Then quiet returned. He'd left.

Light-headed with terror or blood loss, Sally still refused to move. Every bit of her hurt from the beating she'd taken. Stars popped in her vision.

He'll be back, she thought. *To anoint me the Final Girl.*

All that mattered to her was she'd go on surviving.

Then she remembered why.

"Oh God," she groaned, adding shame to her damage list.

Nicholas.

Max and his murderous camera were headed his way. She couldn't just let him die. It was this kind of every-man-for-himself thinking that allowed the director to win. They needed to fight for each other.

She needed to correct her mistake.

Meanwhile, Dan was coming. She only had to fight a little while longer.

Sally took inventory of her body. She cataloged a patchwork of cuts, scratches, and splinters all throbbing with hurt. Her fingers came away sticky with blood. She suffered, but she could still move.

Could still fight.

Sally wasn't strong like Clare or crafty like Nicholas, but she had one simple thing going for her: She was willing to try.

In fact, her survival wouldn't mean much if she didn't.

She'd lost her stick during the nightmare, but it didn't matter. The house was literally made of sticks. They protruded everywhere from the rubble in which Clare now lay entombed. She selected a thin slab of wood and hefted it. This one wasn't flimsy at all. A formidable club. She felt strong again.

I'm ready, she thought.

Setting her aching jaw, Sally took a step toward her destiny—

And froze, unable to budge another inch.

She'd always thought the Final Girl had been aptly named, as the audience ended up thinking, *One of the characters is Finally not acting like an idiot and is Finally doing something.* She now understood how hard that is for the Girl, especially after she has seen the monster's power.

A movie wasn't anything like real life. All the experience in the world didn't prepare you for the brute shock of real horror. Horror the way Max understood it. Yes, Sally had toughened up over the past few months. She'd suffered real things for the first time in her life, and they'd made her stronger. She'd sworn that next time she faced horror she wouldn't freeze up, and she'd act.

But this...

This electric, paralyzing fear. She might not want to live with herself if she did nothing, but she felt absolutely certain that she didn't want to die.

Sally wasn't actually the Final Girl, though. That wasn't her character. She wasn't the Bad Girl either, not really.

She was Sally Priest, and she was doing this.

The most challenging role of her life. Gripping her club, she stomped across the wreckage and returned to the night.

THIRTY-EIGHT

Leaning on her club, Sally hobbled through the dark, following the splashes of light leading back to the actors' trailers standing at base camp.

I'm coming, Nicholas, she thought.

No plan this time, only a fierce determination to end this nightmare.

Reaching her trailer, she grunted up the short steps and gripped the handle. From inside, she heard Nicholas begging for his life.

"I told you," he howled. "Sally went that way! Take her!"

Sally's hand froze. Only for a few seconds, but it was enough.

Max murmured his incantations.

She flinched as something heavy struck the wall with a resounding boom, leaving a bulge. The trailer shuddered at the impact and kept on shaking as everything inside, everything Sally had brought with her to the desert, tumbled around to crash against the walls. Everything plus Nicholas.

The battering stopped. The rocking trailer resettled on its tires.

She was alone now, in every sense of the word.

Turning, she limped back to the beach. Dan and the cop were on the way, but she didn't care about being saved anymore. The show must go on, but it always concluded. Max's movie needed a final battle between good and evil, and she'd deliver. Spotting a splash of light near the shore, she headed toward it.

The place her scene card had planned for her to die under the all-seeing eye.

Outside the pool of illumination, Sally gazed out at the Salton Sea glittering in the moonlight. Water lapped at the piled bones. Reduced to posts, the docks jutted from the sea like giant deformed teeth.

Max called out for her, and she heard her stage name escape with the wind across the waters. As for her battered body, it stayed put a moment longer, and then she pivoted to return to the light.

Lightning flickered across the scene. Thunder rumbled to the southwest.

"I'm on my mark," she said.

The director huffed into view grinning.

"That was amazing," he said. "What a crazy night!"

"Amazing," Sally echoed in a dull voice, leaning on her stick.

"*You* were amazing."

"I was...?"

"The performance of a lifetime. I couldn't have done it without you. You brought my vision to life. Sally, we just made the perfect horror movie!"

The director shed the equipment he'd been hauling around all night. He planted the boom microphone in the sand and tossed aside the tripod. Cradling the camera like a football, he managed a stretch.

"Yup," he groaned. "It's a young man's game."

"So, what happens now?" she asked.

"Now we get the other camera and shoot the coda. I know you're probably in a lot of pain—" He inspected her torn clothes, bleeding scrapes, and the rat's nest of splinters in her hair, and pulled a face. "But we can use that."

"I'm up for finishing the movie," Sally said.

"Of course you are, you're a pro. We finish the movie, we tell the police a story, and then we get our perfect movie cut and distributed. Me? I know I'm finished as a director after this. But for you, the sky's the limit now."

She stared at him in wonder. Just minutes ago, he'd leered at her while she'd fought a losing battle against cosmic forces. She'd witnessed his bloody work, the other actors pulverized or left punctured and bloody and headless.

The entire cast massacred.

Now here he was, talking as if they hadn't been adversaries all along but instead willing collaborators on a grand creative project.

"Okay." Sally hobbled toward him. "I'm ready to finish it."

Raising the stick, she whacked him across the face.

"Hey! What—"

She bashed him again.

Then again, laying into him with everything she had left in her.

At last, the camera fell to the sand. Still, Sally didn't stop, swinging until the director dropped to the ground cowering and sobbing.

Sally flung the stick aside and picked up the camera. He made his own grab at it, but she kicked him back into the dirt.

"No, please," he said. "If it's broken, they'll all die, really die—"

"I'll be careful," she promised.

Then she aimed the lens at him.

Cupping his battered face, he blanched in terror. Blood poured from his nose.

"Don't! I'm going to make you a star!"

"Maybe," said Sally. "Either way, you're going to pay for what you did."

Killed by his own camera. Pure horror justice.

She pressed the start switch.

Arthur Golden's occult machine whirred to life and fixed the director in its malevolent gaze. The film started rolling.

Crying out, Max flinched into a quivering ball, arms covering his head.

Nothing happened.

Slowly, he lowered his arms.

"Oh," he said. "I see."

Almost like he'd been hoping for a different result. Frustrated, Sally ignored his reaction, focusing her will into the viewfinder.

Do it, she raged. *Do it before I lose my nerve!*

Behind Max, a police cruiser roared into the frame, lights strobing. Dan had finally arrived. Like in a movie, the cavalry showed up too late. But unlike in a movie, he'd also come too soon, as the monster had not yet been destroyed.

Come on, you piece of shit. Work!

Dan jumped out of the cruiser. A giant cop charged out the other side, weapon drawn and ready to shoot.

Dan lunged toward her, arms outstretched. "Sally!"

Please, just give me one more minute!

"Dear Sally—"

The world turned white, accompanied by the loudest boom she'd ever heard. A wave of electric shock crackled through her body and left it quivering.

Dazed, she saw Dan Womack belly flop out of the air like a flaming rag doll.

In the aftermath of the lightning strike, an awful ripping sound. Snarling.

The cop's pistol cracked in a deafening report once, twice. Then he disappeared screaming under a pile of wild dogs.

Watching in amazement, Max shook his head.

"There go both my nemeses," he said.

Sally winced at the camera. She wanted to fling it into the sea.

The director turned back to her.

"You're a real natural with it. But you don't know how it works. Give the camera to me. Hand it over, and we'll finish the movie together. You'll own Hollywood. You'll have everything you ever wanted."

"Screw you, Max."

His bruised face darkened. He pulled off his bucket hat, revealing his wild hair, which during the night had finally gone almost completely white.

"I still have Ashlee's coda in the can," he said. "I'll have to leave the plane engine scene on the cutting-room floor, but the story will still work."

Planting his hands on the dirt, he started to rise.

"Stay back," she warned, aiming the camera at him again.

The director appeared immune to its effects.

"I mean, I can always put it in a bloopers reel," he said.

Sally's gaze darted to the cop lying in a ravaged heap next to his strobing cruiser. The dogs had scattered. The man's gun lay on the ground nearby. She'd never make it in time. Max would catch her first.

She didn't need a gun, though.

She raised the camera over her head.

"I'll smash it to pieces."

Max's eyes widened. He settled back onto the sand.

"Please don't do anything we'll both regret."

"Stay right there."

"Look. I'm not moving."

"Good."

"Good," he echoed. "So, what now?"

She'd missed something. Some secret sauce that powered the movie magic.

What was it?

"Jeez, this angle," the director murmured. "At this angle, you're a goddess."

"Shut up, I'm thinking."

"I love you, Sally."

"You what?"

"I think I did ever since I met you at the premiere party. I've never encountered a human soul that so fully embraces being alive. The camera didn't inspire me. You did. Everything I did in this film, I did it for you."

"Oh," she said in surprise.

Sally understood.

Max asking her to teach him how to develop empathy in acting. Max thanking her after Jim Foster's death for making all of this possible.

"You were always the Final Girl to me," he said.

To end this, she'd have to act again. Act like her life depended on it.

"But I'm not, Max," said Sally. "I'm the Bad Girl."

She summoned everything she knew about acting like a superpower she'd spent a lifetime cultivating and was now ready to unleash upon the world.

"We could have it all," he said. "You might even learn to love me back."

"I do," she said.

Max brightened with an eager, hopeful smile.

"You do?"

Sally pressed the start switch again.

Camera speeding. Film rolling.

"I love you too, Max."

The cosmic roar surged all around them, the angel of death descending.

The ground dissolved under the director. He sank into the earth, his face morphing between joy and despair like ancient Greek theater masks.

Then the sinkhole collapsed, and Max Maurey disappeared.

The sand poured into the grave and filled it. Silence returned to Bombay Beach. Sally sighed in the sudden stillness.

Her fight was over.

As for *If Wishes Could Kill*, it had finally wrapped.

But there was still one thing missing. Something important she'd forgotten to do. Had intended to do all night, but she'd never had the perfect chance.

Balling her fists, Sally screamed across the black sea.

RELEASE

Horror is as healthy as eating carrots.
It's therapy for the human condition.

Max Maurey
Director, *If Wishes Could Kill*

THIRTY-NINE

Sandwiched between a massage parlor and a run-down motel, the Night Owl once stood as a proud nickelodeon bringing the novel magic of cinema to the people living in Los Angeles's Hollywood district.

Long ago, the marquee proudly announced showings of great silent films like *Napoleon* and *Metropolis*. Slowly dying ever since, it reinvented itself as a revival house in the sixties and a grindhouse in the seventies. These days, it survived by showing the X-rated likes of *New Wave Hookers* and *Café Flesh*.

Tonight, however, the seedy little theater offered something new. Something truly nasty and startlingly taboo, a shocking film that brought the Moral Majority types screaming outside its doors for two weeks running.

TONIGHT'S MIDNIGHT MOVIE
IF WISHES COULD KILL

FORTY

Sally Priest cut through the handful of protesters chanting their defiant hymns and entered the Night Owl's dim, stale interior. Ignoring the concessions stand fragrant with popcorn, she passed through a dark curtain and walked into the little theater, where rows of grungy, sticky seats faced a projection screen.

The air smelled dusty. The decor was outdated and appeared not only tired but utterly exhausted. The theater hadn't received a proper cleaning in ages. It wasn't even close to the kind of venue she'd imagined one day displaying her acting talent, but beggars didn't get to be choosers, no. Not in this town.

The theater staff had draped yellow tape over the two front rows, stringing together RESERVED signs. Sally picked a seat in the front row, center. She hadn't watched any of the movie outside a Moviola. This would be her first time seeing it from start to finish and in an actual theater. She hadn't wanted to see it at all ever again.

If concerned moms and clergy couldn't stomach *If Wishes Could Kill*, imagine being the only actor who survived its filming.

Instead, Sally had bought these seats in advance and walked here to see the horror film in all its shock and grimdark glory. Tonight, she had to bear witness again, as it wasn't only about her. Just as she'd had to see it finished.

Tonight would be something of a premiere, in fact.

She groaned a little as she settled into the polyurethane foam seat. Even now, parts of her ached from her ordeal at Bombay Beach four months ago. Over time, the cuts and bruises had healed, but her inner wounds might take years to mend. Badges of horror. Sally had finally gained the experience she'd craved to inform her performance as a Final Girl. She'd gotten her suffering.

Careful what you wish for, right. She still dreamed of scorpions and snakes boiling out of the ground, rustling toward her feet.

When she'd at last have the chance to play the Final Girl in a future film, she'd be able to run her lines without acting. And the offers were coming.

Everyone wanted a piece of her now. A real live Final Girl in a true-life horror movie. America's scream queen. The media ate it up, from the snobs at the *New York Times* to the cheerful blasting TV morning talk shows to Howard Stern. Overall, they didn't know whether to canonize or crucify her. She was the victim who'd fought back against an evil director who'd lost his ability to distinguish fantasy and reality, and she'd won. She was also the pariah who'd realized that director's vision by finishing his snuff movie and wrangling distribution for it.

Louise had been a substantial help on that last part, bringing in bookkeepers and lawyers and yelling over the phone, *We gotta make hay! Make hay while we can!* Sally had imagined her in black jacket and overalls like the farmer in Grant Wood's *American Gothic* painting, but instead of a pitchfork she held a scythe, sweeping the flashing blade not through wheat but through bodies, all the cast and crew, and then the scythe turned into the blades of Harry Stinson's crashing Bell 47.

Ever since Bombay Beach, Sally's imagination traveled to dark places.

It's what they would have wanted, she'd told *Good Morning America*, referring to her movie's murdered cast. The same answer she gave all the newspaper reporters and radio shock jocks and TV talking heads. It wasn't about the money for her but instead honoring the dead in their glorious final roles.

She wasn't lying.

Sally had inherited the cursed camera, and it came with debts.

Heavy footsteps thudded in the theater aisle. She craned her neck to see. A man lurched down the gentle incline, grunting and groaning. His face glowed pale and ghoulish in the dim lighting. The blazing eyes met hers, and he shambled over to plop into the seat next to her with a ballooning puff of desert dust.

He managed a strangled moan.

Sally answered with a smile.

"Hi, Max," she said.

FORTY-ONE

S ally said, "I'm glad you came."
  The director bent over, choking like a cat working
through the world's largest hairball. At last, he hocked up a massive
pile of watery sand and sat back gasping.

"Wouldn't miss it for the world," Max said, his voice like wet
gravel.

She'd visited the dead every full moon during the months following the Bombay Beach massacre, but he'd always walked off
sulking.

"I'm sorry I killed you," she said. "Really sorry."

He picked a sand fly from his teeth and flicked it. "Jordan was
right about one thing. The living dead don't have much to worry
about."

"I just wanted to live."

"It's why I loved you. Like I said, you were always the Final Girl
to me."

"And I always respected you, Max."

For all the dead didn't care, Sally could tell hearing this
pleased him.

"I used to loathe people," he rasped. "Even my own audience.
Now I kind of miss them. Funny, isn't it? The dead hate solitude
more than anything."

"I understand."

"Yes." He cleared his throat. "No. That's not quite right. What we probably hate the most is having no story. We aren't in the script anymore. We're the audience now."

Max no longer existed as a creator god of dark worlds but a mere citizen, plagued by ennui. He'd gained what he'd always craved, a life of horror. Only the horror came from an eternity of being stuck with Hollywood people for company and without an audience.

"Well, your movie got finished," Sally offered. "You made history. You've got an audience tonight."

"Do people know about the camera?"

"No one but me. Dorothy might, but I don't know for sure."

"She doesn't. Have you spoken to her?"

"She's not speaking to anyone."

The writer had gone back to Big Bear Lake and secluded herself, apparently happy to have escaped the movie business alive and return to her safer, solitary art.

"If you're the only one who knows, that's probably for the best."

"The world thinks you somehow rigged the set to murder everyone and then died in one of your own traps," Sally explained. "They see you as some kind of evil genius, the Houdini of horror."

Again, Max appeared pleased.

"Perfect movie," he murmured.

Sally wondered if it was all worth dying but didn't ask. She knew what he would say. Worth dying, sure. Worth killing too.

"Thank you," Max added. "For bringing it to life."

"You can thank Jordan," she said.

Across the full moons she'd spent visiting the dead, the producer had walked her through everything. How to access the remaining funds, who to call for editing help, and how to bring it to market. He shared a few dark secrets about his brother Joseph—now the owner of Lyman Entertainments' surviving assets—which helped Sally gain a clear legal road to finishing the movie, signing a deal that made Lyman a silent investor.

Under Jordan's guidance, *If Wishes Could Kill* launched with limited distribution at indie and X-rated video stores nationwide as well as a handful of grubby little theaters in major markets like Los Angeles and New York. Since then, distribution and ticket sales had grown by leaps and bounds. It would take some time to turn a profit, but the movie had legs, propelled by sensational media coverage and attempts by various city governments to ban it, which produced court battles over free speech. Foreign rights and video sales, meanwhile, kept climbing. The French and the Japanese apparently couldn't get enough of it.

An instant cult classic.

The air smelled like ash and cigars. The producer arrived like royalty, carried down the aisle on his litter by charred, faceless mannequins that were once Arthur Golden's crew. They hoisted him into the seat on the other side of Max and shambled away smoking and ashing.

Smirking behind his mirrored shades, Jordan lit a fresh cigar and got right to business.

"How are we doing, Sal?"

She shared the release numbers. The producer whistled. The movie, he said, would start generating profit in a matter of weeks on its current trajectory.

"You should think about getting into producing," he added.

"No, thank you." Managing people and budgets was nerve-wracking. She might have discovered herself as a fighter and survivor, but she'd never enjoyed conflict. "Now that the movie's done, I want to get back into acting."

"What's in your pipeline?"

"A lot of opportunities, actually." In fact, it seemed every horror director under the sun wanted to cast her in a starring role.

"I'm not surprised," he said, puffing on his cigar. "Right now, you're hotter than Elvira, babe. You should be pouncing on anything that moves."

The old Sally would grab it all with both hands as fast as she could. She'd have exploded at the mere possibility of gigs like these. The new Sally found it overwhelming. She could sleep for a year. Dorothy had been right; horror might birth in violence, but it lingered in grief, trauma, and memory.

"I needed time to heal," she said.

Max cleared his throat again, sounding like an outboard motor trying to start. "Getting back to it is how you heal."

"Look at you two," Raphael said as he stomped onto the scene lugging a massive cardboard box. "Final Girl and director together again, as God intended."

The Final Girl the surrogate for the audience, the monster the surrogate for the director. Together, they told an ancient story of creation and annihilation. Life and death. Light and darkness. Order and chaos. Irresistible wind and immovable rock.

Opposing forces of nature ever locked in cosmic yin-yang struggle, played out in horror movie formula as mythic theater. One not able to truly exist and become its true self without the other. And while death may appear to be all-powerful and have the final say, life always triumphs simply by enduring.

An endless story about survival in a hostile world.

A rusty shape blurred into the scene and burst onto Max's lap. Licking her chops, Lady Susan gazed hopefully at her owner with her head slouched to the side.

He scratched her back, sending her bum into happy windmilling. Even Max smiled. The dead hated being alone.

"Who's still my good girl?" he asked. "Who? Is it you?"

"I...be...row," a muffled voice said inside the box.

Raphael grinned. "Oh, sorry."

After he opened the flaps, the voice became strident as a trumpet: "Is this the front row? I *hate* sitting in the front row."

"These are the seats we got, my dear," he said.

"I'm the star of this movie," Ashlee railed. "I had the best death. I should be able to sit where I goddamn please!"

Raphael laughed. While the actor went on shouting, he hefted the box and threw Max a glare. "*This* is your idea of bringing me Ashlee Gibson?"

Max shrugged with an impish smile, a shrug that said, *Oopsie*.

Helga Frost elbowed past the special makeup effects artist. "Miss Priest. You have not yet destroyed the camera. Are you still considering it?"

"Every day," Sally answered honestly.

Though, like its previous owners, she wouldn't.

"Yeah," Raphael enthused. "Ending our existence is a *great* idea."

Helga pivoted to peer up at him from her sideways head. "Indeed—"

"*Not*," he added, tossing Sally a wink with his one working eye.

Ashlee carried on with her diva rant.

"At least take what's left of my head out so I can see what's—"

"Okay, okay." Raphael chuckled. "Let's find a seat in the second row."

"I *said* I *want* the *back row!*"

Helga frowned down at Sally. "We will talk again, I am sure."

Johnny Frampton limped down the aisle, propping up a tottering Jim Foster with one arm, rags wrapped around his middle to hold in his guts. Jim was scarcely recognizable after being struck down by racing steel, living among the revenants as one massive weeping bruise with broken bones jutting from his flesh.

"I still love you, Wanda." He grinned through missing teeth. "I always will."

"I love you too, Brad. In my own way."

Sally had honored him as well by jury-rigging his death scene into the film.

He eyed her with undying hope. "Can I sit with you?"

"Sorry, I'm saving this seat for someone else."

His eyes took on a look of quiet desperation. Stuck being Brad for eternity, Jim was still trapped in there, screaming to be freed.

"Come on, my dude," Johnny said. "We don't want to miss the movie."

Nicholas arrived next. He regarded Sally with a sad smile, the smile itself an apology. She smiled back and nodded. All was forgiven.

Then his shoulders lilted in a mischievous shrug. The dead didn't really care. Even the living only cared so much. He'd done what he'd had to do to try to survive, and because he was Nicholas, what he'd done hadn't been that difficult a decision.

Sally understood. She'd done the same, only she'd done it differently. By making better choices, the Final Girl provided her own solution to survivor's guilt. A good answer to the question of why she alone survived while the others didn't.

"I used to hate seeing my face on a screen," he said.

"I love it and hate it," said Sally.

"Now I'm curious what I looked like when I was alive."

A gruff voice intruded. "Well, look who decided to finally show."

Officer McDaniel regarded Max with a triumphant grin that grotesquely clashed with the rags of still-dripping flesh hanging off his large frame.

"Oh no," Max deadpanned. "My archnemesis is here."

Sally had made a point of not staring or jerking her head to avoid looking at the camera's victims, but even for the dead, the cop was hard to look at. The wild dogs had eaten parts of him and savaged the rest.

"I was right," Dan said, wearing a dazed look. A charred smear ran from his shoulder to his hip, still sizzling and bubbling from the lightning bolt that ended his life. Wavy black lines like tattoos radiated from it across his skin. His hair smoked. "I tried, Sally. I really tried. I was right all along."

"Thank you," Sally said. "For trying to save us. And sorry."

She'd said it before to him many times. She couldn't say it enough.

"I was *right*," Dan insisted. "I *tried*. But then everything… turned white…" Then he grimaced, both because he remembered and because he couldn't.

"She hears you, big guy." McDaniel shot her a sympathetic look. "You know how he gets stuck in a loop sometimes when he first wakes up. The lightning fried a few circuits."

They moved on, revealing Bill Farmstead waiting his turn to say hello.

"Hey, you," he said.

"Hi, Bill." It always hurt to see him like this.

Though, even dead, even holding his severed head in place to avoid grossing her out, he was still the same charming, hunky devil.

"I'm realizing we never did talk about, you know."

The unspoken potential.

"We never got the chance," Sally said.

"I just wanted to tell you we would have been fire."

She laughed. "It's true."

"Let's pretend it happened," he said. "I'll have memories to keep me company, and you can move on. You have your whole life ahead of you."

"Deal," said Sally with a bittersweet smile.

Bill plucked the head off his shoulders as if doffing his hat to a lady. Tucking it under his arm, he ambled off to find a seat.

"Hello, love," said the towering punk.

"Clare!" Sally swallowed back tears; it was turning out to be a very emotional night. Out of all the camera's victims, she missed Clare most. "I saved you a seat."

The punk sank into it. "We need more women here. Look at all these dicks. The after-party is going to suck."

"Congratulations. Your first movie."

"I just hope I don't look stupid during my death scene. The whole thing is a blur now. I hardly remember it."

"You looked great," Sally assured her.

"Well. Either way, we all put on a hell of a show."

Clare reached across to nudge Max while he extracted handfuls of wet sand from his jacket pockets and dropped them onto the floor.

She said, "I almost had you that night, fucker."

He smirked and said nothing.

"You know, we should put on a play or something," she added. "You could direct."

For a while, he didn't answer that either.

Then he said, "That's not a bad idea. Watching the living is pure tedium."

"It'd be something to do. Maybe *Hamlet*."

"No. Grand Guignol. Realistic murder and mayhem seven nights a week."

Sally said, "It's in the blood."

Her way of saying his distant relation, who'd once directed the infamous horror theater in Paris, would be proud.

"In the blood," he agreed.

The one big thing they'd always had in common.

Behind her, the Night Owl had filled to capacity. A sold-out show. Most of the moviegoers looked excited. A few bragged that they'd seen it before. Others seemed anxious, no doubt wondering what they'd gotten themselves into. All had come to see the blood-curdling car crash they couldn't look away from.

Sally spotted her mother sitting in the back row.

The lights dimmed. The theater darkened like a warning. Some young guys whistled and hooted in anticipation, which set off a wave of nervous chuckling among the rest. Whistling not past the graveyard but straight into it. Because this was no mere movie but an experience, and a dangerous one at that.

The movie's sound came to life with a thump, followed by utter quiet.

Black screen. No music.

A single simple credit appeared in white blocky capitals:

A FILMS OF THE CRYPT PRODUCTION

Several long seconds of ominous, thickening silence. The words vanished.

And then:

IF WISHES COULD KILL

"Yes," Max hissed in the dark.

Sally patted his cold and lifeless hand.

"Thank you for casting me in your movie, Max."

Then she got up and headed for the exit.

FORTY-TWO

Sally anticipated hating seeing her overbite blown up to vast proportions on the silver screen, but that wasn't why she wanted to leave.

She couldn't bear to see them all die again.

Besides that, she dreaded the point in the film where she'd stopped playing a role. Because it didn't matter how talented you were. You could be Meryl Streep or Al Pacino. You could never act as well as the real thing when it came to naked terror.

The one time she'd ever gotten her performance truly perfect.

Jordan released a cloud of cigar smoke as she passed. "Sally Priest."

"Yes?"

"The camera. It's still safe?"

"Yes." She'd stashed it and the spell book.

"On the next full moon, let's do a general," the producer said. "I've got some fresh ideas for it that will put you on top."

Though free of desire, the dead remained hungry, and these particular spirits offered a dedicated production studio specializing in lethal freak accidents.

"I love it." Sally smiled. "My people will call yours."

As things went in Hollywood. People lied all the time.

She moved up the aisle to watch her mother watch the movie.

Like the others, Sally was invisible tonight, her mortal coil tossing and turning in her bed back in her apartment. *Astral travel*, Raphael had called it during a previous visit to the dead. He was the one who'd taught her to tie her body to the bedframe to prevent it from trying to follow her spirit. To the moviegoers, the two front rows sat empty, occupied by a foreboding presence they instinctively avoided testing.

On the screen, *If Wishes Could Kill*'s inciting incident scene marched to its climax, making way for the rest of the story. Clutching her purse as if ready to bolt at a moment's notice, Maude stared with her face set in a mortified mask, a grimace of social death. Her only daughter in America's most notorious horror flick, a production that had almost killed her. Maude's idea of real horror.

You were right, Sally mused. *Horror movies really can create violence.*

Light and dark flickered across her mother's features as if trying to imprint themselves. Sally heard her own voice on the theater speakers, joined by Clare's. Her first scene in the movie had appeared. Though she faced away from the screen, she could see it in her mind. She and her friend lying shoulder to shoulder on a bed at a soundstage in Burbank.

She stiffened, expecting Maude to stage a bitter and tearful walkout.

Instead, her mom's lips curled into a slight smile.

All along, Sally had missed an important fact hiding in plain sight. Her mother had always been proud of her. She'd never realized until now.

Seeing it in action was priceless.

Priceless, though a bit too late.

She didn't care that much about Maude's approval anymore. Bombay Beach had burned that need out of her. Her own little hero's journey complete. While the dead shed their worries, the living traded up for entirely new ones.

When it came to hang-ups, survivors had way bigger fish to fry.

"I love you, Mom," Sally said. "Regardless of what you think. I'm glad you're here. But I'm a scream queen. You'd better get used to it."

Scripts kept arriving on Louise's desk. Now that *Wishes* had slouched to Hollywood to be born, Sally could start thinking again about the future.

Horror directors wanted her. Other directors did too for everything from romantic comedies to action movies. Even studio heads like Chazz Morton, whom she'd enjoyed rejecting. Sally had ample choices, but she'd already decided to stay in horror. Despite what Max had done, the genre remained playful, accessible, boundary breaking. She'd scream again, and the audience would love her for it.

It was also therapeutic. Max had been right about that.

The desire to revisit her trauma to confirm she had in fact survived. Hoping that the next time, she'd understand it.

Like Max, Sally would stick with the genre that let her play with her demons. She'd relive the horror until at last the monster couldn't hurt her anymore.

That's how the Final Girl truly won.

And if that didn't work, well, she always had the other option.

Always Arthur Golden's cursed camera, craving fresh souls.

FORTY-THREE

Max sat in the dark with his magnum opus, the culmination of his life's work, the sum of his artistic ambition as a horror creator.

On the silver screen, the players frolicked and fought their petty squabbles, beautiful and larger-than-life, brimming with youth and dreams, unaware they were all doomed to die horribly. An ancient mythic script now rendered in history's most wonderful optical illusion, the product of persistence of vision when viewing a series of images flashing by at a high rate. In this case, film recorded at twenty-four frames per second and played back at the fusion frequency of forty-eight hertz. The science and magic of cinema, rooted in humble beginnings in the zoetrope and cartoon flip-books, on to Edison and Dickson and all the way to the slasher flick and horror's final incarnation: *If Wishes Could Kill.*

By buying a ticket, the audience had summoned the players back to life like reanimated souls haunting a stretch of film. The living sat stacked behind him, they and the whole human race, all of them playing out their own dramas, similarly doomed. Each of them alone but also not alone. The screen the campfire, the movie a story about survival, the surrounding darkness filled with predators that still lived in the genes. They'd come for horror, a psychological room where they could share and face their collective fears, traumas, and taboos—both the rational and mundane kinds inflicted by the current zeitgeist and the illogical kind lurking deep in the soul. And feeding these fears, there were the horror creators like Max, inch by bloody inch carving out new spaces promising fresh scares and thrills.

He'd certainly faced his own fear. The horror of seeing his father drop dead at the dinner table after telling a joke. A moment demanding endless repetition and awe. At last, in creating *Wishes* and dying for it himself, in being reborn into this loveless and fearless afterlife, he'd vanquished his lifelong trauma.

Even if he weren't dead, he'd have no regrets. Not a one. Max had gained what Hollywood's storytellers would call a positive character arc, where the protagonist gets exactly what he needs and becomes a complete person.

He'd made the perfect horror movie.

The cherry crowning a long, venerable history of horror cinema. From the experimental early shorts exploring the medium's innate strangeness to the silent horror films, flicker and shadow, murky and ominously mute, which led to the dreamy desolation of German Expressionism following the Great War. Universal Studios birthing the monsters of the Great Depression in the thirties, from Dracula to Frankenstein, making horror less artistic and more accessible until the horror-comedies of the forties and the next innovation: psychological horror. On to the mutant monsters of the atomic fifties, the psychos and witchcraft of the psychedelic sixties, and the closer-to-home terrors of the paranoid seventies. Right up to the romping eighties with its slashers and seemingly everything else on the menu.

One could read the dark and stormy history of the twentieth-century American psyche in these films, which like bad dreams purged the nation's lusts and fantasies and paranoias and collective fears. All of it led up to tonight, this movie, where the story was real and the real was story and you were a part of it. Where reality and fiction rutted to become a surreal waking nightmare, a nearly two-hour night terror, a psychic tattoo you'd carry with you forever like a liminal STD. What you are about to see is real, viewer discretion advised.

And he was the visionary who'd made it.

Max sighed. He wanted nothing.

He was done.

When Jim Foster disappeared in the glare of a truck's headlights, the crowd sucked in its breath. A reverent pin-drop silence fell upon the theater, a tangible church hush, so quiet the dead heard the rattle in the projector booth and the living the blood rushing in their ears. When the climax kicked off with Johnny Frampton impaling himself, a few broke down sobbing.

Do you see now? he thought. *Do you understand horror the way I do?* His audience had just witnessed, close-up and personal, real death in all its drab and startling pageantry. Surely, they comprehended the awful respect horror demanded, the delicious pain it delivered, now that it had displayed its full power.

The camera lingered on Johnny's bleeding corpse, the bag of Lay's Italian Cheese Potato Chips partially visible in the corner of the frame.

"Yum," someone called out, provoking a wave of nervous chuckling.

Yeah, okay, thought Max.

They laughed because they were scared, he knew that. They were young and didn't think they'd ever die. They laughed at death.

He still didn't like it. They could laugh at eternity and try to fill it up with wishes all they wanted, but Max demanded they gaze into the void.

As if powered by its bleakness, the movie inexorably carried on toward the next death. The camera jerking and wobbling in a dizzy abandonment of convention, the sound ranging from terrible to nonexistent, the abrupt disregard for production quality practically breaking the fourth wall. It only made the movie grittier. The real even realer. As if the movie no longer cared if you watched, and if you looked away, if you so much as blinked, you might miss what was coming.

Max turned in his seat and scanned the gawking teen faces shining in the movie glow. Kids who used to be his core audience. They were riveted, but he could tell that jokey *yum* and giggle had broken the spell. *It's only a movie*, they thought. They could at last breathe again, clutching their oversize Cokes and crunching their nonpareils and dipping into their greasy tubs of popcorn. Many were too young to be here in the first place, but an X rating didn't stop these boys and girls from taboo. One trope the horror movies always nailed on the head: Tell a bunch of teenagers something is forbidden, and they'll run a race right at it.

Grumbling, Max crossed his arms and sank deeper into his seat.

The next death struck like a bullet: Bill Farmstead's head popped off to produce a collective *whoa* that came out an anguished empathetic groan. *Holy shit*, someone yelled, which produced another smatter of anxious chuckles. To Max's utter delight, at least half the audience stood and fled the theater. Among those who stayed, however, the chuckling became general, took on an angry note of defiance.

When the jet engine tumbled out of the darkness to plow Ashlee in a vast wave of dirt, a group of boys cheered from the back row.

"No," Max said.

"Do you hear that, Nicky?" Ashlee called out in the dark. "They love me!"

With her spectacular on-screen demise, the atmosphere changed, a subtle shift in the power dynamic. A few more moviegoers trickled out, but the remainder stubbornly held on. The heavy despair and constant on-edge nausea and terror dissipated. Some had seen the film several times and shouted out lines, turning *If Wishes Could Kill* into an impromptu *Rocky Horror Picture Show*.

"Quit that," Max snarled. "Shut up!"

As if in defiance, the audience roared louder, braying like hyenas. His cast got into the act, cheering their on-screen deaths. Even the thickening darkness in the theater, the presence Raphael called the Beast, powerful and intangible as Hollywood, chortled along with them.

"Stop it!"

Jordan tilted his head. "You're talking over your own movie."

"They're *laughing* again."

"They're surviving, babe," the producer said. "It's called proof of life."

On-screen, Max told Sally he loved her and disappeared into the earth. Gales of laughter filled the theater.

"What have I done?"

Jordan smiled behind a puff of cigar smoke.

"You raised the standard, killer. I salute your genius."

Max howled into the flicker.

Horror wasn't horror unless it was real.

ROLL CREDITS

Who's laughing now?

Bruce Campbell as Ash Williams
Evil Dead 2: Dead by Dawn

ACKNOWLEDGMENTS

As an art form, horror is not a modern invention. Its origins can be traced to humanity's earliest storytellers. Roman author Pliny the Younger, for example, tells a story of the philosopher Athenodorus, who bought a house in Athens and quickly learned why it had been such a steal: It was haunted. The discovery of an unmarked grave in the yard resulted in the bones being given a proper burial, and the ghost subsequently departed.

Then there's ol' William Shakespeare, widely considered one of the greatest storytellers in the English language, who gave us a brutal little Elizabethan tragedy titled *Titus Andronicus*. That play contains enough murder, mutilation, cannibalism, and revenge to stand alongside the most grisly eighties splatter flick.

The list goes on. As fear is such an old and base human emotion, it's no wonder that horror has endured as both an element of fiction and a genre itself, from the campfire to the modern screen. Good horror thrills us, breaks boundaries, makes us confront our fears, asks disturbing questions, induces wonder, and makes us check under the bed, you know, just in case.

Outside of art, however, horror is an emotion that most of us do our utmost to avoid. Why do we eagerly seek it out on the page and screen? And while we can all recognize horror as a feeling, why is it so hard to define as a genre? What makes good horror? When horrifying an audience, how far is too far?

It was these eternal questions that in large part inspired *How to Make a Horror Movie and Survive*—a love letter to the horror genre in general and horror filmmaking in particular, shown through the lens of one of the great periods in horror history: the slasher era.

While writing this novel, I became captivated by the evolution of it all. I reflected on my own place in it as a horror writer. And I realized what I owed both to all those who came before me and to the amazing horror creators who influence my life today in what is arguably a new renaissance in the genre.

So with utmost gratitude, I'd like to acknowledge first and foremost fellow horror writer Chris Marrs, my life partner, who is so wonderfully supportive and is always willing to talk me through a difficult page.

I'd like to thank all the colleagues who have become stout friends ever game for a marathon of shop talk, people I love watching achieve success with every book they write, notably Peter Clines and John Dixon.

I'd like to thank Bradley Englert, my fantastic editor and a fellow horror fan, as well as the rest of the team at Hachette Book Group, who enabled the dream of this novel to become real.

I'd like to thank the entire horror community, both past and present. The Horror Writers Association offered me a found family, a warm and welcoming community of writers I respect and have learned so much from.

And last but certainly not least, I'd like to thank you for joining me on this journey by reading my work—with a promise that I will keep telling stories as long as you keep reading them.

MEET THE AUTHOR

Jodi O

CRAIG DILOUIE is an acclaimed American–Canadian author of horror and other speculative fiction. Formerly a magazine editor and advertising executive, he also works as a journalist and educator covering the North American lighting industry. Craig is a member of the Horror Writers Association, Imaginative Fiction Writers Association, and International Thriller Writers. He currently lives in Calgary, Canada, with his partner, Chris Marrs, and two wonderful children.

if you enjoyed

HOW TO MAKE A HORROR MOVIE AND SURVIVE

look out for

EPISODE THIRTEEN

by

Craig DiLouie

From the macabre mind of a Bram Stoker Award–nominated author, this heart-pounding novel of horror and psychological suspense takes a ghost hunting reality TV crew into a world they could never have imagined.

Fade to Black *is the newest hit ghost hunting reality TV show. Led by husband-and-wife team Matt and Claire Kirklin, it delivers weekly hauntings investigated by a dedicated team of ghost hunting experts.*

Episode 13 takes them to every ghost hunter's holy grail: the Paranormal Research Foundation. This brooding,

*derelict mansion holds secrets and clues about bizarre
experiments that took place there in the 1970s. It's also famously
haunted, and the team hopes their scientific techniques and
high-tech gear will prove it. But as the house begins to reveal
itself to them, proof of an afterlife might not be everything
Matt dreamed of. A story told in broken pieces, in tapes, journals,
and correspondence, this is the story of Episode 13—and how
everything went terribly, horribly wrong.*

Fade to Black Blog
Matt Kirklin, Lead Investigator

Jackpot! We got it, gang.

Foundation House for lucky thirteen.

During my five-plus years as a paranormal investigator, I've always wanted to check out this house. In our little community, it's pretty infamous. Not for the haunting, which is honestly kinda run of the mill, but for the general weirdness.

This place has some wild lore connected to it. Seriously, I could write a book.

Nobody's ever been given access until now, a real stroke of luck. You heard me right. It's never been investigated. *Ghost Hunters*, eat your heart out!

Built in 1920 near the historic Belle Green Plantation a few miles from the little Virginia town of Denton, the mansion is a throwback to antebellum architecture. Picture large, wrap-around porches where you sip mint juleps while you enjoy the sunset. The house was built by Jared Wright, heir to a sugar company. When he died in the sixties, it stood intestate until the Paranormal Research Foundation, or PRF, bought it and moved in.

That's when Wright Mansion became Foundation House.

In 1972, while the Republicans renominated Nixon for president, the last American troops left Vietnam, and Bobby Fischer became the first American world chess champion, five paranormal all-stars lived in this house and recruited dozens of people to take part in weird experiments.

Their motto was "Where there is smoke, there is fire." They believed paranormal powers reside in all of us, dormant in our DNA. They were members of the Human Potential Movement, which believed humanity only used a fraction of its potential intelligence and ability. They wanted to identify paranormal abilities in people, discover the underlying mechanisms, and learn how to train and develop them to make a utopia.

In short, they were wacky as hell, but see it through their eyes for a minute. They envisioned a world where people could talk to the dead. Could read minds, control objects remotely, travel out of their bodies, know the future. And they weren't stereotypical hippies. They were some of the leading scientists of their time, and two of them— Shawn Roebuck and Don Chapman—were certified geniuses.

As for the researchers, we know they went missing in 1972. The police files themselves vanished in the Election Day Flood of 1985.

So what are we investigating, exactly? Over the years, neighbors driving past the property reported seeing the ghostly apparition of an abnormally tall woman appearing in the upstairs window. Local kids using it as a party hangout said they heard invisible feet stomping on the grand staircase, experienced cold spots, and witnessed strange flashing lights in the woods around it.

In Episode 13, *Fade to Black*'s crack team will spend seventy-two hours at Foundation House. According to the owner, nobody's lived in it since 1972, so we are hoping to find it more or less how the scientists left it.

Using cutting-edge techniques and the latest technology, we'll investigate the paranormal claims and also see what we can learn about the Foundation itself. Which makes a great opportunity for me to brag about my team.

As our camera shooter, Jake Wolfson is the eyes of our little operation. Because the show is unscripted, we have to be careful about what we shoot so we don't flood out postproduction. Hence his motto: "The most story for the least footage."

Camera shooters are usually pretty stressed out. They track the action on their little black-and-white viewfinder while being aware of everything that's going on and anticipating what will happen next. Jake's a solid pro, though. Nothing ever seems to faze him. He's a big, muscly guy with a braided gold beard and runic tattoos running down his arms. A real badass in look and deed.

Then there's our tech manager, Kevin Linscott, the man with the mustache, our operation's ears and technical wizard. He helps set up all our gear and monitors it while mixing audio for the show. If the camera doesn't see it, the audio catches it.

Kevin's a retired Philadelphia police officer who did a lot of ghost hunting with me at Ralston Investigates the Paranormal (RIP), an amateur local ghost hunting group, before joining the show, and he's got all these great stories. When Claire tells me to trust the equipment, Kevin reminds me to trust my instincts and senses.

Jessica Valenza is our understudy and protégé. She's a professional actress the producers added to the show to round out the team. She has turned into quite the paranormal investigator, and she fits right in.

For a reality show, we keep things lean and mean, as we don't want people crowding around bumping into stuff and producing false positives on our instruments. Jessica not only helps with the investigating but does a lot of behind-the-scenes stuff for the show, a real jack-of-all-trades.

And then there's Claire, my wonderful wife. The best of the best. Adorable and smarter than a bullwhip, she graduated magna cum laude from Virginia Tech with a PhD in physics. She designed all our ghost hunting protocols and is a crack investigator.

I honestly couldn't do this without her.

Working together, we're a team. But more than that, we're family. A family that explores the unknown with a spirit of comradeship and a whole lot of scientific curiosity to solve the oldest and greatest of human mysteries: What happens to us when we die?

Oh, and I should give a shout-out to one more person who makes all this work.

You.

Seriously, without you, there's no show, so as always, thank you for watching and participating. This show is heaven for me, as I get to earn a living doing what I love doing most, something I'd be doing either way.

So really, it's about you. I'm proud that you're on our team.

And I hope you're as excited as we are about Episode 13.

It's going to be amazing.

Foundation House, here we come!